Environment

FUNDING GUIDE

Denise Lillya

Contributors:

Anna Adams
Jessica Carver
Sarah Johnston
Amy Rosser
John Smyth
Tom Traynor

Fourth edition

DIRECTORY OF SOCIAL CHANGE

Published by
Directory of Social Change
24 Stephenson Way
London NW1 2DP
Tel. 08450 77 77 07; Fax 020 7391 4804
email publications@dsc.org.uk
www.dsc.org.uk
from whom further copies and a full books catalogue are available.

Directory of Social Change Northern Office
Federation House, Hope Street, Liverpool L1 9BW
Policy & Research 0151 708 0136

Directory of Social Change is a Registered Charity no. 800517

First published 1989
Second edition 1993
Third edition 2000
Fourth edition 2010

ISBN 978 1 906294 37 3

British Library Cataloguing in Publication Data
A catalogue record for this book is available from the British Library

Cover design by Kate Bass
Text designed by Kate Bass
Typeset by Marlinzo Services, Frome
Printed and bound by Page Bros, Norwich

Contents

Introduction

The fourth edition

> 'We've got to pause and ask ourselves: How much clean air do we need?'
> *Lee Iacocca, CEO/Chairman, Chrysler Corporation, 1979–1992.*

This statement, breathtaking in its arrogance, hopefully would not be made today. Even the CEOs of leading companies realise that our environment is important to the public (their customers) and its resources are finite. We have come a long way in a short time and it is the work of environmental groups – large and small – their funders and supporters, and public opinion that has forced change.

The scope of this book and why it's been written

Environmental issues cover a wide range of topics, from the air we breathe, deforestation and the threat to the African mountain gorilla, the pollution caused through importing food and the counteraction of sustainable local communities, to the preservation of historic buildings, wildlife sanctuaries and all things in between. This guide, however, is focused on topics relevant to the UK. Our aim is to inform fundraisers in their search for money and support for the environmental work their groups carry out.

Throughout the guide there are case studies showing the part that environmental groups, with their funders' support, play in the wider scheme of things, especially in helping bring new heart to disadvantaged communities and providing fresh ideas to improve our natural and built environment.

During the research for this book on grant-making charities and other funders, it has been encouraging to see the abundance and diversity of those funders and the environmental organisations they support. These groups, run by people who are passionate about our planet, from preserving the local badger sett to making their own small contribution to combat global warming, make a real difference and it is inspiring that funders recognise their innovation and their practical contribution to improving our lives by awarding them grants and support.

The guide deals with the range of fundraising possibilities and how best to exploit them. It is primarily aimed at grassroots and medium-sized organisations that are working towards a clean, healthy, sustainable, diverse and cared-for environment.

New edition

In this, the 4th edition, our aim has been to help fundraisers in all aspects of making applications to the various funding sources. The guide includes new chapters on getting started, developing a strategy, recruiting a fundraiser, preparing a budget, project fundraising, writing a good application, campaigning issues, environmental organisations and charitable status and tax requirements and benefits.

A separate chapter has been included on obtaining money from the Landfill Communities Fund which, since it started in 1996, has helped 2,528 organisations that in turn have spent over £804 million on environmental projects, improving the lives of communities living near landfill sites.

As with the 3rd edition, there is detailed information on some of the largest grant-making charities and companies that support environmental issues. and guidelines on how to apply to them.

Funding sources

One of the challenges in accessing funding for environmental work is that often it is not clearly categorised as such. For example, *The Funders' Almanac 2008* (DSC) records that just over 10% of grant-making charities gave to 'environment and animals' whilst 44% gave to 'general charitable purposes'. Despite not being classified by funders as being for environmental work, this huge proportion of general funding is certainly worth exploring when looking for support.

However, with a vast range of possible definitions of 'environmental causes', researching prospective funders is critical. One funder might support wildlife, heritage, preservation, conservation, architecture, farming, biodiversity and the effects of global warming. Another might support wildlife, conservation and climate change but exclude heritage, architecture and farming. The permutations are endless.

Different funders also take different approaches to what they will support. Some will support those projects concerned with changing our day-to-day behaviour, for example, the 'sustainable living awareness campaign' aimed at local schools; others will fund grand projects such as The Eden Project.

Further information on the grants made by trust funders can be found in the *Where The Green Grants Went* series of reports available on the Environmental Funders Network website (www.greenfunders.org).

A new way of living

We are increasingly taking personal responsibility for our own space on the planet and recognise that individual action is at the heart of social change.

A comprehensive survey by leading think tank The Future Laboratory highlights that Britons now realise they can have a greater impact than government, with 49% stating it is down to the individual to take the lead. Thirty-two per cent of young people aged 18–24 think being environmentally aware is a matter of personal politics, 41% believing individual action is the only way forward to combat climate change.

According to the research, 68% of those surveyed said that the notion of 'green' would soon become obsolete – not through any lack of interest but rather that the majority viewed behaviours such as recycling (91%), switching lights off (66%) and driving hybrid cars (51%) as becoming standard practice within the next 20 years.

This is encouraging for the groups that have been struggling for years trying to convince the public and funders to engage with the idea that the damage done to our environment, and the responsibility to redress it, must start with the individual playing a part. Because of this, and despite the current recession (which has seen funders losing millions from their portfolios and a consequent reduction of income to award grants with), you can at least be assured that you have public support.

Thanks and acknowledgements

In addition to the contributors credited on the title page, we would like to thank Jon Cracknell of the Environment Funders Network for his encouragement and for writing the Foreword to this book.

Thanks also go to the Charity Commission, ENTRUST, the Environment Agency and all those organisations that allowed us to reprint case studies in order to illustrate funding potential.

Good luck with your applications and appeals and to all of you working in environmental groups – thank you for your work, which benefits us all.

The research was done as fully and carefully as possible, but there may be funding sources that have been missed and some information may be incomplete or will become out of date. If any reader comes across omissions or mistakes in the book, please let us know so that they can be rectified in future editions – email the Research Department of the Directory of Social Change at research@dsc.org.uk or ring 0151 708 0136.

Foreword

As we rush towards a full world of more than 9 billion people, pressure on the Earth's resources and life systems continues to intensify. For everyone on Earth to live a North American lifestyle we would somehow need to find another four planets worth of resources. Since we only have one planet to work with, there is an urgent need for social and political change.

Martin Luther King Jr once observed that: 'Human progress is neither automatic nor inevitable. We are now faced with the fact that tomorrow is today. We are confronted with the fierce urgency of now. In this unfolding conundrum of life and history, there is such a thing as being too late ... We may cry out desperately for time to pause in her passage, but time is deaf to every plea and rushes on. Over the bleached bones and jumbled residues of numerous civilizations are written the pathetic words: Too late.'

This guide is designed to help those concerned by the 'fierce urgency of now'. It outlines the principal UK sources of funding for environmental projects, and will help fundraisers to navigate the grants market. The better this market functions, the greater the chance we have of addressing our environmental challenges. With this in mind I greatly welcome the publication of this new guide by the Directory of Social Change.

Jon Cracknell
Coordinator
Environmental Funders Network

How to use this guide

The first six chapters of this guide give you the basic tools to start fundraising and to increase your chances of success. Chapters 7 to 15 outline funding sources with details of some of those that support environmental work and including a chapter on raising money for campaigning issues. Chapter 16 gives information on charitable status, the legal implications of becoming a registered charity and how to register your group with the Charity Commission. Chapter 17 deals with tax and tax benefits.

The main sources of funding and support are:

Grant-making charities

These charities exist to give money to other charities. Some are particularly interested in environmental concerns, others in certain geographical areas. Most support salaries and project costs for up to three years; others give small one-off grants for equipment or individuals.

For further information, see Chapter 8 *Raising money from grant-making charities*.

The National Lottery

This supports good causes through its distribution boards. Some of these give mainly capital grants (building, equipment, etc.); others give revenue grants as well (i.e. salaries and running costs).

For further information, see Chapter 9, Raising Money from The National Lottery.

Landfill Communities Fund

The Landfill Communities Fund (LCF) is a government scheme which provides funding for community or environmental projects in the vicinity of landfill sites. The LCF encourages landfill operators and environmental bodies to work in partnership, create environmental benefits and jobs, promote sustainable waste management and undertake projects that improve the lives of communities living near landfill sites.

For further information see Chapter 10 *The Landfill Communities Fund.*

Members, friends, the local community and the public

The public is still one of the largest funders of charitable work through sponsored events, buying raffle tickets and contributing to collections and subscriptions. This funding tends to come with fewer strings attached. There is a list of useful addresses and sources of information at the end of the guide.

For further information, see Chapter 7 *Raising support from the public.*

Local authorities

Support for project costs, programme development, equipment, salaries and so on can still be raised from your local authority. Each will be different and there are guidelines for making your approach. Contractual arrangements are increasingly entered into with local authorities for the provision of services, and the nature of this funding has both increased and become more dependent on conditions.

For further information, see Chapter 12 *Raising money from local authorities.*

Central and regional government

Support is available through various government departments which can help with project costs that meet their clearly defined priorities (for example, regeneration, rural development, social inclusion).

For further information, see Chapter 13 *Raising money from government.*

European money

There is a variety of schemes available from Europe. Programmes usually require matching funding from other sources, and many are tied to geographical areas, economic outcomes or capital projects.

For further information, see Chapter 14 *Raising money from Europe.*

Companies

Company support is extensive and varied and is not just about cash. Links with a company can secure donations, gifts in kind, professional advice and expertise, profile-raising and sponsorship.

For further information, see Chapter 11 *Winning company support.*

1 Getting started in fundraising

Background

This chapter looks at how to begin to develop a sustainable organisation and the different approaches that can be employed when fundraising.

Fundraising today

Every organisation needs money to meet its running and project costs – to pay staff salaries and office overheads, to maintain any buildings or vehicles and, importantly, to develop programmes for the future.

Given the short-term nature of most current grant regimes, many organisations find themselves continually involved in fundraising, whether by holding fundraising events or making formal applications to other organisations.

Part of the challenge of being involved with a charity, whether as a member, volunteer, member of staff or trustee, can be the fundraising aspect, with charity workers involving the public in their enthusiasm and commitment by holding events designed to publicise the charity's aims, vision and work and to involve the public in its goals. These events can be productive in ways other than financial gain and can show the general public the charity's successes, imagination and creativity.

Fundraising by application to grant-making bodies, companies or other organisations is much less fun and requires a more formal and structured approach.

Fundraising in general has become more difficult in the competition between charities for donations and grants. New statutory regulations following the Charities Act 2006 impose further requirements on charity trustees to ensure the integrity of their fundraising methods and the protection of charity funds.

It is important for charity trustees in their fundraising to be aware of, and sensitive to, public opinion and to manage and control their fundraising by adopting the highest standards to protect the monies raised, the integrity of their charity and the sector as a whole.

It is also important for fundraisers to be accurate and truthful when applying for funds, whether by way of appeal, collection box or application to grant-making bodies. They also need to decide on, and make known, the contingency provisions if the money raised is insufficient for the purpose or if there is a surplus.

A planned budget with regular forecasting is a necessary management tool to show the amount of money you plan to spend, the amount already raised or promised and the extra you will need to meet your outgoings for the year.

Fundraisers should monitor your progress in fundraising by keeping records of all money received or promised, and by preparing and discussing management accounts with your trustees at regular management meetings. If your income isn't coming in as planned, then you will need to take some sort of action – step up your fundraising programme, find and develop new sources of funds, cut costs, defer planned projects or agree to subsidise the deficit out of your reserves.

Creating a viable and sustainable organisation

Fundraising is about helping to create and maintain a viable and strong organisation which is able to sustain itself in the future.

There are many ways of doing this. One is to build a substantial and active donor base – getting people to support you who sympathise with your aims and who will continue to give their support over a long period. Other ways include:

- organising fundraising events (which can create a regular and continuing source of income)
- creating capital within your organisation, such as a capital fund for buildings or equipment (especially when this reduces your need for running costs or can help you generate an income)
- developing income generating schemes for the organisation itself.

Many organisations are addressing long-term needs – for example, through community development, which will not yield immediate results, or in campaigning over environmental health issues which would be a long-term goal.

You need to create an organisation that is financially strong in the long as well as the short term, rather than one that is unstable and running in crisis mode from year to year or month to month. Financial concerns can affect the morale of the whole organisation. Crisis fundraising is time consuming and difficult – and in the end you will find you run out of goodwill. You need to find ways of strengthening the financial position of your organisation and this means developing a sensible fundraising strategy for the future.

Your supporters

Your supporters are a very useful resource to you. They may provide financial help or attract financial support from other sources. Importantly, they can volunteer or by their efforts and enthusiasm encourage friends who are also willing to support you. They provide an indication of the level of support that your organisation is attracting and therefore can add extra resources for your organisation and strength to any lobbying and campaigning work.

You need to think about what kind of supporters you would like to attract and who your work will appeal to: they might be students or activists, people from minority backgrounds, from a particular type of profession or perhaps retired people with some spare time to give. You will need to think about how best to identify them, the sort of message they will respond to and in what format this should be.

Reducing dependency

Many organisations are funded by only one or a handful of donors or funders. If one of the grants is withdrawn or sponsorship ceases, this can create a financial crisis. It may also be difficult to determine your own agenda if you are constantly having to adapt to the priorities or terms and conditions of a key donor or funder.

Broadening your fundraising base can reduce this dependency. You need to decide whether your organisation is too dependent on any one source. You might then see if you can build some stability by developing alternative sources of income. See 'Developing independent sources of funding' on page 14.

Key principles

Asking for money

When asking for money you need to be clear about exactly what you want, whilst being aware of what that particular donor may be able and/or willing to give. You must also make it as easy as possible for the donor to respond.

The personal approach

The general rule is that the more personal you make your approach, the more effective you will be. Consider the following methods, starting with the most effective.

- Ask someone face to face.
- Telephone someone to ask for support.
- Write a personal letter to someone asking for support.
- Give a presentation to a group of people.
- Organise a meeting at your project where the prospective donor/s can see your work and meet some of your user group.
- Put out a request on your website (the people who visit it are likely to be interested in what you are doing).
- Ask someone with a high profile who has already given, such as a business leader or expert in the field, to make the approach on your behalf. This can be more effective than a request from your fundraiser or project leader as it shows that someone with a reputation to maintain endorses what you are doing.
- Send an appeal to lots of people. Many fundraisers prefer to send letters asking for support and this is sometimes the only way to reach a large group. However, this is not the most effective way of asking.

Understanding the donor's viewpoint

The funder or donor will have their own set of criteria by which your application or appeal is assessed. Grant givers will have the responsibility of dealing with charitable or public funds and need to ensure that these are used in line with their own purposes. They are accountable and need to be able to demonstrate transparency in their giving. They also need to be confident that there is a good chance of the project succeeding in its aims and outcomes. They will use their own set of criteria – who and where they want to benefit, the financial procedures they require an organisation to have in place, procedures for how you will monitor and evaluate your project, and what the outcomes are expected to be, etc.

A donor may have personal reasons for wanting to give. They might support an environmental project which advises on eligibility for energy efficient grants because they themselves have been helped through this sort of group, or a charity combating environmental illnesses because a relative has benefited from a similar organisation. They may feel strongly about an issue – such as climate change – and want to do something about it.

In supporting your cause they are also supporting *their* cause, doing something they feel needs doing and that they want to see done. You need to recognise this and try to discover what will trigger a positive response from the person/ organisation you are asking.

Fundraising is all about people

People give to help other people or because they want to create a better world and your job as a fundraiser is to show how you can help them to achieve this. One way of doing this is through case studies – illustrating your work with examples of who you have been able to help, how you have been able to change their lives and the difference that a donation has made.

Another way is to focus your fundraising on particular aspects of your work: the 'Going carbon neutral' project that will improve the lives of the community and of future generations, or the schools project which aims to establish wildlife habitats on and around school sites. By focusing on specific projects rather than the overall work of the organisation, it makes it easier to excite and enthuse your donors.

Fundraising is selling

Fundraising is a two-stage process. It is about showing people why your work is important and effective and only then persuading them to give. You should demonstrate that there is a need for the work you are undertaking and that you can do something useful to address it given their support. If they agree with you that the need is there and that your organisation is capable of doing something to make a difference, then provided you meet their criteria, they will want to support you – your success will also be their success.

Credibility and communication

People prefer to give to organisations and causes they have heard about and think well of. Your organisation's credibility and reputation are important. Media coverage of your work, making known your successes in the newsletters you send to supporters and getting endorsements about the quality of your work from experts and prominent figures can all help give people confidence that you are doing a worthwhile and successful job. This then makes it much easier for you to ask for support.

How to ask a donor

There are various ways of asking for money and you might want to consider some of the following:

- Ask for a specific sum to cover a particular item of expenditure (for example, £500 to purchase gardening equipment for your allotment project.)
- Give a shopping list of different items at different prices (for example, if you are equipping a wildlife hospital, you can list all the items you will need to purchase, put a price against each and ask a donor to contribute to one or more). Break down your appeal total into numbers of gifts of different sizes that you need if you are to reach your target. This technique is commonly used in major capital appeals.
- Show the cost per client in your user group as a unit cost, and ask the donor to support one or more units (for example, at a summer environmental club, show how much it costs for a child to attend for a week, and ask a supporter to sponsor a child for a week or throughout the summer holidays).
- Give examples of gifts already received.
- Provide a list of items supporters could provide and update it regularly.

Example shopping list

British Trust for Conservation Volunteers (BTCV) is the UK's leading practical conservation charity. It connects people with places, builds healthy sustainable communities and increases people's life skills. BTCV aims to create a better environment where people from all cultures feel valued, included and involved. Its mission is to create a more sustainable future by inspiring people and improving places. This shopping list gives examples of what donations will buy:

- £5 protects 10 trees
- £15 buys a bowsaw to coppice woodland
- £20 buys a garden fork
- £35 buys 50 native woodland trees
- £50 creates 150 sq metres of woodland flowers and grasses.

Case study

The Barn Owl Trust

The Barn Owl Trust is a small charity working very hard to conserve one of the most beautiful birds on earth. Anyone who has ever watched a barn owl hunting at dusk has surely been touched by the experience but sadly these magical birds have become increasingly rare – and the reasons are all man-made. Lack of food due to intensive farming, the loss of roost and nest sites, road mortality, and a host of other factors are to blame.

The Trust was founded by a small group of volunteers who believed not only that they could reverse this decline through practical conservation work, but also that they could use people's interest in the barn owl to increase environmental awareness. Thus the Trust's two-pronged approach and slogan 'Conserving the barn owl and its environment' was born.

Despite having a small team of professional staff and being consulted by government, the Barn Owl Trust is still a grassroots voluntary organisation that prides itself on the sheer amount of practical work it does. From erecting nesting boxes to creating ideal habitats, providing quality care for casualty owls to innovative research, and thought provoking educational work to specialist training for professionals – the Barn Owl Trust leads the field.

Do you have something we need?

Rather than (or as well as) giving the Trust financial aid, you may be able to contribute by giving us something we need. Some of the items are quite small and you may have them lying around at home doing nothing. Others might be a bit more of a challenge to find. You will notice that the list changes from time to time as people give us things and as we add new items.

In past years we have been given diverse items: from a caravan to use at county shows to a set of office desks; from a microwave to heat up our meals to a shovel – not to mention things that help us to raise money for our grand draw and the odd raffle prize now and again, so please read through our list and see if you can help.

continued...

- A microwave that has a defrost function
- Copy of A Manual for Wildlife Radio Tagging *by Kenward & Walls (2001) ISBN 10: 0124042422*
- *Empty film canisters to hold a single owl pellet*
- *Foreign change (please enclose a note of the type of currency)*
- *A roll of new, hardwearing office carpet, suitable for gluing to the floor*
- *Wild bird food — mainly sacks of black sunflower seeds, also peanuts and plain canary seed*
- *Wood for making outdoor nestboxes — sheets of 9 or 12mm tanalised softwood ply and lengths of 25x 50mm tanalised batten*
- *A4 and A3 recycled paper and card, both coloured and white*
- *A box trailer in good working order*
- *Inkjet cartridges for HP Deskjet 3820 and HP Deskjet 930*
- *Lawn rakes/garden rakes*
- *A small petrol-driven power-drive lawn mower (for use in Forde Orchard)*
- *Twelve stackable office chairs*
- *Postage stamps (both new and used commemorative)*
- *A metal detector*
- *Wildlife rehab group looking for somewhere to release house sparrows (we have the perfect release site)*
- *Good quality barn owl winter scenes, either photographic or illustrative, for Christmas card images*
- *Empty inkjet cartridges and old mobile phones for recycling*
- *Wild barn owl pellets (we can never have too many)*
- *Anyone in the Ashburton area who could occasionally provide temporary lodging for a Barn Owl Trust volunteer, at a reasonable rate*
- *Small plate compactor*
- *Emulsion paint (pale colour) sufficient to paint an office*
- *Set squares for woodwork use.*

Saying thank you

Saying thank you is extremely important. It recognises and values the donor's generosity, it makes the donor feel better about your organisation and it might also encourage them to give again.

Telephoning or writing to your donors saying how thrilled you were to receive their gift and how it is to be used makes the donor feel that they or their organisation are doing a good job and that their money will have a real impact. This is a very personal approach to thanking your supporters and may not be something you are practically able to do. However, even if you can't show your appreciation for every gift made, you should make sure you thank your donors periodically – at least once or twice a year.

Long-term involvement and commitment

What you really want are people who will give to you regularly and substantially. The effort you make in finding a donor and persuading them to give will be most effective if they continue to give over a few years, maybe increasing their level of giving over time. To achieve this means getting them involved with the work of your organisation and committed to its success by:

- saying thank you immediately and telling them what you plan to do with their money
- regular reporting back, showing them what you have achieved with their contribution
- sharing your ideas and hopes for the future
- encouraging them to visit you and meet some of the wildlife they have been helping
- inviting them to meet with the staff and volunteers who are actually doing the work.

Accountability and reporting back

When you accept a donation from somebody, you are responsible for seeing that the money:

- is spent on the purposes for which it was raised – failure to do this is a breach of trust
- is well spent and actually achieves something
- follows an audit trail.

You should always report back to the donor to show them that you have used their money effectively, and that their support has made a difference. You can do this by telephoning, sending a personal letter, a project report or a newsletter, by post or by email. This is not only polite, it is good fundraising practice – an enthusiastic donor who has seen the money make a difference may consider becoming a more committed supporter.

You should be aware that with the growing variety of methods and media used by charities to fundraise from their existing supporters and the general public, such as face-to-face 'clipboard' fundraising, emails and SMS, the accountability and transparency of charities is essential.

Different approaches to fundraising

Besides funding the work, you will also need to fund the organisation and its future. There are several factors to consider.

1) Capital developments

Capital developments, such as acquiring new buildings or IT systems, can have an impact on future fundraising needs in four ways. On the plus side:

- they can reduce operating costs
- they can generate income from fees and charges (for example, from letting out space)
- they can generate a greater capacity to fundraise (for example, when organising a major appeal you will be building a database of important contacts which you can utilise later on for further support).

On the minus side:

- they may increase your revenue costs if they require extra people to run them.

2) Endowment

Some organisations want to develop an endowment – that is, a capital reserve which can be invested to produce a regular income for the organisation. Some approach major donors for contributions to this fund; others set aside some of their income each year. They feel that this will give them greater financial security, remove some of the fundraising pressure or act as a reserve in times of unexpected difficulties. However, most grant-givers and companies will prefer to fund your work directly rather than have their money tied up as an investment.

Case study

The following case study gives a detailed example of endowment fundraising and is a good example of the need for, and how to set up, an endowment fund.

Tusk Trust

Tusk Trust has become one of the leading African wildlife conservation charities based in the United Kingdom and has successfully initiated, funded and supported a wide range of important conservation programmes across the African continent. While Tusk's primary objective is to promote the protection of endangered species, it also recognises that education, sustainable rural development and the involvement and support of local communities are all essential ingredients for the long term success of conservation.

A large number of the conservation projects supported by Tusk involve assisting rural communities to establish sustainable development programmes, many of which are linked to ecotourism or other businesses. These initiatives not only provide valuable employment, but also help to alleviate poverty and generate alternative revenue to improve healthcare, schooling, water supply and security in otherwise very poor and remote areas. In turn, these projects directly benefit wildlife conservation and have led to a dramatic reduction of poaching and a rehabilitation of natural habitat.

Tusk also regards the broadening of environmental education amongst young Africans as a cornerstone for the survival of wildlife and its diminishing habitat. The charity supports a number of dynamic education centres, which act as 'bush classrooms' and expose children to the need for sustainable management of their natural environment. Tusk's successful PACE [Pan African Conservation Education] education resource pack has now been adopted right across the continent.

Tusk strives to provide practical, logistical and financial support to a diverse range of projects. In the past this has included the purchase of vehicles, aircraft, radio equipment, as well as the construction of primary and secondary schools, clinics, water improvement schemes, roads, buildings, bridges and airstrips,

continued . . .

as well as covering the direct costs of rangers. The charity enjoys a reputation for being financially efficient with an average of 85% of the net funds raised reaching the field.

Tusk Endowment Fund

The chairman and trustees of Tusk, with the full support of our Royal Patron, Prince William, in 2008 launched a targeted appeal to establish a permanent endowment fund for Tusk, to be called the Tusk Foundation. The aim is gradually to build the capital held in this fund to £1 million over the next three years and thereafter continue to increase it to £5 million.

The thinking behind the endowment fund (the 'Fund') held within the Tusk Foundation is that:

- *it should represent a permanent financial endowment for Tusk*
- *its investment policy should be focused principally on the preservation of capital and the distribution of income only to support the charitable activities of Tusk*
- *the initial primary destination of the income should be the financing of the administrative costs of Tusk (including staff costs) within its budget plan approved by the board*
- *the establishment of the endowment fund should not divert donor funds which are raised for the ongoing delivery of financial support for the core day-to-day project needs.*

Fundamentally, the concept of building a permanent financial endowment is intended over time to grow to a sufficient size that the income from the Fund would ultimately cover (as its minimum primary objective) the administrative cost base of the charity, thereby allowing all general funds raised from donors to be invested directly into Tusk's portfolio of projects. Ultimately, the trustees plan that this form of financial security will ensure the longevity of Tusk and its work beyond the current generation. Depending on the size of the endowment the Fund may, in time, also be able to support other secondary objectives, such as ongoing programmes supporting the main charitable objectives of Tusk.

Endowment funds are often referred to as the future lifeblood of any charity. Providing for the long-term financial success of Tusk, the Fund will also act as a buffer in times of financial and/or fundraising reversals.

continued ...

The Fund will act as an appropriate destination vehicle for individuals, and trustees of grant-making trusts, who wish their gifts to be given in perpetuity. The capital of the endowment will remain untouched and managed on an extremely cautious and low risk investment strategy, and only the income, except in exceptional circumstances, will be used to underwrite the charity's administration and ongoing programmes and services.

It is important to note that the endowment fund held within the Tusk Foundation differs from the charity's reserve funds, where the principal and the income may be expended by the trustees. The charity's reserves are held in accordance with the recommended policy of the UK Charity Commissioners.

A gift that keeps on giving

An endowment fund is extremely valuable for a charity as it can supply a steady and dependable source of income. It is a timely and responsible initiative by the trustees to embark on this drive for greater self-sustainability. A contribution towards the Fund is 'a gift that keeps on giving' and will also create a lasting testimony.

Since its formation in 1990 Tusk has generated enough revenue each year to finance both its growing number of field programmes and its modest administration (overall revenue in 2007 amounted to £1.75 million). The charity prides itself on its enviable record for investing in the field. Our goal is to build the endowment so that it is large enough to underwrite an average administrative overhead equivalent to 15% of net revenue, and thereby ensure that as close to 100% of what Tusk raises each year as possible may reach the projects.

If you would like to support the endowment fund held within the Tusk Foundation please contact the charity's finance manager, Andree Hall, via email on andree@tusk.org or by calling the Tusk office on +44 (0)1747 813 005. Registered charity no: 803118

It takes a lot of hard work and time to raise an endowment and there may be other, more suitable ways of fundraising for your organisation to raise the money you need.

3) Developing independent sources of funding

There is a fundamental difference between an organisation that receives all its money from one source, and an organisation that receives money from several or many sources, each contributing towards the total requirement. Over-reliance on one source might give that donor too much influence over what the organisation should be doing and where it should be going. It creates a risk of failure – which the organisation will not be able to survive if the grant is cut back or withdrawn.

You need to decide whether your organisation's funding base is too narrow and, if it is, how you can broaden it. You will need to think about all the possible sources of income, and decide which are the most sensible for your organisation to develop.

On the other hand, although it is good to have a broad base of support, there is a danger of taking this principle too far and having so many small-scale donors that all your fundraising energies go into servicing them without being able to develop your fundraising further.

4) Developing a membership and a supporter base

A strong membership or supporter base helps create financial independence by:

- creating a constituency of support (the number of people who support you adds to your credibility as an organisation and gives you lobbying power)
- building a local base for your organisation (your relationship with your local community will be much closer if the funding is drawn from it rather than obtained externally)
- creating opportunities for further fundraising. Each donor can be asked to give regularly and more generously, to recruit other donors, to volunteer their time and skills, to donate items of equipment, or even to leave a legacy. The more people who are supporting you, the more opportunities you will have for developing your fundraising.

Some key issues

Before deciding who to approach there are some more general issues to think through.

- **Be cost conscious.** You need to monitor the money you spend carefully. Many charities exist to provide a service to their user group that is free or highly subsidised. This means that the amount raised determines the volume of work that can be undertaken. However, you may be able to charge for your services and you need to decide if that is appropriate for you and your users. Alternatively, in the current contract culture, statutory bodies may be able to pay for the services you deliver. Either way, you must cost what you do carefully and accurately. Someone has to pay for it – your funders, your sponsors, your donors or your users.

- **Avoid risks.** The cash that you spend on your fundraising is intended to generate money to spend on your work. You shouldn't be speculating with it on high-risk fundraising schemes where there is a real possibility that it might be lost. Fundraisers must minimise risk. You might need to pilot or test a new fundraising idea. You should identify the worst case scenario and take whatever action you can to avoid it, insure yourself against it or even scrap it if it looks set to fail.

- **The long-term approach.** You can simply concentrate on getting cash now, or you can devote some of your fundraising resources to ensuring the longer-term flow of funds into your organisation. For example, committed giving by individuals and appeals for legacies have high costs in the short term, but their long-term value usually far outweighs that of casual giving.

- **The multiplier approach.** A good way to maximise fundraising results is to 'cascade'. A sponsored run can bring your organisation to the attention of a large number of people. Every runner will sign up sponsors, and some of these may subsequently become interested in becoming a member or a regular donor (rather than in simply sponsoring a friend). This cascade effect will multiply the number of people supporting you and the amount you raise.

- **Sustainability.** In an ideal world, your organisation would be structured so as to minimise the need for permanent fundraising. Even if this seems ambitious to you in your current situation, there are a number of ways of making yourself more sustainable and therefore financially more secure:
  - Develop a range of income-generating activities.
  - Develop partnerships with larger bodies capable of giving larger sums – government, for example.
  - Raise an endowment fund.

continued...

- Recruit volunteers and get support donated in kind.
- Develop income sources that continue over many years, such as a membership.
- Organise events that are repeatable, so that if they work they can be done again and again with less cost – and be even better next time.

■ **Time.** You need to be realistic about how long things will take. To go from £0 to £100,000 a year from grant-making charities may require years of patient fundraising effort. To land your first major company sponsorship requires professionalism and good relationships that you may not yet have. To get your first 1,000 supporters is far harder than getting the next 1,000. Everything can take longer than you expect and there is a danger of being over-optimistic.

Accounting for fundraising

The following extract is taken directly from CC20 – Charities and fundraising on the Charity Commission website:

The costs of fundraising are a legitimate matter of public interest. Trustees should ensure that these costs are shown properly in the accounts. They include publicity costs associated with fundraising or raising the profile of the charity. They do not include costs of purely educational material produced by the charity as a way of achieving its purposes.

For those charities producing accruals accounts the Accounting and Reporting by Charities: Statement of Recommended Practice *(SORP 2005, revised July 2008) provides more detailed guidance.*

Appeals for funds
Whatever type of appeal is chosen by trustees to raise funds there are certain points that trustees should bear in mind:

■ *The purpose of the appeal should be clearly expressed. Where the appeal is for general funds then any specific project mentioned in the appeal document should be clearly identified as an example of the charity's work. Care needs to be taken so as not to mislead donors into thinking that their money will only be used for a particular project identified in the appeal literature where this is not the case.*

■ *If the appeal is for a specific project then it is very important that there are plans to deal with any unspent money and that these are reflected in the fundraising document. This will enable trustees to deal with any surplus funds that are raised over the appeal target or if the appeal fails to apply the money which was raised.*

We recommend that any funds raised for a special appeal be accounted for separately. One way to do this is to arrange for a separate bank account.

- *All contributions, as far as possible, need to be made directly to the charity and be under the control of the trustees.*
- *Where possible set an end date for the appeal.*

[Further information explaining in detail what to do if insufficient or surplus funds have been raised and plans have not been made is given on the Commission's website.]

Registered status to appear on certain documents

Trustees of registered charities with a gross income of £10,000 or more in the last financial year are required by section 5 of the 1993 Act to state, on a range of official documents, that the charity is a registered charity. The documents on which the statement must appear include notices, advertisements, material placed on websites, and other documents issued by or on behalf of a charity intended to persuade the reader to give money or property to the charity. This includes the solicitation of membership subscriptions.

If your club or organisation is not a registered charity, it is still prudent to follow the advice provided by the Charity Commission, as donors, supporters and sponsors will, rightly, still expect accountability and transparency.

Case study

Illustrate the work you do

This is an excellent example of how to attract readers to your organisation/ project/appeal. It appears on the Badger Trust's website: www.badger trust.org.uk.

Badger Trust

Badger Trust promotes the conservation and welfare of badgers and the protection of their setts and habitats for the public benefit. We are the leading voice for badgers and represent and support around 60 local voluntary badger groups. Badger Trust provides expert advice on all badger issues and works closely with government, the police and other conservation and welfare organisations.

Pounds, shillings and pence appeal – Badger Trust – Sussex

Three orphaned triplets were exposed to the elements of a cold March day when workmen clearing an overgrown garden in an urban seaside area of Sussex moved a large shipping container. Fortunately for the cubs, the container stood 30cm above the ground and they were unharmed when it was rolled away from its site. A quantity of hay and other bedding material was then observed on the flat ground, together with three very small badger cubs. Unfortunately, this occurred during the early morning and it was a further six and a half hours before a call

continued...

was made, at 4.30pm, to Jackie on the Badger Trust – Sussex's hotline, whose response was swift, although initially the caller was reluctant to divulge the address.

Tony, the local field officer, arrived to assess the situation and decided that, for their own protection, the cubs should be removed. A tom cat was prowling hungrily nearby, Tony knew there were foxes on site and the temperature was dropping very rapidly. There was no sign of the mother. As Tony was on his way to work he contacted Jeff and Pat, [two of the board of directors and on duty volunteering that day], and arranged to meet them in the car park of a local pub in order to hand the cubs over.

The rapid response Land Rover kindly loaned to the group by the Born Free Foundation was deployed and the tiny cubs in their nest of bedding, covered with a soft blanket for additional warmth, were transferred to the heated front seat of the vehicle.

Jeff and Pat made the 30-mile journey to the group's local wildlife hospital as quickly as possible and handed the cubs into its care at approximately 6.45pm. The cubs were very vocal during the journey, constantly wickering [a noise between growling and squeaking that badgers use when they interact]. The hospital had been alerted and a warm incubator was ready and waiting for the two little girls and their baby brother.

They were as cold as ice when found and it is doubtful that they could have survived outside for very much longer.

Annette and Dave, who run Folly Wildlife Rescue (see www.follywildliferescue.org.uk) left them to warm up for two hours before giving them their first feed of a special milk formula, which closely replicates the mother's milk.

When admitted, each weighed c. 340g and were estimated to be approximately two weeks old. As is usual at that age, their eyes were still closed, they had a sparse covering of soft hair and surprisingly long toenails. They survived the night and when the group made an anxious call to the hospital the next morning, they found all was well; all three cubs were eating for England and were still wickering.

The babies are fed at intervals of three hours, day and night, their weight has increased steadily and in addition to the milk, they are

continued...

receiving antibiotics as a precautionary measure. The milk powder is really expensive and, sadly, in the coming weeks there will be other young cubs found in similar circumstances all over the country and each youngster will require similar attention.

A substantial amount of money will be needed to rear these three cubs, who have been named Copper and Penny for the females and Bob for the male, hence the name of the appeal. Apart from the costly milk powder, they will need other nourishing food once weaned. There will also be all the expenses associated with finding a suitable release site and the building of an artificial sett. Following release in early autumn, they will need supplementary feeding for a short while until they acclimatise to their new surroundings.

The trustees of Badger Trust – Sussex have decided to mount a fundraising appeal towards the expense of rearing not only Copper, Penny and Bob but also other orphaned cubs requiring similar help during 2009. We are full members of Badger Trust who have kindly permitted us to put this message on their website. You can help by making a donation for the benefit of motherless cubs. No matter how small the donation, every penny collected will help cubs such as Copper, Penny and Bob and we should like to thank all donors in advance for their kind assistance.

Of course, the ideal situation for all cubs is that they remain with their mother in the wild and are reared by her. But accidents happen: perhaps mum is run over, and sometimes in such circumstances a cub will struggle out of the sett and be lucky enough to be found and cared for. Our aim and that of Folly Wildlife Rescue is to rear the cubs as wild animals in order that they can be returned to the wild. Copper, Penny and Bob will be bottle-fed by one person only and once they are weaned they will be put into an outside pen where they will receive minimal human contact. We would do them no favours by making pets of them. If these three cubs all survive, they may be joined by one or two more and the entire group will be released into a suitable site during the autumn, helped with a little food initially and then left to fend for themselves as nature intended.

Finally, if you ever find a young cub that appears to have been abandoned, please do not delay. If you know the number of your local Badger group, ring them immediately.

continued . . .

Contact details for Badger groups can be found online on www.badgertrust.org.uk. Otherwise, ring the national organisation, Badger Trust, on 08458 287878, who will be able to assist you to make local contact. If you feel you may be able to offer a potential release site, the national organisation will be delighted to hear from you.

Thank you for reading this and for any donation you feel able to make. We hope you like the photographs and shall update this note with further pictures of Copper, Penny and Bob so you can enjoy watching their progress.

How to donate
You can either:

- send a cheque payable to Badger Trust – Sussex, c/o PO Box 708, East Grinstead RH19 2WN, or
- pay your donation direct to HSBC, Sort Code 40-24-37, Account No. 81216260, or
- donate online by going to our online shop and purchase the 'Orphaned Triplets Appeal' and then add your donation. This will ensure that your donation is identified for the cubs.

BADGER TRUST – SUSSEX
Registered Charity No. 1113434
March 2009

2 Developing a fundraising strategy

It is essential to spend time before undertaking any fundraising exercise to develop a strategy: some forms of fundraising can be costly and it is important to be sure that the costs will be justified in terms of a realistic return. The strategy will need to cover the following points.

- **The level of funding:** are funds required for a special project or part of the charity's rolling programme of work? How much is needed? Would it be possible to collaborate with other charities operating in the same field to meet the need?

- **Possible sources of funding:** for example, grants from local or central government, grant-making charities or companies.

- **The resources available to support fundraising:** fundraising costs money. Costs can range from producing appeal literature to equipping a fundraising office and organising fundraising events.

- **The proportion of gross receipts that will be left after fundraising costs have been met:** the trustees should agree in advance the likely proportion of the gross receipts that will be spent on the costs of fundraising. Actual performance needs to be monitored against that target and the trustees should satisfy themselves that the expenditure is justified.

Strategy is about organising your ideas to produce a viable plan to take you forward beyond the current year. If you just need a small amount for equipment, for example, all you may need to do is approach an individual or business sympathetic to your cause or organisation. However, if you have wider hopes and new projects to fund, you will need to spend some time and be creative in developing a sustainable fundraising strategy.

Your fundraising strategy is an integral part of your business plan and it should indicate where your organisation is expected to be in a specified number of years. Business plans should be flexible and should be updated every year to incorporate changes and new ideas. You will also need to revise your strategy every two to three years.

There are few quick fundraising fixes: getting funding for a project takes time. It can take nine months or more to prepare, apply for and receive a grant from one of the larger funders. It may take years to build up to a really big event. Be realistic from the start about how much time you have and how much time it will take.

Planning your approach

Spending time on planning your fundraising strategy is a good investment: forward planning can save time and resources and prevent difficulties later. It is also a sign of a proactive charity and this is attractive to funders.

The starting point for your strategy should be to define the needs of the organisation. This can be done at three levels.

To continue at the current scale of operation

For the organisation to continue at its present level, how much funding do you need? How much is already in place or assured and how much do you need to raise to meet spending requirements?

Expanding to meet a growing need

Most organisations would easily be able to target and benefit more beneficiaries if they had the resources. They often face a growing problem, which means there is a wish to expand the organisation to meet the need.

It might be helpful to ask yourself the following questions.

- What is the current level of unmet need?
- What will happen if nothing is done?
- How and why are the needs growing and what changes do you foresee over the next few years?
- What should your organisation be doing to respond to the challenges of the future?
- Who else is tackling the need?
- How does your plan fit in with what others are doing?
- Is your idea an effective way of addressing the need?
- Could or should you be providing solutions to the problem rather than simply addressing the need?
- Are there ways of collaborating with others that could combine efforts and resources to save money and make a greater impact?

■ Is it just a case of expanding what you are already doing or do you need to develop new mechanisms to address the problem?

■ Will staff or volunteers need further development and training?

Expanding and developing your organisation's work

Organisations need to be flexible and forward thinking if they are to meet the needs of their user group and develop in order to meet changing needs. For example, changes in demographics caused by immigration into a particular area or the closure of industries resulting in people moving away from an area will require changes in the organisation's services.

It may be necessary to extend or adapt your work, evaluate your impact, undertake research, experiment, innovate and perhaps campaign. This all requires extra money and the resources to raise it.

Fundraising for projects

It is far easier to raise money for something specific than to appeal for administrative costs or general funds. Donors prefer that their money is going to fund something they are genuinely interested in and specific, such as buying specialist equipment for your conservation project on the local village school site.

Many funders say they won't fund organisations, only their individual projects, and this is one reason to think of your work in project terms. The project should include the core costs necessary to run it, but it is discrete from the organisation's general funds.

It is easier to design, develop, market, monitor and control a specific project with its own budget and set outcomes than to do this for an entire organisation.

You should simply focus on a particular piece of work or activity instead of the whole organisation. A fundable project should be:

■ **specific**, an identifiable item of expenditure or aspect of your work

■ **important**, both to your organisation and to the need it is meeting – long-term impact is an added bonus

■ **realistic and achievable**, giving the funder confidence that you will be able to deliver the intended targets and outcomes

■ **good value**, so that it stands out in a competitive funding environment

■ **topical**, looking at current issues and concerns

- **relevant to the donor**, meeting their known interests and priorities
- **a manageable size**, so that it won't overload the organisation.

To cost a project properly, you need to include all the direct and indirect costs that can reasonably be attributed to the running of the project; for example, an appropriate percentage of management salaries, the cost of occupying the building, using the phone, photocopying and so on. This is known as full cost recovery.

Projection of financial need

The next step is to make a financial projection of the resources you will need to undertake your planned programme of work over the next three to five years. This must take in all planned expenditure and all probable income. It should show you two things: the funding gap that needs to be met, and possible fall-back options if funding is not received. This is illustrated by the following example.

Example of a funding projection for a small organisation

Source of income	Current year	Next year	Two years' time	Three years' time
Current local authority grant	10,000	10,000	5,000	nil
Grant from charitable trust	2,500	2,500	nil	nil
Membership subscriptions	250	250	250	250
Total committed income	**12,750**	**12,750**	**5,250**	**250**
Reserve at start of year	500	2,050	2,050	2,050
Current operational costs	10,000	12,500	15,000	15,000
New project costs	1,200	3,500	5,000	5,000
Projected fundraising target	**nil**	**3,250**	**14,750**	**14,250**

The example shows that the funding position for the current year is good, and that there is a small target to meet next year which is a realistic goal for fundraising. However in two years' time, as the major grants run out, these will need to be replaced or new ways developed to fund the organisation

Six key points to consider in your fundraising strategy

Most donors, whether they are large grant-making charities, major companies or individual members of the public, receive many more requests each year than they can hope to respond favourably to. How are you going to construct your case so that it stands out from the others? Before you start to fundraise, you need to ask yourself:

- **Who are you?** Are you reliable and professional, with a strong track record of good work successfully completed?

- **What is the need that you intend to meet?** This should not simply be an emotive statement, but should include factual evidence about, for example, whether the situation is local, national or global; how many people it affects; why it is urgent.

- **What is the solution that you offer?** This is where you can describe what you intend to do, the results you expect to obtain and how these will be monitored and measured. You may want to use examples of how similar projects have worked.

- **Why should you do it?** This is where you establish your credibility. What other work have you done? Have you had good publicity for this? Do you involve volunteers and/or your user group in your work? Do you have a good track record in attracting funding?

- **How much do you need?** You need to have a clear idea of the total, who you intend to approach for the money, and how the total could be broken down for donors who want to contribute but could not possibly fund the whole thing.

- **What future do you have?** If you can show that you have thought ahead and have attempted to achieve long-term stability, funders will be more inclined to support you.

Once you have the answers to these key questions, you will be able to use them in your fundraising, when you write an application to a grant-making body or company or when you appeal to the public.

Measurement and control of fundraising

Your fundraising strategy should be flexible and you should update it from time to time to take account of changes, both inside and outside your organisation. You should aim to review that strategy each year and rewrite it every three to five years.

The first step with a new or revised strategy must be to ensure that all your committee members, staff and key volunteers understand it and accept it. It will not be possible for everyone to be involved in producing the strategy document, so before you finalise it, make sure that all the issues have been widely discussed. This process of consultation will help everyone feel more committed to the outcome.

Monitoring progress

Without a strategy and a detailed plan, it is hard to monitor how you are getting on.

Why monitoring is important
- To check your overall returns.
- To compare the effectiveness of different aspects of your fundraising.
- To justify the level of investment the charity is making.
- To help assess and review your fundraising performance.

You will need to keep a particularly close eye on:
- costs incurred by each fundraising method
- cash received
- pledges of future support received
- offers of help and support in kind received.

Monitoring is often easier for a small organisation. It can be surprisingly difficult for many larger organisations if their financial systems have not been designed to produce the information that fundraisers require.

To compare the effectiveness of each fundraising initiative, the fundraiser needs to know exactly how much time and money is being spent on it and what income it is producing.

Monitoring sheet for .... month/year

Source	Direct income from source this month	Budgeted income from source for this month	Direct income from source for year so far	Budgeted income from source for year so far	Direct costs	Indirect costs	Cost: profit ratio
Collections							
Postal appeal							
Sponsored event							
Totals							

Signed: ....   Dated: ....

Detailed measurement of fundraising

You can measure the effectiveness of your fundraising in a number of ways, although not all measures are appropriate to all situations. The most common measures are the cost ratio and the profit. You might find the sample table above useful when making your calculations.

- The cost ratio is calculated by taking the direct income generated by the activity and dividing it by the total costs that can be attributed to that activity (including an estimate of the indirect costs). This is then expressed as a ratio (for example, 5:1). The main problem is that it does not give you the full picture.

  For example, you may discover that your public speaking to a wide range of local groups and appealing for support raised £2,380 and cost only £340 (a ratio of 7:1). On the other hand, you raised £17,200 from grantmakers at an estimated cost of £6,500 (a ratio of 2.6:1). This makes the latter look less successful and can be misleading. You may have exhausted all the local speaking possibilities and so you cannot repeat your success, even if this has been your most cost-effective method of fundraising.

  The cost ratio is an important management tool for controlling costs, but on its own it is not a sufficient measure of fundraising success. There are other measures which you can use.

If you are using the telephone to fundraise, you need to know how cost effective this method is. The first indicator is the response rate to your request (divide the number of successes by the total number approached). This method can similarly be used in postal appeals and payroll giving campaigns.

However, knowing how many people have responded is not enough, you also need to know how much they have given or pledged. It may be good to get 10 people in 100 saying yes; but if they only give £5 each, this has not been cost effective in terms of time and money spent. You can then try to increase both the response rate and the average donation. For example, when you ask a supporter to renew their membership, why not suggest that they increase the level of their giving? When organising a sponsored event, you can ask people to sponsor by the minute rather than by the hour, and they are then likely to give more. If you ask a supporter to pay monthly contributions, you are likely to receive more than if you ask for quarterly or annual contributions.

■ Another measure is the yield. This is the income received divided by the number of people approached. So, if you mail 1,000 people and receive £550 in donations, the yield would be 55p per donor mailed.

You will need to have some way of measuring the impact of long-term or open-ended commitments. Your fundraising commitments have gained you a donor; you can measure the donation they have made, but many of them will go on to give further support, and the costs of getting this further support will generally be much lower than the costs of getting the first donation. A very few may even go on to make a major gift or leave you a legacy.

■ Measuring the 'lifetime value' of a donor is useful because it helps you justify a higher level of initial expenditure on promotion and fundraising. For example, you mail 1,000 people and get 20 responses and a total of £550 in income. You predict that those 20 people on average will each make two further donations of the same amount. The total income you expect to receive from these donors is £1,650. The total cost is the cost of the initial mailing to 1,000 people plus the additional cost of further mailings to your 20 new supporters. From this you can calculate the lifetime value of these 20 donors and demonstrate that the costs of acquiring them, in this instance, were reasonable.

- Gross profit percentage is a key ratio for many types of trade, such as retail selling of bought-in goods (not donated goods), mail order selling, Christmas card sales and other forms of merchandising. Calculate the gross profit percentage as follows:

$$\frac{\text{Gross profit}}{\text{Sales}} \times 100$$

Different rates of gross profit can be expected for different types of goods, but monitoring the percentage, both overall and for individual lines, will provide useful management information about performance.

Selecting appropriate measures to assess your fundraising is extremely important. It enables you to manage the process better – to control costs, to try to generate more income and more supporters, and to retain these supporters for longer periods. It enables you to see what works and what doesn't work, to develop new and better fundraising techniques, and to test out new ideas. It is important that you succeed in generating the money you have committed to raise and that you do this within your agreed budget. It is also important that you continue to improve your fundraising skills.

Useful tips for a fundraising strategy paper

- Review of the current position, including:
  - strengths and weaknesses
  - past fundraising experience
  - existing fundraising resources.
- Who will undertake the fundraising.
- Projection of fundraising needs.
- Overall funding strategy.
- Proposed new sources of income.
- Suggested methods to meet fundraising targets.
- Resources needed to do this.
- Timeline for implementation.

3 The fundraiser

It is very important to get the person with the right attitude, commitment and skills to undertake fundraising for your organisation. In theory, anyone can be a fundraiser – they don't have to belong to a professional body, have formal qualifications or even have had vast experience in fundraising. They do, however, require exceptional skills to raise money effectively and to be an appropriate representative of your organisation. This chapter looks at those skills and the procedures the organisation should have in place when employing a fundraiser.

Please note that there is a difference in this chapter between 'fundraiser': a person who has been given the job of fundraising and 'professional fundraiser': a person who carries on a business for gain (see further details on page 32).

Who should fundraise?

This is one of the first considerations when developing a fundraising strategy and there are several options to consider.

The trustees

The people who are legally responsible for the administration and management of the charity and protecting its funds (the managing trustees, committee of management, board of directors, etc.) are required to ensure that the fundraising is carried out efficiently and effectively and to bear in mind all the legal requirements and best practice. They can carry out fundraising themselves, although this is more likely to happen with smaller charities.

The chair

In larger charities the chair, with the chief executive or manager, may be involved in meetings with businesses or larger grant-making charities in trying to secure funding. The chairs of smaller organisations will often undertake much of the fundraising themselves.

The chief executive or manager

The chief executive or manager is in the unique position of having a good knowledge both of the charity and its workforce and the legal requirements and responsibilities of the trustees. They are usually good networkers and often aware of other charities' events and sometimes their fundraising plans, and of the latest funding possibilities. They are also in a senior position and are able to make decisions on behalf of the trustees within certain parameters. They are, however, often very busy and if they are to manage a fundraising project will need administrative and other support.

A member of staff

Often, where fundraising is a high priority, charities may create a post of fundraiser to ensure that fundraising is ongoing rather than for one-off projects or events that happen from time to time.

Fundraising, whether by appeal, events or making applications to grantmakers, requires specific skills, imagination, creativity and a good knowledge of the charity and of the legal requirements surrounding fundraising. Members of staff employed to fundraise should be required to give frequent progress reports in order to ensure they have adequate support and are on track to meet their target goals.

Volunteers

Volunteers often have direct knowledge of the charity's user group and the commitment and enthusiasm necessary for successful fundraising. They may have more time to give but will probably need support from the staff and trustees. Very often volunteers will be given responsibility for one aspect of a fundraising strategy. Targets should be set and agreed and regular monitoring should be in place to ensure they are adequately supported.

A professional fundraiser

The following definition is taken from the Charity Commission website:

> A **professional fundraiser** is any person (apart from the charitable institution or a company connected with such an institution) who carries on a fundraising business for gain which is wholly or primarily engaged in soliciting or otherwise procuring money or other property for charitable purposes; or any other person who solicits for reward money or other property for charity apart from:
>
> ■ any charity or connected company
>
> ■ any officer or employee of a charity or connected company

- *any charity trustee*
- *any public charitable collector – other than promoters*
- *people who solicit funds on TV or radio*
- *any commercial participator.*

In addition, the definition of professional fundraiser does not apply if the fundraiser receives £500 or less by way of remuneration in connection with a particular campaign or £5 per day or £500 or less per year where there is no specific venture.

*A **commercial participator** is any person who carries on a business for gain, and which is not for fundraising, but who in the course of that business engages in any promotional venture (i.e. any advertising or sales campaign or any other venture undertaken for promotional purposes) in the course of which it is represented that contributions are to be given to or applied for the benefit of a charity.*

When employing a professional fundraiser or consultant you should consider whether the charity can afford their fee and consequent administration costs and whether their employment will increase the resources of the organisation in a significant way. Not many organisations are able to acquire sponsorship for a professional fundraiser and so their costs have to be met from funds they generate. It may be that you consider that it is necessary to employ them as no one else within the organisation has the time or the skills and expertise to take on the task and that without a dedicated person the organisation will not have the capacity to raise the income necessary to continue. However, you should be extremely selective in the recruitment process in order to achieve your aims cost-effectively and find the right person for the job.

People prefer to give to organisations and causes they have heard about and think well of. Your organisation's professionalism, credibility and reputation are important and your fundraiser is, in effect, an ambassador for your group.

Recruiting a fundraiser

If you decide to recruit a fundraiser you should circulate information about the job opportunity to your staff, supporters and volunteers and advertise in all the usual press, journals and recruitment services or via the Institute of Fundraising.

Once you have decided to recruit a fundraiser, you should consider the following objectives and skills required.

Objectives

What are the objectives for the fundraising post? Is it to:

- develop alternative sources of funds to replace grants that are coming to an end?
- launch an expansion programme?
- run a major capital appeal?
- develop independent and local funding?
- create a large and active membership?
- develop corporate support?
- organise high profile events that will raise awareness as well as money?

You need to be clear about your objectives. This will help you to write a job description and a person specification so that you recruit someone with the experience and ability to do a good job. The objectives must be realistic: they should recognise your need for money, the opportunities that exist to raise it and a reasonable timetable for doing this which is achievable.

There is always a learning process at the very start when the fundraiser is undertaking background research and developing contacts (and getting familiar with the work of the organisation if you have recruited externally). It is important, nonetheless, that results begin to flow reasonably quickly.

The skills required in a fundraiser

There are a number of key skills and qualities required of the fundraiser in order for them to achieve success.

Commitment and enthusiasm

These are two important qualities for the job of fundraiser. They must believe in the organisation's work and the cause it is addressing. Some people have the ability to raise significant amounts through their enthusiasm, personality and commitment to the user group and will encourage others to support them and add to the fundraising effort.

Persistence

Fundraising can be a hard and dispiriting business and many fundraisers will give up too soon. If your application or appeal is based on a worthwhile project, with realistic outcomes and where there is need in that area, it is worthwhile trying to persuade people of your belief in the organisation's ability to succeed and the positive contribution they could make.

Funders or donors want to be involved with projects that meet their own aims and which have a good chance of success. If the fundraiser feels that a potential funder would benefit from giving you money, it does no harm to persuade them of this even if the initial approach has been turned down (this is of course assuming that your project meets their criteria).

Truthfulness and realism

It is essential for fundraisers to be truthful and not exaggerate the need or promise outcomes that can't be delivered. The fundraiser should present a truthful case, making it attractive and powerful enough to persuade donors to give and using sensitivity and honesty.

There can be a temptation to present the user group as victims, which is patronising and not appropriate for people who are trying to reach their potential, or a specific goal, often despite disadvantage.

There can also sometimes be a temptation to promise unrealistic outcomes in order to get money, or to say what you think the donor wants to hear in order to illicit sympathy or to meet criteria. This is not a good idea: even if you get the money this time, the organisation will not be able to meet the targets set, budgets will be problematic, monitoring and evaluation will be very difficult and outcomes will not be met. The funder has to rely on the information supplied and needs to be able to trust that it is accurate. The fundraiser should raise money for what you want and for what you know you can deliver.

Knowledge

This can range from the detail of a current project – what the targets are, who will benefit and the costings for the project – to the overall aims and mission of the organisation. The fundraiser should also have a good knowledge of the organisation's finances; for example, how much is spent on administration and what the staffing costs are. When talking to potential donors, the fundraiser must be able to answer their questions.

Contacts and networking

The fundraiser should be aware of who they should be in contact with in your local area and who it might be useful to know. They should find out about local umbrella charities, councils for voluntary service, community foundations and which groups these organisations support. It would be helpful to attend local events and find out about other organisations, their current projects and long-term goals, their difficulties, their successes and who has funded them.

Training courses or conferences run by the Directory of Social Change or the Institute of Fundraising are both informative and useful for the fundraiser and a place where they will meet people in similar situations.

Good social skills

A good fundraiser needs confidence, patience, tact and diplomacy. Any appeal or application needs to be compelling and this requires confidence when dealing with questions from potential donors. They should be confident in the success of your group's appeal and the aims of your organisation. They will require patience, tact and diplomacy when asking for donations face to face – they are representatives acting on your behalf and need these skills to reflect the professionalism of your organisation.

Good organisational skills

Good organisational skills are essential for achieving success in any job and when fundraising it is equally important to keep accurate financial records, copies of all correspondence and appeal literature and notes of all meetings held in connection with the fundraising project. It is also important that clear and detailed records are kept of every donation given (where possible), so that no act of generosity is forgotten or unrecorded. This is good customer care and also contributes to transparency with public funds.

Imagination and creativity

Your organisation's work should be presented by the fundraiser in an imaginative and creative way. Your appeal needs to stand out from the others to inspire existing supporters and catch the attention of potential donors. Your organisation will be constantly evolving and the fundraiser can use these changes to identify new approaches. They should try not to rely too much on what has been done in the past, but to use fresh and innovative ideas to encourage people to think about and want to support your organisation's aims.

Opportunism

The good fundraiser makes things happen. For example, the difference between an adequate event and a really successful one could be the fact that a person of real standing in the community or a 'celebrity' is invited. This gives the event a higher profile and prestige and makes it much easier to market.

You should, however, be very selective in who you approach. Your invited special guest would need to have views sympathetic to your cause and be someone who you would want your organisation to be associated with.

Sometimes, despite all your best efforts things can go horribly wrong. In 1997 an internationally known model appeared in an anti-fur campaign for PETA, the animal rights organisation. Just seven months later the model was on a catwalk in Milan draped in a fur coat...

Case study

Select your fundraiser with care

The following extract is taken from *Charities Back On Track* 2007/08 published by The Charity Commission.

Offers to fundraise on their behalf may seem like a dream come true for hard-pressed charities, but making sure you do your homework is key to ensuring your gift horse does not become a Trojan horse.

The Summertime Trust

This charity was set up to provide holidays, transport and other facilities for disabled children. They were approached by a professional fundraiser, who offered to sell competition tickets, pens and badges on their behalf during a ten-year contract.

The deal involved the charity getting 20% of the money raised, with the fundraiser keeping 80%. The fundraiser would also receive one-third of any donations made to the charity as a 'management fee'. The charity took no professional advice about whether this agreement was in the best interests of the charity.

We soon started receiving calls from local authorities and supermarkets alerting us to the fact that the fundraiser was collecting without the necessary licences or permission. These were followed by complaints about the low level of charitable expenditure in relation to the amounts being raised.

Concerned about the charity's apparent inability to monitor and control these fundraising activities, and whether the contract between the fundraiser and the charity complied with the Charities Act and the Charitable Institutions (Fund-Raising) Regulations 1994, we opened an inquiry. We found that the contract did not comply with the law, that the terms tied the charity to a one-sided exclusive contract for a decade and that the ratio of money going to the charity was very small. For example, in one four month period the fundraiser raised nearly £250,000 but the charity received less than £50,000.

Money raised was not paid gross to the charity, and the trustees were completely unaware of how much was being raised and of the regular breaches of legal requirements. After receiving our advice and guidance, the trustees put various controls in place to monitor the fundraising activity and ensure it complied with fundraising

continued...

---

regulations. However, as the fundraiser refused to cooperate, the trustees gave him notice to terminate all further fundraising in the charity's name. Our intervention had effectively enabled the trustees to disrupt the potentially long-term financial exploitation of the charity by the fundraiser through a deficient contract agreement, as well as to alert others to this and similar previous activities by him.

After the closure of our inquiry, it came to the trustees' attention that the fundraiser carried on fundraising in the charity's name. The trustees reported the matter to the police, whose enquiries were ongoing at the time we published our inquiry report in January 2008.

Over a year after our inquiry closed, the trustees decided to dissolve the charity due to lack of funds.

Trustees should be actively involved in making key decisions in relation to agreements with professional fundraisers. In addition to our guidance Charities and fundraising *(CC20)*, the following may help:

Is the organisation legitimate?

- Is it a member of a trade body, such as the Public Fundraising Regulatory Association, the Institute of Fundraising and the Fundraising Standards Board? If not, you may want to know why.

- Ask for references and take them up.

- Does it have the necessary local authority licences for public fundraising?

- Do an internet search to see what public information there is about the organisation – you never know what may come up.

Is the agreement fair?

- How do you know how much is being raised? Does all the money get paid over to the charity, from which the charity then pays the fundraiser? Fundraising guidance says it should be paid gross, and be recorded gross in your accounts with costs shown separately.

- Does the agreement provide for you to see the fundraising in action (for example listening in to telephone fundraising or visiting the offices), review the fundraiser's performance, books and records and amend the contract accordingly?

- It is always a good idea to put any potential agreement out to open tender to ensure you're getting best value. Take independent legal advice on the terms of any fundraising agreement.

- *Does the agreement tie you in solely to this company? If so, why and for how long?*

Are you getting a good return?

- *£20,000 a year may seem a lot, but not if the fundraising organisation is bringing in £100,000. There is no recommended level for a return on investment but you should ensure you are getting at least a reasonable amount for the use of your charity's name.*

- *Are there high upfront or ongoing fundraising costs? Why? Who is paying for them? Can the fundraisers justify them to you and – importantly – will you be able to justify them to your donors?*

Do you like their methods?

- *How are they planning to raise your funds? Cold-calling businesses to buy adverts in charity wall-planners? Tin rattling? Make sure you set clear boundaries and are happy with their proposals.*

- *Check they are clear about making the required solicitation statement stating both that they're professional fundraisers and how much they will get out of donations.*

- *If they propose fundraising material for your charity, make sure you get final sight and sign-off – after all, you're probably paying for it.*

- *Consider both your charity's brand and the reputation of charities generally. Being mired in controversial fundraising methods could cost you a lot more in lost support than the £10,000 you are getting from the company.*

Employing a fundraiser

Once you have a fundraiser in position you must provide the structure, guidance and resources they need to do their job.

Setting targets and monitoring progress

Targets should be agreed with the fundraiser rather than imposed and progress should be monitored regularly. It may not be the fundraiser's fault if targets are not being met – you or they may have been overly optimistic, or one large donation may have failed to materialise. Regular monitoring and adjustment of targets will help to ensure that any problems are addressed quickly.

The organisation should try to learn from past mistakes. You may want to create a small fundraising advisory group that will take a particular interest in the fundraising and with whom the fundraiser can discuss issues or refer problems.

Keep track of the time and effort put into each fundraising initiative. Too much time can be spent chasing after marginal or unlikely sources and too little developing those central to your future. Fundraising events can take up a lot of time for little financial return. Time is usually your most expensive asset, so your fundraiser must use it effectively.

Budget

Your fundraiser will need to be provided with a budget for equipment, operational costs and promotional activity. Without such a budget they will be unable to do their job properly. The following box gives a list of headings that you will probably need to include.

Budget headings (employing a fundraiser)

- Recruitment and training
- Salary, national insurance and pension contribution
- Computer and printer
- Mobile phone
- Stationery, printing and photocopying
- Share of office overheads
- Travel
- Subscriptions to professional organisations, magazines, etc.
- Purchase of directories or CD ROMs, etc.
- Design and print of leaflets and a presentable annual report
- Mailing costs

Equipping a fundraising office

Some items and pieces of equipment are essential for a fundraiser; others are extremely useful. The main items that should be made available are as follows.

- **Annual reports and brochures** If you are a registered charity you have to produce an annual report by law. However, it is also an important fundraising document, as many funders or donors will want to see your report and accounts. They do not need to be expensively produced but should be well prepared and presented. A small range of information leaflets for the public that include reply coupons will encourage a direct response.

- **Books and websites** Books or websites on fundraising, sources of funding and technical information on tax are all very valuable. Directories of trusts and companies that list the major givers and provide information on their grant policies are essential (visit www.dsc.org.uk for information on DSC's range of publications and subscription websites).

- **Cash collection facilities** You must have a bank account so that you can pay in donations. If you expect to have large sums on deposit for any length of time you should have a high interest account. If you plan to do door-to-door or street collections you will need to have the appropriate envelopes or collection boxes. You will also need to be aware of new regulations regarding this following the Charities Act 2006. Please refer to the Charity Commission website – see *Useful contacts and sources of information* on page 409.

- **Computer** A computer together with a basic software package such as Microsoft Office (or OpenOffice.org, which is free) will help you produce high-quality letters and proposals as well as storing your database of supporters and perhaps your budget and financial records. You will also need a good printer, and as part of your start-up package you may be offered a scanner, which can be useful when producing material such as publicity leaflets.

- **Display equipment** Fairs, exhibitions and shop windows can be good ways of gaining more interest in your work. You will need attractive (not necessarily expensive), informative display material.

- **Email and the internet** More and more information is sent by email, and most funders now have websites. You may want to have a second telephone line for a fax. All sorts of package deals are now available from telecoms companies and internet service providers (ISPs).

- **Fax** From time to time you may need to fax a document. You can get a fax machine that will also do small volumes of photocopying.

- **Letterheads** Letterheads need to include certain information (name and address, website, logo, legal status and charity registration number, etc.). The design of your letterhead is important; it is the first point of contact for many people. You can also spread your message through a strapline explaining your aims or mission. You might also want to consider whether you need business cards, compliments slips and reply-paid envelopes.

- **Photocopier** This will help you to prepare large volumes of printed material for circulation to supporters. If you don't have access to a photocopier, try to make arrangements with your local copy shop and ask them to give you a good price.
- **Telephone** This is essential. Ideally you need a line for the fundraiser only, because of the volume and length of the calls, and to have it in a quiet place, so that calls can be made in privacy. Fundraisers are often out of the office, so you need to ensure either that someone is there to answer the calls or that there is a voicemail facility. You should also be able to track the cost of calls in order that you can compare this with the budget.

Setting up an office can be expensive. You may be able to borrow some of the equipment from friendly organisations or supporters; other equipment you might get cheap or second hand. You can also try to get equipment donated (local companies often have surplus equipment or furniture), or ask local suppliers for a good discount.

You could also use a recycling scheme or check to see if a Freecycle scheme operates in your area. If you are a member of NCVO (National Council for Voluntary Organisations), you can take advantage of discounts it has negotiated on a range of products and services for its members.

You might want to prepare a shopping list of your needs and present it to a major funder as an investment package. It is in the funder's interest to help you set up a fundraiser's post – it will reduce your dependency on them.

Keep your donors committed

Remember, getting money is only the start of the process. First-time donors are more likely to give again if your project is a success and you can back this up with the targets you have met, i.e. the people and/or community you have benefited. Your fundraiser should keep your donors or funders informed of how you are progressing and how the quality of your user group's lives is improving as a result.

4 How much do we need?

A guide to basic budgeting

Success in raising money depends to a large extent on research, showing evidence of that research, planning and presentation. All of these are involved in drawing up a budget for a project. You want to be confident that what you are asking for is realistic in terms of what the funder can give, but also that you have asked for enough to meet your project's needs. Funders often say that projects have been under-costed and applicants should have asked for more – the required amount to achieve success. An under-costed budget is as unlikely to succeed as an over-priced one: both show that the budget has been poorly planned.

A budget will help your organisation with:

- planning
- accountability
- setting objectives
- directing funders
- raising money for core costs.

Who should draw up the budget?

There are undoubtedly people who cope with figures more confidently than others and hopefully there is at least one person in your organisation who has this expertise. However, the process of budgeting should also involve those who will actually carry out the work, as they are likely to have an idea of what will be involved and they will carry the burden of an under-funded project if the costing is not realistic. Consultation also encourages accountability. Where people have been involved in drawing up estimates for income and expenditure they will have a better idea of what resources are really available and why they should keep to their forecasts.

What needs to be included in the budget?

How much a project really costs

Before looking at any income that will come to the project, you need to look first at how much the project will cost to run. There are obvious costs and other costs that are hidden. Some items such as equipment may seem easier to fund than others. Don't leave less attractive elements out as these are part of the real cost of running the project. This is an opportunity to apportion core costs to a project and raise money for salaries, running costs and depreciation.

Some organisations are nervous about this approach, worrying that funders may be scared off by large amounts that seemed to have been 'smuggled in'. Full cost recovery was endorsed in *The Role of the Voluntary Sector in Service Delivery: A Cross Cutting Review* (HM Treasury, 2002), which states:

> All voluntary and community organisations have fixed or overhead costs. There is a strong view within the voluntary and community sector (VCS) that funders are often unwilling to finance these costs and a common perception by funders that other sources of finance are already being used for this purpose.

> But there is no reason why service providers should not include **the relevant portion of overhead costs** within their bids for service contracts. These are part of the total costs of delivering a service. To do this, the VCS needs to be able to apportion overhead costs effectively. But there is no reason why service funders should be opposed in principle to the inclusion of relevant overhead costs in bids. Clearly, different providers will want the autonomy to decide how to structure individual bids and funders will want to award service contracts on a best value basis.

The same principle applies when making applications to grant-making charities – you should ask for the full cost of delivering your project, or your organisation or club may struggle to meet the targets set.

Funders who have a feel for the business of sifting applications will recognise a realistic project costing when they see one. (If you are applying to funders whom you suspect may not appreciate this approach you can explain your figures more fully, or simply present a shopping list of items for them to choose from.)

If you ask for too little you may not be able to run the project at all, or if you do, benefit fewer in your user group and only run it half as well as you would have done if you had allocated costs properly. Cost items realistically and have confidence in your budget. If the proposal is well thought out and it needs £20,000 to see it through, you should apply for £20,000.

Having a realistic grasp of how much a project will cost means allowing for:

- any capital costs (machinery, equipment, buildings, etc.)
- running costs (salaries, rent, heating, depreciation, decoration, etc.).

Whether you are budgeting for a capital item or the running costs of the project, the processes will be the same.

Capital costs

If you are planning a capital project (an extension to your existing facilities, or a new computer suite for your educational project, for example), you need first to list all your costs. These may include all or some of the following:

Land and buildings

- How much will it cost to buy the land?
- How much will it cost to provide access or facilities for people with disabilities?

Professional charges

- Accountant
- Architect
- Feasibility studies
- Quantity surveyor
- Solicitor
- Structural engineer

Building costs

- Site works before construction
- Construction cost (as on contractor's estimate)
- Furniture and fittings
- Security system
- Decoration
- Equipment

You should add to this list as necessary. However, these are only the costs of *building and equipping* your extension or new suite. They do not show how you will pay for the long-term costs (such as maintenance, heating, lighting, security and insurance). These ongoing costs should be included in your revenue budget, as shown on the following page.

No budget will be 100% accurate. It is your best estimate, with evidence if appropriate, at the time you are planning the project of how much money you will need. You may wish to put in a contingency for unforeseen costs, if you feel this is a sensible precaution.

If at a later stage it appears that your figures are no longer accurate, you can always revise your budget so that it reflects the financial situation as you then know it. Remember though, that you will probably not be able to get any extra money from your funder to cover this.

The list also assumes that you will be paying for everything. In fact, it may be that a friend of the organisation who is an architect may reduce their fees as a donation; you may be able to get your members to paint the extension with donated paint from a local factory; and your furniture may be given by a firm that has recently had its offices refurbished. All this should be taken into account and your budget adjusted as necessary. It helps when applying to funders to show how much you have raised from your own resources. Gifts in kind (such as donated furniture or reduced solicitor's fees) should be costed and their financial value recorded.

Revenue costs

These are your main running costs and will include all or some of the following:

Premises

- Rent
- Rates
- Maintenance of the building, inside and outside
- Heating
- Lighting
- Health and safety measures
- Security
- Insurance
- Depreciation of equipment

Administration

- Salaries (including national insurance)
- Telephone
- Postage
- Stationery or printing
- Cleaning or caretaking
- Book-keeping, audit and bank charges
- Training courses
- Childcare
- Volunteers' expenses
- Miscellaneous (travel, tea, coffee, etc.)

Project costs

These are the costs of running individual activities or pieces of work that take place in the building or as part of your remit as an environmental organisation. Where you can, split your work up into separate units that can be costed individually. You can then look at what a project costs, which includes capital items and revenue costs such as those listed previously.

By costing projects separately you can keep track of individual project costs and allocate some of your general running costs to projects when preparing funding applications. (See Chapter 5 *Fundraising for projects.*)

Drawing up a budget: estimating your income

Your budgeted costs set out what you need to spend. The other side of a budget needs to show where you intend the money to come from.

Look at each source of income you can expect (for example, your local community foundation, local authority, subscriptions, fundraising events) and list them as you did your expenditure. The project itself may produce an income and you should provide evidence of your research into this and how much is expected to be generated.

You will need to look at where this year's income came from and make a reasonable guess about what will happen next year. Most of this is common sense and an awareness of local issues. You can look at opportunities as well as threats to your funding. Is there a new source of support that has opened up? Do you have more members this year than you did last year? Do you have a new group of volunteers? Has your funding been affected by local government reorganisation?

Monitor your income frequently and carefully and allow for any shortfall in your expected income quickly. For example, if you had expected to raise £30,000 from the Big Lottery Fund to expand your support service for people with physical disabilities but your application fails, you then have to make some decisions. Do you have reserves, and do you want to use them for this? Can you borrow the money and can you afford to? Can you raise money through cutting expenditure in other areas? Do you have time to find another funder? Should you abandon the scheme and, if so, what are the consequences for your user group?

When forecasting income it helps to list both definite and hoped for funds. For example:

Source of income	Budget	Certain	Probable	Possible
Local authority	£25,000	£25,000	–	–
Membership subs (i)	£2,000	£1,200	£600	£300
Grant-making charities (ii)	£5,000	–	£3,000	£2,000
Local companies (iii)	£250	–	£250	–

1) **Membership subs:** Say you have 100 members paying £12 each. You can enter £1,200 in the 'certain' column for next year. You estimate you can accommodate more (although you will have to work out any significant increases in expenditure that this will cause). You have a waiting list of around 50, and you predict that they are all likely to join, so enter £600 in the 'probable' column. You also hope that some publicity will bring in an extra 25, but you are not sure, so put £300 in the 'possible' column.

2) **Grant-making charities:** Your budgeted £5,000 can be entered in the 'probable' column if you are confident of the charity (for example, the grant is recurrent). You would put the figure in the 'possible' column if you know less about it and felt less hopeful.

3) **Local companies:** Similarly with companies, if you have a good relationship with local businesses or they are represented on your management committee, the £250 can go under 'probable'. Otherwise enter under 'possible'.

Income versus expenditure

Having listed your projected spending and income you will now have an idea of where you stand. This process can give an overview for the whole organisation but can also give the picture for individual projects. Try to make sure that you are not too optimistic about your sources of income and that you haven't missed some areas of expenditure or under-costed them.

If your income is below your projected spending you will need to look carefully at the reasons for this. Is the snapshot year you are looking at exceptional in some way? Do you have a large number of one-off start-up costs related to a big project (such as building work, feasibility studies, equipment costs, etc.) that will not be repeated in following years, or does the deficit come as a result of regular income failing to match routine expenditure? Wherever there is a shortfall you will have to do some planning immediately. What you should *not* do is ignore the problem.

Look carefully at the figures again and satisfy yourself that they are reasonable. Decide whether the shortfall is short-term or long-term.

Look at what you can afford to do, and decide whether you can manage the deficit by some cutting-back or whether you need to take more drastic action. You may need to scale some things down or wait a while longer to start other things. You will need to allow for time to elapse if you are cutting expenditure; the effect will not necessarily be instant. You may have to cut some activities altogether or use successful projects to subsidise other under-funded ones.

Whatever you decide, make sure that it is realistic and that it is clearly understood within the organisation.

Cash flow predictions

The final phase of this part of budgeting is looking at your cash flow. This is where you try to forecast when the money will come in, and when it will go out. Will there be any significant changes in costs or income during the year? This is particularly important if you have a building project where large bills have to be paid. Will you have enough money to cover them?

Take all the different areas of expenditure that you have listed and work out in which month each will be paid. For example, salaries are paid evenly throughout the year; rent is paid quarterly; insurance is due in October; deposit for the residential activity week is to be paid in February; and the printing bill for the summer schools' club is due at the end of June. Once you have done this, try then to allow for the events and items of expenditure that will be extra this year. If you have some flexibility, you may want to plan them in months where other expenditure is relatively low. Once you have done this, total up each month's expenditure.

You should now do the same with your expected income. Again, this may be erratic and difficult to predict. If you have a grant, payment is probably made on a fairly regular basis (provided your project is meeting its targets) and you will know when to expect it to be paid into the organisation's account; membership subscriptions may be collected throughout the year; government money for your recycling project may be paid in a particular month; and your second year's funding from, say, the local community foundation is sent after its February trustees' meeting. These are the sources you can predict.

There may be others such as the various award schemes that change each year and make planning difficult. If you have a source of money that is new to your organisation, you will have to become familiar with the timing of payments – phone them and ask.

By matching the expected monthly spending with the expected monthly income you will spot any gaps where there is little or no money to meet expected bills. You need to plan and take action for this. You may be able to renegotiate your payment terms for some items. You may need to arrange an overdraft facility. If you are hiring equipment you will want to schedule payments in months that have less expenditure.

Forecasting becomes particularly important if you are planning a large capital project. Some funders will award you your grant but will only pay in stages when work has actually been completed; you need to reach agreement with your builders over this. Funders will rarely consider applications for work that has already started, and before embarking on a large capital project you should apply for money for a feasibility study and surveys before you make your application for the build itself.

Having worked out your budget you should have a good idea of how much you need, what you need it for and when you need it by and you will have evidence to support your figures. You are now in a position to approach funders.

When you are implementing your budget, review and monitor it regularly and try to stay within the budget headings. Where these change because of an anticipated over- or under-spend, and you think it best to modify, ask for approval from your funder and keep them informed of any changes before you implement them. Similarly, the management committee (your trustees), will need to be informed where money allocated under one heading is to be used to subsidise another.

Budgeting – a five step plan

Step 1 Estimate your costs (these are very often higher than you first think).

Step 2 Estimate your income (this is often lower than you first think).

Step 3 Predict your cash flow.

Step 4 Make adjustments as necessary.

Step 5 Implement your budget, monitor it and make it work – reviewing the budget and forecasting should be a standard item at management committee meetings.

5 Fundraising for projects

Fundraising is about getting hold of enough money to meet the day-to-day and/or capital costs of your organisation, plus the resources required for future development. However, it is far easier to raise money for something specific than to appeal for administrative costs or general funds. This is because donors can then match the support they give to a specific piece of work that they are really interested in and for which they can see direct outcomes. This way they can see that their money is actually making a change and that they have made a real contribution.

Asking for money towards the upkeep of your preservation society may (just) work with your local authority; it won't get very far with the Heritage Lottery Fund. They will only want to fund a particular project or part of your work, for example: your new work with young people aiming to improve local green spaces, community gardens and allotments.

Your members will also respond much better to an appeal for one specific item (such as a new piece of equipment) than for a generous contribution to your overall expenses.

Thinking of your work in project terms and designing projects that will attract support is the basis of successful fundraising.

Make your project sound exciting

One of the great advantages with project fundraising is that you can highlight particular areas of your work that will interest the person you are writing to. Make sure you do everything that you can to show that the work is worthwhile, worth funding and will be enjoyed by your user group and others in the community.

A fundable project should be:

- **specific** – an identifiable item of expenditure or aspect of the organisation's work
- **important** – both to the organisation and to the cause or need it is meeting. If there is some long-term impact that will be an advantage

- **effective** – there should be a clear and positive outcome
- **realistic** – the work proposed should be achievable
- **good value** – it should be a good use of the donor's money
- **topical** – it should be looking at current issues and concerns
- **relevant** – it should be relevant to the donor and the donor's particular funding concerns
- **manageable** – it should not be too large or too small for a donor to support, although the cost might be shared through several smaller grants.

Identify a project

Case study

Our village Heritage Society

This group conserves, regenerates and promotes the restoration of its local area.

Its activities include the restoration of local woodlands and the maintenance and improvement of a community garden for the village, created from an unregistered piece of land which had become derelict.

The society needs to generate another £3,000 a year to cover its costs. It also wants to erect a large, secure shed on the site of the garden in which to store its gardening tools and equipment. It has £950 in the bank. What can it do?

- Put up the members' subscriptions to cover the £3,000 annual deficit. However, many members would resist an increase in subs and might leave, so this could result in making the problem worse.
- Have a one-off special appeal to members and users. This would solve the problem but is not sustainable.
- Apply to the local authority for a grant. It might fund this as a one-off grant but the group would not be able to rely on the grant permanently.
- Organise an annual fete. This might bring in sufficient profit but it's a bit ambitious and who is going to organise and fund it?
- Write to local charities and companies to fund the deficit. Unfortunately, they wouldn't fund running costs that you simply couldn't meet.

continued...

Clearly there are problems with all the above strategies. The society could try to divide its needs into more attractive projects and apply for funding for these individually.

- It could apply for funding to expand the membership to include local schools. This would attract funds from various groups interested in the welfare of children and young people. It could also be run on a fee-paying basis, like an after-school club, to bring in extra money.
- It could develop specific activities for people with disabilities. This would widen the range of possible funding sources.
- It could set up research activities, including surveys, on the local flora and fauna and on how the village residents would like the group to develop and improve the local environment. Again, other funding streams could be available for this research.
- It could provide training on horticulture and environment awareness topics and charge a fee.

The advantage of breaking the work down into projects is that you can appeal to a wider range of funders. You are no longer restricted just to those concerned for say, local heritage, you can apply to people interested in children, education, health, family life and people with disabilities. Having done this, running and developing the society and its capital requirements is a much easier proposition because: the society is clearly being used for the benefit of a wide cross-section of the community; and this brings in a number of potential new funders.

By breaking the bigger picture up and dividing it into projects, you can focus on activities (for example, conservation awareness courses, research projects) rather than your own core needs (money for bills), widen the range of possible funders (you are no longer just about your current users) and force yourselves to be a bit more creative in your fundraising.

Full project funding – how to cost it

Costing a project

Imagine you are running training courses in environment awareness (i.e. this is your project). You will have two basic categories of costs – direct and indirect.

The direct costs will include the equipment, publicity and tutors' fees – these are usually fairly easy to identify. The indirect costs (sometimes called support costs or hidden costs) can be harder to pinpoint. They generally include items such as staff time for those not involved on a day-to-day basis in the project (for example, a manager, admin worker or finance controller), depreciation, use and maintenance of the building (including rent, rates, heat and light), insurance, post, telephone, stationery and other office costs.

A difficult area is how to calculate the central or office costs. Obviously, you cannot work out in advance exactly how many telephone calls will be made or the stamps or office stationery that will be needed. The best way to come to a reasonable estimate is to try and work out how much of your organisation's time and facilities will be taken up by the project.

So if your project will be the fourth one in the organisation and it takes up the same amount of space as the others and requires the same amount of the manager's supervision time, then it would be reasonable to allocate a quarter of all your central costs to the project. However, if it is only taking up a tenth of the organisation's time and facilities, then allocate a tenth of these costs. Remember, you are not expected to predict things down to the last pound; rather, the funder simply wants to see a sensible way of calculating the full cost of doing this work.

In a climate where it is more and more difficult for groups to get funding for the less glamorous parts of their work, it is vital that applicants cost projects appropriately and that includes all the costs needed for running the project – they must include core costs. This is what full project funding is all about – trying to identify the real cost of the work you are doing, including all the costs needed for running the project.

If you are successful, funders may require detailed accounts of how the money was actually spent to compare this with your initial budget, which will have been a reasonable estimate. More and more funders expect to see these central costs included in a budget. They see it as a sign of good management and of a well planned piece of work, rather than the applicant trying to apply for 'double funding'.

To cost a project properly, you need to include all the direct and all the indirect costs that can reasonably be said to be necessary to the running of the project. This means you should allocate a proportion of your central (or core) costs to the project. The process of costing a project has several stages.

Describe the project
Be clear about what the project is. You should identify what the project will do for its users rather than how it will solve your funding problems. For example:

'We will develop our existing environment awareness course into more structured educational training through the provision of IT equipment. This will enable trainees to design and produce information sheets, fliers, posters and a colour calendar showing the growing seasons'.

The direct costs

Write down a list of all the direct costs. For the educational project these could include:

- staff costs
- extra tables and chairs
- pens, paper and other necessary stationery
- kitchen equipment
- refreshments
- advertising and publicity
- computers and software.

The indirect costs

Write down a list of all the relevant central costs. This is where you need to be more focused in your thinking because you must include all the hidden costs. At this point you are trying to establish how much the project actually costs to run.

The classes cannot run without a building; the building needs heat, light and insurance; the tutors and any support staff will need the use of a telephone and photocopier; they may need supervision, training and so on.

Your list of indirect costs will include:

- rent and rates
- heat and light
- postage and telephone
- management and supervision of the project
- book-keeping
- insurance
- cost of training courses for staff.

You should think of your work as a series of projects and build your full overhead costs into each of these. You should recognise that if the overhead costs have not been applied for, the project will not be fully funded and will fail.

Include the relevant central costs in each project budget. You can then use the attractiveness of the project to get the unattractive administrative costs paid for.

Costing the costs

Put a figure against all the areas of expenditure. This is pretty straightforward for the direct costs, although make sure you get more than one quote on each cost. The difficulty is how to cost the indirect expenditure. You cannot put a precise figure on this; all you can do is be reasonable. You should try and work out what proportion of the central costs the project needs.

Say your organisation as a whole currently uses premises for 40 hours a week and you intend to run the training courses for ten hours a week. This means the project will be using the building 25% of the time. Say that it will occupy half the centre's rooms. Putting these two figures together you can then say that it takes up 12.5% of the centre's building costs. So allocate 12.5% of all the rent, rates, heat, light, postage, telephone, etc., to the project.

If you have one manager who has responsibility for all the activities, you will need to work out how much time this person will spend supervising the project and allocate the salary and national insurance costs accordingly. So, for example, if the manager works a 35-hour week and will spend on average 3.5 hours per week on the project, allocate 10% of the salary and national insurance to that.

Is it reasonable?

Ask yourself: 'Does the total figure look reasonable?' Does it look real value for money?

Some of the costs you will put down will be difficult to put a precise figure on, so the budget is flexible. The key thing is that you can justify how you have arrived at those figures if a funder questions you about them.

Finally

You now have to decide who will pay for what. Are you going to ask one funder for the whole amount of the project or are you going to ask various funders for different parts of it? Are you going to allocate some of your own money to the project (for example 10% of your local authority grant)? Remember:

- apply to a funder who is interested in your kind of work
- ask for an amount they can conveniently give
- stress the benefits of the project to your existing and potential beneficiaries and the community and show how it is real value for money
- more than one funder requires more than one set of monitoring and evaluation procedures – account for this in your budget.

Sample budget

Project name: It's Easy Being Green – Accredited course on current environmental issues.

Course duration: Two days a week for six weeks. Non-residential.

Number of participants: 10

Number of tutors: Two

Costs:

1) *Equipment:*
   Purchase of 10 laptops £
   Video camera hire £
   Video cassettes £

2) *Staff:*
   Tutors (a) £
   Part-time project director (b) £

3) *Building use:*
   Heating £
   Electricity £
   Training room (c) £
   Publicity £
   Office expenses £
   Caretaking/cleaning £

4) *Overheads:*
   Insurance £
   Depreciation (d) £
   Miscellaneous £

Total costs £ ....

Notes

(a) Requires two people working ten hours per week for six weeks at £ ....
    per hour

(b) A part-time post for two months @ £ .... per month

(c) 25% of current facilities for 12 days, so allow 25% x 12 x £X room hire per
    day

(d) Equipment if bought is usually depreciated over three years so you would
    need to allow 33% of the purchase price of the equipment each year – this
    is so that you build into the budget the cost of replacing out-of-date or
    broken down equipment.

6 Preparing and writing a good application

Your fundraising application is the introduction of your organisation, which needs support, to those who can provide it, and you only get one chance of giving a first impression, so it needs to be good. This is the opportunity to sell your idea to someone who has the means to make it happen. The easier you make it for the funder to assess your application (by providing relevant information and evidence, including of meeting their criteria), the more they will be inclined to help you. This help may be a one-off cash donation, a grant spread over a number of years, the sponsorship of an event, gifts for a raffle, time and expertise from a member of staff or an item of equipment.

Your task is to make the funder interested in and engaged with your vision and ideas, aware of the good practice your organisation has in place, including stringent and transparent financial procedures, good governance and the ability to deliver the targets set for the project.

Before you begin your application

Writing successful applications is a skill. You might write the clearest, brightest, most engaging application, but if it misses an essential point or fails to meet the funder's criteria, you will not be successful.

Before you start, you need first to have prepared thoroughly. Most funders receive hundreds of requests each year; think carefully about how you can make your application stand out from the others. Look at any previous successful applications for a guide, and at failed applications for any feedback you have received.

There are many ways of asking for funding. You can ask face to face; you might make a presentation to a group of business people or a meeting of supporters; you might consider it best in certain circumstances to use the telephone. Wherever possible, make a personal contact, it's surprising how few people are asked personally for money when in some circumstances this would be the best way to gain their support.

The funding bodies outlined in this guide would most likely require an application letter or completion of an application form. This chapter will look at what to include and also how to improve your presentation.

Most of the effort of application writing goes into condensing a full account of the project and organisation and providing evidence of need, numbers of beneficiaries (including those who were not supported before), an exit strategy (how your project will continue when the funding ends), administrative and financial procedures including an audit trail, provisions for monitoring and evaluation and feedback from your user group and others.

It is important not to provide reams of unnecessary paperwork but to stick to the criteria required and be concise and accurate. Funders have many applications to look through and cannot spend time reading and interpreting vast amounts of information.

It isn't possible to tell funders everything; generally they do not have the resources to consider all that you know about your organisation and the proposed project and many find that application letters are far too long. Put yourself in your reader's place and consider what it is you would need or want to know if you were responsible for public or charity money and wanted to fund a successful project.

A general rule would be one and a half sides of A4 maximum for a letter to a grantmaker and one side maximum to a company. Local authorities and central government departments may give you more space on their forms – generally speaking these officials will be more used to reading long project descriptions. This gives you the opportunity to provide more detail about the benefits of your project. You should still maintain a clear, positive and succinct style.

Funders that provide application forms should also give you guidelines on how long your answers to their questions should be and what they need to know.

Your approach

Most of the larger grantgivers publish guidelines on what they will and will not fund. It is important to read these before applying to see if what you are proposing fits within their policies, meets their criteria for the programme to which you are applying and does not fall within their exclusions.

In your letter or application, select and concentrate on your main selling points and the set outcomes of your project, emphasising those which will be of most interest to the particular person or funder you are writing to. Don't ask funders to support your organisation. Instead, ask them to support the people you help, the work that you do and, preferably, a specific project.

Believe in what you are doing and be enthusiastic – positive messages are more inviting than negative ones. Try not to go in for the sympathy vote by focusing on the gloomy consequences of not getting the money. Paint an exciting picture of all the things that will happen when you do get the money. You need to enthuse people and make them want to be a part of your work.

Be aware of the traps that could prevent your application getting the attention it deserves; for example, asking for too little by not budgeting properly or writing what you think the funder wants rather than giving an honest, well thought through account of your project. A major grant-making charity states in its guidelines:

> *A thoughtful and honest application always stands out in the crowd! Tell us clearly what the problem is, and how your project will do something about it. Give us relevant facts and figures, please don't use jargon, and don't be vague. You don't need to promise the moon, just tell us what you can realistically achieve.*

> *Your budget should show that you've done your homework and know what things cost.*

> *A thoughtful and honest application isn't a hurried and last minute dash to meet our deadlines with something dreamed up overnight. It is a serious and sincere attempt by your organisation to use its experience and skill to make a positive difference where it is needed.*

You will need to make a number of key points that will catch the reader's attention, arouse interest in the work, and sell your proposal to them. Ask yourself:

- Why should anyone want to support us?
- What is so important about what we are doing?

In other words what is unique about your work – what makes it different, why is it necessary and what will it achieve? Importantly, why should this particular donor want to support it?

You should try your answers and application out on a friend who does not work in the same field and has little knowledge of your work. Your application letter should tell any reader everything they need to know about your appeal in a short time. Assume they will not read anything else you send. After reading the letter, if your friend cannot answer the following questions, then nor will your potential supporter be able to.

- What is your organisation about, what does it need and why does it need it?
- What good will the project do, why would they want to be associated with it, where will other funding come from and what will happen when their support has finished?

Funders need to feel they know the context you're working in and what you're trying to do and you need to reassure them by explaining your ethos, aims and activities in a way that is clear. An outsider's view can tell you whether you are assuming too much about your reader, whether you need more or less information to make your case and when you have got it about right.

Eight essential elements of an application

1) What your organisation believes in and wants to achieve
2) Why you are writing to this particular funder/donor
3) The need you wish to meet
4) The solution you offer
5) Why *your* organisation should do it
6) The amount you need
7) The future you have – your project's exit strategy and future plans
8) Your organisation's monitoring, evaluation, financial and administrative procedures

1) What your organisation believes in and wants to achieve

The funder wants to know what kind of organisation they are dealing with and it is helpful for them to know:

- what your ethos is – what drives your organisation
- how long you have been operating
- what your key activities are
- what you have done that has been especially worthwhile or innovative.

Show the funder that your organisation is professional, creative and one that they would want to be associated with.

2) Why you are writing to this particular funder or donor

It seems to be standard practice to tell the funder or donor how much you are requesting in the introductory paragraphs and you might want to stick with this standard form of approach. It may be, however, that you would prefer your funder to know what your organisation is about and who you benefit and also that you know something about their organisation before asking for money. An example of your opening sentences might then be:

> Let'sGoGreen is a charity set up to address the problems of climate change through a commitment to the production of food by local people for local consumption, and to the recycling of waste products. Our organisation is a network of local people, environmental and other charities, social enterprises, businesses and schools who are working together to increase the production and consumption of local food in the town.

> The aim is to make our town 75% self-sufficient in vegetables and fruits within the next five years and 100% within the next eight. Alongside this we aim to raise awareness of the problems surrounding waste and educate our community in the advantages of recycling, starting with programmes aimed at our schoolchildren and young adults.

> Your organisation is well-known for supporting innovative and creative new projects in our area, with a particular focus on the benefits of recycling, and I am writing to ask if you would consider supporting us in this aspect of our work.

3) The need you wish to meet

All voluntary organisations exist to meet a particular need – to make society better in some way. You need a brief and clear explanation of the need or problem that you exist to deal with and how your particular project will extend or add to this work. Your research should inform the funder about how widespread the need is and if it is local or has regional, national or international implications. If it is local, say what special features of the community make it special or interesting to support. Point to who will be helped by your work, which can often be a wider group than just the people involved in the project. If you have user involvement you should emphasise this.

You should provide evidence, if you can, of the further need that will be met and how many more members of your user group you will benefit if your project goes ahead.

Emphasise any elements that are special or unique in the need you are trying to meet. Explain the problem, however complex, in a concise and compelling way and explain to the funder how important and urgent the need is and how you know this. Provide evidence if you can.

You may want to highlight what would happen if you were not doing anything about the problem. Do not be over-emotional or portray your beneficiaries as victims; this is an opportunity to give your reader assurance that something constructive can be done. However, do not undersell yourself or assume that 'everybody knows this is a problem'. If the funder thinks that it is not very pressing, they will find something else that is and if they do not think that you understand the problem, they will assume you cannot solve it either.

You need to do the following.

- Describe the problem.
- Support this by evidence.
- Say why this is important – is the problem you are addressing worse than others? Or is the solution you are offering better than others?

4) The solution you offer

Once you have made clear the need and said how important it is to do something about it, you then need to show that you can offer a particular solution. For example:

> *We will initially provide eight part-time trainers to 10 of the schools in our area, and two will be assigned to our local youth clubs. Our aim is to engage 1,000 children and young people over six months. The trainers will provide structured programmes on conserving and promoting local wildlife habitats and will include workshops, practical indoor exercises, a field trip for each class, debating groups and one-to-one advice sessions for those wishing to become more involved in our activities following training.*

Be constructive
When making your case don't assume that the need you know about is obvious to the reader. If there is a need for a local wasteground to be developed into a

community garden, say why it is needed, how you know this and in what way it will improve the lives of people in your community. If you haven't properly identified the need you cannot offer a solution.

You need to point to the actual or expected results of your work and how these will be measured (often referred to as outcomes and monitoring and evaluation). This may be, for instance, how many people will volunteer, how resources will be shared with other groups, how an information pack will be distributed to local schools and organisations, if litter will be reduced and what other benefits there will be.

Be realistic

Make sure that what you want to do is workable, that it can be done in a reasonable time, by you, and that it gives *value for money* (a favourite phrase of funders). Don't promise what you can't deliver. If anything, err on the side of modesty and then you can broadcast the additional benefits that come from the project when the work is finished.

You should define clearly how you will overcome any problems that may come as a result of running the project (for example, for a furniture recycling project: safety, trading standards, insurance, storage, etc.).

Support your case

Good arguments to support your case would be to look at other communities where a similar project has led to visible benefits, for example where young unemployed people had been encouraged to become involved in the marketing and distribution of furniture for a similar project in another town so that their skills in these areas were developed. You might be able to show that they had been motivated to access training courses following their work with this group and you could detail the numbers of older people, or single parents, or families on low income who had benefited from the service.

In short, the donor should now be saying: 'I can see there is a real need and the project would certainly make things better'.

5) Why *your* organisation should do it

You now need to establish your credibility. Why should your group run the project? Why should the funder trust you? What is different about the way that you do things? How effectively will you manage the project?

Sell your case

Think about your plus points. Do you use volunteers creatively? Do your trustees come from the local community? Do they participate in leadership training qualifications? Do they have a story to tell that would interest a funder? There must be something about your group or your work that is attractive and fulfilling to those who help. By training local leaders, for example, you have given the community a vital resource and encouraged people to discover commitment and talents that may otherwise have been left unused. This builds credibility by showing commitment to all in the community, not just your own user group.

Provide evidence of your successes

Do you have examples of media coverage that give positive images of your organisation's work or have any of your users achieved something as a result of your activities? Have you helped raise money for other causes in a committed and imaginative way? Has your group or an individual gained an award or recognition for a scheme or achievement?

A report in the local paper can help to support your case. Has your group produced a community leader? Do you have a famous former member who regularly supports events? Positive publicity can show the often life-changing results of working on environmental projects and the importance of what you do; it can also show that you are here to stay, with a record of making things happen.

Are you successful in raising money from other sources? Do you have a mixture of supporters from a number of sectors? Do you have good working relationships with agencies, local businesses, schools, local authorities, etc. and what have these partnerships achieved? Financial stability will impress any funder and this is one of the keys to establishing trust with their money. The more secure your funding portfolio is, the more likely you are to be entrusted with other grants.

Strong links with other groups and organisations give a good indication of how integrated you are and further proof of how much added value your activities bring to the community – funding your group may bring knock-on benefits to other local groups.

Generally, can you show that your work is good value for money and more cost-effective than the alternatives? What makes your organisation's people the right people to be meeting this need? Is your approach an example of good practice that could be copied and applied elsewhere?

You should be able to come up with a number of good reasons why your group should be supported. The more you can do this, the more credibility you have. The more credibility you have, the more likely donors are to trust you with their money. Success can breed success, and funders will be attracted to a confident, enthusiastic approach. Your plus points will all help to sell your case, so make them clearly and confidently in your application.

6) The amount you need

Funders are keen to know about the project and the value and benefits of the work. But you also need to tell them very clearly what it will cost and how much you expect them to give. Some applications tail off when it comes to asking for money but by now you should have made a good case for someone to support you and proved that you can be trusted with their money.

There are different ways to ask for what you want and you should think about the type of funder you are applying to. Where you are asking a funder for a small amount or where you think they would like to see some specific, immediate benefit from their donation, you can produce a shopping list. This can be very effective when raising money from companies: you can give a range of items, with costs starting at a level that all those you are writing to can afford and then suggest an item from the list that you think the supporter would like to pay for. By including more expensive items you can hopefully persuade them to give more. If you are looking for gifts in kind rather than cash this is the best way to give supporters an idea of what you want.

7) The future you have – your project's exit strategy and future plans

Make sure that you emphasise your long-term viability as this underlines your credibility and why funders should support you. If your future is not at all sure, funders will be reluctant to take risks and will think their money would be better used elsewhere.

Show how the project will be funded once the grant has been spent. If you are applying for money for a new facility, who will pay for its running costs once it is opened? How will you continue a project when the three-year grant has finished?

8) Your organisation's monitoring, evaluation, financial and administrative procedures

For organisations that have been successful and received a grant, funders will want to know, sometimes during and always at the end of the project, how their money has been used and whether you have met the targets and reached the beneficiaries as promised in your application. You must have monitoring and evaluation procedures in place to be able to provide this evidence when it is

66

required. This not only helps you with further projects, identifying need, etc., but will also predispose your funder to consider favourably any new application from you. These procedures do not have to be complex, they simply have to provide proof of how you have achieved your targets and spent the money.

As well as monitoring procedures, any funder will expect your organisation's financial and administrative procedures to follow good practice. All money in and out of the project must have a clear audit trail, showing which budget line it came from and how it was spent. The simplest of tasks, like keeping all receipts, can become problematic at the end of a grant if procedures haven't been followed. Also, your administrative requirements should be contained in your governing document (constitution, memorandum and articles of association, trust deed or rules) and should be followed as a matter of course in all your organisation's dealings.

How to ask for money

- You should state clearly how much the overall project will cost.
- Give the funder a clear idea of how much you would want them to contribute.
- Show how much other organisations have so far given, or committed, to the project.
- Show where the rest of the money is coming from (for example, 'The overall project will cost £30,000. We expect to raise £15,000 from our members and supporters, £5,000 from other fundraising events and £10,000 from grant-making charities. I am therefore writing to you and eight other major grantmakers to ask for a total of £10,000').

This will give the funder more confidence that you know what you are doing, and show that you are not solely reliant on one funder and can raise the necessary money.

The application

Only approach organisations, including companies, that you want to have associated with your organisation. Make sure that they are appropriate for your user group, your ethos and your long-term aims.

Remember to ask first if the funder has an application form to fill out, as there is no point spending time writing the perfect letter of application only to find that you have to rewrite the whole thing on an application form. If you are unsure about the information required on the form, contact the funder for clarification. Sort out all the problem areas on the form before you ring and go through each in one phone call as this will save time for you and the funder.

The application letter

Now that you have done your research and pulled all your selling points together you need to put them into some kind of order. There are no golden rules for writing proposals, no perfect letters of application. What works for the club down the road will not necessarily work for you: try to inject some of your organisation's own personality into the proposal.

The following is a structure that many have found to work, and this can be a starting point for your own letter.

1) Project title

This can be really effective, especially if it is catchy and quickly describes what you want to do.

2) Introductory paragraph

This is the first part of the application to be read so it is important that it makes the funder want to read on. It should tell readers what the application is about and why it is likely to be relevant and interesting to them.

Try not to make your applications generic, they should be adapted to accommodate the aims and sympathies of the funder.

3) The introduction: what your organisation believes in and wants to achieve

Many applications say little or nothing about what the organisation is about; instead, they just state what the applicant wants. You should assume that readers know nothing about your organisation. What would they need to know to trust you with their money? You need to show you are good at what you do, reliable, well-used and well-liked – in three or four sentences.

4) The need: why something needs to be done now

The next stage in your application is to explain what the need is, how you know it exists and why it is important that something is done now. Remember, people are mainly interested in what your group does and how you benefit your user group or community. Don't ask people to support you; ask them to support your work and the people that you help.

Tips: plus points that make you better

Write down as many selling points for your group as you can. Below are some possible categories that may help you to see the strengths of your group.

People: What's different, good, or extraordinary about your volunteers, members, workers, etc.?

Financial stability: What's sound and reliable about your finances? What's successful about your fundraising?

Personal achievements: Has anyone achieved something notable through your activities? Have your users, members or volunteers gained experience, qualifications, employment, training, etc. through being part of the group? Do you have a local, regional or national profile?

Partnerships: Who have you linked up with? What has been achieved?

Mention the plus points that give you an edge such as:

Publicity: Have you had any coverage in the local press? Have you been successful at recruiting new members and leaders through outreach?

Perseverance: Do you have a good track record? How long has your group been running?

Performance: Has your group developed activities or projects that have been adopted and been successful elsewhere? Explain why your work is innovative, creative and used as a model by other groups.

Explain how you meet the following:

- The needs we meet are particularly important because ...
- Our solution is new and groundbreaking because ...
- We are different/unique because ...
- Our other strengths are ...
- If we did not exist then ...

You need to show your organisation is unique. Be confident in your successes; list your five greatest successes in the past five years and then select one that's appropriate for your application letter.

And finally, to build your confidence further in preparation for the application letter, complete this tie-breaker in 20 words or fewer:

'We are the best there is in our work on climate change because ...' Perhaps you could ask your user group to help with this.

5) Your proposals: what you intend to do about the problem

You now need to show what you intend to do and how you intend to do it. Make sure you include your targets (outcomes) and how you will reach them. (If you are having problems with this part, maybe you could try predicting what the organisation will be like in two years' time and how things will have changed.)

6) Why your organisation should do it

You have so far said what your organisation believes in and wants to achieve, the need you want to meet and how you are going to meet that need. Now you need to show why you are the best people to take this on.

The funder will want to know that they can trust you to deliver what you say you can and that you have thought the project through to the end, including what you will do when their funding stops. Your solution to the problem should be clear and practicable and your monitoring and evaluation procedures effective. Use your plus points to show your ability, professionalism and good track record to get the job done well. Quotes, especially from those benefiting from what you do or from those who have previously used your services are always helpful here.

7) The budget: how much you need

This is how much you intend to spend on the project and is an extremely important part of your application. You should have clear evidence of costs and these should clearly fit in with what you are paying for, such as staff hours. It should also relate to your outcomes; for example, seven staff will provide awareness training for 14 local schools. Your budget will include the direct costs of the project and overheads. (See Chapter 4 *How much do we need?* and Chapter 5 *Fundraising for projects.*)

8) Funding plan

You need to show the funder where you intend to get the money from. It may be that you are asking this funder for the whole amount or you may be getting it from a variety of sources. Therefore, you need to say something like: 'The total cost of this project is £50,000. Our local authority has agreed to give us £5,000 and this will be matched by European money of £5,000. We aim to raise £10,000 from local supporters, £20,000 from the Big Lottery Fund and £10,000 from grant-making charities.'

You also need to show how you intend to meet the longer-term costs (see Chapter 1 *Getting started in fundraising* for detailed information on this).

9) The rationale: why the funder might be interested and what their role is

There are many reasons why the donor may be interested:

- You are running a good project that is right at the heart of their stated aims and priorities.
- You have already received support from them and this further grant will allow you to build on that success.
- There is a personal contact (which it will pay to highlight).
- There is a particular benefit to the donor that you want to stress. (This is especially the case with companies, which will want to see a business or public relations return on their money.)

Sometimes, people sum up on a negative note: 'Wouldn't it be a tragedy if all this good work came to an end?' or, 'If we don't raise £30,000, the project will have to close.' Avoid this kind of negative persuasion. You've made a good, convincing case with positive reasons for supporting your work. There is no reason to assume you will not get the money, so be positive: your letter should leave the reader feeling optimistic and enthusiastic.

10) The signatory: who puts their name to the application

This person should be sufficiently senior

Whoever signs the application must be sufficiently senior with a good knowledge of the project. For example, the project leader, fundraiser, chair of the management committee, an appropriate director or an appeal patron. This shows you are treating the application seriously and gives it the necessary authority.

Be knowledgeable

Funders may well ask for more information. The person who signs the letter should be able to tell them what they need to know, including the overall financial position of the organisation. If the name on the letter cannot give this information it will seem as though the application has not been well organised and the project not well thought through. If you have a patron who signs the letters but does not know about the day-to-day running of the project, you should include the contact details of someone who will be able to answer more detailed questions.

Be available

Again, if funders want more information they don't want to have to leave a whole series of messages before they get the details they need to make a decision. Make sure your contact details are clear and that you have made provision for someone to take your messages and for them to be passed on quickly to you or for a voicemail facility to be in place.

Be open

Leave your potential supporters with plenty of opportunity to talk to you, find out more, or visit. Many will decline your invitations to come and look at the work or meet members of your user group, but an invitation shows confidence in your work.

Start making sense – a guide to writing simply

- Look at the layout critically. Would it entice you to read further? Look at line spacing, point size and font selection: are you put off by long sections of text? If you are, so will your reader be. Always avoid jargon – although you might understand what you are talking about, outsiders generally will not. Remember to explain acronyms.

- Be direct and try not to repeat yourself – it adds to the flow of your application and keeps the length down.

- Use personal pronouns such as 'we', 'our', 'you' and 'your' rather than 'the organisation/association' or 'the users' etc.

- Use strong verbs and tenses, rather than weaker passive ones. 'Our group works closely with local schools' reads better than 'Local schools have become involved with the activities organised by the members of our group.'

- Weed out waffle. Say something sincerely, simply and succinctly.

- Read, re-read and rewrite.

A skeleton application letter

There is no such thing as a model application letter. Write your letter in your own style, in a way that is tailored to the funder and shows your work in its best light.

Here is an outline that we hope will be helpful when first drafting your application letter.

Dear .... [Wherever possible use the name of the correspondent. If you do not know it, make every effort to find out. It's important that you show you have done some research in order to direct the letter to the appropriate person.]

continued...

I am writing on behalf of .... Our organisation was set up in .... by .... to provide .... Our major initiatives have included .... and recent projects have seen ....

I am writing to you about our .... project. Your organisation is well known/well known locally for supporting .... and we have seen the successes of groups similar to our own that you have funded in the past.

The need we are meeting is particularly important, having carried out research on .... and potential beneficiaries who state that ....

We know the project will be effective because [talk about your innovative approach/new ideas, etc.] ....

We consider we are the best people to do this work because ....

The project will cost in total £.......... and we intend to raise the money as follows: ....

We hope that you will want to be involved in this exciting new work for our group and I am writing to you for £....................., which will provide ....

At the end of the grant we expect the project will be funded by .... /be self sustaining.

We would be more than happy for you to visit our organisation to see the work we do and to discuss this application, although I appreciate your time must be limited. If you require further information or you wish to discuss this application please contact me on ....

Yours sincerely

Ann Other

Chair ....

What do you send with the application letter?

If the funder has an application form this will provide instructions on what you should send to accompany it. If you are writing an application letter, you should send the following supporting materials:

- A set of your most recent accounts or a budget for the year if your organisation is new.
- A budget for the particular project you want support for, including estimated income and expenditure.
- An annual report (if you have one). If you have not done so before, think about your annual report as a fundraising tool; it is not only a statement of your financial activities, trustee body, etc., it can also say as much about your activities and success stories as you want it to.

You can also enclose anything else that will support the application (for example, you could provide one or two of the following: newsletters, press cuttings, videos, photos, drawings or letters of support). However, don't overwhelm the reader, pick an appropriate selection, and don't rely on these extra bits to get you the money – they will not compensate for a hopeless letter. Assume that funders will only read your application letter and the financial information (budget and accounts). They should be able to get the complete picture from these. If in doubt, ask yourself:

- Is this relevant to the application? Is it absolutely essential or a nice extra?
- Will it help the funder to make a decision in our favour?
- Does it present the right image? (Is the additional material so glossy that it implies you are a rich organisation? Can you get publicity material sponsored?)

Remember, everything is for a fundraising purpose. If the accompanying information does not help the application, do not include it.

What do you do with the application letter?

Think about your different supporters. You will have to take into account what each funder will be looking for and why. A company, for instance, will be looking at the commercial possibilities of linking up with you; i.e. what is good for its business. It may look for more tangible benefits in the short term than, say, a grant-making charity or local authority.

It may be best to send the application out in stages. Write to a few of your key supporters first (adapting the letter as necessary) and see if they will lead the appeal (that is, give you a grant that then encourages others to do the same).

When some of these have committed themselves to supporting you, then write to the rest saying that first, you have already raised £10,000 of the £20,000 needed and second, that X, Y and Z funders gave it to you.

Money tends to attract money. The more you raise, the easier it is to raise more. Highlight any money that has already been raised or pledged. Sending applications out in stages can improve your chances because you concentrate initially on those most likely to support you. Then you widen the net to include those who don't know you as well but will take their cue from other funders' confidence in you. However, this approach is more time consuming and needs more planning. It may not be the remedy for your project or for crisis funding when you are desperate to get money in as soon as possible.

What to do after the application letter has been sent

You should keep a simple record of what you have sent and where, including the supporting materials you have sent or the events you have invited funders to. You might want to include an sae with your application or send it recorded delivery to be sure it has been received. Apart from that, there is little you can do but wait for the outcome.

You can never be sure how funders' offices will respond to phone calls asking about the progress of your application. Some will discuss what stage your application has reached and when you might expect to hear a decision; others will not welcome any follow-up contact: they will not have the time or inclination to answer your enquiries, however general.

If you are unsuccessful, you may not realise for some time. You might not even get a rejection letter or telephone call, let alone an explanation of why you did not get a grant. It is, nevertheless, always worthwhile asking for feedback on your application so that you will know where you went wrong (with that particular funder) for next time. Some may refuse to provide this, others will be extremely helpful and some may tell you that your application was good but that they ran out of funds.

If you are successful

If you get a positive response, write to say thank you immediately and put this funder on your mailing list for the future. Keep them informed of your progress.

Note any conditions on the grant that have to be met (such as sending a written report to the funder each quarter year) and make sure you keep to them. It is important that if there is any variation in what you have been given the money for and what you are actually going to do, you should inform the funder and check this is acceptable.

You will want to go back to those who have supported you for help in the future. Keep them interested in your progress and how the money has been spent (with their permission). If individuals have benefited, personal accounts and progress reports can be an easy and friendly way of keeping funders interested and enthusiastic about what their money has helped to achieve.

Don't give up...

If you haven't heard regarding your application for some time, you might want to send those funders still considering your appeal a further letter to update them on progress (if you have anything further to add, such as a recent success story).

The letter can be quite short, saying: 'We understand you are still considering our funding application for our project "...................". However, you may be interested to know that we have so far raised £10,000 of the £20,000 we need. This has come from .... Please contact me if you need any further information about the project.'

Don't be afraid to go back to people who have previously turned you down, unless they have said they would never support your kind of work. There may be many reasons why you have not been awarded money: they may have funded something similar the previous week; they may have run out of funds; they may have had a deluge of brilliant applications and yours was next on the list; they may have never heard of you before and are not prepared to take a risk.

Remember that while it is your job to get money to continue and develop your organisation's work, it is the funder's job to give funds to well thought out, creative, well budgeted, worthwhile and potentially successful projects whose organisation is sound managerially and financially and operates with good business practices.

Application checklist

- Does it have a personal address? Do what you can to find an individual's name.
- Does the first paragraph catch the reader's attention?
- Are you clear about what you want and why you want it?
- Is your work likely to be interesting to the donor?
- Is it clear how much the donor is expected to give? Is this reasonable?
- Is the application well presented? Does it attract the eye with short paragraphs and no spelling mistakes?
- Does it back up what it says with good supporting evidence?
- Is it positive and enthusiastic?
- Does it take account of guidelines published by the donor? Does it make a connection with the supporter's interests?
- Is it written in clear, plain English and free of jargon?
- How long is the application? Remember it does not have to say everything, but it has to say enough.
- Crucially, is the application appropriate? A brilliant letter to the wrong people will not get support.

7 Raising support from the public

Until relatively recently, in terms of the history of charities, many small and medium-sized organisations raised money largely by asking those involved with the group, their relatives and friends and anyone else who would turn up, to support small fundraising activities such as a garage sale, coffee morning or car wash. Now the emphasis is more on spending dedicated time on an application or polishing up presentation skills to appeal to a major funder. However, the general public is a vital resource and while statistics change from year to year, it is generally accepted within the voluntary sector that it is the largest group donating to charities. While you are chasing the grant, don't forget also to appeal to the general public: figures suggest that around a third of the money available to charities comes from this source.

Fundraisers should keep in mind that while grants are now a major part of charities' income, getting the public to support your group can be more effective in terms of time and resources spent. If you need, say, £500 for a laptop, it might be more efficient to ask the local community rather than applying to a grant-making charity or company. The right appeal targeted to 200 people might be less time consuming and produce more immediate results. It also helps to make your case to other funders if you have a well-established track record of successful fundraising from the public.

Fundraising in this way can also bring good publicity to raise the profile of your group locally. However, you need to assess the scale of any proposed event or appeal, the help you can rely on and its expected return.

This chapter will give some pointers to planning, some money-making possibilities and some pitfalls to avoid.

Who might give

Every donor to an organisation has their individual motivations and preferred way of giving. The fundraiser must be clear about which individuals they want to approach for a particular type of gift and how to plan to attract the support of that group of people.

There are all sorts of reasons why people support and give to good causes, for example:

- **They are already involved with and sympathetic to the cause.** Your user group, their families and friends, helpers, organisers and patrons, for instance. These are usually the most dedicated fundraisers and donors. You should not have to convert them to your cause, they should already be aware of what you are doing and its importance.

- **They have previously been involved.** People who have been involved with the group in the past, for example, former members, volunteers, staff and trustees and people who have benefited from your group, are likely to want to support your initiatives. Occasional reunions, particularly if combined with an anniversary, can be a way of focusing their financial support. Past members will, hopefully, have some affection for the organisation and fond memories and they might be persuaded to support the present activities.

- **They know someone involved with the work.** Sponsored events are a good source of fundraising and the network of extended family and friends connected with those taking part will want to sponsor the individual they know.

- **They think the organisation is worth supporting because of the work it is doing.** This is an appeal to those who do not have any personal contact with your organisation but value the work that you do. Your activities may tie in with their interests in some way such as health promotion, education, job prospects, social skills or crime prevention.

- **Individuals connected with established institutions.** Churches and other faith groups, schools and colleges, philanthropic groups of local business people and trade unionists might want to support your work because environmental issues, conservation and heritage are also important to them.

- **Employers.** Employers might be pleased to associate their name with your cause and through them you can often reach a large number of individual employees. This sort of contact can often bring gifts in kind and time as well as financial donations.

- **People in specific regions.** Often people will have an affinity to a particular village, town or city and be pleased to give their support.
- **Where the organisation will attract press coverage and people will want to help.** The humorous advertisement below with topical references, will bring attention to the Keep Britain Tidy appeal for a celebrity to head their new campaign.

Keep Britain Tidy
is seeking a clean-living celebrity who may not have much time on their hands but must be blameless and extremely cheap.

The organisation has taken the unusual step of advertising in the Guardian *for a celebrity to follow in the litter-picking footsteps of Morecambe and Wise, the Queen Mother, Marc Bolan and Abba.*

The working conditions are not arduous – despite the fact that after half a century of campaigning Britain seems to be sinking under a rising tide of cigarette butts, burger boxes and chewing gum, they want only two days a year of their celebrity's time.

Candidates must 'be famous not infamous', said a spokesman, which probably rules out Jonathan Ross and Russell Brand, and are promised 'by taking on this role you'll be forever linked with our efforts to inspire people to make their communities better places to live'.

No salary, never mind a pension or floating duck island, is offered, 'but we still reckon it's a pretty good deal'.

More than 50 years since it was launched, and 25 years since it became a limited company, the organisation has taken another radical step and changed its name – to Keep Britain Tidy.

The campaign, founded in 1954 by the National Federation of Women's Institutes, changed in 1987 from Keep Britain Tidy to Tidy Britain Group, but since 2001 it has been called Encams, short for Environmental Campaigns.

'I think most people always did call us Keep Britain Tidy', Phil Barton, the new chief executive, said. 'We did a survey and found that name got 85% recognition, and only 12% knew what Encams stood for – and, to be perfectly honest, I'm surprised it was as many as that. So we've gone back to basics.'

There may be more than one reason why people connect with a cause. Some of the runners in the London Marathon, for example, will be involved because of any or all of the reasons previously listed.

Planning any fundraising should first take into account the support networks your group is immediately in touch with. You can then look at the wider audiences who may be attracted to the event and your cause.

Why people give

People support organisations for many different reasons. However, the more your fundraising message ties in with an individual's personal motivation, the more successful that approach will be.

The following are some of the reasons why people give to charity.

- **Being asked.** They have been impressed with your approach and what you are doing for your user group and the wider community and want to give.
- **Concern.** This is a strong motivator for many donors. They may be worried about a particular group, say, young people, and want to help to channel their energies into specific projects. Making a donation provides them with an opportunity to do something positive for a cause they believe in.
- **Duty.** Another strong motivator, particularly for older donors. Many faiths promote the concept of charity, with some recommending that their members allocate a certain share of their income each year for this.
- **Personal experience.** People with children at school may want to support their child's awareness of environmental issues; or someone may want to 'give back' to the community they live in.
- **Personal benefit.** Some people like the status or recognition that comes when their generosity is publicised, or like to be involved with the charity world.
- **Peer involvement.** When people know that their friends and colleagues have given or when these people are asking them to give and explaining the aims of their cause, it can be the motivation for them to contribute as well.
- **Tax benefits.** These are unlikely to be a prime motivator for giving, but can be an important factor in encouraging people to make certain types of donation and to give more generously.

It is important to understand why supporters and potential donors might want to give to your particular organisation. You can then tailor the message to make it more relevant and interesting to them.

You also need to be aware of why people don't give and whether the reasons need addressing by you. They may not be interested in your organisation and what it stands for or they may have given to something similar recently. Other demotivating factors might be that:

- your cause has had some bad publicity
- your cause appears to have high administration costs
- there is a concern that the money is not getting to the intended beneficiaries
- you have not looked after your donors particularly well in the past.

Creating support

The clearer you can be about who your organisation's potential supporters are, the more successful you will be in reaching them. Start with your existing supporters: for example, a survey could help to find out what sort of people have supported your organisation in the past and why. If you have a database of your supporters, you could start your analysis there.

Those at the very heart of what you are doing – your user group, volunteers and staff – are probably your most enthusiastic supporters. They are the people who understand what you want to achieve to make life better.

Next in line will be previous members and organisations and agencies that your group has links with. These can include other charities, church groups, the local authority, schools and colleges as well as leaders in your community. These people do not know your group so well, but they have some affinity with it, as well as an interest in seeing it prosper.

You can also appeal to the wider community, such as companies you have business links with. (Is there a coach company you use regularly? Who do you bank with?) Is there a local event you could attend where you could provide refreshments at a stall run by your members? They could provide information on what you do and make people aware of your aims and past successes.

Finally, you can organise events in the high street or shopping precinct, such as simple collection boxes or having street entertainers outside the entrance of your local supermarket: anything to attract the public's eye and put them in a generous mood. These will bring in people who may know nothing about your group but are attracted by the activity. If you are considering this type of fundraising you should consult the Charity Commission website as the Charities Act 2006 makes new provision for collections. You should also refer to the relevant Institute of Fundraising Codes of Practice.

If you think creatively about venues, activities and audiences you can increase your chances of success.

Even when you've raised core funding for your organisation, it makes sense to continue to raise money from the local community. It heightens your profile and nurtures local links, giving your project deeper community roots and a strong local identity.

Making contact

Here is a suggested five point plan to follow when starting to approach the public.

1) Identify your potential supporters: those people whose background and motivations make them likely to want to support your cause.

2) Create the right message to appeal to them, which:
   - starts from their understanding of the cause

   - builds on their motivation

   - takes account of their natural hesitations or reasons they might have for not giving.

3) Direct that message to those people in the right way. For example, if senior business people are your audience, they can be reached by a variety of means: through the business press, local rotary clubs, chambers of commerce and other associations of business people or through personalised letters, or by asking business people who already support you to ask their colleagues and peers directly.

4) Make it easy for them to make their donation. Any materials that aim to get people to support you should include a clear means by which they can respond (whether by post, phone, fax, email or through a website) and clear contact details.

   To increase the likelihood of someone making a donation, if your organisation has the means, you could also consider the following options.

   - A dedicated telephone line for credit card donations and enquiries, with a named person on promotional literature and at the end of the line. This makes the facility more personal and shows a concern for customer care. You might also consider a freephone facility.

- A CharityCard donation facility for Charities Aid Foundation (CAF) clients, which includes approximately 100,000 individual donors and about 2,000 companies. Around 4,000 charities now welcome the use of the CharityCard and are listed with their telephone numbers in a CAF directory and on the CAF website (www.cafonline.org).

- A secure website, so that donations can be made online.

- A freepost facility. However, almost all organisations now suggest that if a stamp is used this will save the charity money.

5) Support your fundraising with good publicity, as people are more likely to give to your organisation if they have heard about its work and the importance of the cause. Public relations is a key ingredient of successful fundraising, so if your organisation does not have a press officer, you will need to spend some time promoting the organisation and publicising its work.

Five things to remember when fundraising from individuals

1) State clearly how much money is needed for the project.

2) Express the need in human terms, giving images of the issue being tackled and examples of your successes. Avoid abstract statistics unless a particular point needs to be emphasised. The more people can understand and identify with a problem, the more they will feel they are helping to address a real need and the more successful the appeal will be.

3) Ask for exactly what you want. Prospective donors will not necessarily know the size or nature of the donation expected of them. It is also useful to suggest a range of values, so the donor can choose their own level of giving. If relevant, a 'shopping list' might be used showing what different amounts can achieve – see Chapter 1 *Getting started in fundraising.*

4) Target the appeal carefully, making the message as personal and relevant to the donor as possible. When approaching existing supporters, refer to their previous generous support and what has been achieved with it, or if approaching local people, focus on the local benefits of your organisation's work. The more targeted the message, the more successful it will be.

5) Make your approach positive and forward thinking.

Building a supporter base

It is far easier to build on a base of existing supporters than to start from scratch. An existing donor is much more likely to support your organisation again than someone who has never given. However, if you have few or no current donors there are various methods you can use to acquire them.

Promotional or fundraising leaflets

Produce a leaflet giving details about your cause and illustrating your need for funds. This does not have to be expensive. Sometimes the simplest leaflet is most effective – for example, an A4 sheet, printed in two colours and folded to make a four-page leaflet with photographs of the organisation at work and a reply coupon so potential supporters can express interest or make a gift. You could ask your group to design it.

You might also give people options for how they would like to get involved: for example, by giving money, becoming a member or volunteering their time. Remember to include your website address, if you have one.

A membership or supporter scheme

Developing a scheme of this type can bring people closer to your organisation and keep them in touch with news and success stories. It can also provide a legitimate reason for communicating on a regular basis. See 'Membership schemes', page 92.

Supporter-get-supporter

Ask existing supporters to help by recruiting a friend, a colleague or a family member (see page 91).

Local newspaper, radio and TV coverage

A paper, radio or TV station might be interested in running a feature about a local charity. To make this opportunity as effective as possible, you should make sure that the contact details are for the best person possible to deal with the media.

Door-to-door collections or face-to-face fundraising

If your organisation is not well known, one way of addressing this is to approach people face to face. This can be particularly effective for a local cause. The term 'door-to-door collections' includes visits to pubs, factories and offices to collect money or to sell things, on the basis that part of the proceeds will go to a charity. If you are considering this type of fundraising, as previously mentioned, you should consult the Charity Commission website as the Charities Act 2006 makes new provision for this. You should also refer to the relevant Institute of Fundraising Codes of Practice.

Events

Potential supporters may be attracted to an event where they have the opportunity to visit an exclusive venue, hear a well-known speaker or participate in an entertaining evening. Once there they might well be receptive to hearing more about the cause that the event is to benefit. Once a donor has been recruited, the aim is to keep them involved so that they continue to give and, hopefully, develop their relationship with your organisation in other ways.

Major donors

Some of your donors may have the potential to do much more for you than others. They might identify themselves by making a significantly larger donation than the amount you asked for, or you might find out that they have greater potential through researching your supporter base. You might then decide to set up a fundraising programme specifically for these people.

Firstly you should make a decision about the point at which you will begin to treat people as major donors: this will be different for different organisations.

For a small charity a major donation from an individual might be £250 or even less; for a larger organisation with a developed strategy for encouraging big gifts, its major donor programme may only kick in with those giving several thousand pounds. To help you make this decision look at your current range of donations by value. You will probably find that there is a clear cut-off point above which donations become scarcer. Once you have identified these people, you need to decide whether they will get similar communications to your other donors but with higher levels of gift asked for, or a totally different type of letter concentrating on more ambitious ways in which they can help you. Either way, you should aim to make them feel more involved rather than simply sending a standard donor appeal.

You might organise special events and visits for them or get them involved in the fundraising itself – you will find the guidelines *Major Donor Fundraising* produced by the Institute of Fundraising a useful guide if you plan to concentrate on this group of your donor base. Visit the Institute's website at www.institute-of-fundraising.org.uk for information on this best practice guide.

Major donor programmes

If you feel that there are sufficient numbers of people who are or might become major donors, you could set up some sort of club to encourage them to increase their commitment to you. You could ask your existing key donors to advise you on who else you might approach, or ask them to approach their friends, colleagues and networks to ask for support. You need to make sure that this is going to be cost-effective for you, as these people are likely to take more of your time to look after, or steward, than your other supporters. Also, they may require particular types of benefits in return for their support, such as meetings with your chief executive or board members, crediting in your literature (such as your annual report) and even having some influence on the future of the organisation (you need to be particularly aware of such potential implications when considering this type of condition).

Encouraging giving

Individuals can support you in a wide variety of ways, for example with cash gifts or gifts in kind, or by buying raffle tickets, attending events or volunteering their time. The following sections look at the main methods by which you can encourage people to donate money.

One-off donations and appeals

Asking existing or prospective supporters for a one-off donation to support a cause is a key method of raising funds for many organisations. This can be done on a large scale by approaching hundreds of individuals through direct mail or, more directly, face to face with individuals or small groups of people, particularly when asking for a high value gift.

One-off donation appeals are often used to encourage new donors to support you. Once that first donation is made you might go back and ask for another or offer other methods by which you can be supported, for example, by making a committed gift. You will find that some people who have supported you with a single donation will be happy to become more committed if they can see the benefit of their original gift. However be careful not to ask too soon or to alienate them with too many appeals for their money. You need to engage them with your work and show them results over a period before you make further requests.

Legacies

Legacies are an important source of charitable funds. Legacy fundraising can often seem a mysterious activity which generates large sums with apparently little effort from the fundraiser. In fact, some of the largest legacy-earning charities have carefully planned strategies for developing this income. Like other forms of fundraising, what you get out depends on what you put in. You should:

■ decide whether you are the sort of charity that might expect to receive legacy income, bearing in mind that most legacies come from people who are aged 65 and over

■ find out who has left you legacies in the past, if they supported you during their lifetime and why they gave.

You should consider whether to go for existing supporters, which is where you are most likely to find support, or whether to target the general public. You might also consider adding the name of your organisation to the CAF database, which has information helping people who would like to set up a legacy and a database of charities that might be supported. For full information see CAF's website www.cafonline.org.

One aim of having a supporter base is to build up a good understanding amongst your members of how they might help you. If some form of regular committed giving is a natural successor to occasional one-off gifts, then a legacy may be a step up from regular giving. In the process of communicating with donors, you will over time build relationships which might enable you to discuss legacies, but take care with this, it is a highly sensitive issue.

For further information on legacies see *The Complete Fundraising Handbook* published by the Directory of Social Change.

Committed giving

Committed or regular giving is one of the most valuable and consistent ways your donors can support you and will provide one of the best financial returns for any direct marketing activity. Getting people to give their first donation can be expensive, but it is often the necessary first step in building up a base of supporters.

Follow-up mailings are what generate the real revenue – people who have already given respond much better to any appeal than those who have never given.

Getting your donors to commit to regular giving creates a continuing income stream, broadens your fundraising base and enhances your organisation's sustainability. Also you can apply income from regular givers to those parts of your work which are hardest to raise money for. To encourage people to make committed gifts you need to:

■ stimulate their concern for the cause and interest in your work

■ help them recognise the importance of long-term support – your work may take time to yield results and you depend on them continuing to give

■ make it easy for them to give regularly: one way is to set up some form of membership or friends scheme, with pre-set levels of giving

■ ensure that, where possible, donations are paid tax-effectively through the Gift Aid scheme (details given on page 97)

■ reassure them regularly about the continuing value of their committed support.

This list will provide you with an agenda to develop your direct mail and donor acquisition programme, and then turn a new donor into a committed and enthusiastic long-term supporter.

Mechanisms for committed giving

There are three main ways in which committed giving can be developed.

■ Through regular, usually monthly, payments which can be made tax efficient with Gift Aid.

■ By means of a membership scheme. This will not always be tax-effective as there are restrictions on the level of benefit the member can receive. Some schemes are concerned primarily with generating income, others aim for high membership numbers to enhance the credibility and campaigning ability of the organisation.

■ Through payroll giving, which is also a tax-effective way of giving.

The specific mechanisms available for the actual transmission of money are as follows.

■ Using a banker's order or standing order, where the payments are sent from the donor's bank to you.

■ Using direct debit, which reverses the control of the transaction. You, the charity, claim the payments from the bank when they fall due.

■ Regular payments via a donor's credit card.

■ Cash or cheque payments, though these are not so efficient to administer as you will usually need to remind donors when to send their payment.

Promotion of committed giving

Not every donor will want to enter into a long-term commitment with you, but you should give all of them the opportunity to do so. Your strategy will depend on your answers to the following questions:

- What are the interests and motivations of your supporters?
- How much income do you need to raise and how much are your donors prepared to give?
- How will you encourage your existing supporters to increase their commitment?
- Can you identify any other potential committed supporters?
- What opportunities do you have for reporting back to your committed givers, so as to maintain their enthusiasm and support?
- What else can you do to get them to feel more involved in the work of the organisation and the cause it is addressing?
- Are you able to administer and steward such a programme?

It is important not to take your committed givers for granted. Keep in regular touch and tell them what you are doing. Always recognise their commitment so they understand that you are contacting them because of their regular donation.

You can report back to your committed givers regularly through a newsletter, magazine or personalised letter from you or your chief executive or chair. Committed givers tend to want to see their donations going to the cause rather being used on expensive communications, so it's good to keep expenditure here to a minimum.

Some charities hold events where donors can meet staff and members of the user group and see the organisation in action. This not only provides a good opportunity to thank them, but also enables the most committed to become even more involved, get more information, meet other supporters and, importantly, the people benefitting from your group's activities.

The following are some of the promotional techniques you can use.

Approaching active givers

Analyse the response to your appeals. A number of your donors will have given more than once. These are your priority targets for committed giving. Contact them to point out the advantages of giving regularly and offer to send the appropriate forms. If there are only a few prospective targets, then contact them by telephone or try and arrange a meeting with them.

Promoting committed giving more widely to your donor base

One strategy is to undertake an annual appeal to promote regular giving and encourage payment by standing order or direct debit. Another strategy is to mention the value of committed giving in each mailing, pointing out that it helps the organisation plan for the future and allows people the opportunity to opt into giving in this way.

Regular upgrading of donation value

Once you have donors giving on a regular basis you might think about asking them to increase the value of their donation (but be careful not to ask them too soon, or for too much). It is administratively easier to do this if you have set up their donations via direct debit rather than a standing order, as the latter will require filling out a new form.

Using a sponsorship programme

Here the donor is linked to a specific project or community over a period. Such an approach can work well in fundraising terms, but read carefully the terms and conditions of the sponsorship.

Recruiting large numbers of supporters with a low-value regular gift by direct debit

Some organisations such as the NSPCC use this very successfully. Once donors are giving monthly donations, there is the opportunity to go back to them after a suitable time has elapsed and tell them what their donations have achieved and what could be done if they increase the value of their donation.

'Welcome mailings'

These are sent following an initial gift to an organisation from newly recruited donors. There is a two-fold purpose to these mailings: to welcome new donors and tell them more about the cause they have given to, and to ask them for more and regular support, often suggesting a regular monthly gift through their bank.

'Member-get-member' or 'supporter-get-supporter'

This is simply an invitation to an existing member or supporter to nominate or recruit another. This method relies on the personal enthusiasm of existing members and their ability to persuade their friends and colleagues, but the technique generally works well.

Membership schemes

Many voluntary organisations have membership schemes. Some are aimed primarily at people who are interested in becoming more involved – helping the organisation to campaign, attending cultural events, volunteering their time – but also giving money. Membership schemes of this type may have their annual subscription levels set deliberately low to encourage as many people as possible to join, therefore increasing the organisation's influence and campaigning ability.

Some membership schemes have a fundraising purpose – the primary aim being to generate income for the organisation.

Benefits of membership

1) Membership is a means by which you can ensure committed and long-term support.
2) Membership can enhance your campaigning ability. Organisations like Amnesty International and Friends of the Earth invite people to become members to harness their support for the cause.
3) Membership can open up the organisation to democratic control through annual meetings, giving the members some control over the direction of the organisation.
4) Your membership list is also a good place to look for donations. These people have demonstrated their commitment to the cause and so qualify as perfect prospects for obtaining further financial commitment.
5) Membership can easily be structured to invite different levels of contribution (to reflect people's commitment, ability to pay, etc.).

Why people become members

There are a number of reasons why people will sign up as members of your organisation.

- **Personal benefit:** the member joins principally because of the benefits they will gain. Examples of this are the RSPB and the National Trust, which give members discounted entry into their reserves or properties.
- **Support:** the member joins to express support for the work of the charity. In this case membership is organised to encourage members to subscribe at affordable rates as a way of making their contributions on a continuing basis.
- **Campaigning:** members are signing up to show their support for particular policies or causes.

- **Influence:** members often join local organisations simply to be able to influence their affairs. This will be done through regular meetings and AGMs.
- **Clubs:** the member joins a club – such as the 'Friends of the Save Our Red Squirrels Group' – to signal their support for the work and also to receive benefits from membership. Subscriptions may be higher in such cases and there may be expectations of involvement in activities and events.

Membership and regular giving

The value of membership subscription income depends on the following factors.

- **The number of members:** the more you have, the better. Once you have established a scheme, your aim should be to find ways of recruiting new members economically.
- **The annual subscription level:** this will depend on your objectives, whether it is primarily to make money or, alternatively, to involve as many people as possible. Some organisations give members a choice of subscription levels.
- **The cost of running the scheme:** this includes the cost of member acquisition, collecting membership fees and communication costs (such as sending newsletters and annual reports). You need to analyse costs very carefully to establish the real net value of the scheme.
- **The value of any additional income** that is generated from further appeals to members.

It is most common to ask people to give on a monthly, quarterly or yearly basis. You might suggest a certain level of donation and ask the donor to select the frequency. The value of encouraging regular giving is something that can be tested quite easily in a mailing. Usually requests for monthly or quarterly giving will be no less effective than an annual payment, and can produce much higher average annual donations.

Categories of membership

One of the key issues in this area is the way in which membership and committed giving are priced and styled. Membership fees have to take into account the possibility of attracting large numbers of people who are prepared to be identified with your organisation. They also need to allow concessions to people on low income and encourage higher levels of support from wealthy supporters, benefactors and corporate members.

Many organisations have several categories of membership with different levels of annual subscription. Other categories of membership can be created such as a sponsor or a patron. Some organisations have three categories – 'Friends', 'Good

Friends' and 'Best of Friends'; others have 'Gold', 'Platinum' and 'Silver' membership. The fundraiser's challenge is to lift members from one category to the next.

Life membership is an opportunity to get a single large payment in one go, as well as enabling a member to be seen as an important benefactor of the organisation. But life means life, unless you state otherwise, and you are committed to servicing the membership for the duration without any expectation of an annual income. Therefore the price needs to reflect this.

Administration

The administration of a membership scheme demands a high degree of organisation, especially if you wish to maximise the benefits of your fundraising efforts. There are several issues to consider.

How do you get members to renew their subscriptions? The best system is where the member has to do nothing – the membership continues until cancelled, and the subscription is paid automatically through the donor's bank account by direct debit (or via their credit card).

If there is a fixed-term commitment and this comes to an end, you will want to ensure that as many people renew as possible. The usual way to do this is by sending reminder letters, preferably a couple of months before the expiry, giving them time to renew.

The telephone is also a valuable tool for renewal. You will need to decide at what point in the renewal cycle you use the phone – before or at the renewal date. It is also a good medium for asking a donor to increase the value of their donation. You can also gather useful information at this time about why members may not be renewing.

Membership renewal can be done on one fixed date each year (for example with annual membership running from 1 January to 31 December). Those that join through the year will pay pro rata.

An alternative is that each member's membership expires exactly 12 months after the annual subscription was paid. This requires more efficient organisation, as you will be dealing with renewals on a rolling basis throughout the year.

If you have a large membership you will need a reliable computer database to help you handle renewals. A key issue is the ability of the system to identify renewal points so that you can mail not only on the point of renewal but also before, to stimulate the highest possible renewal rate.

Raising the subscription rate: Changing the annual subscription rate can be a very laborious process, because members have to be informed of the change and any standing orders you are administering will need to be cancelled and replaced with new ones for the appropriate amount. As a result, some organisations review their subscriptions quite infrequently (perhaps once every three or four years) and take a conservative view of the need to increase rates. This means that membership fees can often lag behind inflation.

One way around this problem is to ask for subscriptions to be paid by direct debit. You will still need to inform your members in advance of any rise in the subscription, giving them a chance to cancel if they do not want to pay the higher amount, and you have to agree to reimburse any sums debited from a bank account in the event of a dispute.

Making membership payments tax efficient: Under Gift Aid, any payment can be made tax effectively provided the donor is a UK taxpayer and has declared (by ticking a box or filling out a form) that they wish the charity to reclaim the tax paid on all their donations.

If you want to make membership payments tax efficient you will need to check with Her Majesty's Revenue & Customs (HMRC) to make sure it accepts that the membership benefits you offer are within the current limits. If your primary aim is to generate funds, it makes sense for you to make your scheme tax-effective and encourage as many members as possible to pay in this way. In addition, if the member is a higher rate taxpayer, they will benefit from higher rate relief.

VAT liability on membership subscriptions: When more than an annual report and a right to vote at the AGM are offered to a member in return for their subscription, HMRC will treat the subscription payment as being partly a payment for a service, and some or all of it may be taxable (for those organisations registered for VAT, or where the taxable subscription income takes them over the VAT registration threshold). Many organisations are keen to offer benefits to encourage people to subscribe. If you are unsure about the tax implications, you should consult HMRC before finalising your membership scheme. More information can be found in *A Practical Guide to VAT* by Kate Sayer and Alastair Hardman, published by DSC in association with Sayer Vincent.

Maintaining donor records: Your committed givers and members will be giving money to you regularly and possibly supporting you in a number of other ways. You need to keep track of their support to identify people who might give you extra help when you need it, or to invite to special events such as receptions, or simply to personalise your appeals to them. All this information needs to be on one record, not only in order to develop a full picture of each donor's support, but also to avoid any duplication of mailings. If you are not yet ready to invest in one of the big tailor-made databases, the 'How to' guide *Building a Fundraising Database Using your PC* by Peter Flory, published by DSC, will provide you with a step-by-step introduction to setting up a simple database using Microsoft Office.

In collecting any data about your supporters you must of course ensure that you comply with the requirements of the Data Protection Act. For more information on this, refer to *Data Protection for Voluntary Organisations* by Paul Ticher, published by DSC in 2009, or visit: www.ico.gov.uk.

Payroll giving

Giving at work has been around for some time in Britain. Originally it involved large numbers of factory workers giving a few pence per week and signing an authorisation to have the amount deducted from their wages each pay day.

Luke FitzHerbert, former co-director of the Directory of Social Change, led a project in the mid 1980s to launch payroll giving in Britain. In 1987, the government created a new scheme for tax-deductible payroll giving as part of its policy of encouraging charitable giving. This was seen as an opportunity for charities to mobilise support from the millions of people in employment and gave what had been a very marginal form of giving, a completely new lease of life. In the past the scheme has not delivered anything like what was expected of it and still does not generate as much revenue for charity as it could.

Payroll giving is, however, continuing to grow and raised almost £109 million for UK charities between April 2007 and March 2008, an increase of 22.5% from the previous year. In the same period almost £109 million was received and distributed by the Payroll Giving Agencies to UK charities from employees donating from their pre-tax pay. More than 717,000 employees donated through payroll giving between April 2007 and March 2008, an increase of 11.5% from the previous year. It is now an established way of giving and provides charities with a mechanism for regular committed income.

Most recently the Institute of Fundraising has been working with HMRC to promote this tax efficient opportunity for giving. As part of this scheme grants and matching funds have been offered to employers who wish to initiate payroll giving for their staff, as well as the award programme the Payroll Giving Quality Mark. More information on this can be found at www.payrollgivingcentre.org.uk.

Tax-effective giving

Gift Aid

Under the Gift Aid scheme, UK charities can claim back the basic rate tax that an individual has already paid.

Gift Aid is a way for charities or community amateur sports clubs (CASCs) to increase the value of monetary gifts from UK taxpayers by claiming back the basic rate tax paid by the donor. It can increase the value of donations by a quarter at no extra cost to the donor.

The following is an extract from the HMRC website:

> *Gift Aid is an easy way to help your charity or CASC maximise the value of its donations, as you can reclaim tax from HMRC on its 'gross' equivalent – its value before tax was deducted at the basic rate. This is 20 per cent from 6 April 2008. You can work out the amount of tax you can reclaim by dividing the amount donated by four. This means that for every £1 donated, you can claim an extra 25 pence.*
>
> *In addition, HMRC will automatically pay your charity or CASC a further three pence for every pound donated. This 'transitional relief' – to adjust to the fall in basic rate tax (from 22 per cent to 20 per cent) – is available on Gift Aid donations made from 6 April 2008 until 5 April 2011. This means that for every £1 donated, your charity or CASC can receive 28 pence, so the total value of the donation is £1.28.*

Donations that qualify

Gift Aid can only be claimed on gifts of money from individuals, sole traders or partnerships, in any of the following forms:

- *cash*
- *cheque*
- *direct debit*
- *credit or debit card*
- *postal order*
- *standing order or telegraphic transfer.*

Gifts made by cheque only count as received once the cheque has cleared. Your charity or CASC can accept gifts of money made in sterling or any foreign currency.

Payments that don't qualify for Gift Aid

These include:

- *donations of money from a company*

- *donations in the form of a loan waiver or debt conversion – for example, an individual may lend money to your charity or CASC and then, at a later date, agree that it does not have to be paid back – this is not a gift of money, it is the waiver of a loan*

- *gifts made on behalf of other people, for example a membership subscription paid on behalf of somebody else – this is a gift of membership from the payer to the member, not a gift made to the charity or CASC*

- *gifts that come with a condition about repayment*

- *gifts with enforceable conditions about how your charity or CASC should use the money – for example on condition that it buys goods or services from the donor*

- *payments received in return for goods or services – these are not gifts – for example payment for admission to a concert, payment for a raffle ticket or an entrance fee for an adventure challenge event*

- *a 'minimum donation' where there is no choice about payment – this is simply a fee for goods or services, it is not a gift*

- *gifts made using 'charity vouchers' or 'charity cheques' provided by another charity.*

Gift Aid declarations

Before your charity or CASC can claim tax back on a donation made by an individual, you need to obtain a Gift Aid declaration from that donor.

A Gift Aid declaration can be made in writing, electronically or verbally, and must contain certain information about the donor. You also need to show that you have advised the donor that they will need to pay sufficient UK tax at least equal to the amount that your charity or CASC will reclaim on their donation(s).

You must keep these records in support of your Gift Aid repayment claims. Each donation included in a claim must be supported by a Gift Aid declaration.

A Gift Aid declaration can be made either in writing or orally and may cover donations made since 5 April 2003 and all future donations. The donor needs to understand that they are giving you authority to reclaim tax from HMRC on the gift.

Any payment made to a charity by a taxpayer is eligible for tax relief as long as:

- *the donor fills out a Gift Aid declaration which is then kept by the charity*
- *the charity maintains an 'audit trail' linking the payment to the donor – the charity needs to record each donation separately and be able to prove to HM Revenue & Customs how much each donor has given.*

Not all charities take advantage of Gift Aid, in particular the UK's smallest non-profit organisations (those with a voluntary income of less than £100,000). Therefore it appears that there is still work to be done in terms of promoting the benefits of Gift Aid to this group.

You can get further advice on implementing a Gift Aid programme by visiting HMRC's website – www.hmrc.gov.uk/charities (see also www.tax-effective-giving.org.uk, which is a part of the Institute of Fundraising website). Here you will also be able to find exactly what information is required to be included in a Gift Aid declaration, and a model form.

The Gift Aid declaration can state that it covers all donations from the date of the current gift onwards (and going back up to six years prior to the date of the declaration), so one declaration can cover all future claims, although the donor can cancel this at any time.

The level of benefits the donor can receive are limited to 25% for a donation or subscription up to £100, £25 between £101 and £1,000, 2.5% above £1,000, with an overall maximum of £250. So, in theory, you can add 25% (on 2008–09 tax rates) to the income from, for example, a sponsored run if:

- *all your sponsors are taxpayers*
- *they all complete or have completed a Gift Aid declaration*
- *you can prove that they have made the payment.*

Once you have proper record keeping in place, the system is now so simple that you can reclaim tax on almost any donation, whatever the size, as long as the donor is a taxpayer.

You should be aware that there is now a time limit for making claims for tax on donations made by Gift Aid. Any charity which is a company for tax purposes must make any claim within six years from the end of the accounting period to which the claim relates; while a charity which is a trust for tax purposes must make any claim within five years of 31 January in the year following the end of the tax year to which the claim relates.

Charities Aid Foundation accounts

Another method of giving tax effectively is where the donor uses CAF's services. Here they pay a sum to CAF as a charitable donation and tax is reclaimed on this. The total amount, made up of the value of the donation and the tax reclaimed, less an administrative charge to CAF and a compulsory donation to NCVO (which set up the scheme), is kept in an account for the donor. The donor can then make charitable donations from the account, either using vouchers which they give to the charity as they would a cheque, by quoting their CharityCard number, or by asking CAF to make regular direct payments to a charity from their account.

Gifts of shares to charity

Since April 2000, individuals (and companies) have also been able to get tax relief on gifts of certain shares and securities to charity when calculating their income for tax purposes. The tax relief applies where the whole of the beneficial interest in any qualifying shares or securities is disposed of to charity either by way of a gift or by way of a sale at an undervalue.

The following categories of shares and securities can be donated using this relief:

- shares and securities listed or dealt in on the UK Stock Exchange, including the Alternative Investment Market (AIM)
- shares and securities listed or dealt in on recognised foreign stock exchanges
- units in an authorised unit trust (AUT)
- shares in a UK open-ended investment company (OEIC)
- holdings in certain foreign collective investment schemes – broadly, schemes established outside the UK equivalent to unit trusts and OEICs.

NB

Definitions of AIM, AUT and OEIC are given at the end of this chapter.

To check whether the shares or securities qualify for the scheme, contact HMRC for advice.

Where an individual makes use of this relief, they are able to deduct the 'relevant amount' from their total income for tax purposes. The relevant amount is either the full market value of the shares (where the transfer is a gift), or the difference between the market value and the actual cash received (where transfer is a sale at an undervalue). This figure is then adjusted by adding to it any incidental costs of disposing of the shares – for example brokers' fees.

Tax relief can be claimed at the donor's top rate of tax via their self-assessment tax return, and for capital gains tax (CGT) transfer is deemed to have taken place at cost (so no CGT is payable) unless the shares are sold at an undervalue, where the sale price is taken as being the transfer price.

Since April 2002, the same tax relief has been available for donors who give land and buildings to charity.

Looking after your supporters or stewardship

Your donors and supporters are a key part of your fundraising future. They have demonstrated their commitment to you through giving, and you should try to retain this commitment and strengthen their ties to your organisation. This is often referred to as donor or supporter care, stewardship or customer relationship marketing. This section concentrates on two aspects of developing your supporter relationships – thanking them and increasing their involvement.

Thanking your donors

Being thanked makes donors feel good about their giving, and tells them that their donation has been received and is being put to good use. Thanking your donors gives you the opportunity to find out the depth of their interest, and perhaps some of the reasons why they support you. It can also enable you to tell them more about your work and your future plans, and all this will hopefully help you to get further support from them.

Your best prospects for a donation are those people who have already given to you, so when and how you thank them can be crucial. There are several ways of saying thank you.

By post

Some charities reply to all donations, while others reply only to certain types or levels. It can be expensive to thank people for every donation whether large or small, especially if there are a lot of them, but there are important advantages in thanking donors at some point, even if you do not do it every time. If you are concerned about saving administrative costs, you might ask donors to tell you if they do not want an acknowledgement from you every time they give.

When you do say thank you, try to do it soon after the donation is received. Try and make the letter as personal as you can, recognising how long the person has been supporting you and their level of giving. It might be useful to develop a set of generic letters which you can then adapt as necessary. Some organisations get their chair or director to sign the letter. This is not necessary except for very large donations. Your smaller and regular donors may be more interested in getting to know you (the fundraiser) or a donation administrator, whom they will be able to contact if they have a query or want further information.

By telephone

If you want to respond quickly and personally, particularly for larger donations, the telephone is ideal. As soon as you receive an exceptional gift, ring the donor and thank them personally.

By email

If you know a supporter's email address (and this is something you should be collecting along with their postal address and telephone number), this can be an immediate way of saying thank you and also has the advantage of being very cost-effective.

Face to face

Personally visiting important donors can be a time consuming business. However, it can also be worthwhile. The visit should be made by an appropriate person. Depending on the level of donor, this might be the fundraiser, a member of the management or fundraising committee or a trained volunteer. Be careful not to impinge too much on the donor's time – they might not appreciate taking time from their schedule to meet with you and a visit might be counter-productive, so make sure that it is welcomed.

Donors may be wary about the object of such visits until they have actually received one. A simple chat to tell the donor more about your work and to thank them for their gift will sometimes naturally lead on to discussing other ways they can help without your having to introduce the subject yourself or ask directly. There might also be something you were unaware of that your group could do for them.

Through an event

If a face-to-face visit is not appropriate, another way of meeting and thanking supporters is by setting up an event, such as a reception or open day. A senior person from the organisation might attend and give a short talk; then staff, committee members or other volunteers can be on hand to talk to those who have been invited to the event. This requires careful planning and briefing of your staff, committees and volunteers to ensure that everyone is spoken to.

You might hold the event from where your organisation operates – people are often interested in seeing how an organisation works and meeting the people who work there. Or you could organise a site visit to see a project at work and enable the donors to meet some of the members of your user group and the local community.

By public acknowledgement

You can also thank people through a public announcement – such as an advertisement in a newspaper or a mention in your newsletter, magazine or annual report. Think carefully about your annual report. Not only can you credit your donors, but this also sends signals to others that you need donations and will publicly acknowledge any support you receive. This gives credibility – 'If those people have given, then they must have faith in the organisation'.

As an organisation grows, the number of donors may get too large to list everyone, but the major donors should still appear. Taking paid advertising to thank donors might be expensive but can be worthwhile if there are other messages to communicate (for example that the cause has widespread or prestigious support). Remember to *get the donor's permission* before you do this and also check how they wish to be credited, as some will not want to see their names publicly in print.

Challenges for the fundraiser

- To get the donor to give again.
- To persuade the donor to give regularly and frequently, ultimately on a committed basis.
- To encourage the donor to increase their level of giving.
- To get the donor to give in several different ways.
- Possibly, to encourage the donor to leave a legacy.

Fundraisers should never allow fundraising to become divorced from the advocacy work. It is important to ensure that there are a number of ways for people to support an organisation: giving money, volunteering, fundraising and campaigning. Some people will only be able to do one of these. However, many may want to do more – and by becoming more involved, this will strengthen their concern and commitment to you.

Recruiting volunteers from your donors

It is sometimes assumed that volunteers and donors are two separate categories of supporters which should not be mixed. Many charities feel that they should not ask their donors to volunteer, although they may want to. It might be a question of not feeling confident, or of waiting to be asked. Even if they do not wish to volunteer, their support may be all the stronger when they are made aware that their time would be valued.

Other fundraising ideas

Local fundraising

It can be worth approaching local bodies that may be able to help your fundraising by raising money on your behalf. Some will welcome presentations from you. Local groups include: chambers of commerce; community foundations; faith communities, for example churches, synagogues, mosques, temples and gurdwaras; inner wheel clubs; lions clubs; local businesses; local colleges/schools; local police and fire brigades; masonic lodges; rotary clubs; local round tables; and student committees.

Distinctive, attractive appeals work best, as do requests for small amounts of money.

Fundraising events

Before organising your event you need to be sure of why you are asking people for money. It will help to decide the type of event and the way it will be run if you have considered why people will want to give. As mentioned above, people give for a number of reasons which can be simplified to four:

- they like the *organisation*
- they like the *people*
- they like the *cause*
- they like the *event*.

Make sure you know who the event is aimed at and that it will be attractive to them. Once you have decided on your event you then need to answer some key questions. A small team of people can help to think through these points and share both the organising and administrative load.

- Why are you doing this? Is the event attractive in itself, or is it the cause?
- What are the risks to you in organising this event? (How easily could it go wrong? How much money do you stand to lose?)
- Who are you raising the money for, yourselves or for an outside cause?
- Who will organise the event?
- Who will come to the event?
- What is the local competition likely to be, especially around certain times of year?
- Where will it be held?

- Is it safe?
- Have you considered whether your insurance provisions are adequate?
- Do you need permission? Have you checked for any statutory regulations that may apply?
- How much money do you hope to raise?

This last question becomes increasingly important the higher your initial outlay. It will be no good to you or your group if you organise the best event ever if you cannot guarantee a paying audience. The people from your group may learn much in the process about teamwork, creativity, organisation and marketing, but if your organisation is seriously out of pocket, you will have difficulty recouping the loss.

Remember too, that all outside events are at the mercy of the weather and you should make contingency plans.

There are basically two kinds of fundraising event:
- ticket events where money is raised through ticket sales
- participation events where money is raised through sponsorship of those taking part.

It may be best for you to start event fundraising in a small way if you are new to this. People sometimes start with a great idea for a grand scheme but are over-ambitious. You should do what you know your group can achieve and build from your success. Organising a car boot sale may not have the appeal of a music festival in the park, but for a first 'event' will be easier to run and have fewer risks attached.

Sponsored events – a guide
Asking people to sponsor someone for an event is the most common way that groups and individuals raise money from the public. It is easy to see the advantages:
- easy and quick to organise
- easy to contact supporters
- reaches a potentially large number of donors through personal contact
- includes participants who are members of the group and helps the group's identity
- they're fun
- can have little initial outlay
- almost unlimited number of activities that can be sponsored
- can raise large sums

- can be used to focus on areas of interest: for example, a treasure hunt to support your anti-litter campaign or gardening for people in sheltered housing to improve their and the community's environment.

With imagination and enthusiastic volunteers, you can take a sponsored event and do something different with it. If you can give the activity a new twist you build new enthusiasm for the event itself.

Publicity can also be increased if the event is even slightly off the wall. You could for example, hold a fancy dress football match, or shave a trustee's head (pay to watch). Not only does this maintain the momentum of long-term fundraising, it also keeps interest from flagging. This is an important factor when people are doing the hard work of raising money and where interest and enthusiasm can soon be lost. Fundraisers have to be imaginative and have different, creative ideas for events to keep interest high.

Organising a fundraising event is probably not the time to raise money for core costs such as the rent or salaries. There may be exceptions to this rule, but generally you will be more successful if you are raising money for equipment or a specific activity or trip that directly benefits your user group.

Publicity

Attractive publicity materials can give any event an added boost and place it firmly within your specific context. Comic Relief, which organises the Red Nose extravaganza, is among the leaders in the field. Their website says:

> *Red Nose Day is a UK-wide fundraising event organised by Comic Relief every two years which culminates in a night of extraordinary comedy and moving documentary films. It's the biggest TV fundraising event in the UK calendar. On Red Nose Day everyone in England, Scotland, Wales and Northern Ireland is encouraged to cast inhibitions aside, put on a red nose and do something a little bit silly to raise money – celebrities included. It is an event that unites the entire nation in trying to make a difference to the lives of thousands of individuals facing terrible injustice or living in abject poverty.*

You might want to visit Comic Relief's website for ideas on events: www.comicrelief.com.

Publicising and celebrating the success of the group after any event and showing how the amount raised will be used will keep motivation and enthusiasm high for those who have been involved.

You might try something like the following:

Dear Sponsor

Ourlocalvillage Allotment Group has been set up with the aim of designing an allotment and garden specifically for the clients of our two local day centres. As you are probably aware, both council-run centres offer quality therapy for people with disabilities who live in and around our area.

Following our agreement with the local council that we could rent the land (which was fast becoming a waste-tip) at a peppercorn rent, and with a much appreciated grant from our local community foundation, we have levelled the land and made it accessible for everyone.

We now need to buy specialist equipment and accessories to start us off with our planting.

With your kind help we aim to buy:

10 x kneelers – lightweight and portable seats which double as kneelers	£25.10 each
10 x long-reach garden tools	£29.15 each
10 x gardening tool kits for our volunteer helpers	£25.00 each
10 x easy to use garden tools to minimise stress on the wrist	£10.40 each
10 x bird feeders	£4.10 each
6 x bird tables	£20.00 each
6 x hanging baskets	£7.00 each
6 x hanging basket water attachments for easy watering	£7.00 each
3 x garden hoses	£35.00 each
2 x bee logs for pollinating fruit, vegetables, herbs and flowers	£15.00 each
2 x wheelbarrows	£34.95 each
Seeds, plants, shrubs, herbs, compost etc., for planting	£250.00

Total amount to be raised: £1,595

Most of the equipment we intend to buy is specifically designed for people with disabilities, is robust and sturdy and bought with the intention that it will last for many years.

You have generously donated to previous fundraising events and we hope you will encourage our eager gardeners with a donation towards our new project.

continued...

We will be formally opening our Allotment Garden on June 25 2010, with a talk from a celebrity gardener. Refreshments will be available. We hope to see you there, even if you are not able to give this time.

Very best wishes

Ann Other

Chair

Ourlocalvillage Allotment Group

Helping people to give

The public are no different from other donors when it comes to wanting to be told how to give and even how much. Many will not have much idea when handed a sponsorship form of how much they should sign up to.

Give donors the option of sponsoring a total amount as well as the number of units. It is always a good idea to give a total amount, rather than sting the sponsor after your group's efforts. If the sponsor has pledged 50p a length of the pool, a claim for £25 after 50 lengths by a new Olympic hope might be more than they anticipated and you might even have trouble collecting your hard-earned money. You should also think about the type of unit – 10p a kilometre, for instance, will generate more income than 10p a mile.

You might want to offer a small incentive for the participants but these should only be token. Certificates or badges to be presented may well be enough.

Do the right thing – do you need a licence?

The regulatory hurdles you will have to clear will depend upon the event you are running. It is also worth doing a risk assessment on your event. The Health and Safety Executive (Infoline: 0845 345 0055; website: www.hse.gov.uk) can give guidelines.

Depending on the event you are running you may have to consider the following:

- Bye-laws – check with the local authority's leisure and recreation department, or other authorities such as rivers, waterways, footpath, coastal and heritage.
- Car boot sales – contact the licensing office of the local authority for guidance.
- First aid, fire and police regulations – contact the appropriate body.
- Food hygiene and safety – contact environmental services at the local authority for guidance.

- Health and safety – check all aspects of your activity with the local authority and the local health and safety office.
- Premises licence – this provides for the sale of alcohol by retail, provision of regulated entertainment or provision of late night refreshment. Contact your local authority for guidance.
- Lotteries – see information from the Charity Commission's website. The Gambling Commission also has information on regulation.
- Public liability and other insurance – check with your insurer.
- Safety certificates – where you are organising fairground rides, motorised tours, balloon rides or the like you need to apply for appropriate licensing. The leisure and recreation department, environmental services or the licensing office of your local authority can give guidance.
- Street closures – you need to apply for a street closure order from the local authority.
- Sunday trading – contact the local authority to find out the current regulation.

Please also note the following guidelines taken from the Charity Commission's website:

Telephone fundraising and broadcast appeals

Where the telephone is used to raise funds it is the trustees' duty to ensure that the public are clear which charity the funds are for, what percentage of the donation will be spent on the objects of the charity and also to ensure that all funds raised are transferred directly to the charity. (See also [the paragraph on page 112 on professional fundraisers and commercial participators] which affect telephone fundraising and broadcast appeals.)

The Institute of Fundraising has produced a code of practice for telephone fundraising – visit the website at: www.institute-of-fundraising.org.uk.

Chain letters

Chain letters are not illegal but their use is generally discouraged by us [the Commission] and the Institute of Fundraising because they can be difficult to control. Once started they are difficult to stop and can give rise, when the appeal target has been met, to claims that the charity is misleading the public.

Statutory provisions controlling fundraising

The Charities Act 2006 is a major piece of legislation affecting charities and the following paragraphs are taken from *A Guide to the Main Provisions which Affect Charities* at the Commission's website – www.charity-commission.gov.uk.

You should be aware that at the time of writing not all of the provisions had been put into place and you should check with the Commission for the current requirements. The Office of the Third Sector has published an implementation plan outlining when each part of the Act will come into force. This can be found at: www.cabinetoffice.gov.uk.

Fundraising solicitation statements

Currently professional fundraisers and commercial participators fundraising for charities must have a written agreement with the charity, and must make a statement telling potential donors that they are getting paid when they ask for money. This is so that potential donors can make an informed choice about giving.

The Act makes two main changes to these 'solicitation statements':

- *They will have to include the amount the professional fundraiser or commercial participator will be paid for fundraising for the appeal, or if the specific amount isn't known, to give a reasonably accurate estimate of what they'll receive.*

- *Slightly different statements will also have to be made by employees, officers and trustees of charities who act as collectors. This doesn't apply to volunteers.*

Public charitable collections

The Act provides for a new system for licensing charitable collections in public. It applies to all such collections, including face-to-face fundraising, involving requests for direct debits.

There is a new role for the Commission in checking whether charities and other organisations are fit and proper to carry out public collections and we will be responsible for issuing 'public collections certificates', valid for up to five years.

We need to develop the right regulations and guidance so that we can take on this new role. We also need the necessary resources to set up the new systems and this will take time to set up. We don't envisage taking on this function for a few years yet.

Collections in public places

Previous legislation referred to 'street' collections. The Act extends this to collections in 'public places' which includes some privately owned land, such as railway station ticket halls and supermarket forecourts. Once a charity has a public collections certificate it will be able to apply to a local authority for a permit to hold collections at certain times in certain places in that local authority area. Local authorities will ensure that there are not too many collections taking place at the same time, in the same place.

Door-to-door collections

Previous legislation referred to 'house-to-house' collections. The Act refers instead to 'door-to-door' collections, to make clear that this includes business premises. A charity with a public collections certificate will be able to conduct door-to-door collections without permission from a local authority, but it must inform the local authority that the collection is taking place.

Local, short-term collections

Some collections will be exempt from licensing and will not require either a certificate or permit, but organisers will have to notify the local authority that the collection is taking place; so small-scale activities like carol singing should not be disproportionately affected.

Lotteries

There are two main types of lotteries of interest to charities, both regulated by the Lotteries and Amusements Act 1976 as amended by the National Lottery etc Act 1993:

- small lotteries
- society lotteries.

Small lotteries

Small lotteries do not need to be registered but they have to be incidental to an exempt entertainment. Exempt entertainments are defined by the 1976 Act and include fêtes, bazaars and dinner dances. Certain conditions have to be met which include no cash prizes, the sale and issue of tickets and announcement of the results must be carried out during the entertainment and on the premises where it is held and no more than £250 can be spent on buying prizes. Trustees are advised to seek professional advice if they are in any doubt.

Society lotteries

Where a charity is promoting the sale of lottery tickets which will exceed £20,000 in value (or if taken together with sales from previous lotteries in the same year will exceed £250,000) it will be necessary to register with the Gambling Commission. Charities conducting lotteries below these thresholds are required to register with the local authority.

There are detailed statutory regulations about the conduct of lotteries covering accounts, age restrictions, the maximum price of tickets and the amounts which may be paid out in prizes and deducted for expenses. Trustees are advised to consult the appropriate local authority or the Gambling Commission for further advice.

Competitions and gaming
Competitions such as bingo and the use of gaming (slot) machines are mainly regulated by the Gaming Act 1968 [repealed by the Gambling Act 2005] and trustees are advised to consult the Gambling Commission.

Professional fundraisers and commercial participators
Where trustees decide to raise funds by employing a professional fundraiser or by entering into a promotion with a commercial participator they need to be aware of the provisions of Part II of the Charities Act 1992 (as amended by the Charities Act 2006) and The Charitable Institutions (fundraising) Regulations 1994 (SI 1994/3024).

These extracts were taken from CC20 – *Charities and fundraising* and *A Guide to the Main Provisions which Affect Charities*. You should refer to the Charity Commission's website for further advice.

Prominent figures
Working with someone who is well known can help to raise the profile of your event or your organisation. There are a number of advantages to attracting a 'name' to your cause:

- increased media coverage, locally and nationally
- more people may come to an event
- other funders may attend a celebrity event
- a morale boost for those participating and organising the event
- this person can act as a positive role model
- you may be able to obtain discounted rates or items from suppliers
- this person may have contacts and links with other groups and 'names'.

If you do not already have a well-known and respected person connected with your fundraising, look at whether you have a patron, notable trustees or any famous names who once had a connection with your organisation. They will rally to your cause if they:

- like and trust the group and agree with what you are trying to do
- have some connection with you
- like the event.

Ten tips on working with the famous

1) Think about your audience.

2) Choose someone your audience knows and likes and **who you are pleased to have associated with your group** – you should be very selective in this.

3) Choose someone who is sympathetic to your cause, ideally someone with first-hand knowledge and who has a connection with your organisation.

4) Contact any celebrity well in advance of any event.

5) Be very clear about what you want their involvement to be.

6) Offer to pay expenses (mileage, materials, meals, accommodation, etc.) and budget accordingly.

7) Brief them well, and advise them about any press coverage.

8) Make sure those who will be meeting and those introducing them know what to do.

9) Don't overrun, unless they initiate it.

10) Say thanks and keep them in touch with what you are doing.

For further information on working with famous people refer to *Patrons, Presidents and Personalities* by Eileen Hammond, published by DSC.

As with everything else in fundraising, you need a mixture of the tried and trusted with the new and eye catching.

In general, fundraising from the public is one of the most exciting ways of raising money – it can be a lot of fun. Remember though to start small, start early, be realistic, cover all your health and safety requirements and make sure you have contingency plans for when things go wrong.

Checklist – how to organise an event

Lancashire Community Futures (a community council) has produced a checklist to cover planning, preparation and running a village event. You can adapt the following to your own activity, but remember this cannot cover all eventualities and you should use this as the start for your planning, rather than the last word.

If you are thinking of holding an event, a logical approach to the planning process will always produce a better organised, safer and more enjoyable event. This list has been designed to be a step-by-step guide and checklist, taking an organising committee through all the stages necessary in planning a wide range of community events.

The list follows the logical order of event planning, starting with:

1) Feasibility – the following points should be considered to ascertain the feasibility of your event before planning starts.

   ■ What type of event are you planning?

   ■ Why are you holding it?

   ■ When will you hold it? Will it clash with other events?

   ■ Where will you stage it (safely)?

2) Once you are satisfied that the event is feasible, the next stage is to plan it.

3) After deciding that your idea is sound and getting committee approval the final task is to appoint an event coordinator – who has overall control – and an organising committee with a clear remit, set targets and clearly assigned responsibilities.

Organising a community event

Planning

Agree the date of the event, and set realistic timetables for preparation. Consider the main areas of planning. The outline plan for your event should cover at least the following areas.

Safety	Assigned	Finalised
Insurance	☐	☐
Risk assessment	☐	☐
Health and safety	☐	☐
Safe site	☐	☐
Occupier's Liability Act	☐	☐
Health & Safety at Work Act	☐	☐

Budget		
Draft budget and contingency	☐	☐
Break-even point	☐	☐
Sponsorship/grant aid	☐	☐
Costs/sales	☐	☐
Trade/concessionaires	☐	☐
Reinstatement deposit	☐	☐

Publicity		
Sponsors' requirements	☐	☐
Trade adverts	☐	☐
Advertising costs	☐	☐
Publicity material costs	☐	☐

Programme	Assigned	Finalised
Time/date – other local events	☐	☐
National events	☐	☐
Holidays	☐	☐
Legal considerations –		
Food hygiene	☐	☐
Planning permission	☐	☐
Licences – alcoholic drinks	☐	☐
Music/dance	☐	☐
Personalities/guests	☐	☐

continued...

115

Site

Mains services

Car parking

Access to/from

Marquee hire

Reinstatement

Staffing

Numbers required

Paid

Volunteers

Preparation

Having planned the event and agreed the timetable for preparation, you must assign tasks to members or sub-groups, and arrange dates for their completion. For larger events, sub-committees for each area of preparation, e.g. safety or publicity, should be set up. The event committee must meet regularly to make sure everything is going to plan – or to iron out any problems. Members of the organising committee should take responsibility for individual areas. Completion dates should be set.

Safety	Assigned	Completed
Signs		
Barrier hire		
First aid personnel		
PA systems/radio		
Public liability		

Budget

Costs – services

Staff

Site

Equipment

Supplies

Income – sponsorship

Admission charge

Trade stands

continued...

Advertising on site/programme ☐ ☐
Tickets/programme sales ☐ ☐
Insurance ☐ ☐

Publicity
Radio/TV ☐ ☐
Programmes ☐ ☐
Press release ☐ ☐
Sponsors' requirements ☐ ☐
Handbills ☐ ☐
Posters ☐ ☐
Photographer ☐ ☐

Programme

	Assigned	Completed
Start/finish times	☐	☐
Food hygiene	☐	☐
Planning permission	☐	☐
Insurance – high-risk activities	☐	☐
Specific items	☐	☐
Third party claims	☐	☐
Consequential loss	☐	☐
Cancelled event	☐	☐
Damage to site	☐	☐
Weather insurance	☐	☐
Catering/bars	☐	☐

Site
Signposting ☐ ☐
Site plan ☐ ☐
Electricity/water ☐ ☐
Toilets – disabled access ☐ ☐
First aid post ☐ ☐
Lost children area ☐ ☐
Seating – fire/safety regulations ☐ ☐
Car park – disabled/vehicle recovery ☐ ☐

continued ...

117

Staffing

Recruitment – parking, tickets,
officials, catering, security

Uniforms/bibs

Expenses/meal tickets

Troubleshooters

On the day

Arrive early – earlier than you think you'll need. Ensure individual members know their delegated tasks. Check all tasks have been completed. Run through the event and the volunteer jobs. The event coordinator should not be tied to one job, but should be free to assist and troubleshoot where necessary.

Safety	**Assigned**	**Checked**
PA/radios and coded messages	☐	☐
Marshals – bibs	☐	☐
Barriers – secured	☐	☐
Signs – Keep Out, Exit, etc.	☐	☐
First aid post – signposted	☐	☐
Experienced personnel	☐	☐
Firefighting equipment	☐	☐
Police	☐	☐
Electrician	☐	☐

Money

Float

Prize money/cheques

Secure cash boxes

Tickets – start no.

End no.

Publicity

To the event signs

Programmes on sale

Radio/TV on the day

Banners/flags

Reporters/photographers

continued...

Site	Assigned	Checked
Car park – security disclaimer	☐	☐
Toilets – clean, check regularly, well positioned, accessible	☐	☐
Lost children area – staffed, signposted	☐	☐
Seating – set out, checked, anchored	☐	☐
Electrical supply/generator	☐	☐
Water/drainage	☐	☐
Catering outlets – clean and priced	☐	☐
Bars – plastic glasses: clean and priced	☐	☐

Staffing

	Assigned	Checked
Easily identified	☐	☐
Briefed/specific duties	☐	☐
Given meal tickets/expenses	☐	☐

After the event

Thank your team but try to maintain momentum to ensure that all post-event jobs are completed. Discuss problems and how the event could be improved next year. Start planning now!

	Assigned	Checked
Return site to original condition	☐	☐
Extra litter collection	☐	☐
Thank you letters	☐	☐
Debriefing	☐	☐
Press release/photographs	☐	☐
Bank money – prepare accounts	☐	☐

Remember – this list cannot cover all eventualities. Space has been left for you to fill in the individual requirements specific to your event.

Produced by: Lancashire Community Futures, 15 Victoria Road, Fulwood, Preston PR2 8PS Tel: 01772 717461

A sponsored event checklist

Make sure you plan and set objectives well ahead.

1) Choose the right activity for your target audience and cause.
2) Set a date and find a suitable venue.
3) Get any permissions you need, such as permission to use a public place.
4) Produce sponsorship forms.
5) Involve other organisations, as they can be a good source of participants.
6) Organise local publicity and get media sponsorship.
7) Get local business sponsorship to cover costs and pay for any prizes being offered.
8) Prepare for the day: ensure you have all the stewards, equipment and information that you need for the event.
9) Prepare simple monitoring and feedback forms for evaluation at the end of the event and decide how you will distribute and collect them.
10) Thank everyone.
11) Chase up all uncollected pledges.
12) Make Gift Aid claims.
13) Log all details on your database.
14) Evaluate the results against your objectives.

A number of websites have ideas for events and activities, and tips on how to run them, including Save the Children. Send for, or download, its free guide at: www.savethechildren.org.uk.

Glossary

AIM is the London Stock Exchange's international market for smaller growing companies. On AIM you will find a wide range of businesses, ranging from young, venture capital-backed start-ups to well-established, mature organisations looking to expand.

AUT A unit trust scheme authorised by the Financial Services Authority (FSA). A UK unit trust must be authorised before it can be offered to the general public in the UK.

OEIC stands for an open-ended investment company, which works in a very similar way to a unit trust except that an OEIC is legally constituted as a limited company (plc). OEICs have been operating outside the UK for some time but only since 1997 has it been possible to operate an OEIC in the UK. OEICs are not trusts and do not therefore have a trustee. However they have a depositary, which holds the securities and has similar duties to a unit trust trustee.

8 Raising money from grant-making charities

Grant-making charities give to a great many causes and often their purposes are wide in order for them to be as flexible as possible. Many will have 'general charitable purposes' as their stated objects and will only be specific about their targeted groups in their grant programmes or in their criteria for grantgiving. Many will be interested in supporting the work of environmental organisations even if they have no legally stated preference for this area of work.

This chapter provides a listing of charities interested in supporting environmental issues, often with significant grants. The list is not definitive, as there are too many to detail in this guide.

We hope to show you how you can strengthen your approach and make the most of the wide variety of resources that are available. It should be read along with Chapter 6 *Preparing and writing a good fundraising application.*

About grant-making charities

Grant-making charities are set up to give money away in grants for charitable purposes. As with all charities, they are founded for a variety of reasons and with different legal frameworks. Their social and political perspectives vary, as do their approaches to grantmaking; their income usually comes from investments or their own fundraising. There are various key factors that influence how each one operates, and you need to develop an understanding of these in order to increase your chances of success.

Grant-making charities are extremely diverse in their purposes, vision, aims, activities, assets, structure and procedures. One of the largest grant-making charities is the Wellcome Trust, which gives over £300 million each year but mainly to medical and scientific research, and so is not relevant to the majority of fundraisers.

The Garfield Weston Foundation has a wide range of purposes and will fund projects involved with the environment, community and education.

In 2007/08 the charity awarded almost £1.5 million in 195 grants to community groups supporting a wide range of activities of benefit to the community, including furniture recycling, volunteering days involving litter-picking, repainting run-down community spaces, renovating a grade II listed building to enable a wider a wider range of activities and participants, and restoring a former Miners and Mechanics Institute for use as a gallery space and multi-use community facilities.

The Foundation distributed £34.8 million in 142 grants for educational purposes. These included upgrading key buildings and infrastructure in Oxford, including new facilities and accommodation to support academic and communal life, preserving and enhancing the historic fabric of colleges and halls, building a new conservation centre to preserve ancient manuscripts and texts, using both the latest technologies and traditional approaches, grants to the Mary Rose Trust in Portsmouth for the ongoing conservation of Henry VIII's favourite warship, which requires highly specialised preservation techniques to secure the ship and artefacts for future generations. A new visitor centre and educational facilities in a purpose-built home for the ship have also been built, bringing all the artefacts onto the same site as the ship itself. The National Museum of Scotland, visited by over 800,000 people a year, received £500,000 for access, facilities and a learning space for its collections in art, science and the natural world.

The Foundation gave 32 grants totalling £842,000 for environmental activities, including £100,000 each to Painshill Park Trust, the Woodland Trust and the United Kingdom Antarctic Heritage Trust and £50,000 to the Father Thames Trust for restoring and conserving historic gardens and public spaces along the river. The Tree Council received £20,000 towards its tree warden scheme and the Little Ouse Headwaters Project was granted £10,000 for restoration of grazed wet fen and wet meadow. A similar amount was provided to the Royal Society for the Protection of Birds to help reintroduce the red kite into Northern Ireland.

At the other end of the scale are much smaller (usually local) bodies that may have as little as a few hundred pounds a year to distribute but are worth approaching if you operate within their area of benefit.

There are funders that operate internationally, nationally, regionally or only locally; some will only give to organisations, others only to individuals, many will only support registered charities and, surprisingly, some national charities make purely local grants. Many have a particular interest in supporting projects close to where they are based.

Some also have defined areas of the country where they give their local support (on the basis that it is more effective to concentrate their resources on a particular area, and that it is difficult to assess applications from all parts of the country). Such grantmakers usually also want to focus on need, so any local project should try to make a convincing case that local needs are particularly pressing; comparative local data can be useful and you should contact your local authority for your ward profile, which provides useful demographic information.

If you live in an area where funders are sparse, you could try making a case to a national charity based not just on need, but on the lack of available local funding to meet that need.

Part of the skill in tailoring an application lies in identifying an area of work that a grantmaker will support and highlighting that aspect in your proposal. Most grant-making organisations say they receive many more applications than they can support but that often the standard is not good enough for them to consider awarding a grant. Generic letters are often sent by groups without being tailored to each grantmaker's particular interests and priorities – these are generally rejected. You need to make sure that each application you send is relevant to the particular charity from which you are requesting funds and that you ask for the amount needed, backed up with evidence.

Many grant-making charities see their role as being to support innovation – new ideas, new ways of approaching or tackling a problem, new needs and new projects. They will be careful not to fund anything that could be interpreted as being a statutory responsibility even if cuts have been made and there is a need there.

Grantmakers will also be reluctant to fund your core costs over a long period. Some organisations owe their existence to grantmakers that were prepared to shoulder whatever risk there may have been during the early stages of an organisation, but this is not the norm. In order to obtain funding beyond the initial start-up period (usually a maximum of three years), organisations are required to repackage their work into new projects, even if they are still addressing the same long-term need. Whilst this involves extra work for an organisation, it also necessitates a review of its future aims and target areas and this can often result in an innovative project and a realistic and current overview of the whole organisation.

Successful fundraising from grantmakers requires identifying suitable funders, finding out as much as you can about them, finding an aspect of your work that they will want to support, trying to get them interested in your work (sometimes even before you approach them for a grant) and persuading them that your project is workable and value for money.

How are grant-making charities run?

The running of a grant-making charity will depend on the provisions set out in its governing document, whether that is a will, trust deed, constitution or memorandum and articles of association. It is basically the set of rules by which the organisation is run and will set out its objects, provisions for its administration and management, membership (if any), trustee body and future appointments, amendments and dissolution provisions (in the event that the charity needs to be wound up). The following information will help you to understand how most grant-making charities carry out their work.

The donor or founder

The charity may have been set up by the will of a benefactor, a donation from a philanthropist or by funds raised by local people or given by a local businessperson. Often the name of the charity will indicate this. Many are established with a capital sum provided by a founder during his or her lifetime or in their will. This could be cash, shares in a company or even land. The founder could be a successful businessperson – such as Paul Hamlyn or John Moores, who both set up foundations – and some are set up with donations from the public such as the Diana, Princess of Wales Memorial Fund, which was founded in her memory.

Some have no permanent funds, but rely on continuing fundraising to provide them with money for distribution; two of the largest of these are the BBC's Children in Need and Comic Relief, both of which raise money through major television appeals.

Companies may set up a charity as a vehicle for their own charitable giving; that is, instead of donating money to an established charity, or having a 'charity of the year', they establish their own through which they give grants to other charitable organisations. Depending on the way it is set up, such a charity can be truly independent of company influence, while others are obliged to follow grant-making policies that are in the interest of the company (in which case you should probably approach them in the way that you would approach a company – see Chapter 11 *Winning company support*).

How a charity is founded can have a significant impact on its grantmaking and although the declared area of interest may simply be recorded as 'general charitable purposes', the founder's wishes will guide the trustees in their giving. The founder and his or her family may often play a leading role in the charity's affairs as trustees, supporting concerns and projects which particularly interest them. Like other charities, all charitable grant-making organisations in England and Wales must be registered with the Charity Commission and file their annual accounts according to the requirements of the statement of recommended practice (SORP) and other financial regulations. In Northern Ireland eligible charities will need to be registered with The Charity Commission for Northern Ireland and in Scotland *all* charities must be registered with the office of the Scottish Charity Regulator. Over time, the founder's influence can diminish as outside trustees are appointed, which has happened, for example, with the Joseph Rowntree and Nuffield Foundations.

Examples of major charities established by successful business people

- Esmée Fairbairn Foundation (Ian Fairbairn, M & G Group, unit trusts)
- The Gatsby Charitable Trust (David Sainsbury, J Sainsbury, supermarkets)
- The Paul Hamlyn Foundation (Paul Hamlyn, publishing)
- The Mackintosh Foundation (Cameron Mackintosh, musical theatre)
- The Tudor Trust (Sir Godfrey Mitchell, Wimpey, construction)
- The Wates Foundation (the Wates family, builders)
- The Garfield Weston Foundation (Garfield Weston, Associated British Foods)
- The Westminster Foundation (Duke of Westminster, landowner)
- The Wolfson Foundation (Sir Isaac Wolfson, retailing)

Trustees

The trustees are the people who are ultimately responsible for the administration and management of the charity and they make the grant decisions. They can have different titles, including managing trustees, committees of management and boards of directors, and they should meet on a regular basis, depending on what their governing document provides for. In the case of grant-making charities the meetings will include considering applications, recommendations from their staff (if any) and awarding grants.

Staff

The majority of the larger and medium-sized charities have paid staff; they are not trustees and will rarely make the final decision over whether a project should be funded. However, they will consider correspondence, visit applicants or request more information and then make recommendations to the trustees about whether a grant should be awarded. The trustees will, in almost all cases, have the final say on what is and is not supported.

Policies

Most funders will have some sort of grant-making policies. Some will set up specific and changing programmes, others will have stated preferences for the types of organisation they want to fund. The policies should state:

- what kinds of activity they will support: for example, sports clubs, youth organisations, environmental charities, projects for minority groups, wildlife charities
- where they support them: for example, throughout the UK, only in Merseyside, or within five miles of a city centre
- what kinds of grant they like to give (capital or revenue)
- what they will definitely not support (exclusions).

Charities with such policies rarely give grants outside their stated policy and if you don't fit the criteria, don't apply unless you have a project that you feel they would be specifically interested in.

Written applications

Most grantmakers receive written applications on a form that they have provided or by letter. On the basis of these applications they decide who they will give a grant to, for how much and for how long. Some, however, do not consider any applications at all – they go out and find the projects they want to support. When a grantmaker states that it does not respond to unsolicited applications or that it only supports projects known to the trustees, it's probably best not to apply as you will be wasting their time and your own. If you have a personal contact with one of the trustees or you're confident that the trustees would not want to miss out on the opportunity to fund your new and innovative project, then you could telephone and make enquiries or write with a brief description asking if they would be interested.

Some dos and don'ts when applying for grants

Do

- Plan a strategy
- Plan ahead
- Select a good project
- Believe in what you are doing
- Select a target
- Write an application tailored to the needs of the funder you are approaching
- Use personal contact where you can
- Prepare a realistic and accurate budget for the project
- Be concise
- Be specific
- Establish your credibility
- Keep records of everything you do
- Send reports to keep the grantmaker informed
- Try to develop a partnership or long-term relationship
- Say thank you

Don't

- Send a duplicated mailshot
- Ask for unrealistic amounts, whether under or over budgeted
- Assume funders will immediately understand the need you are addressing
- Make general appeals for running costs
- Use jargon
- Convey any sense that your beneficiaries are victims
- Beg

What kind of funding do grant-making charities give?

Cash

Most grantmakers simply make cash donations and these vary in size depending on their annual income. Environmental grants can range from a few hundred pounds to several million and small local trusts may give as little as £50 or less.

Short-term/pump priming

Most grants are given for one to three years, as the trustees want to keep themselves free to respond to new requests. Many have a maximum grant limit. They also want to feel that, unless you are proposing to eradicate a problem totally, the work will continue after their support has ended. A few grantmakers may venture beyond this and invest significantly in an organisation over a longer period, but this is not the norm. Neither do they see their role as paying for core services for a long period, they prefer to kick start new and exciting projects and look for sustainability. Your application should include a feasible exit strategy showing that the members of you user group will be provided for when the grant has finished.

Once you have come to the end of your grant, the grantmaker will rarely give more money for the same thing. However, you can go back for funding for a different project. Therefore, unless you are new or very small, do not ask them to support your organisation as a whole, ask them to support a particular piece of work or meet a specific need. (See Chapter 5 *Fundraising for projects.*)

Revenue and capital

Grants can be awarded both for revenue (such as salaries, rent and rates) and for capital (such as building and equipment costs), although not all grantmakers will give for both and you should check this before making an application. If you are applying for revenue costs, try to show how the project will be sustainable once the grant money runs out. If it is for a capital project, show how well the facility will be used, how the running costs will be met and if it will provide a new source of revenue for you.

Innovation/difference

One of the most important parts of any application is where you show what is new about your proposed project. What makes it stand out from the rest? Is it a brand new project? Are you moving into a new area? Do you have a new approach to a problem? Are you reaching a new group (for example, people with mental health problems)? Are you using new ways to solve old problems (for example, targeting young people to engage in an anti-litter project)? Are you giving people new skills (for example, encouraging local people from deprived communities to take part in training)? Do your activities break down barriers in communities in new ways (for example, organising events specifically targeted to bring communities together)?

This approach will help to keep your own organisation flexible and looking forward to meet current and potential need in different ways.

Non-statutory funding

Grant-making charities will not fund what they consider to be the responsibility of the state (i.e. that central or local government should be funding). Just because the state is cutting back on its commitments, it does not mean that grantmakers will or can step in.

The Charity Commission has published a leaflet called *Grant Givers and Funding of Public Services* which explains the position of the Commission on charities providing services on behalf of public authorities. A copy of this can be downloaded from the Commission's website – www.charity-commission.gov.uk – and should be read in conjunction with leaflet CC37 *Charities and Public Service Delivery*. The following is taken from the Commission's website.

Organisations are advised to ask themselves the following questions:
- *Are you relieving a statutory duty?*
- *Is it an effective use of charity funds?*
- *Is it in the interests of the charity's beneficiaries?*
- *What value will it add, or what enhancement will it provide?*

Statutory duties can be hard to identify and grantmakers should decide what they will and will not fund and set a policy. They should separate legal from moral questions and take advice from the Commission if necessary.

When considering applications for grants they should determine that it's within the applicant charity's purposes and whether the grant should be ring-fenced.

In general trustees should consider whether there is a statutory duty to provide the service in question, whether statutory funding is available, if this is a proper and effective use of charity funds and an effective way of helping beneficiaries and what added value the grant will make.

The Commission's advice to charities is:

- *We are neutral – it's a decision for the trustees.*

- *You should be paid the full cost of delivering services for government – know your full costs.*

- *Defend your independence.*

- *Think about the value you can add.*

- *An effective, working Compact is needed.*

To summarise, in order to have the best chance of success, make sure that your application matches the following.

- **The grantmaker's policies and priorities.** There is no point sending an application to a funder which has no interest in the work that you do.

- **Its scale of grantmaking.** The grant-maker might be structured to consider either small or large grant applications and you will need to pitch appropriately.

- **Its ethos and approach.** You will have the greatest success with those that share your outlook and values.

Which grant-making charities give money for the environment?

There is a large number of grantmakers that might give to your organisation. They may respond to your application if your activities are educational, have social welfare objectives, or just because you work with issues concerned with the environment and they want to support that. It might also be that you are within a geographical area of interest to them.

Even if a grantmaker doesn't have a stated priority to give to environmental projects, your work may still be eligible. For example where it gives support to education, you may be eligible if you work with, say, those who have been excluded from school or for an innovative approach to vocational training. Similarly, where a grantmaker is concerned with drug abuse, your project set up to tackle drug related litter, may fit well with an aspect of its work.

Local grant-making charities

Generally, it pays to find local charities to apply to first, as these will have geographical limitations on the number of organisations that they can help. A great deal of local giving is done on a friendship basis where trustees give to projects they know and like. You should make a real effort to get to know local trustees personally and send them regular information on your current activities and recent successes. It is beyond the scope of this book to list all local grant-making charities, although a few larger ones have been included as examples of the great work that these charities carry out. You can find out about local trusts in a number of ways:

Word of mouth

Ask your own trustees (management committee/board of directors), volunteers, staff or neighbouring groups. Where someone has been successful with a local grantmaker, build on their experience.

Your local or regional association headquarters

If you have one of these it may have details of grantmakers in the area.

Your local council for voluntary service (CVS)

Your local CVS is a good source of information on which organisations give in the area and to whom. Details can be found at www.navca.org.uk.

Local directories of trusts

These are produced locally by CVSs and nationally by the Directory of Social Change. DSC publishes a range of grant directories on trust giving for fundraisers, including its own *Guides to the Major Trusts Volumes 1 and 2* which include the results of independent research and analysis of what the trusts actually give to in practice. DSC also produces *Guides to Local Trusts* and the *Directory of Grant Making Trusts* (DGMT). All of DSC's information on trusts and foundations can also be accessed via the www.trustfunding.org.uk subscription website.

The local press

Some grantmakers advertise their application procedures and closing dates through local papers or community networks, and donations to local organisations may be covered in news stories.

Community foundations

Community foundations work in a specific geographical area to provide grants for local charitable activity. They have been active in the UK since the 1980s, although the idea originated in America in 1914. They raise money from industry and other grant-giving bodies to distribute in the local area.

Community foundations operate in two main ways:

- by building an endowment of capital given by charities, companies and individuals in their area, and from legacies. The income from this is then used to make grants
- by working with other donors to help them distribute their money more effectively. Donors can direct their funds to a favoured cause or within a specified geographical area. Themed funds can address a particular issue, such as crime prevention, and projects can be supported with donations from several sources.

Community foundations are promoted, supported and trained by the Community Foundation Network (CFN) which 'aims to promote the concept of community foundations in the UK, stimulate and support their growth and best practice, and give support to individual community foundations and their networking with others. CFN's objective is to ensure a network of thriving community foundations throughout the UK, each one able to strengthen their local community through strategic grantmaking and excellent service provision to donors'.

A growing network of approximately 60 foundations is now established across the country. According to the Network's website about 90% of the UK population has access to a community foundation.

Details of your nearest community foundation can be obtained from the Community Foundation Network 020 7713 9326; www.community foundations.org.uk or through your local council for voluntary service.

Local environmental projects will be a natural area of interest to community foundations. You should let them know what you are doing and find out how they can support you.

National grant-making charities

Where there is no local charity that works in your area you will have to look further afield and approach national charities. These organisations usually have more money but are the most heavily applied to. Circular letters to them almost always fail; carefully targeted applications have a much greater chance of success.

Ten large grantgivers to environmental work

The following have stated an interest in supporting environmental work. Their priorities differ greatly within this field. All have entries included in the listing at the end of this chapter.

Grantmaker	Grant total	Environmental/ heritage grants	Year
Arcadia	£20 million (approx)	£20 million (approx)	2007/08
Esmée Fairbairn Foundation	£21.5 million	£4.4 million	2008
The Roddick Foundation	£3 million	£3 million	2007/08
GrantScape	£2.1 million	£2.1 million	2007/08
The Shetland Charitable Trust	£13.8 million	£2 million	2007/08
The Sigrid Rausing Trust	£17 million	£1.9 million	2007
The Prince's Charities Foundation	£21.9 million	£1.6 million	2007/08
City Bridge Trust	£17 million	£1.5 million	2007/08
Pilgrim Trust	£1.9 million	£1.3 million	2008
The Headley Trust	£2.9 million	£876,000	2007

Who to apply to and how to do it

Almost all grant-making charities receive far more applications for projects than they can fund. This does not mean that you should not apply but rather that you will have to put time and effort into making a good application to an appropriate organisation and you should be selective in this.

Most of the larger charities publish guidelines as to what they will and will not fund. It is important to read these before applying to see if what you are proposing fits within their policies and does not fall within their exclusions.

The crucial question in deciding whether to make an application is: 'What do we and the grant-making charity have in common?' What you want to do must meet with what the grantmaker is seeking to fund. This may be in terms of geography, where you operate in the same area, or there may be a particular target group (for example, older people) who you want to involve in your activities and who the grantmaker wants to help.

The activities may be an area where the grantmaker has a long-standing interest, such as crime prevention, if so, you need to engage them with what your vision is and how you hope to achieve your aims.

Presenting your case

For grantmakers without application forms, you need to present your case clearly in an application letter and we would suggest it should be no longer than two sides of A4. In many cases it is all the funder has to go on to make a decision and so you need to include all relevant information including: who you are; what you are going to do; how you are going to do it; who is going to do it; what difference it will make; how much it will cost; and how it will be financed when the grant ends.

Documents such as annual reports, a recent set of audited or independently examined accounts and details of other funding that has been raised or pledged should be attached, but this is supporting material – don't rely on it. The case you make in your application letter should be compelling to the reader. Pass the letter to someone who doesn't know your organisation – if they still don't know what you do and intend to do by the end of the letter, you need to re-draft.

The eight essential elements of an application (given in Chapter 6 *Preparing and writing a good fundraising application*) are all highly relevant to grantmakers. However, before you start drafting your letter or form, you should consider the following suggestions.

Find out what charities your organisation has already applied to and whether it was successful

For those applications that failed, look at why and how you can improve a second application. Those that have supported you are likely to support you again, especially if you have done a good job and reported back to them your achievements. They will be unlikely to fund you for the same project but would probably be pleased to consider a new one.

Devise one or a series of projects for which you need money

Unless you are very new or very small, it is unlikely that a grant-making charity will support your entire organisation; they will want to support a particular piece of work that fits in with their specific interests, hence the emphasis on projects. Also, make sure you can show how your project fits into the charity's grant-making policies.

Work out what is new about this work

Does it give new opportunities to young people? Does it try to solve a longstanding problem in a new and exciting way? Is it developing a new service in that town or village? If there is nothing new about the project, your chances of raising significant grants are less favourable.

Decide how the project can be funded in the long term

Grantmakers generally only give grants for up to three years. It could be argued that if they were to make very long-term grants they would be tying the hands of future trustees and would not be able to adapt to change. However, they do like to see long-term benefits and you will need to persuade them that you can pay for the work once their funding has run out. A well thought out exit strategy will show the grantmaker that you have considered the sustainability of your project and how your beneficiaries will be provided for when funding for the project has come to an end.

Maximise the impact of your personal contacts

Ask around your organisation, your user group, members, volunteers, supporters, management committee (trustees) and staff. Does anyone know any charity trustee or administrator of a grant-making charity personally? If so, get them to make contact and see how the land lies. Personal applications are always the best.

Look through the guide books, this one and others

There are various trust directories to look at and the local CVS will have details of them. DSC publishes an extensive range.

Get hold of the grantmakers' guidelines

This is crucial to a good application. Read them carefully and address the points they raise in your application. For example, if the guidelines ask how the project will be evaluated, you need to give a clear idea of what procedures you have in place to record: how many have used the project, if your targeted groups have been reached, what their feedback said, what they feel the benefits have been and how this information will inform future decisions and activities.

Where the grantmaker has paid administrators, you can ring them to discuss your application

You could ask: would it be eligible, do you have to be a registered charity, when would it be considered, do you need to fill out an application form? Most of the larger grantmakers are prepared to have a preliminary chat over the phone. However, if you get the impression that they don't want to talk, ask whether they would prefer you to write an initial letter, or how it would be best to make an approach.

Write to the charities you have identified as having a common interest with you

The letter should not be more than two sides of A4. In this letter you should state clearly:

- who you are
- what you do
- why the project is important
- what you need
- what it will achieve
- where you will get the money from
- how it will be monitored and evaluated
- how it is sustainable.

You should also send a budget for the particular project, a set of accounts for the organisation as a whole, an annual report and maybe one or two other documents to support your application, such as a recent newspaper cutting.

Monitoring and evaluation

Monitoring and evaluation are important tools, not only to collate information for the report to your funder at the end of a grant but as a way of keeping track of the progress of your project and informing your decisions on future activities. Some grantmakers ask for nothing from an organisation following a grant being given, however, most do. Some will ask for a narrative report and some will ask for detailed analysis of the project, together with targets met, budget lines and the difference the grant has made.

A handful, unfortunately, may have monitoring requirements that look similar to those of the European Social Fund and require monitoring and evaluation requirements totally disproportionate to the amount awarded. However, the grantmaker is a charity itself, responsible for the best use of its charitable assets and required to demonstrate its public benefit, an audit trail for its expenditure and transparency and accountability in its work. Applicants should take this into account and include the administration costs of monitoring and evaluation in the project's budget.

These suggestions will help you with the basic elements to include in your application.

You should now consider what will make your application stand out from all the others and here are some ideas to help you with that:

Build contacts

You will probably be able to identify 10 or 15 key charities from which you have a good chance of getting support, maybe now or maybe in the future. If you can, send some information before you actually write to them for money. This could be your annual report, some press coverage or a newsletter. The main purposes are: (1) to show yourselves in a positive light; (2) to try and get your name known before you write for money; and (3) to show that you are committed to a longer-term relationship with them.

Many grantmakers complain that the only time they hear from people is when they want money and that they actually like to hear about an organisation's activities and new initiatives from time to time. Some of the major charities may themselves seek out projects to support and if they already know about you, you will feature more prominently on their grant-making radar.

Supporting material should be professional but not expensive and glossy. Most grant-making charities are run by busy people with little time to wade through long project descriptions and brochures. A letter saying: 'In May last year you supported us with ...., and we are now pleased to say that ....' is all you need. Remember, this is not an appeal letter; you are not asking for money at this stage. Be brief, enthusiastic and informative. Send the funder this kind of information once or twice a year. If you don't know people personally, this is the next best thing.

If the project is new or unknown to the potential grant-making charity

Ask well-known sponsors or supporters, or local community leaders to say how well-run the organisation is and how much the project is needed. This helps create a bridge between you and the grantmaker.

Offer to visit the potential funder to explain your work

Or better still try to get them to come and see you. Put them on your guest list for events you may be running. They probably won't have the time to attend but if they do, hopefully your application will look familiar when it arrives for consideration. Take time to show them round, introduce the kind of people they want to meet and generally get them enthusiastic about what you are doing.

When you do get a grant, remember this is the beginning of the relationship, not the end

Keep them informed of how things are going (they will probably ask for monitoring information anyway). Always try to be positive and enthusiastic. If you get one grant and spend it well, you have a good chance of getting another grant for something different later on; funders often base decisions on the effectiveness of a previous grant.

Tips for applying to a grant-making charity

One national grant-making foundation gives the following guidance to those applying for grants:

In making your application it is important to realise that yours is one of many competing for limited resources. It is helpful to us if your application is:

- clear, concise and to the point – say what you do or propose to do, how much it will cost and how it will impact on your clients

- transparent, open, direct. Do not try to hide what you want funds for in the guise of something else

- realistic – don't just pick a figure out of the air and work your project/programme around it.

Starting with the need, justify the need and outline a tangible response to meeting the need that makes sense.

We have found that projects are very strong in telling us about their aims and objectives, but weak in telling us what they do and how it impacts on their user group.

Grant-making charities supporting environmental organisations

The following list includes large grant-making charities that have made environmental issues a priority in their grant distribution. Most give throughout the UK, with the exception of the City Bridge Trust, the Shetland Charitable Trust, Lancashire Environmental Fund and the Yorkshire Dales Millennium Trust.

Arcadia

Contact
David Sisam, Director of
Administration, Fourth Floor,
192 Sloane Street, London SW1X 9QX
email: david.sisam@nyland.org.uk;
website: www.arcadiafund.org.uk

Trustees
Charities Aid Foundation; Dr Lisbet
Rausing and Peter Baldwin (Donor
Board).

Areas of work: The preservation of the
environment, heritage and culture.

Total grants: See below

Environmental grants: £20 million

Beneficial area: Worldwide.

General
Formerly the Lisbet Rausing Charitable
Fund, Arcadia was set up in 2001 and
operated in parallel with the Lisbet
Rausing Charitable Fund until that fund
was officially wound up at the end of
2008. Full information about Arcadia
and its activities is given on its website,
some of which is reproduced here:

*From 2009 onwards, Arcadia's key mission
is to protect endangered treasures of culture
and nature. This includes near extinct
languages, rare historical archives and
museum quality artefacts, and the
protection of ecosystems and environments
threatened with extinction. Although no
longer part of our remit, we have
historically donated to charities working to
protect free societies and human rights, to
encourage education and to promote
philanthropy.*

How we operate
*Grants are made only to charitable
institutions. The donor board concentrates
on a few themes. These are identified on
the basis of its members' own scholarly and
practical interests and experience, and
informed expert advice. The donor board is
solely responsible for the choice of
programmes or fields to be supported,
and* **we do not consider uninvited
applications.**

*The general criteria for a grant decision
include its scholarly and/or practical
importance; the expertise of those receiving
the grant; and the urgency of the relevant
issue. All grants are subject to detailed
terms and conditions. Regular reports are
requested, and careful financial
administration enforced.*

*Arcadia's mission is to protect cultural
knowledge and materials, such as near
extinct languages, rare historical archives,
and museum quality artefacts. These are
efforts we feel are vital and yet often
neglected. We are also committed to saving
natural treasures, and we support
ecological conservation through
organisations including Fauna & Flora
International, Yale University, Cambridge
University, Conservacion Patagonia and
The Whitley Fund for Nature.*

*We have historically funded in several
areas that are no longer part of our key
mission work. This includes the defence of
human rights, as demonstrated by our
repeat grants to Human Rights Watch.
Other past grant areas include higher
academic training and research and the
promotion of philanthropy.*

Recent grantmaking
*By February 2009, Arcadia had invited ten
organisations to apply for new grants in
2009 totalling $25.8 million (approx
£18.4 million). Nearly all of these grants
are multi-year commitments, and include
the following:*

- *$5 million (approx £3.5 million) to
  each university library of Harvard,
  Yale, and UCLA*
- *$5 million (approx £3.5 million) to The
  Wende Museum*
- *$1.5 million (approx £1.1 million) to
  Birdlife International*

■ *$1.2 million (approx £857,000) to Royal Botanical Gardens – Kew Seed Bank.*

One of the most exciting grants for 2009, although one of the smallest, is an initial grant of $85,000 to the Early Manuscripts Electronic Library. This grant is to support the survey work for a potential five year project to recover the palimpsests held at St. Catherine's Monastery at Mount Sinai, Egypt.

Details of Arcadia's grants can be found on the fund's website as they are announced.

The fund currently makes grants to organisations in the fields of environmental conservation and cultural knowledge, with large grants being made to high profile projects and organisations. As mentioned above, the fund is keen to stress that unsolicited applications are not considered.

Information available

Information was taken from the fund's website.

Applications

Unsolicited applications will not be considered.

The Ashden Trust

CC no. 802623

Contact
Alan Bookbinder, Director,
Allington House, 1st Floor,
150 Victoria Street, London SW1E 5AE
Tel: 020 7410 0330; Fax: 020 7410 0332;
email: ashdentrust@sfct.org.uk;
website: www.ashdentrust.org.uk

Trustees
Mrs S Butler-Sloss; R Butler-Sloss; Miss Judith Portrait.

Areas of work: Environment, homelessness, sustainable regeneration, community arts.
Total grants: £799,000 (2007/08)
Environmental grants: £623,000
Beneficial area: UK and overseas.

General

This is one of the Sainsbury Family Charitable Trusts, which share a joint administration. They have a common approach to grantmaking which is described in the entry for the group as a whole.

Sarah Butler-Sloss (née Sainsbury) is the settlor of this trust and she has been continuing to build up its endowment, with donations and gifts in 2007/08 of £719,000. Total income during the year was £1.7 million including investment income. Its asset value stood at £26.4 million. Grants were paid during the year totalling £799,000.

Grantmaking

This trust's main areas of interest are (with the value of grants paid in 2007/08, including support costs as list in the accounts):

Category	Value	%
Ashden Awards for Sustainable Energy	£351,000	39%
Environmental Projects UK	£178,300	19%
Environmental Projects Overseas	£117,000	13%
Sustainable Regeneration	£93,400	10%
People at Risk	£77,000	8%
Environmental and Community Arts	£62,300	7%
General	£35,400	4%

Four grants were paid during the year. They were to: Dartington Hall Trust (£33,000), towards Schumacher College's capital appeal; Sainsbury Archive (£1,100), towards core costs; East Tytherley Church, Romsey (£750), annual donation; and Humanitarian

Assistance for the Women & Children of Afghanistan (£500), towards the Fund for Nadia in Afghanistan.

The following information about the trust's grantmaking in 2007/08 is taken from its helpful and descriptive annual report:

Environmental Projects UK

The trustees initiate and support work that can reduce the speed and impact of climate change including energy efficiency and renewable energy technology, aviation and transport policy, and the wide ranging benefits of sustainable agriculture.

In the area of climate change and sustainable energy, the trustees aim to take a broad approach supporting research, practical action, awareness-raising, education and organisations that aim to influence policy in the field. This year they have supported the Green Fiscal Commission [£10,000] to make the case to policy makers that environmental taxes and incentives must form part of the government's long-term strategy and Green Alliance's report 'The way we run our homes: the buck stops where?' [£15,000] which identifies policies that are urgently needed to drive mass environmental change amongst householders, and to advocate these measures to government and the opposition.

To encourage institutions and individuals to take action on climate change, trustees have supported Forum for the Future's work [£20,000] to develop new funding mechanisms that will allow Local Authorities to create their own, innovative responses in order to meet emissions targets and Green Thing's website [£15,000 approved] which makes sustainable living accessible and fun for individuals across the globe.

Environmental Projects Overseas

The trustees continue to support community-based renewable energy projects which aim to equip people with the knowledge and tools to help themselves in an environmentally sustainable way. These projects help to alleviate poverty by using renewable energy technologies for the enhancement of income generation, agriculture, education and health. This year a grant to RETAP [£70,000 over 4 years] will train teachers, school children and managers to grow their own woodlots to provide a sustainable source of fuel for cooking in energy efficient cook stoves. The improved stoves use far less wood and are smoke-free, eradicating the harmful effects of smoke on kitchen staff. Allavida's work [£10,000 approved] in an informal settlement in Nairobi trains and supports young people to develop environmental businesses. The recent conflicts in Kenya following the elections in December 2007 were especially damaging to this community yet these small enterprises offer hope and opportunity to the motivated young people who are involved in the project.

The trust is interested in the uptake of appropriate technology and this year has supported Potters for Peace [£5,000]. This organisation trains local entrepreneurs in Latin America and Africa to produce and sell ceramic water filters. These can be made from local materials and eradicate almost 99.9% of water borne disease agents found in drinking water.

Grants to the Beijing Earth Village [£5,000] and PANOS [£7,500] will train and encourage the reporting of news stories on environmental issues. Despite the fact that climate change will be felt most acutely in developing countries, few people are aware of why weather patterns are changing. More stories in local newspapers and radio broadcasts will allow people to understand and take action on this critical issue.

People at Risk

Grants are made to organisations which help people at risk to access support, secure permanent accommodation, regain economic independence and reconnect with important family and social networks.

Over several years the trustees provided considerable help to homelessness projects which recognise that providing housing is only part of the solution, and therefore provide a range of additional support services. In 2003 the trustees commissioned Dreams Deferred from the research company Lemos & Crane, who identified homeless people's own aspirations for personal development. This led to the creation of Support Action Net, a network of agencies working with people at risk, offering toolkits, examples of good and effective practice, and training and organisational development. The trustees encourage this by funding awards for the most effective and innovative agencies.

In this and the Sustainable Development [Regeneration] category, the trustees aim to support projects that are pioneering fresh approaches, such as: self-help and peer support groups, education and training projects, and the provision of employment or work experience for people at risk. This year the trustees have been especially concerned with the needs of struggling young people, preventing early signs of risk developing into long term health, substance abuse and homelessness problems.

[Notable beneficiaries this year included: Project 58 – Torquay (£25,000), towards the development of the Reversing Trends and Moving On Crew's work; and Broadway (£20,000), towards a model new advice service and training for dealing with people from Eastern European EU accession countries in London.]

Sustainable Regeneration

Funding in this relatively new category aims to bring together the themes of social exclusion and environmentally sustainable development in ways which can help local communities make the most of their resources and develop new skills and competencies. In many cases, projects will reflect the themes of the trust's

environmental work, such as the promotion of cycling or sustainable agriculture, and its work with people at risk, including support for employment and enterprise.

The trustees are keen to support projects which link people to the natural environment in a variety of ways. This year they have funded Farms for City Children [£10,000], Surrey Docks Farm [£16,000 approved] and Food Up Front [£18,000], all of which link fresh food and nutrition to inclusion and regeneration. Farms for City Children introduces pupils from inner-city primary schools to life on a working farm. A typical day for children staying at one of the farms might include milking, egg collecting, mucking out, weeding, fruit-picking and apple pressing all fuelled by meals grown and harvested on-site. Surrey Docks Farm provides opportunities for trainees, volunteers and school children to learn about farming at this working site in Rotherhithe, East London. Food Up Front is a new organisation that supports London residents to grow fresh vegetables on unused pieces of their property – front gardens, balconies, window sills or door steps. Participants have been inspired by how easily they can grow their own salad leaves and have found the networking with other local growers enormously rewarding.

Grants to the Society of St James [£10,000] and Street Shine [£20,000] both support people to move on from homelessness through enterprise and on to employability and regular work. The Society of St James has developed training and job opportunities for hard-to-reach homeless people in a micro-propagation business supplying nurseries and garden centres around Southampton. By going into top FTSE companies with a welcome shoe-shine service from desk to desk, Street Shine's trained traders at last gain a footing on the employment ladder.

Trustees envisage that research carried out by the Development Trusts Association into the level of environmental activity across its member organisations will identify interventions that could see a dramatic rise in community engagement on this issue.

Environmental and Community Arts

The trust continues to promote awareness of the developing field of environmentalism and the arts, and in particular, the performing arts, through its website, the Ashden Directory of Environment and Performance. The directory can be found at www.ashdendirectory.org.uk.

Within this category, the trust has begun to explore ways that arts organisations can collaborate with one another to address environmental issues, to reduce their carbon footprints and to prepare their public for the implementation of measures which will improve sustainability.

The trust also helps organisations which highlight current environmental issues through the medium of literature and the arts [including: Cape Farewell (£15,000), towards core costs in raising awareness about global warming; and Cardboard Citizens (£15,000), towards a drama-training and performance programme for homeless people and young people at risk to combat and overcome problems linked to homelessness].

Ashden Awards for Sustainable Energy

The Ashden Awards were created in 2001 by the Ashden Trust. The aims of the awards are to contribute to the protection of the environment, the advancement of education and relief of poverty for the public benefit in developing countries, UK and elsewhere, by promoting the use of local sustainable and renewable energy sources. The Awards does this through:

- *raising awareness of small-scale sustainable energy projects in the UK and developing countries*
- *demonstrating how best they can be put into practice, using the winners as best practice case studies*

- *encouraging policy makers, NGOs and other funders, to incorporate small-scale sustainable energy into their agendas*
- *providing financial awards to outstanding projects which are environmentally and socially beneficial.*

The Ashden Awards 2008 comprised eight UK awards (including four second prize award winners) and eight international awards for work in developing countries in the areas of enterprise, food security, health education and welfare, light and power for homes and businesses and enterprise, including an overall energy champion award and an outstanding achievement award. [The trust allocated £200,000 to the awards in 2008.]

UK Awards

Schools category:
- *Ringmer Community College, East Sussex*
- *Sandhills Primary School, Oxfordshire*

Local Authority category:
- *Leeds City Council*
- *Arun District Council*

Energy Business category:
- *Kensa Engineering, Cornwall*
- *Dulas, mid-Wales*

Charity and Community category:
- *Global Action Plan, London*
- *Energy Agency, South Ayrshire*

International Awards

- *Technology Informatics Design Endeavour (TIDE), India (Energy Champion)*
- *Aryavart Gramin Bank, India*
- *Cooperativa Regional de Eletrificação Rural do Alto Uruguai Ltda (CRERAL), Brazil*
- *Fruits of the Nile, Uganda*
- *Gaia Association, Ethiopia*

143

- Kisangani Smith Group, Tanzania
- Renewable Energy Development Project (REDP), China

This year's Outstanding Achievement Award [2007/8] went to Grameen Shakti of Bangladesh. The organisation has made a significant contribution to the spread of sustainable energy solutions – to date it has installed 160,000 solar home systems and is adding around 8,000 new systems each month. Since winning an Ashden Award in 2006 it has diversified into the provision of fuel-efficient stoves, which improve living conditions and save fuel; and domestic biogas systems which bring clean sustainable energy to thousands more.

Full details on the Ashden Awards can be found at www.ashdenawards.org

Information available

Excellent annual report and accounts are available from the trust's website.

Exclusions

The trustees generally do not make grants in response to unsolicited applications. However, see Applications.

Applications

The following advice is taken from the trust's website:

Who should apply?

If your organisation has a proven track record in supplying local, sustainable energy solutions in the UK or in the developing world then you should read the guidelines for the Ashden Awards for Sustainable Energy.

The Ashden Trust is one of the Sainsbury Family Charitable Trusts. Before applying to one of the trusts, please read the guidelines below.

1) The trust does not normally fund individuals for projects, educational fees or to join expeditions. If you apply for a grant in one of these categories, we are afraid the trustees are unable to

help. *If you are a registered charity or institution with charitable status applying for a grant we must warn you that only an extremely small number of unsolicited applications are successful.*

2) Do not apply to more than one of the Sainsbury Family Charitable Trusts. Each application will be considered by each trust which may have an interest in this field.

3) All of the Sainsbury Family Charitable Trusts have pro-active grant-making policies and have chosen to concentrate their support in a limited number of activities. If you have read through the Ashden Trust's website and feel your project fits into the trust's priorities we would be very interested to hear from you by post.

4) The trustees generally do not make grants in response to unsolicited applications.

If you would like to apply to the trust you should send a brief description of the proposed project, by post only [to the director].

The proposed project needs to cover:

- *why the project is needed*
- *how, where, when the project will be delivered*
- *who will benefit and in what way*
- *income and expenditure budget*
- *details of funding – secured, applied for*
- *description of the organisation.*

Please do not send any more than two–four sides of A4 when applying to the trust, at this point additional material is unnecessary.

The Balcombe Charitable Trust

CC no. 267172

Contact
Jonathan W Prevezer, c/o Citroen Wells, Devonshire House, 1 Devonshire Street, London W1W 5DR
Tel: 020 7304 2000; Fax: 020 7304 2020; email: jonathan.prevezer@citroen wells.co.uk

Trustees
R A Kreitman; Patricia M Kreitman.

Areas of work: Education, environment, health and welfare.
Total grants: £356,000 (2007/08)
Environmental grants: £107,500
Beneficial area: UK and overseas.

General

This trust generally makes grants in the fields of education, the environment and health and welfare in the UK and overseas. It only supports registered charities.

In 2007/08 it had assets of £26.2 million and an income of £743,000. Grants were made during the year to 24 organisations totalling £356,000, which is an increase on previous years due to a substantial transfer of assets to the trust several years ago.

Grants made were categorised as follows:

Health and welfare – 14 grants totalling £184,500

The beneficiaries were: Oxfam (£31,500); NSPCC (£25,000); British Red Cross (£20,000); Amnesty International, Cancer Backup and Africa Now (£15,000 each); Leuka 2000 (£13,000); Cancer Care Appeal (£10,000); Family Planning Association (£8,000); Breast Cancer Care (£6,000); Maggie's – Cambridge and Victim Support (£5,000 each); and Heart of Kent Hospice (£1,000).

Environment – 4 grants totalling £107,500

The beneficiaries were: Durrell Wildlife Conservation Trust (£82,500); Andrew Lees Trust (£15,000); and Wildlife Vets International and Bath Preservation Trust (£5,000 each).

Education – 6 grants totalling £64,000

The beneficiaries receiving more than £1,000 were: Action Aid (£20,000); Royal National Theatre (£15,500); Money for Madagascar (£15,000); Trust for the Study of Adolescence (£10,000); and Blackheath Conservatoire of Music and the Arts Ltd (£3,000).

Information available
Accounts were on file at the Charity Commission.

Exclusions
No grants to individuals or non-registered charities.

Applications
In writing to the correspondent.

The Big Lottery Fund (see chapter 9 for full details)

The City Bridge Trust

CC no. 1035628

Contact
Clare Thomas, Chief Grants Officer, PO Box 270, Guildhall, London EC2P 2EJ
Tel: 020 7332 3710; Fax: 020 7332 3127; Minicom: 020 7332 3151;
email: citybridgetrust@cityof london.gov.uk;
website: www.citybridgetrust.org.uk/ CityBridgeTrust/

Trustees

The Corporation of the City of London. Membership of the grants committee: Joyce Nash, Chair; William Fraser; Kenneth Ayers; John Barker; John Bird; Raymond Catt; William Dove; Revd Dr Martin Dudley; Gordon Haines; Michael Henderson-Begg; Barbara Newman; Rt Hon the Lord Mayor Ian Luder; and Simon Walsh.

Areas of work: Welfare in London.

Total grants: £17 million (2007/08)

Environmental grants: £1.5 million

Beneficial area: Greater London.

General

Background

The purpose of the charity was, for many years, to maintain the bridges connecting the City of London to Southwark. It now puts its surplus revenue to charitable purposes for the benefit of Greater London, which it has chosen to do so far by making grants to charitable organisations. It has done so in an unusually open way, with detailed grants schemes and meetings that are open to the public. In all cases priority is given to projects which tackle deprivation or disadvantage.

In 2007/08 the trust made grants totalling £17 million.

Main grants programme

Type of grants

Grants are given for either running costs or capital costs. Grants for running costs can be from one to three years. Projects of an 'exceptional or strategic nature' may then make an application for a further two years; a maximum total of five years in all. The trust will also consider supporting core costs incurred in providing services which meet the funding criteria.

Grants may be awarded for feasibility studies or disability access audits (up to £5,000 per grant) to help organisations

obtain the best advice to develop their proposed projects.

The following guidelines are taken from the trust's extensive website. The trust frequently reviews its guidelines so please see its website for up-to-date details.

There are five themes under the main grants programme, each with its own specific aims and objectives.

- *Access for disabled people*
- *London's environment*
- *Children and young people (those aged up to 25 years)*
- *Older people in the community (those aged 60 and over)*
- *Strengthening the voluntary and community sectors.*

In all cases priority is given to projects which tackle the greatest deprivation or disadvantage. The trust's current programmes are:

- *Accessible London*
- *Bridging Communities*
- *Improving Londoners' Mental Health*
- *London's Environment*
- *Older Londoners*
- *Positive Transitions to Independent Living*
- *Strengthening the Third Sector.*

London's environment

Aims

This programme is designed to improve the quality of London's environment and its sustainable development.

Objectives

- To increase Londoners' knowledge of environmental issues and the principles of sustainable development.
- To enhance London's biodiversity.
- To reduce London's environmental footprint, i.e. the excessive use of natural or non-renewable resources.

Funding Priorities

Your application must address one of the following priorities:

- projects to promote environmental education
- work to maintain and enhance London's biodiversity.

Grants in 2009

Beneficiaries included: Roots and Shoots (£120,000); SolarAid (£90,000); Learning Through Landscapes (£75,000); Bankside Open Spaces Trust (£67,000); South London Botanical Institute (£50,000); Green Thing – Green Thing Trust for Green Thing Ltd (£25,000); Camden and Westminster Refugee Training Partnership (£24,000); Insect Arts Club (£20,000); Friends of Greenwich Peninsula Ecology Park (£18,000); and Long Lane Pasture Trust (£17,000).

Greening the Third Sector

The trust manages a 'Greening the Third Sector' programme which aims to share experience and best practice with regard to improving environmental performance.

The programme has four main aims:

- making specific and measurable reductions in carbon and waste
- establishing the connections between environmental and social action
- promoting other environmental benefits
- embedding and spreading good environmental practice throughout the sector.

Preference will be given to larger organisations, or those with an extended sphere of influence among members or partner bodies. The trust will cover the costs of an eco-audit, training or consultancy provided by our approved consultants. This is likely to take up to about five days' work, and will include:

- visiting your offices and discussions with chief executive, staff and trustees
- review of your energy use, waste, travel patterns and purchasing practice
- review of policies and how decisions are made
- a report and an action plan
- follow-up visit after one year
- a report on the changes and savings achieved.

The trust expects successful applicants to participate fully in the process, and to involve all their staff and board members. It asks that you consider how environmental behaviours relate to your core objectives, and how you will embed these into policy and practice. The trust will also ask you how you will help to spread any useful messages or changes among your stakeholders.

For more information on this programme, contact the trust to discuss your ideas. You will then be asked to write a short proposal explaining why you will benefit from taking part in the programme, and how you can help to spread good practice.

Exceptional grants

The trust occasionally makes grants outside its priority areas. Consideration may be given to applications from organisations which demonstrate that they are:

- responding to new needs and circumstances which may have arisen since the trust fixed its priorities (for example a major catastrophe impacting upon London)
- projects that require short-term assistance to cope with unforeseen circumstances enabling them to adapt to change and move forward (need arising from poor planning will not be considered).

Please note, the trust states that only a small number of grants are likely to be made in this category.

Strategic work

The trust is working alongside other partners in several strategic initiatives including:

- reducing knife crime among young people
- improving the quality of impact measurement in the third sector
- improving communications skills in the third sector
- improving access advice for developing buildings
- reducing the third sector's carbon footprint.

More information on the trust's strategic work is available on its website.

Principles of good practice

The trust expects applicants to work to its principles of good practice. These include:

- involving beneficiaries in the planning, delivery and management of services
- valuing diversity
- supporting volunteers
- taking steps to reduce the organisation's carbon footprint.

Monitoring and evaluation

The trust requires all grants to be monitored and evaluated. Details of the trust's monitoring and evaluation policy can be found on its website.

Information available

Detailed annual report, accounts and guidelines are available from the trust or from its website.

Exclusions

The trust cannot fund:

- political parties
- political lobbying
- non-charitable activities

- work which does not benefit the inhabitants of Greater London.

The trust does not fund:

- individuals
- grant-making bodies to make grants on its behalf
- schools, PTAs, universities or other educational establishments (except where they are undertaking ancillary charitable activities specifically directed towards one of the agreed priority areas)
- medical or academic research
- churches or other religious bodies where the monies will be used for religious purposes
- hospitals
- projects which have already taken place or building work which has already been completed
- statutory bodies
- profit making organisations (except social enterprises)
- charities established outside the UK.

Grants will not usually be given to:

- work where there is statutory responsibility to provide funding
- organisations seeking funding to replace cuts by statutory authorities, except where that funding was explicitly time-limited and for a discretionary (non-statutory) purpose
- organisations seeking funding to top up on under-priced contracts
- work where there is significant public funding available (including funding from sports governing bodies).

Applications

Application forms are available from the trust or downloadable from its website, along with full and up-to-date guidelines. Please note: the trust will not consider applications sent by fax or conventional email.

The John S Cohen Foundation

CC no. 241598

Contact
Mrs Diana Helme, Foundation Administrator, PO Box 21277, London W9 2YH
Tel: 020 7286 6921

Trustees
Dr David Cohen, Chair; Ms Imogen Cohen; Ms Olivia Cohen; Ms Veronica Cohen.

Areas of work: General, in particular music and the arts, education and the environment.

Total grants: £393,000 (2007/08)

Environmental grants: £40,000

Beneficial area: Worldwide, in practice mainly UK.

General

The objectives of the foundation are general charitable purposes in the UK or elsewhere and it is particularly active in supporting education, music and the arts and the environment, both built and natural.

In 2007/08 the foundation had assets of £8.4 million and an income of £508,500. Grants were made to 122 organisations totalling £393,000. Grants are generally for £5,000 or less.

Most of the foundation's beneficiaries by number appear to be arts organisations, although environmental and conservation groups such as the Marine Stewardship Council, the Natural History Museum, Royal Parks Foundation, the RSPB, Trees for Life and the Wildfowl and Wetlands Trust were supported, some with larger grants of up to £10,000.

Information available

Accounts were available at the Charity Commission.

Applications

In writing to the correspondent. The foundation's trustees' report states that 'Grants are awarded after the submission of applications to the trustees. The trustees review the application to judge if the grant falls within the charity's objectives and whether the application meets its requirements in terms of the benefits it gives. Each application is discussed, reviewed and decided upon by the trustees at their regular meetings.'

The Ernest Cook Trust

CC no. 313497

Contact
Mrs Ros Leigh, Grants Administrator, Fairford Park, Fairford GL7 4JH
Tel: 01285 712492; Fax: 01285 713417; email: grants@ernestcooktrust.org.uk; website: www.ernestcooktrust.org.uk

Trustees
Anthony Bosanquet, Chair; Harry Henderson; Andrew Christie-Miller; Patrick Maclure; Miles C Tuely; Victoria Edwards.

Areas of work: Educational grants focusing on children and young people for the environment, rural conservation, arts and crafts, literary and numeracy and research.

Total grants: £1.6 million (2007/08)

Environmental grants: £512,500

Beneficial area: UK.

General

Ernest Edward Cook was a grandson and joint heir to the fortune of Thomas Cook, the famous travel agent. He presided over the banking and foreign exchange business of the firm, and was probably responsible for the successful development of the traveller's cheque. When the travel agency was sold in 1928, Ernest Cook devoted the remainder of his life to the preservation of English country houses, the estates to which they belonged, the paintings and furniture which they contained and also to the well-being of the communities of those estates.

Before his death, Mr Cook had made arrangements for the continuing care of his estates by either The Ernest Cook Trust or The National Trust, of which he was, for a long time, by far the greatest benefactor. He left his extensive collection of paintings to the National Art Collections Fund, for the benefit of provincial galleries.

The Ernest Cook Trust was established in 1952 and is its purposes are to maintain the estates given to it by Ernest Cook and to give grants to support educational and research projects. Many of the schemes it supports relate to the countryside and environmental and architectural conservation, and all are educational in emphasis.

The trust's grants policy is influenced by Ernest Cook's two great passions, namely art and country estates. Grants, which must always be for clearly educational purposes, aim principally to focus upon the needs of children and young people. To that end the trustees are keen to support applications from the UK which educate young people about the environment and the countryside. Projects which introduce pupils to the wide spectrum of the arts are also encouraged.

All applications are expected to link in with either the national curriculum or recognised qualifications and particular weight is given to projects which improve levels of literacy and numeracy.

The following is taken from the fund's annual report:

It is appreciated that sometimes a contribution will be required towards the salary of an education officer, but the trust always expects to be a part funder and does not usually commit funds for more than

one year; successful applicants are normally asked to wait two years before applying for further help.

A few research grants are awarded if the work links in to the trust's purposes.

Grants range from £100 to £4,000 in the small grants category, of which modest amounts for educational resources for small groups form a large part. At the two main meetings grants are mostly in the range of between £5,000 – £15,000, with only a few larger awards for projects closely connected with the trust's educational interests. One award of £50,000 is made annually; application for this is by invitation only.

In 2007/08 the trust had assets of £82.2 million and an income of £4.7 million. Grants were made totalling £1.6 million; environmental grants were made as follows:

Environment – 139 grants totalling £512,500

Beneficiaries included: Oxford University Botanic Garden (£25,000), towards the Oxfordshire 2010 Challenge for schools; Year of Food and Farming (£20,000), towards educational work in the North East and South West; Good Gardeners' Association (£10,000), towards the cost of an education officer; Royal Entomological Society (£9,600), to cover the cost of the school and farm wildlife programme; Rockingham Forest Trust (£8,000), towards the People in the Forest project; Groundwork London (£7,500), towards the cost of an education officer for the Eco Schools project; Yorkshire Agricultural Society (£7,000), towards the cost of the information boards, an education adviser and information packs; Arable Group Ltd (£6,000), for bursaries for students taking part in the TAG Asset programme; and Scottish Seabird Centre (£5,000), towards educational resources for the website. Small grants of £3,000 or less included those to: Marine Connection,

Gordon Infant School, Footprint Trust Ltd, University of London, Conservation Volunteers Northern Ireland and a range of primary schools across the UK towards educational projects.

Information available

Accounts were available from the Charity Commission. Information is also available via the trust's website.

Exclusions

Applicants must represent either registered charities or not-for-profit organisations. Grants are normally awarded on an annual basis and will not be awarded retrospectively.

Grants are not made to:

- individuals
- agricultural colleges
- education work which is part of social support, therapy or medical treatment
- building and restoration work
- sports and recreational activities
- work overseas.

Support for wildlife trusts and for farming and wildlife advisory groups is largely restricted to those based in counties in which the trust owns land (Gloucestershire, Buckinghamshire, Leicestershire, Dorset and Oxfordshire).

Applications

There is no application form. Applicants are asked to send a covering letter addressed to the grants administrator as well as describing their educational project clearly on no more than two additional sheets of A4, specifying how any grant will be spent. A simple budget for that project should be included, noting any other funding applications. The latest annual report and accounts for the organisation should also be provided. Please note: the trust will not consider further supporting material or email applications.

Successful applicants will be asked to complete an agreement which includes the ability to pay the grant by the BACS. The agreement also requires the applicant to submit a report on the funded project; failure to do so will ensure the rejection of any further application and may result in a request to repay the award.

The full board of Trustees meet twice a year, in April and October, to consider grants in excess of £4,000; applications for these meetings should be submitted by 31 January and 31 August respectively. Meetings to consider grants of £4,000 or less are normally held in February, May, July, September and December. Notification about the date of payment of grants is given when the offer is made.

The Peter De Haan Charitable Trust

CC no. 1077005

Contact
Mrs Sam Tuson Taylor, 1 China Wharf, 29 Mill Street, London SE1 2BQ
Tel: 020 7232 5471;
email: stusontaylor@pdhct.org.uk;
website: www.pdhct.org.uk

Trustees
Peter Charles De Haan; David Peter Davies; Janette McKay; Paul Vaight; Opus Corporate Trustees Ltd.

Areas of work: Social welfare, the environment and the arts.

Total grants: £2.6 million (2007/08)

Environmental grants: £800,000

Beneficial area: UK.

General

Background

The trust's website states that:

The objects of the charity are wide-ranging and allow [it] to operate as a generalist grant-making charity.

151

The charity will not exist in perpetuity and the reserves will gradually be spent over a 20 year period from the date of constitution. It is this policy which governs the annual level of donations and this year we expect to make grants of between £2 million and £3 million.

General

In 2007/08 the trust had assets of £23.3 million and an income of £417,000. Grants were made to 169 organisations during the year, totalling over £2.6 million.

The charity's grantmaking currently focuses on three areas:

- social welfare
- environment
- arts.

In all areas, the trustees will consider funding for up to a maximum of three years.

Guidelines

The following is taken from www.pdhct.org.uk

Environment

We are interested in applications which endeavour to enhance understanding of nature and wildlife and which inspire and attract the public interest, thereby investing in the future of the environment.

Charitable appeals should be able to demonstrate the following:

- *practical and sustainable benefits of a significant scale;*
- *effective operation with, or alongside, local communities and cultures;*
- *recruitment, training and employment of a broad base of volunteers.*

We are unlikely to support the following environmental projects:

- *non-UK projects;*
- *conservation of well-supported or non-native species;*

- *enhancement of habitat for sporting purposes where there are no wider conservation benefits;*
- *expeditions or fieldwork outside the UK;*
- *recycling projects;*
- *individual energy efficiency or waste reduction schemes;*
- *local green space projects;*
- *horticultural training or therapy;*
- *playground or school ground improvements;*
- *zoos, captive breeding and animal rescue centres;*
- *work that is routine or low impact.*

Grants for environmental causes totalled around £800,000. Beneficiaries during 2007/08 included: London Wildlife Trust (£400,000); Leicestershire & Rutland Wildlife Trust (£275,000); and Kent Wildlife Trust (£116,000).

Information available

Accounts were on file at the Charity Commission.

Exclusions

The trust will not accept applications for grants:

- which directly replace or subsidise statutory funding
- from individuals or for the benefit of one individual
- for work that has already taken place
- which do not have a direct benefit to the UK
- for medical research
- for adventure and residential courses, expeditions or overseas travel
- for holidays or respite care
- for endowment funds
- for the promotion of a specific religion
- which are part of general appeals or circulars

- from applicants who have applied to the trust within the last 12 months.

In addition to the above, the trust is unlikely to support:

- large national charities which enjoy widespread support
- local organisations which are part of a wider network of others doing similar work
- individual pre-schools, schools, out-of-school clubs, supplementary schools, colleges, universities or youth clubs
- websites, publications, conferences or seminars.

Applications

In writing or via email to the correspondent.

Grants may be for project-based applications or to subsidise core costs.

The following information should be included:

- a statement that you have made reference to the website
- a description of the charity's aims and achievements
- charity registration number
- an outline and budget for the project for which funding is sought
- a copy of the latest financial statements
- details of funds raised and the current shortfall.

Applications are considered on a continuing basis throughout the year. Major grants are awarded at the trustee meetings held quarterly in March, June, September and December.

Notification of the outcome of applications will be by email. Where an email address is not available, no notification will be possible.

The charity states that it is not seeking applications from wildlife trusts.

Dischma Charitable Trust

CC no. 1077501

Contact
Linda Cousins, The Secretary, Rathbone Trust Company Ltd, c/o 159 New Bond Street, London W15 2UD
Tel: 020 7399 0820;
email: linda.cousins@rathbones.com

Trustees
Simon Robertson; Edward Robertson; Lorna Robertson Timmis; Virginia Robertson; Selina Robertson; Arabella Brooke.

Areas of work: General, with a preference for education, arts and culture, conservation and human and animal welfare.

Total grants: £135,000 (2007)

Environmental grants: £27,000

Beneficial area: Worldwide, with a strong preference for London and the south east of England.

General

Registered with the Charity Commission in September 1999, this trust has recently reviewed their grant-giving policy and have decided to support principally, but not exclusively, projects concerned with education, arts and culture, conservation and human and animal welfare.

In 2007 the trust had assets of £5.2 million and income of £83,000. Grants were made totalling £135,000 and were broken down as follows:

Category	Value
Wildlife and conservation	£27,000
General medical, mental health and disabilities	£22,000
Welfare of children and young people	£27,000
General	£20,000
Education	£21,000
Welfare of older people	£10,000
Sports-based charities	£9,000

Grants included those made to: the World Wildlife Fund (£5,000); and International Animal Rescue (£2,500).

Information available

Accounts were available at the Charity Commission.

Exclusions

The trust does not support charities who carry out medical research.

Applications

The trustees meet half-yearly to review applications for funding. Only successful applicants are notified of the trustees' decision. Certain charities are supported annually, although no commitment is given.

The Ecology Trust

CC no. 1099222

Contact
Jon Cracknell, Hon. Secretary,
Unicorn Administration Ltd,
30–36 King Street, Maidenhead SL6 1NA

Trustees
Jeremy Faull, Chair; Charles Filmer; Kenneth Richards.

Areas of work: Ecological and environmental initiatives.
Total grants: £531,000 (2007/08)
Environmental grants: £531,000
Beneficial area: Mainly UK.

General

The following is taken from the trust's annual report (2008):

The objects of the charity are as follows:

■ *The preservation, conservation and the protection of the environment and the prudent use of natural resources*

■ *The relief of poverty and the improvement of the conditions of life in socially and economically disadvantaged communities*

■ *The promotion of sustainable means of achieving economic growth and regeneration.*

Sustainable development to mean development that meets the needs of the present without compromising the ability of future generations to meet their own needs.

Grants will be made both to charities and also to non-charities in support of work that advances the charitable purposes of the trust. The principal objective of the trust, reflected in its name, is to support ecological and environmental initiatives, particularly, but by no means exclusively, around the issues of agriculture, energy, and climate change. The trust also intends to help local community groups working on environmental issues in the UK and possibly overseas, so as to empower people to contribute to policy development and to participate in planning and decision-making at the local level. It will seek to support projects that prevent environmental degradation and that change values and attitudes, both amongst the public and with people in positions of power. In general the trust seeks to address the causes of the environmental crisis that we face, and to tackle these, rather than to make the consequences of this crisis easier to live with.

Agriculture

The trust is keen to help accelerate the transition away from energy-intensive industrial agriculture towards more sustainable farming systems, including organic agriculture. It will support organisations working to bring about this paradigm change by funding work along the following lines:

■ *Raising public awareness of the consequences of current food production systems.*

■ *Supporting research that explores these impacts.*

- *Developing consumer demand and retail opportunities for local and organic food.*
- *Promoting sustainable agriculture.*

Energy and climate change

Scientific evidence of the risks posed by climate change grows stronger by the month, as does acceptance of the need for a rapid reduction in global emissions of greenhouse gases such as carbon dioxide. As with its work in the agriculture field the trust will seek to accelerate the transition towards a more energy-efficient economy and society by funding work along the following lines:

- *Raising public awareness of the need to move to a more energy-efficient way of living.*
- *Supporting the development of renewable energy and the introduction of energy efficient technologies.*
- *Supporting changes to subsidy schemes that encourage this transition.*
- *Promoting changes to transport policy that lead to significant reductions in energy use and greenhouse gas emissions.*
- *Questioning the role of fossil fuels as energy sources in the future.*
- *Encouraging business as well as Government to take on board the need for rapid reductions in greenhouse gas emissions and to implement the necessary strategies.*

Supporting local communities

The trust is keen to provide support to local community groups that are working to achieve sustainable development in their local area. The trust remains committed to looking for ways to help empower these groups and to pump-prime their activity, via the provision of start-up grants, for example. The trust feels it is important that members of the public are aware of their rights in relation to environmental issues, and the trust is continuing to support educational initiatives that broaden public

awareness and provide members of the public with the skills that they need in order effectively to represent local opinion.

The trust will look to fund:

- *Both project and core costs. These will include running costs such as staff salaries and overheads.*
- *Projects with a clear sense of objectives and the specific strategic steps required achieving them.*
- *Innovative projects where it is clear a grant will have a good chance of making a difference.*

In 2007/08 the trust had an income of £1.2 million including over £1 million from the Irish Evening, a fundraising dinner (£183,000 in 2006/07). Grants totalled £531,000 with £633,000 carried forward at year end.

Half of the net income from the Irish Evening was donated to Marie Curie Cancer Care. Other beneficiaries were: Fundacion Ecologica De Cuixmala (£45,000); UK Waste Incineration Network (£15,000); and Highland Foundation for Wildlife (£6,500).

Information available

Accounts were on file at the Charity Commission.

Exclusions

The annual report states that:

The trust is unlikely to make grants to the following kinds of projects:

- *Work that has already taken place*
- *Part of general appeals or circulars*
- *Outward-bound courses, expeditions and overseas travel*
- *Capital projects (i.e. buildings and refurbishment costs)*
- *Conservation of already well-supported species or of non-native species*

■ *Furniture, white goods, computer, paint, timber and scrap recycling projects.*

Applications

In writing to the correspondent.

The John Ellerman Foundation

CC no. 263207

Contact
Barbra Mazur, Grants Manager, The John Ellerman Foundation, Aria House, 23 Craven Street, London WC2N 5NS
Tel: 020 7930 8566 (general)
020 7451 1471 (direct);
Fax: 020 7839 3654;
email: barbra@ellerman.org.uk;
website: www.ellerman.org.uk

Trustees
Richard Edmunds; Dr John Hemming; Sue MacGregor; David Martin-Jenkins; Surgeon Vice-Admiral Anthony Revell; Lady Sarah Riddell; Beverley Stott; Dominic Caldecott.

Areas of work: National UK charities supporting health, disability, social welfare, arts and conservation and overseas projects.
Total grants: £4.4 million (2007/08)
Environmental grants: £471,000
Beneficial area: Mainly UK.

General

The following information is adapted from the foundation's website.

The foundation was established on the death of Sir John Ellerman in 1970 as a generalist grant-making trust. John Ellerman had inherited his substantial wealth from the business interests set up by his father, especially in shipping – the family business was called Ellerman Lines. Sir John and his wife Esther had throughout their lives developed a profound interest in philanthropy.

Today the foundation uses Sir John's legacy to make grants totalling around £4 million a year to about 150 different charities, mostly in the United Kingdom; The foundation makes grants to UK registered charities which work nationally, not locally. For historical reasons it continues to support a few charities operating in Southern and East Africa.

The foundation's mission is 'to be and be seen as a model grant-maker to the charitable sector.' It aims to achieve its mission by managing its funds in such a way that it can both maintain its grant-making capacity and operate in perpetuity, funding nationally-registered charities so as to encourage and support those which make a real difference to people, communities and the environment.

Guidelines

The foundation gives significant grants which it hopes will enable charities to make a difference to the cause they serve. The minimum grant is £10,000 and the foundation aims to develop relationships with funded charities. Requests for a contribution to large capital appeals are not encouraged. The foundation is especially open to receiving applications for core funding. Charities which receive core funding will be expected to account for expenditure and identify what it has enabled them to do.

The foundation will only consider applications from registered charities with a UK office. Under the Health and Disability, Social Welfare and Arts programmes, support will only be given to charities working throughout the UK or England. Applications from individuals, local/regional charities or those just operating in Wales, Scotland or Northern Ireland will not be considered.

The foundation inclines towards supporting charities which:

- offer direct practical benefits rather than work mainly on policy or campaigning
- involve and attract large numbers of volunteers
- co-operate closely with others working in similar or related fields
- do innovatory work
- are small or medium sized (annual income of less than £25 million).

The foundation receives many more applications than it can fund. On average, only 1 in 5 of all appeals within the guidelines is successful. The foundation states that it recognises that preparing good applications places heavy demands on the time and resources of charities, and diverts energies from their ultimate purpose; it therefore has a two-stage application process.

Stage 1

Applicants are advised to read the Guidelines for Applicants and Category Guidelines, available on the foundation's website. Please ensure that you are eligible to apply, and do not appear in the list of exclusions. Send your latest annual report and audited accounts to the correspondent, together with a letter – no more than one or two sides of A4. This should include the following information:

- about your charity – when registered, what you do, who your beneficiaries are and where you work
- about your need for funding – your turnover, reserves, main sources of income, why you need funds now, and, if you are requesting funds for a particular project, rough costings.

All letters are studied by the appeals manager and at least one trustee who recommend whether your proposal should be brought to the attention of the full board. If your application is

not to go forward, the foundation will tell you at this stage, rather than ask you to complete an application form. Please note that circulars are not responded to.

Stage 2

If a proposal is of sufficient interest to the board, you will be sent an application form. You should return this within one month. There are no specific deadlines for applications, as the board meets regularly throughout the year. (The application form is also available on request in electronic format; however applicants are requested to post a printed version when applying.)

Applicants may be asked for additional information and, as a matter of routine, staff and/or trustees try to visit as many organisations as possible. Your application will then be considered at the next available board meeting. These take place every two months and you will be informed shortly thereafter.

Before calling to discuss potential applications by telephone, ensure that you have read the Guidelines for Applicants and are eligible to apply.

Grantmaking

In 2007/08 the foundation had assets of £110 million and an income of £2.3 million. Grants were made totalling £4.4 million.

The foundation makes grants in the following five categories (shown here with details of funds allocated):

Category	No.	Amount
Health and disability	54	£1,200,000
Social welfare	47	£1,200,000
Arts	42	£1,000,000
Conservation	22	£471,000
Overseas	16	£446,000

Conservation – 22 grants totalling £471,000

Conservation of the environment and natural world is a category reflecting the fact that Sir John Ellerman was a distinguished zoologist and expert on small mammals.

At present the focus of funding is UK-based charities working throughout the UK and/or internationally in at least one of the following areas:

- protection of threatened animals, plants and habitats
- promotion of better understanding of and solutions to major environmental issues like climate change and biodiversity (applications for good research by an institute whose primary purpose is research even though its charitable status may come from association with a university are considered)
- development and extension of conservation facilities/sites
- promotion of sustainable ways of living, including renewable energy technologies.

The foundation is particularly interested in charities which can demonstrate all or most of the following:

- practical and sustainable benefits of significant scale
- collaborative work with others and the open sharing of ideas
- effective operation with or alongside local communities and cultures
- recruitment, training and employment of a broad base of volunteers.

Beneficiaries included: Ashden Awards (£65,000); BBC World Service Trust, Global Canopy Programme and Natural History Museum (£30,000 each); Fauna and Flora International and Zoological Society of London (£25,000 each); Buglife and Plantlife

International (£20,000 each); Rainforest Foundation (£16,000); British and Irish Hardwoods Trust and Tree Aid (£10,000 each); and Grasslands Trust (£8,000).

Information available

Accounts were available at the Charity Commission. The foundation has a helpful and informative website.

Exclusions

Grants are made only to registered charities, and are not made for the following purposes:

- medical research
- for or on behalf of individuals
- individual hospices
- local branches of national organisations
- 'Friends of' groups
- education or educational establishments
- religious causes
- conferences and seminars
- sports and leisure facilities
- purchase of vehicles
- the direct replacement of public funding
- deficit funding
- domestic animal welfare
- drug or alcohol abuse
- prisons and offenders.

Because of the volume of appeals received, the trustees do not consider further requests from charities which have had an application turned down until at least two years have elapsed since the letter of rejection. Similarly, funded charities can expect to wait two years from the last grant payment before a further application will be considered. Circulars will not receive a reply.

Applications

In writing to the correspondent following the foundation's guidelines available from its website and reproduced here in brief.

Esmée Fairbairn Foundation

CC no. 200051

Contact
Dawn Austwick, Chief Executive, Kings Place, 90 York Way, London N1 9AG
Tel: 020 7812 3700; Fax: 020 7812 3701; email: info@esmeefairbairn.org.uk; website: www.esmeefairbairn.org.uk

Trustees
Tom Chandos, Chair; Felicity Fairbairn; Beatrice Hollond; James Hughes-Hallett; Thomas Hughes-Hallett; Kate Lampard; Baroness Linklater; William Sieghart.

Areas of work: Social welfare, education, the environment, arts and heritage.

Total grants: £21.5 million (2008)

Environmental grants: £4.4 million

Beneficial area: UK.

General

Background

Ian Fairbairn established the foundation in 1961 (renamed Esmée Fairbairn Foundation in 2000). He was a leading city figure and his company, M&G, was the pioneer of the unit trust industry. Ian Fairbairn endowed the foundation with the greater part of his own holding in M&G, and in the early years the majority of grants were for economic and financial education.

His interest in financial education stemmed from his concern that most people had no access to stock exchange investment, and were therefore precluded from investing their savings in equities and sharing in the country's economic growth. It was precisely this concern that had led him into the embryonic unit trust business in the early 1930s.

The foundation was set up as a memorial to Ian Fairbairn's wife Esmée, who had played a prominent role in developing the Women's Royal Voluntary Service and the Citizens Advice Bureaux before being killed during an air raid towards the end of the Second World War. Her sons Paul and Oliver Stobart contributed generously to the original trust fund, as co-founders.

In 2008 the foundation had assets of £725 million (£938 million in 2007) and an income of £32 million, mostly from investments. Grants were made during the year totalling £21.5 million.

Summary

From January 2008 the foundation has adopted a new, more general funding approach. From the foundation's press release:

Esmée Fairbairn Foundation has launched a new funding approach.

The majority of our funding will now be channelled through the Main Fund which will be an open, less prescriptive way of working, through which we will listen to ideas. We expect to fund a wider range of work than before, although our core interests remain in the fields of culture, education, environment and social development.

As part of our new funding approach we are also running a number of smaller, more focused funding strands. These will be in areas where we think a more direct intervention may have a greater impact.

The following information is taken from the trust's website.

Guidelines

The Esmée Fairbairn Foundation aims to improve the quality of life throughout the

UK. We do this by funding the charitable activities of organisations that have the ideas and ability to achieve change for the better. We take pride in supporting work that might otherwise be considered difficult to fund.

Funding is channelled through two routes, which are explained fully on the trust's website.

1) Main Fund

Our Main Fund distributes about two-thirds of our funding.

What areas do we support?

Our primary interests are in the UK's cultural life, education, the natural environment and enabling people who are disadvantaged to participate more fully in society.

We welcome your suggestions about how we can help your organisation. We are particularly interested in hearing about how the work you are proposing:

- *addresses a significant gap in provision;*
- *develops or strengthens good practice;*
- *challenges convention or takes a risk in order to address a difficult issue;*
- *tests out new ideas or practices;*
- *takes an enterprising approach to achieving your aims;*
- *sets out to influence policy or change behaviour more widely.*

We can only fund work that is legally charitable. You do not have to be a registered charity to apply, but your constitution must allow you to carry out the work you propose.

What type of funding do we offer?

At Esmée Fairbairn we are happy to consider requests to fund core costs or project costs. These may include running costs such as staff salaries and overheads but generally not equipment costs.

New and emerging organisations may apply and we are willing to help finance the early stages of developing a convincing

new idea in order to test its feasibility and give it the best possible chance of success.

We occasionally fund research where we consider it is likely to have a practical impact.

If you ask for our assistance, you should tell us how much you need. The average Esmée Fairbairn grant is worth about £50,000, but we are happy to consider requests for less or more money.

2) Strands

The following four topics are identified for more detailed attention. These will develop over time, and allow the foundation to make a more focused contribution in an area of interest. Others may come on stream in due course. Check the foundation's website for up-to-date information.

Biodiversity *– Supporting practical conservation action and the science which underpins it. The strand will focus on species and habitats that are uncharismatic or hard to fund and aims to support the development of effective conservation approaches. Linking science and practical action, it will prioritise partnership applications involving research organisations, practical conservation charities and voluntary nature societies.*

Food *– The aim of the Food Strand is to promote an understanding of the role of food in enhancing quality of life. It will prioritise the enjoyment and experience of food rather than its production and we seek to enable as many people in the UK as possible to access, prepare and eat nutritious, sustainable food. We are interested in work that influences policy and practice across a range of food-related areas. We expect to support a mix of practical projects that have wide significance, and some research and policy based work.*

Museum & Heritage Collections *– This strand will focus on time-limited collections work including research,* documentation and conservation that is outside the scope of an organisation's core resources. We will prioritise proposals that are at an early stage of development where it may be difficult to guarantee tangible outcomes. We will also prioritise proposals that have the potential to share knowledge with other organisations through partnership working or dissemination.

New approaches to learning – *Devising, testing and disseminating new approaches to teaching and learning that address current and future challenges in state schools and pre-schools.*

Grants in 2008
The Main Fund

Category	Value	No.
Arts, culture and heritage	£4.36 million	70
Environment	£3.82 million	45
Citizenship or community development	£3.02 million	61
Education	£1.82 million	34
Human rights and conflict resolution	£1.62 million	21
Prevention or relief of poverty	£1.02 million	21
Other charitable purposes	£1.57 million	15
Total	**£17.23 million**	**267**

The average grant size from the Main Fund was £64,500; there were a total of 4,824 applications made, which means that just over 5.5% of applicants were successful. The following is a sample of beneficiaries from the Main Fund with an environmental objective or an interest in the preservation of heritage and the purposes for which grants were given:

The Soil Association (£398,000), towards developing membership over three years to increase unrestricted core income; Green Alliance Trust (£225,000), towards core policy work over three years to advance the economics and politics of the environment; British Trust for

Ornithology (£180,000), towards the salary and travel costs of the co-ordinator over five years for the 'Bird Atlas 2007–11'. An estimated 50,000 volunteers will assess changes in distribution and numbers of the UK's birds; London Wildlife Trust (£171,000), towards the salary of the three core biodiversity conservation posts over three years; Third Generation Environmentalism Ltd (£142,000), towards the salary of the global climate change director over three years; Chemicals, Health, and Environmental Monitoring Trust (£114,000), towards the salary of the director and two projects to reduce the impact of chemicals on wildlife over three years; North Highland Forest Trust (£88,000), towards the salaries of the biodiversity forester and part time support staff over three years, promoting sustainable management of biodiversity-rich woodland; Cheshire Wildlife Trust (£74,000), towards the salary of a new head of conservation over two years to stabilise and rebuild the work of this Wildlife Trust; Cornwall Trust for Nature Conservation (£58,500), towards the salary of the project officer over three years to improve protection of the inshore cetacean populations and their wider ecosystems; CleanupUK (£50,000), towards the salary of the chief executive over two years to support volunteer litter collecting groups; Marine Conservation Society (£50,000), towards the launch and first year of the major MSC litter champions campaign to promote local practical action to tackle the increasing levels of marine litter; People's Trust for Endangered Species (£50,000), towards the salary of an orchard mapping officer and costs of data purchase over two years to map England's traditional orchards and raise public awareness of their importance as a habitat for rare species and as a heritage landscape feature; Sandbag Climate Campaign (£31,000), towards salary costs to support the launch of a new public campaign on climate change and emissions trading; People & Planet (£21,000), towards the salary and overheads of a festival stewarding social business to guarantee funds for their environment and global poverty campaigns; The Oil Depletion Analysis Centre (£20,000), towards costs over two years of establishing a network to spread awareness among local authorities of peak oil and to stimulate policies to protect communities against its worst impacts; Bath Preservation Trust Ltd (£12,000), towards fees for the preparation of the business plan; and Rushmere Commoners (£12,000), to carry out heathland restoration within the fringe of Ipswich over three years, involving local community groups and schools in habitat and species recording and investigating the site's cultural history.

Strands

Category	Value	No.
New Approaches to Learning	£1,120,000	19
Food	£642,000	9
Biodiversity	£615,000	7
Museum & Heritage Collections	£583,000	13
Total	**£2,960,000**	**48**

The following are the seven beneficiaries from the Biodiversity Strand and the purposes for which grants were given:

Marine Biological Association (£195,000), towards research costs over three years to improve the design of artificial urban coastal habitats to maximise biodiversity; University of Sussex (£103,000), towards the cost of research validation for reptile survey work in the National Amphibian and Reptile Recording Scheme (NARRS) over two years; Freshwater Biological Association (£90,000), towards the cost over two years of the re-publication of the classic freshwater invertebrate guide and bespoke freshwater fauna online data recording module; University of

Nottingham (£85,000), towards the salary and project costs over two years, to evaluate the impact of anti-parasitic drugs on invertebrates; Roehampton University (£76,000), towards the cost of a survey of groundwater organisms in Devon and Dorset and subsequent design of sampling protocols for other areas; NERC Sea Mammal Research Unit (£49,000), towards the salary of a research assistant and modifications to a photo identification programme for grey seals; and North of England Zoological Society (£17,000), towards the cost of training for new regional volunteer wildlife recorders.

Beneficiaries of interest from the other strands include: Sustain (£204,000), towards the costs of a campaign over three years to introduce legislation requiring public bodies to purchase food supplies from sustainable sources; The Dartington Hall Trust (£50,000), towards the salaries of a conservation co-ordinator and conservation officer, plus a contribution towards specialist materials; and Almond Valley Heritage Trust (£12,000), towards the salary of a collection development officer to work on the shale oil collection.

Information available

Detailed guidelines for applicants and excellent annual report and accounts, all available on the foundation's clear and helpful website.

Exclusions

The following is taken from the foundation's website.

The foundation does not support applications for:

- *individuals or causes that will benefit only one person, including student grants or bursaries*
- *support for a general appeal or circular*

- *work that does not have a direct benefit in the UK, including expeditions and overseas travel*
- *the promotion of religion*
- *capital costs – meaning construction or refurbishment costs or items of equipment (other than those essential to a project we are supporting)*
- *work that is routine or well-proven elsewhere or with a low impact*
- *healthcare or related work such as medical research, complementary medicine, counselling and therapy, education and treatment for substance misuse*
- *work that is primarily the responsibility of central or local government, health trusts or health authorities, or which benefits from their funding. This includes residential and day care, housing and homelessness, individual schools, nurseries and colleges, supplementary schools and vocational training*
- *projects that primarily benefit the independent education sector*
- *environmental projects related to animal welfare, zoos, captive breeding and animal rescue centres*
- *individual energy efficiency or waste reduction schemes*
- *retrospective funding, meaning support for work that has already taken place.*

Applications

Applying for a grant from the Main Fund:

Follow these three steps:

1) Read through the guidance notes, paying careful attention to the sort of work the foundation supports – and what it does not.

2) If you think your organisation's activities could attract Esmée Fairbairn funding, go through the self-assessment checklist for eligibility [available from the foundation's website].

3) If you can answer 'yes' to each of the self-assessment checklist questions, submit a first stage application [available from the foundation's website].

What happens next

The foundation will then get back to you, aiming to acknowledge your first stage application within a week of receiving it. Within a month the foundation will either suggest taking it to the second stage or decline to support it.

If you are invited to proceed to the second stage, the foundation will ask you for some additional information that will depend on what you have already told them and the size and complexity of the work you would like them to support.

The following section is taken from the foundation's *2008 Guidance for Applicants* paper.

How will we evaluate your application?

We receive many more applications than we can support. Therefore, we have to be selective.

As part of our selection process, we look to support work that has the best chance of achieving its objectives or will leave behind knowledge and experience that could benefit others.

Every application for support is different and we examine each according to the likelihood of it making a difference in the applicant organisation's area of work. Depending on the nature of your application, these are some of the criteria we will apply:

- *How strong are your ideas and how well equipped are your people to carry them out?*
- *How well do you understand the issues you are addressing and what is your track record?*
- *Do you have a clear plan or idea and the capacity to deliver it?*

- *What difference would help from us make to your work?*
- *Does your work have the potential to be applied more widely or can it influence the work of others?*
- *Would receiving our support make you more likely to attract help and engagement from others?*
- *How would your organisation be stronger by the end of the grant and how developed are your long-term plans for sustainability?*

There is a different application process for the funding strands. To learn more about the strands and how to apply, visit the foundation's website.

Fisherbeck Charitable Trust

CC no. 1107287

Contact
The Trustees, Home Farm House, 63 Ferringham Lane, Ferring, Worthing, West Sussex BN12 5LL
Tel: 01903 241027;
email: ian@roffeyhomes.com

Trustees
Ian R Cheal; Mrs Jane Cheal; Matthew Cheal.

Areas of work: Christian, homelessness, welfare, education and heritage.

Total grants: £456,000 (2007/08)

Environmental grants: £50,000

Beneficial area: Worldwide.

General
This trust was registered with the Charity Commission in December 2004, and it is the vehicle for the charitable activities of the Cheal family, owners of Roffey Homes developers. The charity's objects are to encourage charitable giving from the extended Cheal family and to apply these funds to the making of grants for the following charitable objects (taken from their annual report):

- *the advancement of the Christian religion*
- *support the provision of accommodation for the homeless and meeting their ongoing needs*
- *the relief of poverty*
- *the advancement of education*
- *to encourage conservation of the environment and the preservation of our heritage*
- *such other charitable objects in such manner as the trustees shall from time to time decide.*

In 2007/08 the trust had assets of £176,400 and an income of £484,000, mostly from donations and gifts. Grants were made totalling £456,000, most of which went to organisations.

Environmental organisations receiving grants included: the National Trust; and Sustrans (£6,000).

Information available
Accounts were on file at the Charity Commission.

Exclusions
Grants are only made to individuals known to the trust or in exceptional circumstances.

Applications
Grants are given in accordance with the wishes of the Cheal family.

The Freshfield Foundation

CC no. 1003316

Contact
Paul Kurthausen, Trustee, 2nd Floor, MacFarlane and Co., Cunard Building, Water Street, Liverpool L3 1DS
Tel: 0151 236 6161; Fax: 0151 236 1095;
email: paulk@macca.co.uk

Trustees
Paul Kurthausen; Patrick A Moores; Mrs Elizabeth J Potter.

Areas of work: Environment and healthcare.

Total grants: £438,000 (2007/08)

Environmental grants: £398,000

Beneficial area: UK.

General

The foundation was established in 1991, and aims to support organisations involved in sustainable development, and increasingly, climate change mitigation. In previous years the foundation had a preference for organisations in Merseyside – it would appear that this is no longer the case as the foundation moves to tackle broader issues.

In 2007/08 the foundation had assets of £6.2 million and an income of £205,000. Grants were made during the year totalling £438,000.

During the year grants were made to 11 organisations involved in sustainable development. They were: Friends of the Earth (£80,000); Sustrans (£70,000); New Economics Foundation (£55,000); Forestry Stewardship Council (£50,000); Centre for Tomorrow's Company (£35,000); Transport 2000 Trust and Cambridge University (£30,000 each); Soil Association (£20,000); Cree Valley Community Woodland Trust (£15,000); Global Canopy Foundation (£10,000); and the Ecology Trust (£3,000).

A grant of £40,000 was also made to the Osteopathic Centre for Children under 'healthcare'.

Towards the end of 2008 the foundation made grants of £500,000 and £200,000 to New Economics Foundation and Friends of the Earth respectively which reflect its increasing ambitions to mitigate climate change.

Information available

Accounts were on file at the Charity Commission.

Applications

In writing to the correspondent, however the trust states that 'the process of grant making starts with the trustees analysing an area of interest, consistent with the charity's aims and objectives, and then proactively looking for charities that they think can make the greatest contribution'. With this in mind, a letter of introduction to your organisation's work may be more appropriate than a formal application for funding.

J Paul Getty Jnr Charitable Trust

CC no. 292360

Contact
Elizabeth Rantzen, Director,
1 Park Square West, London NW1 4LJ
Tel: 020 7486 1859;
website: www.jpgettytrust.org.uk

Trustees
Christopher Gibbs, Chair; Lady Getty; Vanni Treves; Christopher Purvis.

Areas of work: Social welfare, arts, conservation and the environment.

Total grants: £2.5 million (2007)

Environmental grants: £288,500

Beneficial area: UK.

General

Summary

The trust funds projects dealing with poverty and misery in the UK, and unpopular causes in particular.

Grants, usually for running or project costs, are often for three-year periods and can be for up to a usual maximum of about £30,000. There are also a large number of small grants of £2,000 or less.

Few projects are supported in London. The grants for heritage and conservation are few and small.

The trust has continued to increase its level of grantmaking, taking the view that it should start assuming a long-term level of total return on its investments that will ignore short-term fluctuations, especially in gains or losses of capital. Nevertheless the trust remains heavily oversubscribed, with a success rate of less than 10%, no doubt the result of its own accessibility to those working in fields few others are interested in funding.

Background

The trust's 'Guidelines for applicants' says:

The J Paul Getty Jr Charitable Trust started distributing funds in 1986. Since then nearly £35 million has been given to over 3,000 worthwhile causes all over the UK.

The trust was funded entirely by Sir Paul Getty KBE, who died in April 2003 in London, where he had lived since the 1980s. He took a close interest in the trust, but also continued to make major personal gifts to the arts and other causes in England (£50 million to the National Gallery, £3 million to Lord's Cricket Ground, £17 million to the British Film Institute, £1 million towards the Canova Three Graces, and £5 million towards the restoration of St. Paul's Cathedral). These were personal gifts and had no connection with this trust.

Nor has this trust any connection with the Getty Trust in the USA, to which J. Paul Getty Senior left his money, and which finances the J. Paul Getty Museum in California. These two trusts, one very large and one small by comparison, should not be confused by people who apply to us!

In 2007 the trust had assets of £57.2 million and an income of over £2 million. Grants were made totalling £2.5 million, with 137 new awards being made.

Guidelines for applicants

We set out below guidelines for the majority of our grants, which should be followed by those making unsolicited applications. From time to time the trustees invite selected charities to make applications which may not entirely fall within these guidelines. They may also invite selected charities to make applications for larger grants.

There are four main beneficial areas:

- *social welfare*
- *arts*
- *conservation*
- *environment.*

Potential applicants should note that most funding is given under the social welfare heading.

Conservation

Conservation in the broadest sense, with an emphasis on ensuring that fine buildings, landscapes and collections remain or become available to the general public or scholars. Training in conservation skills. Not general building repair work.

Environment

Mainly gardens, historic landscape and wilderness.

Grantmaking in 2007

The level of narrative reporting on the trust's activities in 2007 has reduced significantly on previous years, however the following breakdown of grants by category is provided:

Category	Amount	%
Children and young people	£467,000	19%
Offenders	£413,000	16%
Drugs and alcohol	£387,000	15%
Heritage and conservation	£235,000	11%
Homelessness	£218,000	9%
Mental health	£213,000	8%
Ethnic minorities	£145,000	6%
Women	£134,000	5%
Families	£103,500	4%
Communities	£91,000	4%

Environment and landscape	£53,500	2%
Other social welfare	£47,000	2%
Other	£13,500	1%
Arts (not related to social welfare)	£2,000	0.2%

Beneficiaries during the year, which were uncategorised, included: Tanyard Youth Project – Pembroke (£90,000); Broadreach House – Plymouth (£69,000); Kaleidoscope – Newport (£60,000); Watts Gallery – Guildford (£50,000); Home-Start Oxford (£45,000); Young Enterprise North East – Gateshead (£33,000); Edinburgh Cyrenians (£30,000); Handel House Trust Ltd – London (£25,000); Lancaster & District YMCA (£20,600); Lizard Outreach Trust – Cornwall (£18,000); Conservation Volunteers Northern Ireland (£10,000); St James Community & Support Centre – Birmingham (£6,000); Pestalozzi International Village Trust (£2,000); and National Osteoporosis Society – London (£1,000).

Information available

Accounts were available from the Charity Commission, which include less detail on grantmaking activities than previous years. The trust also has a website.

Exclusions

Grants are not given for:

- older people
- children
- education
- research
- animals
- music or drama (except therapeutically)
- conferences or seminars
- medical care (including hospices) or health
- medical equipment
- churches or cathedrals
- holidays or expeditions
- sports or leisure facilities (including cricket pitches)
- residential or large building projects
- replacement of Lottery or statutory funds
- national appeals
- grant-making trusts or community foundations
- individuals.

Headquarters of national organisations and umbrella organisations are unlikely to be considered.

Past recipients are not encouraged to reapply.

No applications for projects outside the UK are considered.

The project must be a registered charity or be under the auspices of one.

Priority is likely to be given to projects in the less prosperous parts of the country, particularly outside London and the south east, and to those which cover more than one beneficial area.

Please remember this trust has no connection with the Getty Foundation in the USA.

Applications

Applications can be made to the Director at any time. There are no closing dates, and all letters of appeal should receive an initial response within 6 weeks. Please write a letter of no more than two sides long detailing:

- the purpose and nature of the project
- intended beneficiaries
- budget
- existing sources of finance
- other funding applications, including those to statutory sources and the Lottery
- whether you have previously applied to us, successfully or otherwise.

It is recommended that you do not send videos, DVDs, CDs, tapes or bulky reports. They are unlikely to be reviewed and cannot be returned.

Annual accounts will be requested if your application is going to be taken further.

If a project is short-listed for taking forward for a grant over £2,000, it may be visited by the Director before an application is considered by the trustees.

The trustees usually meet quarterly. There is a short-listing process, and not all applications are put before the trustees. Three months is the least it usually takes to award a grant.

GrantScape

CC no. 1102249

Contact
Matthew Young, Senior Grant Manager, Office E, Whitsundoles, Broughton Road, Salford, Milton Keynes MK17 8BU
Tel: 01908 545780; Fax: 01908 545799; email: helpdesk@grantscape.org.uk; website: www.grantscape.org.uk

Trustees
Dave Bramley; Doug De Freitas; Jacqueline Rae; Alan Loynes; Alastair Singleton; Stephen Henry.

Areas of work: Environmental and community-based projects.

Total grants: £2.1 million (2007/08)

Environmental grants: £2.1 million

Beneficial area: UK.

General
GrantScape is a company limited by guarantee and is enrolled with ENTRUST as a Distributive Environmental Body. Its vision is 'to improve the environment and communities by the channelling and

management of charitable funding towards deserving and quality projects.'

Its generic grantmaking policy is as follows:

■ GrantScape will only make grants in line with its charitable objectives

■ Grants will be made on a justifiable and fair basis to projects which provide best value

■ Grants will be made to projects that improve the life of communities and the environment

■ GrantScape will make available specific criteria for each of the grant programmes that it manages

■ All grants are subject to meeting the generic grant-making criteria as well as the specific grant programme criteria.

In 2007/08 it had assets of £4.7 million and an income of £1.3 million. Grants were made across the following programmes, some of which have now closed, totalling £2.1 million:

Programme	Applications closed	Value (approx)
Caird Bardon Community Programme	Ongoing	£300,000 pa
CWM Community and Environmental Fund	Ongoing	£200,000 pa
Biodiversity Challenge Fund	April 07	£2,000,000
Community Heritage Fund (Windmill and Watermill Challenge)	September 07	£600,000
Milton Keynes Grant Programme	June 07	£100,000

New grant programmes are introduced from time to time – check the charity's website for up-to-date information.

Information available

Information was available on the charity's website.

Exclusions

Specific exclusions apply to each programme – see General for details.

Applications

Applications are made electronically via the charity's website.

The Headley Trust

CC no. 266620

Contact

Alan Bookbinder, Director,
Allington House, 1st Floor,
150 Victoria Street, London SW1E 5AE
Tel: 020 7410 0330; Fax: 020 7410 0332;
email: info@sfct.org.uk;
website: www.sfct.org.uk/headley.html

Trustees

Sir Timothy Sainsbury; Lady Susan Sainsbury; Timothy James Sainsbury; J R Benson; Judith Portrait.

Areas of work: Arts, heritage, welfare and development.

Total grants: £2.2 million (2007)

Environmental grants: £876,000

Beneficial area: Unrestricted.

General

Summary

This is one of the Sainsbury Family Charitable Trusts which share a joint administration. Like the others, it is primarily proactive, aiming to choose its own grantees, and its annual reports state that 'proposals are generally invited by the trustees or initiated at their request'.

The trust has a particular interest in arts, heritage and conservation projects in the UK of outstanding creative or architectural importance and has made large grants to museums, galleries, libraries and theatres. There are ongoing programmes for the repair of cathedrals and medieval churches.

General

The settlor of this trust is Sir Timothy Sainsbury. His co-trustees include his wife, eldest son and legal adviser. The trust's staff includes the director of the Sainsbury family's charitable trusts, Alan Bookbinder.

In 2007 the trust had assets totalling £79 million and an income of just over £2.6 million. Grants were made during the year totalling £2.2 million.

Grants approved in 2007 were categorised with the number of grants and their value as follows:

Category	Grants approved	Amount	Average grant
Arts and heritage (UK)	27	£568,000	£21,000
– Cathedrals Programme	5	£149,000	£30,000
– Parish Churches Programme	60	£137,000	£2,300
– Museums' Treasure Acquisition Scheme	15	£21,000	£1,400
Arts and heritage (overseas)	8	£209,000	£26,000
Developing countries	13	£264,000	£20,000
Education	10	£182,000	£18,000
Health and social welfare	36	£630,000	£18,000
– Aids for Disabled	48	£26,000	£540
Total	222	£2,187,000	£9,900

Grantmaking in 2007

The following grant examples are prefaced by the trust's description of its interests in that area taken from its annual report. The grant totals are the amounts paid during the year, and include grants approved in previous years.

Arts and Heritage – UK – £876,000

The trustees respond to a wide and eclectic variety of building conservation or heritage projects in the UK. They also support regional museums with revenue costs or the purchase of unusual or exceptional artefacts, aim to promote educational access to museums and galleries for both the disabled and disadvantaged, and wish to encourage arts outreach and musical opportunities for young people. They continue to be interested in notable archaeological projects in the UK. They wish to encourage both the revival of rural crafts and the continuing richness of the English Crafts movement. The Trustees have made a major commitment to the Victoria & Albert Museum's new Ceramics Gallery which will be one of the most important in the world.

Grants included those to: Hove Museum (£70,000); Common Ground (£60,000); Wildscreen Trust and Durham County Council (£40,000 each); National Trust for Scotland (£30,000); Bowes Museum Trust (£25,000); Christ Church – Spitalfields (£20,000); and University of Manchester (£10,000).

From the Cathedrals Programme

The Trustees also allocate a substantial sum each year for repair work to the fabric of cathedrals and large ecclesiastical buildings of exceptional architectural merit (pre-18th century). Modern amenities, organ repair/restoration and choral scholarships are not normally eligible.

Five grants were made to: Boston Stump Restoration Appeal (£50,000); Ely Cathedral Trust (£39,000); Southwell Minster (£30,000); and Howden Minster and Selby Abbey Appeal (£15,000 each).

From the Museums' Treasure Acquisition Scheme

This scheme was designed to help local and regional museums purchase archaeological artefacts. It runs alongside, and in collaboration with, the Museums, Libraries and Archives Council/Victoria and Albert Museum Purchase Grant Fund. 15 grants of less than £5,000 were awarded during the year, totalling £21,000.

Beneficiaries included: Barbican House Museum – Lewes, Saffron Walden Museum, Northampton Museum & Art Gallery, Charnwood Museum – Loughborough, Epping Forest District Museum – Waltham Abbey, Derby Museums and Art Gallery and Wiltshire Heritage Museum – Devizes.

Please note: this scheme has its own application form, see Applications.

From the Parish Churches Programme

Funding for fabric repair and restoration is considered for medieval parish churches (or pre-16th century churches of exceptional architectural merit) in rural, sparsely populated, less prosperous villages, through a process of review, diocese by diocese. Urban churches are not eligible, and funding is available for fabric only (including windows), not refurbishment nor construction of church halls nor other modern amenities.

Grants of £5,000 or less were made to 60 churches throughout the diocese of Winchester, Guildford, Hereford, Chester, St David's, Ely, and St Edmundsbury and Ipswich.

Information available

Excellent annual report and accounts were available from the Charity Commission.

Exclusions

Grants are not normally made to individuals.

Applications

The Museums' Treasure Acquisition Scheme has its own application form, available from the Headley Museums Archaeological Acquisition Fund website, www.headley-archaeology.org.uk. For information on the small Aids for Disabled Fund, ring the trust on 020 7410 0330.

Otherwise, see the guidance for applicants in the entry for the Sainsbury Family Charitable Trusts. A single application will be considered for support by all the trusts in the group. However, for this as for many of the trusts, 'proposals are generally invited by the trustees or initiated at their request. Unsolicited applications are discouraged and are unlikely to be successful, even if they fall within an area in which the trustees are interested'.

Lancashire Environmental Fund

CC no. 1074983

Contact
Andy Rowett, Administration Officer,
The Barn, Berkeley Drive,
Bamber Bridge, Preston PR5 6BY
Tel: 01772 317 247; Fax: 01772 628 849;
email: andyrowett@lancsenvfund.org.uk;
website: www.lancsenvfund.org.uk

Trustees
Cllr A C P Martin, Chair; P Greijenberg;
D Tattersall; P Taylor.

Areas of work: Environment and community.
Total grants: £613,000 (2007)
Environmental grants: £613,000
Beneficial area: Lancashire.

General

This fund was established in June 1998 from a partnership of four organisations: SITA (Lancashire) Ltd, Lancashire County Council, the Wildlife Trust for Lancashire, Manchester and North Merseyside and Community Futures. The fund enables community groups and organisations throughout the country to take advantage of the funding opportunities offered by landfill tax credits. It achieves this by supporting organisations and projects based within Lancashire, or nationwide research or development with a relevance to Lancashire, which are managed by an enrolled Environmental Body, as recognised by Entrust.

The fund operates three funding schemes:

Community Chest

The Community Chest is available as a small grant for a small scheme usually to support groups who are seeking one-off funding for a project. Applications are accepted for grants between £3,000 and £15,000. The overall cost of the project should not exceed £30,000. The fund may act as Environmental Body for the project and administer the paperwork required by the regulator.

Strategic Fund

The Strategic Fund is available to organisations that are registered as Environmental Bodies with Entrust, the scheme regulator. Applications are accepted for grants up to £30,000 but the overall cost should not exceed £250,000.

Dirtworks

The Dirtworks programme is funding to encourage young people to volunteer and get involved with practical environmental schemes. Applications are invited from organisations with the capacity to supervise and deliver a high quality project with young people. Schemes should cost up to £25,000 with the fund contributing £20,000. The capital works element of the project should be at least 40% of the cost.

Note: The fund does not normally consider applications for 100% funding therefore, support from other grant sources is welcome.

In 2007 the fund had assets of £3.4 million and an income of £813,000.

Grants (paid and payable) totalled £613,000.

At the April 2009 meeting of the board grants totalling £224,000 were approved in support of 11 projects. The beneficiaries were: Parbold Scout Group and Holton Youth and Community Centre (£30,000 each); Lancashire Wildlife Trust (£28,000); Hawthorne Park Trust, West View Community Association and Pilling Memorial Hall (£25,000 each); Heritage Trust for the North West (£19,000); Bolton le Sands Village Hall and Saheli Community Garden (£15,000 each); Freckleton Parish Council (£8,500); and Elswick and District Village Hall (£3,000).

Information available

Accounts were available from the Charity Commission

Exclusions

Funding is not given for the following:

- core costs of an organisation
- retrospective funding
- projects in school grounds
- allotment or food growing projects
- car parks and public conveniences
- recycling projects
- projects within the unitary authority districts of Blackpool and Blackburn.

All projects must satisfy at least one objective of the Landfill Communities Fund. For more information about the scheme contact Entrust, the regulatory body, by visiting its website at www.entrust.org.uk or telephoning 0161 972 0074.

Applications

Guidance notes and application forms for each funding strand are available from the correspondent or can be downloaded from the fund's website. Completed forms should contain all possible relevant material including maps, photographs, plans, and so on.

The board meets quarterly in January, April, July and October.

Staff are willing to have informal discussions before an application is made. Potential applicants are strongly advised to visit the website before contacting the trust.

The Manifold Charitable Trust

CC no. 229501

Contact

Mrs Helen Niven, Studio Cottage, Windsor Great Park, Windsor SL4 2HP
Tel: 01984 497787;
email: helen.niven@cumberland lodge.ac.uk

Trustees
Manifold Trustee Company Ltd.

Areas of work: Education, historic buildings, environmental conservation and general.

Total grants: £1.6 million (2007)

Environmental grants: £368,000

Beneficial area: UK.

General

This trust was established in 1962 for general charitable purposes. It had previously focused much attention on the preservation of churches, however following the death in 2007 of its founder, Sir John Smith, the trust is now allocating most of its grants for educational purposes. The trust still makes grants to the Historic Churches Preservation Trust for onward distribution to churches; however it would seem that the amount has been reduced on previous years.

As noted in the past, the trust continues to make grants in excess of its income, preferring to 'meet the present needs of other charities rather than reserve money for the future'.

In 2007 the trust had assets of £11.7 million and an income of £707,000. During the year there were 124 grants made totalling over £1.6 million, which included an exceptional donation of £1 million to New College Oxford. Grants for heritage and conservation, including grants to the Historic Churches Preservation Trust, totalled around £368,000.

Grants were apportioned roughly as follows:

Category	%
Education, research and the arts	70%
Repairs to churches and their contents	23%
Other causes	7%

Almost half of these grants made were of £1,000 or less, and only 11% of the charities that were funded received over £10,000.

Beneficiaries included: Historic Churches Preservation Trust (£140,000 in total); Eton College (£78,000); Thames Hospice Care (£50,000); Imperial College (£15,000); Berkeley Castle Charitable Trust and Maidenhead Heritage Trust (£10,000 each); Berkshire Medical Heritage Centre (£7,500); Gislingham PCC (£6,000); Household Cavalry Museum Trust (£5,000); Brompton Ralph PCC (£4,500); Morrab Library (£2,500); and Richmond Building Preservation Society, Askham PCC and Westray Heritage Trust (£1,000 each).

Information available

Accounts were available at the Charity Commission.

Exclusions

Applications are not considered for improvements to churches as this is covered by a block grant to the Historic Churches Preservation Trust. The trust regrets that it does not give grants to individuals for any purpose.

Applications

The trust has no full-time staff, therefore general enquiries and applications for grants should be made in writing only, by post or by fax and not by telephone. The trust does not issue application forms. Applications should be made to the correspondent in writing and should:

- state how much money it is hoped to raise
- if the appeal is for a specific project state also (a) how much it will cost (b) how much of this cost will come from the applicant charity's existing funds (c) how much has already been received or promised from other sources and (d) how much is therefore still being sought
- list sources of funds to which application has been or is intended to be made (for example local authorities, or quasi-governmental sources, such as the National Lottery)
- if the project involves conservation of a building, send a photograph of it and a note (or pamphlet) about its history
- send a copy of the charity's latest income and expenditure account and balance sheet.

Applications are considered twice a month, and a reply is sent to most applicants (whether successful or not) who have written a letter rather than sent a circular.

The Ofenheim Charitable Trust

CC no. 286525

Contact
Geoffrey Wright, Correspondent,
Baker Tilly, 1st Floor, Sentinel House,
46 Clarendon Road, Watford,
Hertfordshire WD17 1JJ
Tel: 01923 816400;
email: geoff.wright@bakertilly.co.uk

Trustees
Roger Jackson Clark; Rory McLeod;
Alexander Clark; Fiona Byrd.

Areas of work: General, mainly charities
supporting health, welfare, arts and the
environment.

Total grants: £354,000 (2007/08)

Environmental grants: £40,000

Beneficial area: Worldwide, in practice
UK with some preference for East Sussex.

General

Established in 1983 by Dr Angela
Ofenheim, it is the policy of the trust to
'provide regular support for a number of
charities in East Sussex because of the
founder's association with that area'.
High-profile organisations in the fields of
health, welfare, arts and the environment
are supported with many of the same
organisations benefiting each year.

In 2007/08 the trust had assets of over
£11 million and an income of £391,000.
Grants were made to 60 organisations
totalling £354,000.

Beneficiaries included: World Wildlife
Fund UK (£10,000); the National Trust
(£5,500); Game Conservancy Trust
(£3,500); and the Barn Owl Trust
(£2,000).

Information available

Accounts were on file at the Charity
Commission.

Exclusions
No grants to individuals.

Applications
In writing to the correspondent. The
majority of grants are to charities
supported over a number of years and
the trust has previously stated that
unsolicited applications will not be
acknowledged. Currently the trust states
that the trustees also respond to one-off
appeals from 'bodies where they have
some knowledge'. Trustees meet in
March and applications need to be
received by February.

The Pilgrim Trust

CC no. 206602

Contact
Miss Georgina Nayler, Director,
Clutha House, 10 Storeys Gate, London
SW1P 3AY
Tel: 020 7222 4723; Fax: 020 7976 0461;
email: georgina.nayler@thepilgrim
trust.org.uk;
website: www.thepilgrimtrust.org.uk

Trustees
Lady Jay of Ewelme, Chair; Lord David
Cobbold; Dame Ruth Runciman; Tim
Knox; Paul Richards; Mark Jones; Sir
Alan Moses; John Podmore; James
Fergusson; David Verey; Lord Crisp.

Areas of work: Social welfare and the
preservation of buildings and heritage.

Total grants: £1.9 million (2008)

Environmental grants: £1.3 million

Beneficial area: UK, but not the Channel
Islands or the Isle of Man.

General

The trust's website states that:

*The Pilgrim Trust was founded in 1930 by
the wealthy American philanthropist
Edward Stephen Harkness. Inspired by his
admiration and affection for Great*

Britain, Harkness endowed the trust with just over £2 million. Harkness did not want the charity named after him, so the decision was taken to name the charity The Pilgrim Trust to signify its link with the land of the Pilgrim Fathers. It was Harkness's wish that his gift be given in grants for some of Britain's 'more urgent needs' and to 'promote her future well-being'. The first trustees decided that the trust should assist with social welfare projects, preservation (of buildings and countryside) and the promotion of art and learning. This has remained the focus of The Pilgrim Trust and the current Board of Trustees follows Harkness's guidelines by giving grants to projects in the fields of Preservation and Scholarship and of Social Welfare. Trustees review these objectives every three years.

In 2008 the trust had assets of almost £47.5 million and an income of £1.6 million. Grants were made across both of the trust's programme areas totalling almost £1.9 million, broken down as follows:

Category	Amount
Preservation and scholarship	£1,200,000
Social welfare	£673,000

The trust provides an excellent overview of its current areas of interest and its activities during 2008 in its latest annual report, selected information from which is reproduced below.

Programmes
Preservation and scholarship

- *Preservation of historic buildings and architectural features, especially projects giving a new use to buildings of outstanding architectural or historic importance; the conservation of monuments or structures important in their surroundings, including buildings designed for public performance. Trustees will consider supporting core costs and the cost of initial exploratory*

works for organisations seeking to rescue important buildings.

- *Conservation of works of art, books, manuscripts, photographs and documents, and museum objects, where normal facilities for such work are not available, including records associated with archaeology, historic buildings and the landscape.*

- *The promotion of knowledge through academic research and its dissemination, for which public funds are not available, including cataloguing within museums, galleries, libraries and archives, and institutions where historic, scientific or archaeological records are preserved. Applications for the costs of preparing such work for publication will be considered, but not the publication itself.*

The Trustees' objectives for 2008 were:

- *To commit £1.37 million in grants for spending in 2008 and up to £600,000 for spending in 2009 and 2010.*

- *To allocate 60% of their funding to Preservation and Scholarship and 40% to Social Welfare.*

- *To support projects in all parts of the United Kingdom.*

- *To continue developing long term relationships with organisations and to support these organisations with larger grants over several years.*

- *To establish a new website and on-line application procedure.*

Grantmaking

Trustees committed £1.4 million for spending in 2008 plus £494,000 for spending in 2009 and £97,000 for 2010. They awarded 89 grants with the main grants averaging just over £23,500.

The following table shows how the Pilgrim Trustees committed the Trust's funds during 2008. Although Trustees aim to spend 60% of their grant giving on preservation and scholarship and 40% on social welfare, their commitments must reflect the quality of the applications they receive. They are not bound by these percentages; they are an aim and trustees are free to vary the allocations.

Review of the year

Partnerships

As reported last year, the Pilgrim Trust is keen to work with others so that it can both draw on their expertise and maximise the impact of its grants. The trustees are delighted by the continued collaboration with The National Archives on the National Cataloguing Scheme and the Association of Independent Museums with its Conservation Grants Scheme. The first National Cataloguing Scheme was launched in the spring covering the whole of the UK. Ten grants totalling £331,000 were awarded and these grants will enable collections that have hitherto been hidden, to become accessible to researchers, students and the general public. The Pilgrim Trust continues to be grateful to The National Archives and the funding partners for the Cataloguing Scheme.

Preservation and scholarship

Preservation of secular buildings

During the year the trust has supported a number of projects that celebrate and preserve the history of lost or dying industries. Two were in the north east of Scotland. The Salmon House in Banff is

listed Grade B and on the Buildings at Risk register. It is one of the last salmon bothies still intact in Scotland. It was the coastal net fishing industry was an important employer in Scotland. The Salmon House was used to prepare the salmon caught off the coast and it would be pickled or packed fresh in ice for transport either by ship or rail to market. It was also used to store and repair the nets and had a workshop to repair the boats, with sleeping and cooking space for the workmen. The interior of the building features three large brick lined vaulted chambers – two stored the ice and the third being the fish preparation area. The intention is to retain as much as possible of the interior but use it as an interpretative centre for this important but now defunct Scottish industry. It will also provide a permanent home for the Scottish Traditional Boat Festival. This festival is now in its fourteenth year and is held around Portsoy's seventeenth-century harbour. The Festival drew 18,600 visitors in 2006. Trustees were delighted to help with a grant of £10,000 towards essential repairs and were particularly pleased that the building's new use will give it a sustainable future.

Trustees awarded a grant of £20,000 to the Knockando Woolmill Trust towards the conservation of original textile machinery. The Knockando Woolmill on Speyside has been producing textiles since at least 1784. The buildings, A-Group listed and cited as 'internationally significant' by Historic

The Pilgrim Trust – Grants committed by region and subject area (2008)				
	Preservation and scholarship	Social welfare	Total	Percentage split by region
National organisation	£310,000	£194,500	£504,500	25.27%
Scotland	£168,600	£52,000	£220,600	11.05%
Wales	£75,100	£0	£75,100	3.76%
Northern Ireland	£45,000	£36,000	£81,000	4.06%
London	£258,000	£92,000	£350,000	17.54%
Home counties	£69,100	£0	£69,100	3.46%
Rest of England	£333,200	£362,600	£695,800	34.85%
Total by subject area	**£1,260,000**	**£737,100**	**£2,000,000**	**100%**

Scotland, contain original textile machinery acquired over the centuries. It has always been at the heart of the local community; listed as the 'Wauk Mill' in parish records from 1784, the mill has since maintained its traditions of spinning and weaving through generations of families.

Knockando Woolmill grew gradually as the mechanisation of textile production developed elsewhere in the UK. This is not the large industrial mill of Yorkshire or the Scottish Borders but eighteenth and nineteenth-century farm diversification. When times were good, the Woolmill tenant would buy a new (usually second hand) piece of machinery. He would extend the mill building just enough to keep the weather off the machine; being a thrifty farmer, he re-used doors and windows from elsewhere. This has resulted in the surviving tiny, ramshackle building stuffed full of historic machinery. Spinning and weaving went hand in hand with agriculture at Knockando. There would be little work carried on in the mill during sowing or harvest time but after shearing, local farmers would bring in their fleeces to be processed and take them away as blankets and tweed cloth. Many communities had their own local district woollen mill, but the majority of these disappeared between the two World Wars. Somehow, Knockando survived. The present weaver, Hugh Jones, learnt the craft from his predecessor, Duncan Stewart, and for 30 years has continued to produce tweed, rugs and blankets on the old looms. Using expertise passed down through generations, he has managed single-handedly to sustain the traditions of the UK's oldest surviving district woollen mill.

The Knockando Woolmill Trust was set up in 2000 to rescue the Woolmill. The aim of the trust is to ensure the Woolmill survives for the next 200 years by restoring the buildings and machinery, continue to produce cloth, train a new generation of people to card, spin and weave and to share the Woolmill experience with as many people as possible. However, the philosophy is to restore the site by doing as much as is necessary but changing as little as possible.

Llanelly House is a grand house, in the centre of Llanelli, which has fallen on hard times. The original house dates from 1605 and from then until 1690s it was the home of the wealthy Vaughn family. After this the estate was acquired by the Stepney family and the house itself was radically re-modelled between 1706 and 1714. In the latter half of the eighteenth century the house was let and began to fall into decline. In the nineteenth century the property was divided up and the surrounding gardens were sold for development. Now the house is entirely enclosed by roads and buildings on all sides. By the end of the twentieth century neglect and misuse had reduced it to a state of appalling disrepair and sadly the building continued to be badly affected by its current position next to the town gyratory system. However, it is Grade 1 listed and one of only two Grade 1 houses in Carmarthenshire. According to CADW (the Assembly Government's historic environment division) it is the most outstanding domestic building to survive in South Wales.

Its significance had led the County Council to make the road in front pedestrians only and also to re-design other roads to route them away from the house. Despite over a century of abuse and neglect the CADW listing described the house as 'retaining extensive areas of original panelling' and 'to a remarkable extent the original fittings of an eighteenth-century house'.

Llanelli Town Council plans to restore the appearance and use of the house by working with the Carmarthenshire Heritage Regeneration Trust, which has acquired a 99 year lease from the council. Once fully restored the house will re-open as Llanelly House Community and Heritage Centre and will be run by a newly created trust. The project aims to save and restore the house as far as possible to its eighteenth-century form and create a sustainable centre for visitors and local people. It is hoped that it will offer this deprived area a much needed boost both to the community and to the regeneration of Llanelli town centre. The Pilgrim Trust grant was £20,000.

Trustees have also funded projects to preserve Northern Ireland's historic buildings. The Belfast Buildings Preservation Trust is a cross-community charitable organisation dedicated to the re-use of historic city buildings for which no viable or commercial use can be found. The trust was founded in 1996 and has won several awards for its work. It is constituted as a revolving fund with surplus money from completed projects being 'revolved' to the next building project. It was founded following arson attacks on two of Belfast's most important historic buildings. St Patrick's National School was the last remaining neo-gothic building in Belfast, while Christ Church was one of the few remaining remnants of the Georgian City. Applications were lodged to demolish both buildings following the fires. At the time the regeneration of Belfast's historic buildings did not feature on the political agenda. The Belfast Building Preservation Trust fought to have the significance of the built heritage recognised and was successful in restoring the school while the Diocese restored the Church. The school is now occupied by the offices of the Catholic school authorities and a Diocesan Resource Centre and bookshop. The trust retains one of the old schoolrooms, which it has restored to nineteenth century specification and uses as an educational resource. In addition to these two buildings, the trust has been involved with approximately 20 other historic buildings in Belfast and elsewhere.

The Pilgrim Trust was asked to support the employment of a member of staff for the trust. Until now, the work of the trust has depended upon the pro bono work carried out by its trustee and patron, Fionnuala

Jay-O'Boyle. It is important that work is undertaken between projects, particularly in terms of education and lobbying. Regeneration of historic buildings and the preservation of the architectural heritage of Northern Ireland are far less developed than in the rest of the UK. For the trust it is important that the message is spread and that it works with communities to establish the critical role that heritage can play in regeneration. The most successful building preservation trust projects are those where the community is involved and is prepared to take ownership of the building in the long term. The role of the staff member would be to engage with these communities, as well as to develop new projects. The Pilgrim Trust grant was £35,000 over two years.

Although the Pilgrim Trust is not allowed, by its Trust Deed, to fund projects outside the United Kingdom, it was pleased to receive an application from The Irish Landmark Trust. As well as working in the Irish Republic the trust is registered as a charity in Northern Ireland and therefore is eligible to apply. The trust saves heritage buildings that are abandoned or at risk throughout the whole of Ireland. The trust undertakes their conservation, restoration and maintenance by converting them to domestic use suitable for short-term holiday lettings. Its buildings are varied, from lighthouses, to gate lodges, to tower houses, to school houses, to mews. All of them are individual and even eccentric and are therefore unsuitable as permanent residences. They are often in remote and delightful parts of the country and are ideal retreats for those seeking a short stay in fascinating and sensitively restored buildings.

To date it has restored 15 interesting and architecturally important buildings across Ireland; north and south. The Pilgrim Trust gave a grant of £10,000 to support the repair of the Magherintemple Gatelodge, Ballycastle, Co. Antrim. Magherintemple is the seat of the

Casement family and a descendant of the family still lives there. The Gate Lodge was built in the Scottish Baronial Style in 1874, possibly by the architect S P Close. It is in the same style as the extended main house. It is an attractive building with a steeply pitched roof and crow steps. It has been unoccupied and has a major damp problem, crumbling brickwork and rampant vegetation. The restoration will respect the layout of the building, but will provide two double bedrooms and a living room. The yard walls will conceal the bathroom and kitchen.

Preservation of religious buildings

The Pilgrim Trust has long championed the cause of encouraging the regular maintenance of historic buildings rather than waiting to act until water is running down walls! Regular maintenance is of particular importance for parish churches and other religious buildings. Trustees have given a grant of £25,000 to The Society for the Protection of Ancient Buildings (SPAB) to assist it with training of those responsible for the care of parish churches in the importance of maintenance. The Society was founded by William Morris in 1877 to care for and preserve the UK's architectural heritage. Since its foundation, SPAB has been committed to maintenance matters, in line with William Morris' exhortation to: Stave off decay by daily care.

Faith in Maintenance is a unique project that aims to provide training and support for the thousands of volunteers in England and Wales who help to maintain our historic places of worship. It will provide 30 training courses each year helping over 6,000 volunteers to look after a variety of faith buildings across the country. Along with protecting significant historic structures, the project also encourages more people to become involved in their local community's heritage. One of the key aspects of the scheme is that the training courses are free and are available to any

faith group using a historic building for its worship.

Preservation and scholarship in museums, libraries and archives

Although trustees are endeavouring to give fewer larger grants they recognised that small grants are valuable and can achieve welcome results. One such small grant in 2008 was £5,000 to the Runnymede Trust. The trust developed in the 1960s partly as a response to the growth of racist politics, especially those of Enoch Powell, which looked at the time to be turning into a mass movement, and also as an attempt to create an equivalent to the American Anti-Defamation League in Britain. Since its inception, the trust has worked to challenge racial discrimination and promote a successful multi-ethnic Britain. Its principal function in the early years was to provide briefs, background papers and research data for MPs, civil servants, local government and others concerned with policy.

One of the larger grants given by trustees in 2008 was to the Bowes Museum in Co. Durham. They promised £80,500 over three years towards the employment of a specialist tapestry conservator. This is a continuation of a project that began in 2003 with the employment of a textile conservator and was supported with £60,000 from the Pilgrim Trust. The Bowes Museum holds the greatest collection of European fine and decorative arts in the North of England. It also houses one of the most comprehensive textile collections in the UK. It represents the history of European textiles from the fifteenth to the nineteenth centuries and is of international significance. It includes tapestries, carpets furnishing textiles, embroideries, lace, ecclesiastical vestments as well as printed and woven textiles.

In the 1980s a conservation studio was created in the museum and a qualified freelance conservator was engaged to work two days per month to conserve textiles and to train a textiles assistant to continue the work. However, since the textiles assistant retired in 2000, the conservation facilities had not been used.

The Textiles Conservator who has been employed for the last three years, funded by the Pilgrim Trust, had helped the museum to achieve conservation and cleaning of three major collections, but the impact of the post was more far-reaching than this alone. In particular, the museum was able to put textiles in new displays [that were] properly cleaned, conserved and mounted.

The Bowes Museum then sought a further grant from the Pilgrim Trust to build on the progress that had been made in textiles conservation. The museum wished to employ a conservator to focus on a major part of the museum's textile collection; the tapestries. The conservator is undertaking work on tapestries in particular need or of importance so that they can return to display. Some of this work is taking place within the gallery so that visitors may witness the conservation; the remainder is being executed in the museum's Textile Conservation Studio. A further part of the role will be to organise an appropriate programme of events to raise awareness of this part of the collection; for example, lectures and commentated demonstrations.

Information available

Annual report and accounts were available at the Charity Commission. The trust also has an excellent website.

Exclusions

According to the trust's website, grants are not made to:

- individuals
- non UK registered charities or charities registered in the Channel Islands or the Isle of Man
- projects based outside the United Kingdom
- projects where the work has already been completed or where contracts have already been awarded
- organisations that have had a grant awarded by us within the past two years. Note: this does not refer to payments made within that timeframe
- projects with a capital cost of over £1 million pounds where partnership funding is required
- projects where the activities are considered to be primarily the responsibility of central or local government
- general appeals or circulars
- projects for the commissioning of new works of art
- organisations seeking publishing production costs
- projects seeking to develop new facilities within a church or the re-ordering of churches or places of worship for wider community use
- any social welfare project that falls outside the trustees' current priorities
- arts and drama projects – unless they can demonstrate that they are linked to clear educational goals for prisoners or those with drug or alcohol problems
- drop in centres – unless the specific work within the centre falls within one of the trustees' current priority areas
- youth or sports clubs, travel or adventure projects, community centres or children's play groups
- organisations seeking funding for trips abroad
- organisations seeking educational funding, e.g. assistance to individuals for degree or post-degree work or school, university or college development programmes
- one-off events such as exhibitions, festivals, seminars, conferences or theatrical and musical productions.

Applications

Main Grant Fund

As the trust's primary grant outlet, this fund distributes approximately 90% of its annual grant budget. If the project fits the trust's programme criteria, organisations can apply under this scheme for sums above £5,000.

Small Grant Fund

This fund is reserved for requests of £5,000 or less. Applications to this fund normally require less detailed assessment (though a visit or meeting may be required) but applicants should include the names of two referees from organisations with whom they work.

Full funding guidelines are available from the trust's website. Applications can also be made online or a form can be requested from the correspondent. The trustees meet quarterly.

The Prince's Charities Foundation

CC no. 277540

Contact
David Hutson,
The Prince of Wales's Office,
Clarence House, St James's, London
SW1A 1BA
Tel: 020 7930 4832 ext 4788;
Fax: 020 7930 0119;
website: princeofwales.gov.uk

Trustees
Sir Michael Peat; Philip Reid; Hon. Lord Rothschild; Leslie Jane Ferrar.

Areas of work: Culture, the environment, medical welfare, education, children and young people and overseas aid.

Total grants: £21.9 million (2007/08)

Environmental grants: £1.6 million

Beneficial area: Unrestricted.

General

The Prince's Charities Foundation was established by trust deed in 1979 for general charitable purposes. The foundation principally continues to support charitable bodies and purposes in which the founder has a particular interest, including culture, the environment, medical welfare, education, children and youth and overseas aid.

In 2007/08 the foundation had assets of £1.2 million and an income of £5.9 million from donations and investments. During the year the foundation made grants to 186 organisations totalling £21.9 million (£4 million in 2006/07), including over £20 million to charities in which the Prince of Wales has a particular interest. One of the main beneficiaries during the year was Dumfries House, with the foundation's contribution facilitated by a £20 million loan obtained by the foundation for onward distribution. The following is taken from the trustee's report 2008:

[Dumfries House] was saved from sale and certain break-up by the intervention of His Royal Highness The Prince Charles, The Duke of Rothesay. His Royal Highness organised a group of organisations and individuals to buy the house at a total cost of £45 million. The Foundation contributed £18.3 million, and with £25 million contributed by the Scottish Government and heritage organisations and trusts, the House, its wonderful collection of furniture and estate were saved for the Nation only hours before the expiry of the deadline for sale at auction. Once purchased, the House and its contents were donated to The Great Stewardship of Scotland's Dumfries House Trust, a UK registered Charity.

Grants, made from both restricted and unrestricted funds, were broken down as follows:

Category	Amount
Culture	£19,300,000
Environment	£1,600,000
Medical welfare	£706,000
Education	£554,000
Children and young people	£80,000
Oversees aid	£19,300
Other	£3,100,000

There were 30 grants made over £10,000 each listed in the accounts. Many of the larger grants were awarded to other Prince of Wales charities.

Beneficiaries included: The National Art Collections Fund (£13.8 million in connection with the purchase of Dumfries House); The Great Steward of Scotland's Dumfries House Trust (£5 million); Accounting for Sustainability (£325,000); The Prince's Foundation for the Built Environment (£277,000); The Rainforest Project (£228,000); Northumberland Wildlife Trust (£87,000); Turquoise Mountain Foundation (£71,000); North Highlands Initiative (£65,000); The Soil Association (£35,000); Dartmoor Farmers' Association (£30,000); and The National Trust (£13,000).

Information available

Accounts were available from the Charity Commission.

Exclusions

No grants to individuals.

Applications

In writing to the correspondent, with full details of the project including financial data. The Prince's Charities Foundation receives an ever-increasing number of requests for assistance, which are considered on a regular basis by The Prince of Wales and the trustees.

The Sigrid Rausing Trust

CC no. 1046769

Contact
Sheetal Patel, Administrator,
Eardley House, 4 Uxbridge House,
London W8 7SY
Tel: 020 7908 9870; Fax: 020 7908 9879;
email: info@srtrust.org;
website: www.sigrid-rausing-trust.org/

Trustees
Dr Sigrid Rausing; Joshua Mailman; Susan Hitch; Andrew Puddephatt; Geoff Budlender.

Areas of work: Human, women's and minority rights and social and environmental justice.

Total grants: £17 million (2007)

Environmental grants: £1.9 million

Beneficial area: Unrestricted.

General

Summary

The trust was set up in 1995 by Sigrid Rausing and takes as its guiding framework the United Nations' Universal Declaration of Human Rights. Its vision is 'A world where the principles of the Universal Declaration of Human Rights are implemented and respected and where all people can enjoy their rights in harmony with each other and with the environment.'

The trust made its first grants in 1996 and, from the beginning, has taken a keen interest in work that promotes international human rights. It was originally called the Ruben and Elisabeth Rausing Trust after Singrid's grandparents. In 2003 the trust was renamed the Sigrid Rausing Trust to identify its work more closely with the aims and ideals of Sigrid Rausing herself.

The trust has four funding categories which provide a framework for its activities:

- civil and political rights
- women's rights
- minority rights
- social and environmental justice.

Each programme has a number of sub-programmes, which can be found on the trust's website.

Grantmaking

The trust has five main principles which guide its grantmaking:

- the essential role of core funding
- good and effective leadership
- flexibility and responsiveness to needs and opportunities
- the value of clarity and brevity in applications and reports
- long term relationships with grantees.

The following is taken from the trust's 2007 accounts and explains the trust's grantmaking policy in further detail.

The trust's defining attribute remains its commitment to support groups that work internationally, using a rights based approach. The trustees are interested in groups that address the serious global problems of our age and are aiming for long-term strategic change. There is an understanding amongst the trustees that they are trying to alter the root causes of problems rather than mitigate the effects.

They generally do not fund the provision of services, except where a group can clearly show that it has a new methodology or approach, which could bring about a substantial change in the sector in which it is used.

The trustees tend to make grants for effective and focused advocacy and campaigning work. They also believe in getting funds as close as possible to the problem and have a strong interest in

funding organisations that sub-grant onwards to small grass-roots organisations in the global south.

They lay heavy emphasis on good leadership – they think it is the key to successful social change. This core belief comes out of the trustees 'no nannying' approach. Groups that apply to the Sigrid Rausing Trust are expected to stand on their own feet. They come to the trust with ideas, it does not suggest plans to them, and it believes they are the experts and entrepreneurs best able to judge their own priorities. The trust's role is to take a decision about whether or not it wants to support what is put before it. If it does, then it tries to stand back and let the group pursue its mission.

The trust seeks to provide support in as flexible way as possible, including core funding where this is applicable to assisting a group advance their overall objectives. It is interested in long-term relationships with the groups it supports, subject to a yearly application and review process. Groups that cannot manage the trust's processes and meet its deadlines without being reminded, tend not to be re-granted.

The trust gives two key types of grants:

- Main Grants – between £15,000 and £850,000 for 1–3 years.
- Small Grants – up to £15,000 – for smaller organisations who find it difficult to fundraise from international funding agencies (several small grantees have also gone on to receive a Main Grant).

In exceptional circumstances the trust may also provide Emergency Funds in response to a sudden human rights crisis or in order to protect human rights defenders. Please note: grants under this programme require a recommendation by an existing grantee, another funding agency, or a contact in the field. Existing grantees may also be eligible for an Advancement Grant, designed to support a major infrastructure step change.

Social and Environmental Justice

The social and environmental justice programme supports organisations that are involved in corporate and institutional transparency and accountability, environmental justice and labour rights in the UK and overseas. In 2008 grants were made to 18 organisations under the sub-programme of environmental justice totalling around £1.9 million.

Beneficiaries included: Pesticide Action Network (£300,000); Zero Mercury Campaign – Belgium and European Environmental Bureau – Belgium (£200,000 each); Angelica Foundation – USA (£175,000); International Rivers – USA (£125,000); Centre for International Environmental Law – USA (£80,000); Mines and Communities (£60,000); Corner House (£50,000); Amazon Watch – USA (£40,000); Latin American Mining Monitoring Project (£35,000); and New Israel Fund (£25,000).

Two grants were also made to Friends of the Earth International – Netherlands (£250,000) and Friends of the Earth – USA (£45,000) under the Transparency and Accountability sub-programme.

A detailed breakdown of grantees under each funding stream, including information on individual projects, is available on the trust's website.

Information available

Accounts were available at the Charity Commission.

Exclusions

No grants are made to individuals or faith based groups.

Applications

Applications are considered only from organisations that have been invited to apply. There is, however, an open pre-application process. Applicants should check the guidelines detailed on the trust's website. If you are confident that your work falls clearly within them, and you wish to be considered for an invitation, you should complete the short 2 page enquiry form (for Main or Small grants, as appropriate) available on the trust's website. Completed forms should be submitted by email.

As trustees consider grant applications under each sub-programme once a year, organisations should register an enquiry as early as possible, if possible at least 6 months before the intended start of the project.

The trust does not give grants to individuals and only funds projects or groups that are charitable under the law of England and Wales. The vast majority of the work it funds is internationally based and it is interested in rights based advocacy and not the delivery of services.

Based on the information provided in the enquiry form, the trustees will decide which groups to invite to apply for funding. Applications pass through a careful vetting process. Even if your organisation falls within the guidelines this is not a guarantee that you will be invited to apply. The trust considers grants to cover core costs, and project work. It also considers advancement grants to help groups extend their reach and operating abilities, but only for those organisations with which it has an established relationship.

All those who receive an invitation to apply for a grant are assessed by the relevant programme officer. Applicants should be aware that the trustees take the application process and the meeting of their deadlines seriously. Sending an incomplete application can count against a group. Failing to submit reports on how the grant was spent by the requested deadline will also be taken into account.

The Roddick Foundation

CC no. 1061372

Contact
J Roddick, Secretary, Emerald House,
East Street, Epsom, Surrey KT17 1HS
website: www.theroddickfoundation.org

Trustees
J Roddick; S Roddick; T G Roddick; S C
A Schlieske.

Areas of work: Arts, education,
environmental, human rights,
humanitarian, medical, poverty and
social justice.

Total grants: £3 million (2007/08)

Environmental grants: £460,000

Beneficial area: Worldwide.

General

The foundation was established in 1997
by the late Dame Anita Roddick, founder
of the Body Shop. As stated in its annual
report, it has the following objects:

- *The relief of poverty*
- *The promotion, maintenance,
  improvement and advancement of
  education for the public benefit*
- *The provision of facilities for recreation
  or other leisure time occupations in the
  interests of social welfare provided that
  such facilities are for the public benefit*
- *The promotion of any other charitable
  purpose for the benefit of the public.*

In 2007/08 the foundation received an
income of £734,000. Grants given to 34
organisations totalled £3 million, with 16
grants totalling £1.2 million made in the
key focus area for this year; human rights.
Grants were broken down as follows:

Category	No.	Total
Human Rights	12	£1,200,000
Medical	5	£784,000
Environmental	4	£460,000
Educational and Media	3	£204,000
Poverty and Social Justice	7	£198,000
Arts and Culture	3	£145,000

Beneficiaries in the environmental
category this year were: Soil Action
(£300,000); Friends of the Earth
(£100,000); UK Pesticides Campaign
(£50,000); and Stakeholder Democracy
Network (£10,000).

Information available

Accounts were on file at the Charity
Commission.

Exclusions

The trust states that it is particularly not
interested in the following:

- *Funding anything related to sport*
- *Funding fundraising events or
  conferences*
- *Sponsorship of any kind.*

Applications

The foundation does not accept or
respond to unsolicited applications.
Grants made by the foundation are at the
discretion of the board of trustees. The
board considers making a grant and, if
approved, notifies the intended recipient.

The Shetland Charitable Trust

CC no. SC027025

Contact
Jeff Goddard, Acting General Manager,
22–24 North Road, Lerwick, Shetland
ZE1 0NQ
Tel: 01595 744994; Fax: 01595 744999;
email: mail@shetlandcharitable
trust.co.uk;
website: www.shetlandcharitable
trust.co.uk

Trustees
Bill Manson, Chair; James Henry; Leslie
Angus; Laura Baisley; James Budge;
Alexander Cluness; Alastair Cooper;
Adam Doull; Allison Duncan; Elizabeth
Fullerton; Florence Grains; Iris Hawkins;
Robert Henderson; Andrew Hughson;

Caroline Miller; Richard Nickerson; Valerie Nicolson; Frank Robertson; Gary Robinson; Joseph Simpson; John Scott; Cecil Smith; Jonathon Wills; Allan Wishart.

Areas of work: Social welfare, art and recreation, the environment and amenity.

Total grants: £13.8 million (2007/08)

Environmental grants: £2 million

Beneficial area: Shetland only.

General

The original trust was established in 1976 with 'disturbance receipts' from the operators of the Sullom Voe oil terminal. As a clause in the trust deed prevented it from accumulating income beyond 21 years from its inception, in 1997 most of its assets were transferred to a newly established Shetland Islands Council Charitable Trust, which is identical to the old trust except for the omission of the prohibition on accumulating income. This has now been renamed Shetland Charitable Trust.

The trust was run by the Shetland Islands Council until 2002. The trust is currently administered by its own separate staff.

The trust aims to provide public benefit to and improve the quality of life for the inhabitants of Shetland; ensure that people in need receive a high standard of service and care; protect and enhance Shetland's environment, heritage, culture and traditions; provide facilities that will be of long-term benefit to the inhabitants of Shetland; build on the energy and initiatives of local groups, maximise voluntary effort and input and assist them to achieve their objectives; support a balanced range of services and facilities to contribute to the overall fabric of the community; support facilities and services and jobs located in rural areas and maintain the value of the funds in the long term to ensure that future generations have access to similar resources in the post oil era.

In 2007/08 the trust had assets of £219.5 million and an income of £13.8 million. Grants were made totalling £11.7 million.

The funds are used to create and sustain a wide range of facilities for the islands, largely by funding further trusts including: Shetland Welfare Trust – day care and running costs; Shetland Recreational Trust; Isleburgh Trust; Shetland Amenity Trust; Shetland Amenity Trust; Christmas Grants to Pensioners/Disabled Households; Shetlands Arts Trust; and Independence at Home Scheme Grants.

The trust has submitted a joint application with Scottish and Southern Energy to the Scottish Parliament to build the Viking Energy wind farm project – the largest project of its kind in Europe and one which could generate enough energy to fulfil one fifth of Scotland's electricity requirements. It is estimated that the scheme could make a profit of £37 million per year for the trust and its partner.

Information available

Accounts and annual reports were available from the trust's website.

Exclusions

Funds can only be used to benefit the inhabitants of Shetland.

Applications

Applications are only accepted from Shetland-based charities. The trustees meet every two months.

The Waterloo Foundation

CC no. 1117535

Contact
Janice Matthews, Finance Manager, c/o 46–48 Cardiff Road, Llandaff, Cardiff CF5 2DT

Tel: 029 2083 8980;
email: info@waterloofoundation.org.uk;
website: www.waterloofoundation.
org.uk

Trustees
Heather Stevens; David Stevens; Janet
Alexander; Caroline Oakes.

Areas of work: Children, the
environment, developing countries and
projects in Wales.
Total grants: £1.7 million (2007)
Environmental grants: £855,200
Beneficial area: UK and overseas.

General

The foundation was established in early
2007 with a substantial endowment of
£100 million in shares from David and
Heather Stevens, co-founders of Admiral
Insurance.

It is anticipated that grants will be made
each year totalling in the region of
£2 million.

In 2007, the foundation's first year of
operation, grants were made to 98
projects totalling £1.7 million.

The foundation makes grants under four
areas: child development; world
development; the environment; and a
special interest in projects in Wales. In
2007 grants were split as follows
(including commitments made for future
years):

Category	Value	No.
World development	£722,000	26
Environment	£855,200	20
Child development	£532,200	21
Wales	£218,100	14
Other	£203,500	17

The foundation's environmental
interests are described on its website as
follows:

Environment
*For the first time in Earth's history
humans are altering the natural
equilibrium of the environment. We
hope through this fund that we can help
mitigate the damaging effects that
humans are causing and contribute to a
positive change both now and in the
future.*

Funding priorities
*The foundation is keen to support
initiatives aimed at reducing man-made
climate change and increasing the health of
the marine environment, both in the UK
and worldwide. Under the Environment
Fund, the foundation has two main
themes:*

1) Forests
*The world has around 4 billion hectares of
forests, covering 30% of the world's land
area. Although tropical rainforests
constitute just 5% of this land area, they
play a crucial role in the maintenance of
the world's environment and climate.*

*18–20% of global greenhouse gas
emissions occur as a result of
deforestation, including the burning of
carbon-rich tropical peatlands (42 billion
tonnes of soil carbon are stored in the
forested tropical peatlands of SE Asia
alone). In addition tropical forests help
to generate the rainfall that stabilises
local and regional weather patterns; they
sustain 40% of all life on earth; and
they support approximately 1 billion
people who depend on them for their
livelihoods.*

*Under our Forests programme, preference
will be given to projects which seek to
avoid deforestation in tropical areas,
although reforestation and tree planting
projects will also be considered. Projects
will be considered at both strategic and
local level.*

187

Strategic initiatives could include:

- *Lobbying for forests to be included in carbon markets, and addressing any issues which may exclude their inclusion*
- *Lobbying for the increased awareness of the importance of rainforests*
- *Lobbying against the drivers of tropical deforestation.*

At a project level (projects should address two or more of the following):

- *Localised tropical forest protection and management*
- *Projects which expose and address the local drivers of tropical deforestation*
- *Creating sustainable livelihoods for forest-dependent people.*

2) Marine

Oceans cover more than two-thirds of the earth's surface, and the number of different species living in the oceans is estimated to be at least 178,000. Oceans are crucial to the world's economy, health and environment. Fish is an important source of food – it is estimated that 1 billion people, predominantly in developing countries, depend on fish as their primary source of protein. Also, an estimated 200 million people are directly or indirectly employed in the fish and seafood industries.

However, according to the United Nations 71–78% of the world's fisheries are either 'fully exploited', 'over exploited' or 'significantly depleted'. Some species have already been fished to commercial extinction; and many more are on the verge of collapse.

Under our Marine programme, preference will be given to projects which:

At a strategic level:

- *Lobby for sustainable fishing practices and techniques worldwide*

- *Lobby for action to maintain and improve world fish stock levels, e.g. Marine Protected Areas, No Take Zones, etc.*
- *Provide support for the marine world to stabilise climate change, in particular the uptake of greenhouse gases.*

At a project level (projects should address two or more of the following):

- *Develop marine and fisheries protection and management*
- *Address local drivers which cause over-exploitation of fish stocks and other seafood*
- *Create sustainable livelihoods for coastal and seafood dependent people in developing countries.*

Other interests

In addition to our forest and marine programmes, the foundation may occasionally support water and energy projects.

3) Water

The foundation will consider supporting projects in developing countries which promote water conservation, or increase access to water.

4) Energy

The foundation will consider offering financial support and advice for small-scale community renewable energy projects in Wales only.

Information available

Accounts were available from the Charity Commission. The foundation also has a helpful website.

Exclusions

According to its website the foundation will not support:

- *applications for grants for work that has already taken place*
- *applications for grants that replace or subsidise statutory funding.*

We will not consider applications for grants in the following areas:

- the arts and heritage, except in Wales
- animal welfare
- the promotion of religious or political causes
- general appeals or circulars.

We are unlikely to support projects in the following areas:

- for the benefit of an individual
- medical charities (except under certain aspects of our 'Child Development' programme, particularly mental health)
- festivals, sports and leisure activities
- websites, publications, conferences or seminars, except under our 'Child Development' programme.

Under the Environment Fund, the foundation does not support:

- Initiatives focused solely on biodiversity.
- Projects designed to achieve largely aesthetic environmental goals.
- Projects that are purely educational.
- Testing new renewable energy technology.

Please note all organisations applying under the environment fund will be expected to have an environmental policy.

Applications

The following is taken from the foundation's website:

We hope to make applying for a grant fairly painless and fairly quick! However it will help us a great deal if you could follow the simple rules below when sending in an application (by the way there are no forms as such to complete).

Email applications to applications@ waterloofoundation.org.uk (nowhere else please!). Include a BRIEF description (equivalent to 2 sides of A4) within your email, but NOT as an attachment, of your project or the purpose for which you want the funding, detailing:

- your charity's name, address and charity number
- email, phone and name of a person to reply to
- a link to your website
- what it's for
- who it benefits
- how much you want and when
- what happens if you don't get our help
- the programme under which you are applying.

Don't write long flowery sentences – we won't read them.

Do be brief, honest, clear and direct. Use abbrevns if you like!

Don't send attachments to your email – your website will give us an introduction to you so you don't need to cover that.

Who can apply?

The foundation's website states:

We welcome applications from registered charities and organisations with projects that have a recognisable charitable purpose. Your project has to be allowed within the terms of your constitution or rules and, if you are not a registered charity, you will need to send us a copy of your constitution or set of rules.

We make grants for all types of projects; start-up, initial stages and valuable ongoing funding. This can include running costs and overheads as well as posts; particularly under World Development and projects in Wales. We do not have any upper or lower limit on the amount of grant we offer but it is unlikely that we would offer a grant of more that £100,000.

The Westminster Foundation

CC no. 267618

Contact
Mrs J Sandars, Administrator,
70 Grosvenor Street, London W1K 3JP
Tel: 020 7408 0988; Fax: 020 7312 6244;
email: westminster.foundation@
grosvenor.com

Trustees
The Duke of Westminster, Chair; J H M
Newsum; Mark Loveday; Lady Edwina
Grosvenor.

Areas of work: Church, conservation,
youth, education, medical, arts and social
welfare.

Total grants: £1.9 million (2007)

Environmental grants: £484,600

Beneficial area: Unrestricted, in practice
mainly UK. Local interests in central
London (SW1 and W1 and immediate
environs), North West England,
especially rural Lancashire and the
Chester area, and the Sutherland area of
Scotland.

General

The foundation was established in 1974
for general charitable purposes by the
fifth Duke of Westminster and continues
to make grants to a wide range of
charitable causes. In 1987 the Grosvenor
Foundation, a separately registered
charity, transferred all its assets to The
Westminster Foundation.

The foundation makes over 100 grants
a year, mainly for welfare and
educational causes but with substantial
support for conservation and rather
less for medicine and the arts. A new
category called 'commemorative' has
recently been adopted. Grants appear
to be all for UK causes and perhaps
half by number, though less by value,
are in the areas of church,

conservation, youth, education,
medical, arts and social welfare.

Grants can be for very large amounts, but
generally, all but a handful are usually for
amounts of not more than £60,000 and
most are between £5,000 and just a few
hundred pounds. About half of the
beneficiaries were also supported in
previous years.

The foundation has previously noted in
its annual report and accounts that:

*'It is usual that the trustees have knowledge
of, or connection with, those charities
which are successful applicants. The
trustees tend to support caring causes and
not research.*

*'Grants are directed towards geographical
areas in which the Grosvenor family and
Grosvenor Group have a particular
connection. For example, Grosvenor Group
are major stakeholders in the
redevelopment of the Paradise Street site in
Liverpool [completed in September 2008].
The trustees have previously committed
£500,000 over a period of five years to the
Liverpool One Foundation [previously
known as the Liverpool Paradise
Foundation], a registered charity set up by
some of the stakeholders involved in the
Liverpool development, and this money
will be distributed to a wide range of
charities and organisations in the
immediate vicinity.'*

This is assumed to be a largely personal
trust, created by the present duke. He is
well known in the charity world for his
active personal involvement in many
organisations, and no doubt a significant
number of the regular beneficiaries are
organisations with which he has
developed a personal connection that
goes beyond grantmaking.

In 2007 the foundation had assets of
£38 million and an income of
£3.8 million. Grants were committed to
140 organisations totalling £1.9 million
and were broken down as follows:

Category	Amount	No.
Social Welfare	£1,310,000	65
Conservation	£484,600	13
Medical	£125,000	29
Education	£80,000	10
Youth	£73,000	14
Arts	£13,000	4
Church	£2,200	3
Commemorative	£1,000	2

Grants in 2007

The foundation's accounts list grants made of £20,000 or more.

Conservation

Beneficiaries included: The Wildlife Trust for Bedfordshire, Cambridgeshire, Northamptonshire and Peterborough (£270,000), to help secure the acquisition of the Holmewood Estate which enabled two nature reserves to be linked; The Game Conservancy Trust (£50,000), towards the Upland Predation Experiment at Otterburn; and, the Atlantic Salmon Trust (£40,000 over 5 years), toward the salary of a research officer.

Information available

Accounts were available at the Charity Commission, giving details of grants over £20,000.

Exclusions

Only registered charities will be considered. No grants to individuals, 'holiday' charities, student expeditions, or research projects.

Applications

In writing to the secretary, enclosing an up-to-date set of accounts, together with a brief history of the project to date and the current need.

The Garfield Weston Foundation

CC no. 230260

Contact
Philippa Charles, Administrator, Weston Centre, 10 Grosvenor Street, London W1K 4QY
Tel: 020 7399 6565;
website: www.garfieldweston.org

Trustees
Guy H Weston, Chair; Camilla H W Dalglish; Catrina A Hobhouse; Jana R Khayat; Sophia M Mason; Eliza L Mitchell; W Galen Weston; George G Weston: Melissa Murdoch.

Areas of work: General.
Total grants: £55 million (2007/08)
Environmental grants: £842,000
Beneficial area: UK.

General

Summary

This huge foundation makes about 1,500 one-off grants a year, typically for amounts anywhere between £3,000 and £1 million. Perhaps helped by the fact that the income of the foundation has been rising rapidly, about half of all appeals result in a grant, though not necessarily for the full amount requested. Awards are regularly made in almost all fields except overseas aid and animal welfare.

Probably more than 85% of the money, and an even higher proportion for the largest grants, is for capital or endowment projects.

The published criteria for grantmaking, reported overleaf can be downloaded from the foundation's website. Compared to the general run of trusts described elsewhere, there are relatively few grants to unconventional causes, or for campaigning or representational activities, and more for institutions such as independent schools and charities connected with private hospitals. Nevertheless, almost all kinds of charitable activity, including the radical, are supported to some extent. Grants are rarely given to major charities with high levels of fundraising costs.

The foundation is one of the few which can consider very large grants, a number of which were made in 2007/08.

The charity's ten trustees (all family members) are backed by a very modest staff, but nevertheless the foundation aims to deal with applications within four months of them being received.

In 2007/08 the foundation had assets standing at over £3.7 billion. Its income totalled £42.7 million. As in previous years, grants were made far exceeding income, totalling £52 million (£40 million in 2006/07).

Grantmaking

What are the trustees looking for in an application?

Applications are considered individually by the foundation trustees. In assessing applications, the following issues are taken into consideration so please bear this in mind to ensure your application is able to address these things.

1) The financial viability of the organisation

Organisations that are relatively stable financially tend to be in a better position to run effectively and deliver the quality of services for which the charity was created. Therefore the trustees look for signs that the organisation is likely to remain running – these signs include, but are not limited to, past history, local support, an appropriate level of reserves, statutory and local council funding.

2) The degree of need for the project requiring funding

There are many ways to evaluate this, however indicators include the level of local commitment to the project, evidenced by

such things as fundraising activity, volunteer effort, local authority support, numbers who will benefit etc.

3) The amount spent on administration and fundraising as compared to charitable activities

The Charity Commission indicates a target of 10% for administration.

4) The ability to raise sufficient funding to meet the appeal target

The trustees are keen to assist projects where they can have a high degree of confidence that the necessary funds can be secured from relevant sources, therefore it is important to demonstrate the level of funds already secured and from what sources; as well as the likely targets to address any shortfall.

5) Whether the organisation has appropriate priorities and plans in place to manage its activities

This includes ensuring that core services are adequately resourced and stable before expanding into new projects, locations or services. It also refers to the ability of an organisation to secure appropriate funding for key projects and services and that necessary capabilities are available for operational success.

Grants in 2007/08

Summary of grants paid

Amount by region

Region	Value
South Central	£13,000,000
London	£10,000,000
National (England)	£4,700,000
Anglia	£3,600,000
South East	£3,200,000
Midlands	£3,100,000
South West	£3,100,000
North West	£2,700,000
Scotland	£2,200,000
North East	£1,600,000
Northern Ireland	£485,000
Wales	£348,000

Amount by Category

Category	£20,000 and over	No. of appeals	Less than £20,000	No. of appeals	Total amount	Total no. of appeals
Arts	£5,800,000	44	£523,000	82	£6,400,000	126
Community	£490,000	10	£961,000	185	£1,500,000	195
Education	£34,400,000	59	£511,000	83	£35,000,000	142
Environment	£740,000	15	£102,000	17	£842,000	32
Health	£3,200,000	43	£231,000	35	£3,500,000	78
Religion	£1,000,000	17	£1,600,000	372	£2,600,000	389
Welfare	£2,200,000	46	£1,100,000	192	£3,300,000	238
Young people	£1,100,000	29	£796,000	160	£1,900,000	189
Other	£50,000	1	£10,000	2	£60,000	3
TOTALS	£49,000,000	264	£5,800,000	1,128	£55,000,000	1,392

Environmental organisations may find the 'Environment', 'Religion' and 'Other' categories of particular interest. The following information is taken from the foundation's annual report.

Environment – £842,000 distributed in 32 grants

Grants of £100,000 were provided to Painshill Park Trust, the Woodland Trust and the United Kingdom Antarctic Heritage Trust. In the last fifteen years Painshill Park has researched and restored its eighteenth century landscape and visitor facilities have been provided, including a purpose built education centre. The final stage of the programme of restoration, the ornamental buildings ("follies"), is now under way and the trustees have agreed to help to complete this work. The grant to the Woodland Trust is towards the cost of purchasing an extension to Elemore Woods together with undertaking a three year programme of tree-planting, conservation work, community engagement and public access works.

£50,000 is provided to the Father Thames Trust for the restoration and conservation of the various historic gardens and public spaces along the river. The Tree Council was granted £20,000 towards its Tree Warden scheme and The Little Ouse Headwaters Project £10,000 for restoration of grazed wet fen and wet meadow. A

similar amount was also provided to the Royal Society for the Protection of Birds for helping to reintroduce the Red Kite into Northern Ireland.

Religion – £2.6 million distributed in 389 grants

Religion again accounts for the largest number of grants, the majority being for £10,000 or less for fabric repairs and re-ordering. The exceptions are cathedrals and some important churches with major capital appeals towards which the trustees provided more significant support.

Ely Cathedral received the largest grant, £250,000. As with most ancient heritage buildings urgent fabric repairs were required, and they also aim to build an endowment fund to support the Choir. The trustees helped to provide music scholarships.

Grants of £100,000 were provided to the Cathedrals of Hereford, Bristol and Rochester and £50,000 to the Selby Abbey Appeal, all for capital requirements. Selby Abbey has received previous support from the foundation as the trustees note the ongoing challenge to repair and restore the stonework, much of which has been affected by pollution. The Abbey is the largest parish church in England, founded by William the Conqueror in the eleventh century, and is one of the few great

193

monastic churches to survive the Dissolution of the Monasteries.

£50,000 was donated each to St James's Church on Piccadilly, Worcester Cathedral, Clonard Monastery in Belfast, Llandaff Cathedral in Cardiff and Wells Cathedral. The latter topped up an earlier substantial grant towards a £6 million appeal to open up and restore the medieval spaces, including the Undercroft which was previously not accessible to the public. The appeal aims to improve access throughout, provide purpose-built facilities for the music, a dedicated education space and an interactive interpretation centre.

The challenges facing St Pancras Parish Church are typical of many churches throughout the UK and illustrate the commitment of local communities to raise the funding they need to carry out their ministries. In addition to normal Sunday and weekday services Saint Pancras provides advice and support and runs projects for all ages. In addition there are regular recitals, lectures, discussion groups and social welfare activities. The trustees recognise that this level of community activity can put strain on the facilities so a grant of £25,000 was provided towards improved access, toilets, kitchen facilities and meeting space.

Another typical example is the case of St Mary's Church in Chiddingfold, where the cramped Grade I listed building struggles to meet the growing needs of the community, particularly the expanding Sunday School and youth groups. A new church room, specifically designed to minimise the visual impact on the ancient church, is planned to solve these problems and the trustees provided a grant of £5,000 in support of this.

Other – £60,000 distributed in three grants

The largest grant in this category was to the Landmark Trust which was established to rescue historic and architecturally interesting buildings and their

surroundings from neglect and, when restored, to give them new life by letting them out to stay in as places to experience. The trust has now restored almost 200 buildings, with the holiday lets covering the costs of ongoing maintenance. The current £50,000 grant is towards the restoration of the Grade II listed Silverton Park Stables in Devon, a rare example of an unconverted stable block built in the mid-nineteenth century and in itself the size of a large country house.

Friends of Anne of Cleves House in Lewes, Sussex, received £5,000 towards renovation work and a similar amount was provided to the Heritage of London Trust for the restoration of the Minnie Lansbury bracket clock which hangs in Bow Road, Tower Hamlets. This memorial clock commemorates the brave East End suffragette heroine from the 1920s, who was a Labour councillor in Poplar, and who served a six week prison sentence for refusing to levy full rates in the poverty-stricken area.

Information available

Excellent descriptive annual report and accounts with an analysis of a selection of grants, large and small, and a full list of beneficiaries.

The Yorkshire Dales Millennium Trust

CC no. 1061687

Contact
David Sharrod, Director,
The Old Post Office, Main Street,
Clapham, Lancaster LA2 8DP
Tel: 01524 251002; Fax: 01524 251150;
email: info@ydmt.org;
website: www.ydmt.org

Trustees
Joseph Pearlman; Carl Lis; Brian Braithwaite-Exley; Colin Speakman; Dorothy Fairburn; Hazel Waters; David

Sanders Rees-Jones; Jane Roberts; Peter
Charlesworth; Steve Macaré; David Joy;
Thomas Wheelwright; Lesley Emin;
Margaret Billing; Michael Ackrel;
Andrew Campbell.

Areas of work: Conservation and
environmental regeneration.

Total grants: £786,000 (2007/08)

Environmental grants: £700,000

Beneficial area: The Yorkshire Dales.

Information available

Annual report and accounts were
available from the Charity Commission.
The trust also has an informative website
detailing current and previous projects.

Applications

In writing to the correspondent.

9 Raising money from the National Lottery

The National Lottery (the Lottery) was launched in 1994 and rapidly established itself as a key funder of the voluntary sector. Since it began, £23 billion has been raised and more than 317,000 grants given out for good causes (2008 figures). However, it takes time and effort to put together a good application and the assessment process is a rigorous and demanding one. Many organisations commit a substantial part of their fundraising resources in applying for grants from the various Lottery distribution bodies.

The National Lottery currently funds four good causes:

- charities, health, education and the environment (jointly)
- sports
- arts
- heritage.

In this chapter we give an overview of how Lottery money is spent, who distributes the money to the four good causes, how the various distribution bodies operate, details of current programmes to which groups can apply and information on the Big Lottery Fund (BIG) thinking consultation process.

How Lottery ticket money is distributed

The company in charge of running the game, Camelot, collects the money from the sale of tickets. Camelot was reappointed by the National Lottery Commission (an independent body set up by the government to monitor the integrity of the Lottery – www.natlotcomm.gov.uk) to run the Lottery from 2009 to 2019.

The following is a breakdown of where money goes from each £1 ticket sale:

Lottery winners	50p
Good causes	28p
HM Revenue & Customs	12p
Individual retailers	5p
Camelot	5p

Each 28p for good causes goes initially to the Department for Culture, Media and Sport (DCMS), which is also responsible for the Lottery's policies and the structure within which the distribution bodies work. DCMS has no decision making powers on how Lottery money is given out and grants should be made independently of government departments.

Distribution bodies

Distribution bodies or Lottery funders are the organisations that distribute the good causes' money to local communities and national and international projects. They cover arts, heritage, sport, community and voluntary groups as well as supporting projects concerned with health, education and the environment. They will also be funding the 2012 Olympic Games and Paralympic Games in London and until at least 2012, the diversion of Lottery funds to the Olympics means that there will be less new Lottery money available.

In England the funding bodies are:

- **Arts Council England.** Arts Council England is the national development agency for the arts in England, distributing public money from government and the Lottery.
- **Arts Council of Northern Ireland.** this is the lead development agency for the arts in Northern Ireland.
- **Arts Council of Wales.** This body is responsible for developing and funding the arts in Wales.
- **Awards for All.** Awards for All is a Lottery grants scheme funding small, local community-based projects in the UK. See details on page 218.
- **Big Lottery Fund.** The Big Lottery Fund (BIG) is committed to improving communities and the lives of people most in need.

- **Heritage Lottery Fund.** The Heritage Lottery Fund uses money from the Lottery to give grants for a wide range of projects involving the local, regional and national heritage of the UK.
- **NESTA.** NESTA (the National Endowment for Science, Technology and the Arts) is a non-departmental public body investing in innovators and working to improve the climate for creativity in the UK.
- **Olympic Lottery Distributor.** The Olympic Lottery Distributor's remit is to support the delivery of the London 2012 Olympic and Paralympic Games. The Olympic Lottery Distributor is not currently running any open funding rounds.
- **Scottish Arts Council.** The Scottish Arts Council champions the arts for Scotland.
- **Scottish Screen.** This agency develops, encourages and promotes film, television and new media in Scotland.
- **Sport England.** Sport England invests in projects that help people to start, stay and succeed in sport and physical activity at every level.
- **Sports Council for Northern Ireland.** 'Making sport happen for you.'
- **sportscotland.** sportscotland is the national sport agency for Scotland. Working with partners, it is responsible for developing sport and physical recreational activity in Scotland.
- **Sports Council for Wales.** The Sports Council for Wales is the national organisation responsible for developing and promoting sport and active lifestyles.
- **UK Film Council.** As the lead agency for film, the UK Film Council aims to stimulate a competitive, successful and vibrant UK film industry and culture, both now and for the future.
- **UK Sport.** UK Sport works in partnership to lead sport in the UK to world-class success.

The Lottery distribution bodies are independent; however, because they distribute public funds, their policies are subject to a level of statutory control from government. Their grantmaking is also under close public and media scrutiny and is often the subject of wide-ranging debate.

Currently Lottery funding is allocated to the good causes in the following way:

- charities, health, education and the environment – 50%
- sports – 16.67%
- arts – 16.67%
- heritage – 16.67%.

Big Lottery Fund (BIG)

BIG was launched in 2004 and given legal status on 1 December 2006 by way of the National Lottery Act 2006. It was brought about by the merging of the Community Fund and New Opportunities Fund, and the transfer of residual activities and assets from the Millennium Commission.

BIG is the largest of the Lottery distributors and is responsible for giving out 50% of the money for good causes raised from the Lottery, which provides a budget of about £630 million a year. Funding covers health, education, environment and charitable purposes.

Since its launch it has distributed over £2.8 billion to thousands of projects across the UK.

BIG is also the largest single funder of the voluntary and community sector (VCS) and awards of more than £1.6 billion have been made to the sector since its launch. This represents 77% of the total grant awards made.

Its mission is to be 'committed to bringing real improvements to communities and the lives of people most in need'. To do this, it has identified seven values. They are:

- fairness
- accessibility
- strategic focus
- involving people
- innovation
- enabling
- additional to government.

The Act of 2006 also includes powers for BIG to distribute non-Lottery funding and to make loans. Much of BIG's funding is given in grants made directly to successful applicants, particularly those in the voluntary sector. However, for some programmes such as Children's Play in England, funds are awarded to local authorities that have the responsibility for developing children's play strategies in their areas. There is a requirement that proper partnership arrangements are in place with voluntary and community organisations to deliver the outcomes set. BIG can also make funding available through its 'award partners' – expert intermediaries who act on BIG's behalf. The Changing Spaces programme in England (see page 200) is one example.

In response to complaints about the short-term nature of its funding, a number of BIG's programmes now provide funding for up to five years. Projects are required to provide a realistic exit strategy that plans out how the project will continue after the funding from BIG has finished. One effect of this is that requests for larger amounts and for longer periods are made, which, over time, might lead to BIG funding fewer projects.

Current BIG programmes in England

Changing Spaces

The Changing Spaces programme will invest around £200 million in environmental projects in England, including schemes to improve green spaces, grow local food and help community groups to reduce the amount of energy they use.

BIG is working with five organisations that have the skills and experience to run an effective environmental programme on its behalf. Each organisation is running an England-wide, open grants programme.

Changing Spaces: Community Sustainable Energy Programme

Summary

The Community Sustainable Energy Programme (CSEP), run by the Building Research Establishment (BRE), opened in April 2008. The programme will help community-based organisations in England reduce their environmental impact through the installation of energy saving measures and microgeneration technologies (producing heat or electricity on a small scale from a low carbon source). The scheme will also fund development studies that help community organisations to find out if a microgeneration and energy efficiency project will work for them.

Grants available

This programme will award grants of between £5,000 to £50,000 and will provide £10 million to community-based organisations for the installation of microgeneration technologies.

The grants are broken up as follows:

- Capital grants – projects can apply for up to £50,000 or 50% of the project cost (whichever is lower).
- Project development grants – maximum grant available is £5,000 or 75% of the study cost (whichever is lower).

Deadlines

Capital grant funding rounds:

Funding round	Application deadline (5pm)	Selection panel meeting
1	**Friday 16 May 2008**	w/c 23 June 2008
2	**Friday 15 August 2008**	w/c 22 September 2008
3	**Friday 7 November 2008**	w/c 8 December 2008
4	**Friday 30 January 2009**	w/c 11 March 2009
5	**Friday 1 May 2009**	w/c 10 June 2009
6	**Friday 7 August 2009**	w/c 16 September 2009
7	**Friday 30 October 2009**	w/c 9 December 2009
8	*Friday 29 January 2010*	*w/c 1 March 2010*
9	*Friday 7 May 2010*	*w/c 7 June 2010*
10	*Friday 30 July 2010*	*w/c 6 September 2010*
11	*Friday 29 October 2010*	*w/c 29 November 2010*

NB The dates shown in italics are to be confirmed. Please check the website www.communitysustainable.org.uk or email info@communitysustainable.org.uk for the most up-to-date information and where details of all aspects of the grant application process can be viewed.

Capital grants will be awarded on a competitive basis at quarterly selection panel meetings. Project development grants will be awarded on a first-come first-served basis until all funds are spent.

Eligibility

CSEP will only award grants to not-for-profit community-based organisations in England. This includes: community groups governed by a written constitution, registered charities and trusts, parish councils, schools and colleges, charitable companies with a community focus, mutual societies, church-based and other faith organisations.

Changing Spaces: Ecominds

Grants: £20,000 to £250,000. This programme is for groups that want to encourage people with experience of mental distress to get involved in environment projects.

Summary

Mind has received funds from BIG to run a £7.5million grant scheme as part of the Changing Spaces environmental initiative over five years. This programme is for a range of groups that want to encourage people with experience of mental distress to get involved in environmental projects, such as improving open spaces and wildlife habitats, designing public art and recycling.

Ecominds has been designed 'to help reduce the stigma surrounding mental distress and help create a society that treats people with experience of mental distress fairly, positively, and with respect'.

Grants available

The programme will award grants of up to £250,000. Four levels of grant are available:

- small – up to £20,000
- medium – from £20,001 up to £60,000
- large – from £60,001 up to £150,000
- flagship – from £150,001 up to £250,000 (approximately five grants will be awarded within this category). Note: The flagship grant closed in May 2009.

Deadlines

Ecominds is a rolling programme (it expects to have two funding rounds each year). All projects must be delivered by December 2012.

Eligibility

The following England-based groups may apply to Ecominds:

- mental health, environmental and community groups
- commercial organisations running projects on a not-for-profit basis, including community interest companies and social enterprise companies where project profits are reinvested solely into the Ecominds project.

Exclusions

This programme will not fund individuals, statutory authorities (although applications from organisations working collaboratively with them are welcomed), projects aligned with or co-funded by pharmaceutical companies and applicants and projects based outside England.

For more information on this programme and full details of the application process, please visit the Ecominds website: www.ecominds.org.uk. Please note there are two sets of guidance notes for this programme.

Changing Spaces: Local Food

Summary

Local Food, run by RSWT (Royal Society for Wildlife Trusts), opened in March 2008. It funds a range of organisations that want to carry out a variety of food related projects to make locally grown food more accessible and affordable to local communities.

Grants available

This programme will award grants of between £2,000 and £300,000.

Three types of grants are available (small, main and beacon), ranging from £2,000 to £500,000. NB Beacon grants closed for applications in June 2008:

small grants between £2,000 – £10,000

main grants between £10,001 – £300,000

beacon grants between £300,001 – £500,000.

Deadlines

Small and main grants are available on a rolling basis. All funded projects must be completed by March 2014.

Eligibility

Grants will be awarded to not-for-profit community groups and organisations in England, including schools, faith-based organisations, health bodies (such as primary care trusts) and universities.

See RSWT's website for more information and full details of the application process – www.localfoodgrants.org.

Changing Spaces: Community Spaces

Summary

Community Spaces is an open grants programme managed by Groundwork UK on behalf of an experienced national consortium.

The programme empowers community groups to improve public spaces in their neighbourhood. 'It responds directly to people's aspirations to have better places on their doorsteps – more interesting places for children to play, safer places for people of all ages to sit, greener spaces where people and nature can grow and flourish.'

The Community Spaces programme aims to:

- create better local environments
- increase people's access to quality local spaces for interaction, play and recreation
- increase the number of people actively involved in developing and running a practical environmental project that is visible in their community
- improve partnerships between communities, support organisations and local authorities.

Grants available

This programme will award grants of between £10,000 and £450,000. It will fund community groups that want to improve local green spaces such as play areas, community gardens and parks.

Small grants from £10,000 – £25,000 and medium grants from £25,001 – £49,999 are available until January 2011. Large grants from £50,000 – £100,000 and flagship grants from £100,001 – £450,000 are now closed.

Applications

Applications must show that projects will improve local neighbourhoods and environments. Types of projects can include, for example:

- community gardens and parks
- informal sports areas and multi-use games areas
- nature reserves
- squares and village greens
- churchyards
- ponds and projects which improve the local community's access to green space.

This list is not exhaustive and if you are thinking about a project that isn't listed here, it may still be considered, as long as it meets the eligibility criteria.

There will be some crossover with BIG's other funding streams. For example, projects looking at play areas, orchards, city farms and woodlands will be considered as long as they meet the general criteria of the programme, although there are other of BIG's Changing Spaces programmes that will fund these types of projects.

There are two stages to the application process and all community groups that are successful at stage 1 must agree to work with a facilitator – a trained individual who is able to provide specialist advice and guidance to groups. Facilitators will be able to help groups develop their stage 2 application form and may be able to help successful groups develop and deliver their project.

Applications from youth groups for youth projects are welcomed as it is considered important for young people to be fully involved in projects and where possible be leading projects of direct benefit to them. However, the main applicant and alternative contact must both be aged 18 years or over.

For further information on the application process please visit the Community Spaces website – www.community-spaces.org.uk.

Eligibility

Community Spaces will provide funding for community groups across England that hope to create and improve their local environment. To be eligible to apply for funding groups must meet the following criteria:

- Applications must be from community groups – defined as 'people living in one particular area or groups of people focused on a neighbourhood who are considered as a unit because of their common interests, background, nationality or other circumstances'.
- Projects must be in England.
- Projects must meet the Community Spaces outcomes – see the project outcome/s document provided on www.community-spaces.org.uk. Consideration of your application will depend on your stated outcomes.
- Projects must be within a two mile radius of a residential area.
- Projects must be open to the public 'most of the time' – please see the 'Definitions' page on the community spaces website.

Community Spaces is a majority capital-funding programme designed to ensure that money is spent on making physical and lasting improvements to people's neighbourhoods. You will be expected to split your project costs into revenue and capital expenditure. Small and medium grants will need to ensure that any revenue expenditure does not exceed 25% and capital expenditure is at least 75%.

Deadlines

Community Spaces' small and medium grants will be open for applications until January 2011 and decisions will be made on regular basis throughout the programme's life.

Exclusions

Community Spaces will not fund:

- individuals
- sole traders
- local authorities
- parish or town councils
- schools
- health bodies
- profit-making organisations and other statutory bodies that have not been mentioned above.

Community groups will not be able to apply for funding for the following:

- costs incurred or monies spent on a project before being awarded a Community Spaces grant
- projects without reasonable physical access for the general public
- activities that promote religious or political beliefs
- the purchase, construction, refurbishment of or access to buildings
- the purchase of land
- formal sports pitches
- projects on school grounds
- the purchase of animals
- projects on commercial property
- vehicles for transporting goods or people
- projects based on statutory allotments
- anything that is the legal responsibility of other organisations
- road improvement projects.

Examples of funding

Group name – The GOAL Group (Greasby Outdoor Activity and Leisure)
Project name – Coronation Park Multi-use Games Area
Project – Playground
Grant awarded – £32,392

Group name – Fern Gore Residents Association
Project name – Fern Gore Community Wildlife Area
Project – Recreational activities
Grant awarded – £49,419

Changing Spaces: Access to Nature

Summary

Access to Nature, launched in April 2008, is run by Natural England on behalf of a consortium of major environmental organisations. It is a £25 million grants programme to encourage people from all backgrounds to understand, access and enjoy our natural environment.

It aims to encourage more people to enjoy the outdoors, particularly those who face social exclusion or those who currently have little or no contact with the natural environment. It funds projects in urban, rural and coastal communities across England.

The programme awards grants of between £50,000 and £500,000 to support projects that deliver one or more of the programme's main outcomes. In addition the programme will make a small number of larger grants of over £500,000 for projects that have a national significance or impact.

Grants available

This programme will award grants of between £50,000 and £715,000.

Applications

Before applying for funding for your project, you are advised to read the Access to Nature general guidance notes document to check that what you are planning to do fits the programme. These guidance notes give information on the types of project that will be considered for funding, the types of grants available and full details of the application and assessment processes. The guidance notes should be read in conjunction with the Regional Targeting Plans, which explain the priorities for each region; both can be found on Natural England's website.

All projects must meet outcome 5 (see page 209) and at least one other outcome. For more information on outcomes and these targets, refer to www.natural england.org.uk and enter 'outcomes' in the search field.

The application process is in two stages:

Stage 1 – Outline proposal form

All applicants should initially submit a stage one application form to provide basic information about their project and organisation and there is guidance on the website to help you with this. Receipt of your application form should be acknowledged within five working days. A regional adviser will then contact you within 20 working days to discuss your project in more detail. Applicants should go to the online system at www.naturalengland.org.uk and search for 'access to nature'.

Please note that section 4 (the 'Declaration Form') requires original signatures and will need to be posted in hard copy form. Photocopies, fax and email versions will not be accepted and assessment will not begin until the signed declaration has been received.

Stage 2 – Full application form

If your organisation is eligible to apply and your project is something that might be supported, the regional adviser will tell you how to submit a stage two application form. You should read carefully the stage two guidance notes, which can be found on the website and which explain how to complete the form. A grants officer will assess your application and it will then be considered by the project board (for grant applications up to £100,000) or by an independent grants panel (for grant applications over £100,000), who will decide whether to award you a grant.

Deadlines

Grants: June 2010. For up-to-date information on closing dates for the national and flagship projects see Natural England's website.

Eligibility

Access to Nature will only award grants to not-for-profit community-based organisations in England. This includes: community groups governed by a written constitution, registered charities and trusts, parish councils, schools and colleges, companies with a charitable purpose and community focus, mutual societies, church-based and other faith organisations.

Funding will focus on three main themes:

- community awareness and active participation
- education, learning and volunteering
- welcoming, well-managed and wildlife-rich places.

Within these themes, grants will be awarded to organisations which can demonstrate that their project will deliver one or more of Access to Nature's five main outcomes:

1) A greater number and diversity of people having improved opportunities to experience the natural environment.

2) More people having opportunities for learning about the natural environment and gaining new skills.

3) More people being able to enjoy the natural environment through investment in access to natural places and networks between sites.

4) Richer, more sustainably managed, natural places, meeting the needs of local communities.

5) An increase in communities' sense of ownership of local natural places, by establishing strong partnerships between communities, voluntary organisations, local authorities and others.

For more information on this programme, please visit the Access to Nature website: www.naturalengland.org.uk/leisure/grants-funding.

Contact for all Changing Spaces programmes

Call the Changing Spaces Advice Line helpline on 0845 3 671 671 (opening hours 8am to 7pm Monday to Friday) for further details of any of the Changing Spaces programmes.

Fair Share Trust

Some parts of the UK have missed out on Lottery funding in the past. The Fair Share Programme aims to help provide a better balance in funding.

Fair Share received £50 million of Lottery money, which was put into a trust – the first Lottery model of its kind. The funding is secure and any interest earned on the original sum covers the management costs, which means that the total £50 million will be spent as grants in the Fair Share Trust areas.

Since launching in 2003, the Fair Share Trust (the trust) has established itself in 81 neighbourhoods across the UK through the work of local delivery partners – 'local agents'. The programme in England runs until 2013.

The trust is entirely managed by Community Foundation Network (CFN), the UK's largest independent community charitable grantmaker, which has set up partnerships with its members – community foundations – and other local grant-making bodies to manage the programme locally. These local agents work with the trust communities to prioritise and agree spend, in line with the guidance for delivery.

Selected neighbourhoods in each area are receiving targeted support from these agents in order that local people have the opportunity to make decisions on where the funding goes.

The Fair Share Trust programme aims to:

- build capacity and sustainability – by involving local communities in decision making about Lottery funding
- build social capital – by building links within and between communities to promote trust and participation
- improve liveability – by improving the living environment for communities.

Each local agent set up a local advisory panel, involving people from the communities receiving the funding, to agree local priorities, drawn from neighbourhood assessment documents, based on local strategic partnership data highlighting local community needs and issues.

Once the local priorities were identified, the local agents and local panels began identifying potential funding recipients. Each local agent would vary in their approach of identifying projects for funding, tailoring the approach in line with local circumstances. The initial setting up phase has been completed, grants have been made and now the outcomes are being gathered through monitoring and results evaluated.

For more information on the Fair Share Trust, please visit the CFN website – www.communityfoundations.org.uk.

Reaching Communities: England

Grants: £10,000 to £500,000. This programme has been extended and will run until at least 2010.

Reaching Communities will fund projects that help people and communities, identified by those communities and who are most in need, particularly those people or groups that are hard to reach. Projects can be new or existing activities, or be the core work of your organisation.

This programme is designed to achieve changes in communities as a result of funding. For example:

- people having better chances in life, including being able to get better access to training and development to improve their life skills
- strong communities, with more active citizens, working together to tackle their problems

- improved rural and urban environments, which communities are better able to access and enjoy
- healthier and more active people and communities.

Eligibility

You can apply to Reaching Communities if you are:

- a registered charity
- a voluntary or community group
- a statutory body, (including schools)
- a charitable or not-for-profit company
- a social enterprise – a business that is chiefly run for social objectives, whose profits are reinvested in the business rather than going to shareholders and owners.

In the light of current economic circumstances BIG has relaxed the eligibility criteria for this programme. Please refer to the 'updated signposting guide' on BIG's website.

Applications

There have been high levels of interest in this programme and BIG states that it has had to turn down some very good projects. You should consider contacting BIG before embarking on work for this programme to discuss whether there is another programme to which your project might be better suited. This programme is under regular review to ensure it is meeting those communities most in need.

Contact

National helpline for advice on 0845 410 20 30.
Email – general.enquiries@biglotteryfund.org.uk.
Lottery Funding Helpline on 0845 275 00 00 or go to www.lotteryfunding.org.uk.

Research programme

The Big Lottery Fund is providing £20 million to fund social, medical or socio-medical research led by voluntary and community sector (VCS) organisations in England, Scotland, Wales and Northern Ireland.

The Research programme aims to influence local and national policy and practice by funding VCS organisations to produce and disseminate evidence-based knowledge. In the longer term the programme, through producing sound evidence, aims to help develop better services and support for beneficiaries.

Grants of between £10,000 and £500,000 are available for research projects lasting up to five years.

Applications

This programme has been heavily oversubscribed, with 450 applications to round two, compared with the 35–50 awards that BIG expects to make. As a result, BIG has employed an additional assessment phase (as well as eligibility and completeness checks) that will enable it to score and rank all applications and only progress those that have a realistic chance of success.

New guidance for applicants and application form help-notes are available. These will help applicants make sure you include all the necessary information in their application. Anyone who applied for a grant in round one should read the new programme guidance and refer to the new application form help-notes to make sure they are up to date with the eligibility requirements. Please refer to BIG's website for full details.

The People's Millions

In 2005 ITV teamed up with BIG to launch The People's Millions, allowing people across the UK to vote for projects in their community to win cash from the Lottery.

Since then a total of 229 awards and £13.6 million has been given out to projects around the UK – including skate parks, sensory play areas, woodlands regeneration and even audio sculptures.

BIG wants to fund projects that help communities to transform or enjoy their environment. That means buildings, amenities, public and green spaces and the natural environment.

Priority is also given to local environment projects that get more people involved in the local community and help people in the community who are most in need and are original and innovative.

Films are shown on ITV regional news programmes and viewers are asked to vote for the project they want to see be awarded a grant. If your group would like to be put forward as a beneficiary of this scheme you should visit BIG's website on www.biglotteryfund.org.uk.

The Secret Millionaire Fund

BIG has joined with Channel 4 to create the Secret Millionaire Fund website which will allow applicants to:

- nominate a community project they think would benefit from funding, or
- apply directly themselves.

Successful applicants to the Fund may then be selected for filming by Channel 4 and appear on the website or on the TV programme itself.

The partnership is based on one of Channel 4's most popular TV programmes – The Secret Millionaire – with 4.5 million viewers. Each week a millionaire leaves their luxury life behind, takes on a secret identity and for 10 days lives undercover in a deprived area of the UK. On their final day, the millionaires come clean and donate thousands of pounds to projects they feel will most benefit.

Eligibility

In order to be eligible for application applicants must:

- be a voluntary or community organisation, school, parish or town council, or a health body
- have a UK-based bank or building society account in the name of their organisation that requires at least two people to sign cheques or make a withdrawal.

Projects must achieve one of these four outcomes:

- people have better chances in life, with better access to training and development to improve their life skills.
- stronger communities with more active citizens, working together to tackle their problems
- improved rural and urban environments, which communities are better able to enjoy
- healthier and more active people and communities.

Applications

For further information on how to apply, visit http://secretmillionaire.channel4.com.

Current programmes for Northern Ireland only

Building Change Trust

In November 2008 BOG announced details of the Building Change Trust – a multi-million pound investment to help develop and shape the future of Northern Ireland's community and voluntary sector.

The Building Change Trust will invest £10 million over the next 10 years to help community groups and larger voluntary organisations adapt and develop new ways of working.

It will not make grants in a traditional way, but will look at what resources already exist in communities and identify ways to support communities to develop and change.

The following organisations are responsible for the delivery and operation of the Building Change Trust:

- The Community Foundation for NI
- Community Evaluation NI
- Rural Community Network
- Volunteer Development Agency
- Business in the Community NI

The Trust will identify detailed programmes that promote volunteering and develop the local community infrastructure and leadership skills in rural and urban communities. Part of the money will be invested to offer loans and advice to community and voluntary organisations.

The Community Foundation has responsibility for the day-to-day running of the Trust. For further information visit: www.buildingchangetrust.org.

Current programmes for Scotland only

2014 Communities

2014 Communities is focused on building a 'legacy of wellbeing before and beyond the Commonwealth Games [which are being held in Glasgow in 2014]'. This is a micro grant programme aimed at grassroots sports and community organisations. Through the programme BIG hopes to encourage more people to take part in sport or physical activity, increase the numbers of those volunteering in sport or physical activity, and bring communities together through sport and volunteering.

The programme offers local sports clubs, voluntary and community organisations, community councils and schools grants of £300 to £1,000 to support and stimulate grassroots involvement in sport and physical activity. In year one of the programme (November 2008/09), BIG has £500,000 to award in grants. The programme will continue up to the Glasgow Commonwealth Games in 2014, but the funding focus and delivery may change, based on learning leading up to 2014.

For this programme projects should achieve one or more of the following outcomes:

- more people take part in sport or physical activity
- more people volunteer in sport or physical activity
- more people and communities are brought together through taking part or volunteering in sport or physical activity.

Priorities

Groups such as women and girls, people with disabilities, people over 50 years of age or under 25 years of age and people from black and minority ethnic communities are more likely to receive funding. These priorities may change in the future and will be updated on the 2014 webpage.

Grants

Grants of between £300 to £1,000 will be offered, based on a process similar to the Awards for All model (see page 218). However, supporting documentation such as constitutions or governing documents and bank statements will only be requested once a conditional offer has been made. If the documents are satisfactory the grant will be paid directly into the organisation's bank account.

Eligibility

Grants may be offered to sports clubs, voluntary and community organisations, community councils and schools. Branches of a larger organisation may be eligible to apply, but BIG will ask the larger organisation for written support in the event of an offer. Independent branches may apply in their own right. Groups can only apply for one grant in a 12-month period; decisions will be made within 15 working days.

For further information on how to apply visit: www.biglotteryfund.org.uk/ 2014_guidance_notes.pdf

Investing in Ideas

Investing in Ideas can award grants of £500 to £10,000 to test and develop ideas that could eventually become fully-fledged projects. Investing in Ideas could pay for the preparation and planning that can turn a basic idea into a well-planned project including:

- market research
- feasibility studies

- business planning
- committee training
- exchange visits in the UK to see how other projects work
- community consultation
- professional advice
- technical reports and scheme design studies.

It is important that the idea has the potential to fit with one of four areas of investment:
- growing community assets
- dynamic inclusive communities
- life transitions
- supporting 21st century life.

For further information see the Investing in Communities section of BIG's website.

Current programmes for Wales only

Life Skills Project

The Life Skills project has approximately £14 million available to deliver services throughout Wales that will support targeted groups of economically inactive people (see below) to engage or re-engage with education, learning, volunteering and employment.

The target groups are:
- care leavers
- carers and former carers returning to work
- economically inactive families.

This is the first time that National Lottery money has been matched with European Social Fund (ESF) at source. The ESF funding is being distributed via the Welsh European Funding Office.

The aims of the Life Skills project are to:

- enable participants from the target groups to develop their life skills, increase their confidence and re-engage with, and continue to access, education, learning, volunteering or employment
- develop individual long-term support plans to enable beneficiaries to continue to access and remain in education, learning or employment opportunities, in collaboration with other agencies.

Note: The Life Skills project is not a grant-making programme. The project will follow a strict competitive tender process (the Restricted Procedure Process) in accordance with EU Directives and UK Regulations. For detailed information, including Q&A, visit: www.biglotteryfund.org.uk/prog_life_skills_project.

The pre-information notice and the bidder information pack are available from www.sell2wales.co.uk/notices. Type 'life skills project for Wales' in the search field.

Queries relating to the Life Skills project should be logged via www.biglottery fund.bravosolution.co.uk.

People and Places

This programme will fund capital and revenue projects that encourage coordinated action by people who want to make their communities better places to live. It will support local and regional projects throughout Wales that focus on:

- revitalising communities
- improving community relationships, or
- enhancing local environments, community services and buildings

The main aim is to bring people together to create significant improvements to communities and the lives of people most in need. Projects should be community led: helping people to develop the skills and confidence to become more involved in their community is an integral aspect to this programme.

BIG will encourage organisations to work together, and will accept applications from organisations based anywhere in the UK. However, projects must mainly benefit people in Wales. Organisations not currently working in Wales should be able to demonstrate that they are aware of social and policy issues relevant to the local area and the project.

Eligibility

Grants will only be awarded to voluntary, community or public sector organisations either working separately or together.

The recession

In recognition of the effects the recession has had on communities in Wales, an extra £2 million has been set aside to be allocated in two rounds during the financial years ending 31 March 2010 and 31 March 2011. You can apply for this through the existing People and Places programme for a limited period.

For further details visit:

www.biglotteryfund.org.uk/prog_people_places

Awards for All

Awards for All, England

Awards for All, England offers grants of between £300 and £10,000 for projects that improve communities, and the lives of people within them. It is for voluntary and community groups, schools and health organisations, parish and town councils.

Awards for All, Northern Ireland

Awards for All, Northern Ireland is delivered and funded by the Big Lottery Fund in Northern Ireland and awards funds of between £500 and £10,000 over 12 months.

Awards for All, Wales

Awards for All, Wales is a simple small grants scheme making awards of between £500 and £5,000. The programme aims to help improve local communities and the lives of people most in need.

Awards for All, Scotland

Awards for All, Scotland puts lottery money back into local communities by giving grants of between £500 and £10,000. It funds projects that improve opportunities for people to take part in arts, sport and community activities and can fund a wide range of organisations.

Community Assets

The Community Assets programme is not funded by the Lottery, the funding is provided by the Office of the Third Sector. However, the programme is delivered by BIG, because it was considered to have the necessary expertise. The aim of the programme is community empowerment. It offers capital grants for third sector organisations and local authorities to refurbish local authority buildings in England for third sector ownership.

Community Assets aims to empower communities by facilitating the transfer of genuine assets from local authorities to third sector ownership for the benefit of the community. Genuine assets will generate operational, financial and other benefits for third sector organisations without significant liabilities, over a long-term period.

myplace

The Big Lottery Fund is delivering myplace on behalf of the Department for Children, Schools and Families (DCSF). This is not Lottery funding.

myplace aims to deliver world class youth facilities driven by the active participation of young people and their views and needs. So far, the programme has funded 62 projects across England worth £240 million. myplace offers a significant opportunity to those with the vision, ambition and drive to deliver world class places for young people to go. It will reward those who:

- are developing plans for ambitious, world class places that will offer young people the widest possible range of high quality activities and co-located support services
- are putting young people in the lead to plan and deliver dedicated youth projects driven by their views and needs
- are working in partnership across sectors to develop robust, financially sustainable co-funded projects that respond to local needs and priorities
- require between £1 million and £5 million of capital investment to deliver an outstanding building project.

For more information on myplace, please visit: www.biglotteryfund.org.uk/prog_myplace

Arts Council England

Arts Council England is the national development agency for the arts, supporting a range of artistic activities including theatre, music, dance, literature, photography, digital art and crafts.

'Grants for the arts are for individuals, arts organisations and other people who use the arts in their work. They are for activities carried out over a set period and which engage people in England in arts activities, and help artists and arts organisations in England carry out their work.' Grants for the arts are funded by the Lottery.

Between 2008 and 2011 Arts Council England will invest in excess of £1.6 billion of public money from the government and the Lottery.

The Council has recently simplified its application form and improved its guidance on how to apply. For more details on the plan for 2008–11 and the Council's priorities for the future visit: www.artscouncil.org.uk/plan. An enquiries team is available on 0845 300 6200.

NESTA

'NESTA is the National Endowment for Science, Technology and the Arts – a unique body with a mission to make the UK more innovative.' It invests in early-stage companies, informs and shapes policy, and delivers practical programmes 'that inspire others to solve the big challenges of the future'. For more details visit NESTA's website – www.nesta.org.uk.

Olympic Lottery Distributor

The Olympic Lottery Distributor is an independent body set up by Parliament, its remit is to support the delivery of the London 2012 Olympic and Paralympic Games and their legacy.

> *When making grants, we will seek to ensure that the principles of a lasting legacy, environmental and social sustainability, as set out in the bid which won the Games for London, are put into practice. We are part of a family of organisations concerned with the funding of the Games and to date have grant funded the Olympic Delivery Authority (ODA) and the London Organising Committee of the Olympic Games and Paralympic Games (LOCOG). We will monitor grants to ensure that they are spent effectively and will work with our partners towards a successful London 2012.*

The Olympic Lottery Distributor is not currently running any open funding rounds.

Sport England

Sport England is the government agency responsible for 'developing a world-class community sport system and creates opportunities for people of all ages and abilities to play sport in the community'. In June 2008 a new strategy was launched to help community sport make the most of the opportunities presented by the London 2012 Olympic and Paralympic Games.

Sport England has published the following targets to be achieved by 2013.

- One million people taking part in more sport.
- More children and young people taking part in sport for five hours every week.
- More people satisfied with their sporting experience.
- Twenty-five per cent fewer 16 to 18 year olds dropping out of five sports.
- Improved talent development in 25 sports.

Sport England invests in projects that help people to start, stay and succeed in sport and physical activity at every level. For further information on Sport England and its application processes, visit the website – www.sportengland.org.

UK Film Council

The UK Film Council works with the film industry and government, awarding funds from the Lottery and making policy on issues surrounding film; it aims to stimulate a competitive, successful and vibrant UK film industry and culture, both now and for the future.

Every year the Council distributes around £27 million from the Lottery and the same amount from government to support: script development, film production, short films, film distribution and export, cinemas, film education, culture and archives, festivals, audience support schemes, skills training and national and regional film agencies.

Over 1,600 funding applications per year have been received for Lottery funding since 2000, 80% of which have been unsuccessful. The Council has a target time of 40 days where final approval or rejection is made.

Funding priorities for the three-year plan of 2007–10 have been set and you can find information on these at the Council's website, where related policy and strategy papers are also available – www.ukfilmcouncil.org.uk.

UK Sport

Established by Royal Charter in 1996, UK Sport works in partnership with the home country sports councils and other agencies to 'lead sport in the UK to world-class success'. UK Sport is responsible for managing and distributing public investment and is a statutory distributor of funds raised by the Lottery.

Through its World Class Events Programme, UK Sport distributes approximately £3.3 million of Lottery funding each year to support the bidding and staging costs of major events on home soil, as well as providing specialist support to organisers. For more information visit: www.uksport.gov.uk.

Big Thinking – strategic framework to 2015

The Big Thinking consultation process for funding in 2009 -2015 was the largest consultation ever carried out by a lottery distributor. The process, feedback and evaluation– *What you told us* – was published in June 2009, with BIG's *Strategic Framework to 2015*.

BIG wants its funding to be flexible, responsive and more personalised for applicants. It promises to 'minimise unnecessary effort on behalf of applicants, making decisions as early as possible and communicating them clearly.' We will have to wait and see whether these promises translate to the grant applicant.

From distributor to intelligent funder

The framework will underpin all of BIG's funding programmes to 2015 and 'charts the journey' from where BIG is today to where it would like to be in 2015. BIG's aim is to become a more effective and efficient funder – an intelligent funder – securing greater impact and influence from its work. It describes an intelligent funder as one that:

- offers support (apart from financial) to the organisations it funds
- works with other funders to develop and share leading practice
- promotes the analysis of the impact of its funding to policymakers.

This means being more than just a distributor of money – it means engaging and supporting organisations that apply for funding, building and using evidence of need to inform the development of programmes, sharing this evidence more widely, and learning, developing and sharing good grant-making practice with other funders.

Outcomes

The framework confirms the proposal in the consultation that, to contribute most effectively to successful outcomes, BIG's funding is best placed in three areas:

- reducing isolation
- helping people through certain key transitions (for example leaving care, redundancy)
- assisting more people in communities to feel empowered.

These areas will characterise all of BIG's funding for the next six years.

The framework provides the reasoning behind these hoped-for outcomes and in a general way how they might be achieved. However, it is not clear from the framework document how these areas will be applied to the development of future funding programmes. BIG states that it wants 'to continue discussing our priorities and our direction of travel with you', and hopefully this is what will inform the next set of programmes.

Risk takers

The framework states that 'BIG will be unashamedly assertive in taking risks to address unpopular or challenging issues that have been neglected by other funders, where this fits with our mission'. This will not be easy to achieve as BIG also states that it wants its funding to be 'supported and inspired by the communities we are looking to help' and that public involvement in the Lottery's work is positive and will be expanded. It might be difficult to meet both ideals when the public is often against supporting unpopular issues. However, on the bright side, there was significant support in the consultation feedback for 'local decision-making panels' and little support for armchair voting on TV. Much will depend on how these proposals are developed.

Additionality and the commitment to fund the voluntary sector

The framework offers a renewed commitment to additionality: BIG will 'complement and add value to others' work at a local level, not duplicate or replace it'. This will need to be monitored against practice, as the pressure on public finances and more outsourcing of public services will create even less distinct boundaries between what is 'additional' and what is not.

The framework states that the voluntary and community sector is BIG's 'major partner' and that it will receive at least 80% of its funding. This is an improvement on the previous percentage, even if it will mean less funding in total, because of the contribution to the Olympics. However, given that the remaining 20% will predominantly be provided through partnerships involving voluntary sector organisations, (where the local authority facilitates bids with local groups, for example) this is encouraging.

Partnerships

BIG 'will not force partnerships' but will 'encourage links between organisations working to deliver the same ends'. If BIG can use its position to act as a helpful 'broker' between groups this has the potential to be a positive measure.

Types of funding

The framework states that BIG will deliver a 'mixed portfolio of funding' but that grants will continue to be its main business. It will not deliver loans directly but may explore doing this with partners if 'stakeholders' support it.

In line with its intelligent funder concept BIG is currently focused on delivering existing programmes in a way that responds to the needs of the sector and communities during the recession. The open programmes Reaching Communities and Awards for All are continuing, with Reaching Communities receiving an extra £20 million.

BIG also has also found an extra £43 million, to be invested throughout the UK, which will go towards a recession-related programme, which has yet to be launched. For further information please visit: www.biglotteryfund.org.uk.

Future programmes are still being developed; the new funding portfolio will begin in 2010.

Next steps: UK, England, Northern Ireland, Scotland and Wales

BIG has confirmed that the International programme, which funds UK-based organisations working overseas, will continue. At the time of writing this had been subject to recent consultation and details were due to be announced 'in due course'. Other UK-wide programmes will be considered by BIG's UK Board in the coming months and will be rolled out from 2010.

England

During 2009/10, the open programmes Reaching Communities and Awards For All will continue. BIG also plans to announce smaller scale initiatives during the year, including some aimed at helping communities cope with the effects of the recession.

BIG will continue to develop open, community and targeted funding programmes for the period up to 2015. This will be done by working with partners at national level and through BIG's regional offices.

BIG's new funding portfolio will be launched in 2010.

Northern Ireland

BIG will consult further with stakeholders during autumn 2009, as the next round of programmes is developed. Plans for the first phase of funding programmes for 2009–2015 will be published in early 2010. In the current financial year (2009/10) BIG has promised to commit funding to a number of projects with aims that reflect the current socio-economic climate. BIG Awards for All and the Big Deal programmes are open for applications.

Scotland

BIG will build on Investing in Communities, hoping to improve and refocus it where necessary to take account of the needs and priorities of Scottish communities. This will be done in dialogue with stakeholders and customers, reflecting the policy directions of Scottish ministers. The aim is to open for applications by June 2010.

In the meantime, funding is available through Awards for All, which provides funding of up to £10,000 for a wide range of community and voluntary activity. Investing in Ideas, the ideas development fund, will continue to support the exploration and testing of new ideas, with grants of up to £10,000.

The 2014 Communities programme (see page 214) will continue to offer grants of up to £1,000 for grassroots projects that promote physical activity or sports-related volunteering in local communities in the run up to the 2014 Commonwealth Games.

Wales

Working within the overall UK Strategic Framework, BIG will:

- embark on a new portfolio with a Community Asset Transfer programme later in 2009, which will be launched in partnership with the Welsh Assembly Government
- follow this with a programme aimed at reducing poverty and isolation amongst older people
- launch programmes to promote the citizen's voice and reduce the impact of climate change.

A new demand-led programme will be launched in 2010, responding to the needs of Welsh communities. Whilst very similar to the current People and Places programme (see page 217), BIG will gather intelligence on the projects and areas funded and work closely with stakeholders to ensure that the programme is promoted successfully to those most in need.

Working with stakeholders, experts and policymakers, an Innovation Fund will be set up to support social innovation that will complement the support provided at a UK level and specifically address the Welsh social and cultural context. BIG will continue to welcome applications for funding while developing new programmes, through the small grants scheme, Awards for All (see page 218), with grants of up to £5,000, and the People and Places programme for larger grants for projects that support a wide range of coordinated action by people to make their communities better places in which to live.

In conclusion

The National Lottery's distributors are well known for their complex and rigorous assessment processes and this can sometimes deter groups from applying for funding from them. The process is long and time consuming for applicants and often dreams for a good, innovative new project for the members of their group (and sometimes people's jobs), are pinned on a 'You have been successful' letter. Rejection can be worse than disappointing, it can alter a group's ability to deliver and some may even fold.

While researching this guide, we have been in contact with staff at BIG, the main distributor, through their helpline and it has been encouraging that they have been more than happy to advise on all questions raised about funding and have gone out of their way to be helpful. This was not the case some years ago when staff were actually prohibited from giving all but the briefest guidance.

BIG and the other distributors do want to award the monies that are available, it's their job to get the money out into our communities. However, they are, rightly, subject to public and governmental scrutiny over what they fund and need to ensure that their policies and procedures are transparent and open and that the money they are responsible for goes to sound organisations with a worthwhile and practicable project to deliver.

There is a lot of information available through the Lottery distributors' individual websites and help and advice lines. You should make good use of these resources before you embark on the long road of collecting information and evidence for your bid.

Be imaginative and creative, do your research and collect your evidence, be selective in who you approach and make your project stand out from the rest.

10 The Landfill Communities Fund

Background

Landfill is a method for the final disposal of solid waste on land and a disposal option for wastes that can't be recycled, composted or used to generate energy. The refuse is spread and compacted and a cover of soil applied so that effects on the environment (including public health and safety) are minimised.

An industrial landfill disposes of non-hazardous industrial wastes. A municipal landfill disposes of domestic waste including refuse, and this waste may contain toxins that are used in the home, such as cleaning materials, pesticides, engine oil, paints, solvents and weed killers.

In 1996 the landfill tax was introduced on waste disposal in landfill sites in the UK. The aim of the tax is to encourage the industry to reduce waste and its associated problems, recover some value from the waste and promote a shift to more environmentally sustainable methods of waste management. The initiative enables the landfill operators to pay a proportion of their landfill tax liability to not-for-profit environmental and community organisations close to landfill sites.

The landfill tax regulations came fully into force in October 1996. They apply to England, Scotland, Wales and Northern Ireland and outline various administrative procedures relating to the operation of the landfill tax. Specifically, they deal with the registration of those organisations that intend to make disposals covered by the tax, and the payment of the tax.

All distributors of landfill communities funding are regulated by the organisation ENTRUST, on behalf of HM Revenue & Customs (HMRC).

227

Landfill sites

Landfill sites are where local authorities and industry can take waste to be compacted and buried. They are licensed, regulated and monitored by the Environment Agency.

Landfills are classified according to whether they can accept hazardous, non-hazardous or inert wastes, and wastes can only be accepted at a landfill if they meet the acceptance criteria for that class of landfill. Most wastes must first be treated: there are formal processes for identifying and checking wastes before they are accepted at a landfill site.

Certain kinds of waste cannot be disposed of at landfill sites, for example, waste which, in a landfill, would be explosive, corrosive, oxidising, flammable or highly flammable, or hospital and other clinical wastes, from medical or veterinary establishments, which are infectious.

'Historic landfill sites' are locations were there are records of waste being received to be buried but are now closed or covered.

Landfill operators

Landfill operators (LOs) are the organisations that run landfill sites. They may be private companies, local authority-owned companies, local authorities or sole traders. LOs pay a tax for every tonne of waste they dispose of via landfill. This tax is designed to reduce the amount of waste that is sent to landfill each year. A proportion of the tax that LOs pay can be allocated to the Landfill Communities Fund.

LOs can contribute up to 6% of their landfill tax liability to environmental bodies and reclaim 90% of this contribution as a tax credit. They may bear the remaining 10% themselves, or an independent third party can make up the difference. (See 'contributing third parties' later in this chapter.)

Environmental bodies

Environmental bodies (EBs) are organisations that have registered with ENTRUST in order to receive landfill tax money from LOs or other EBs. They don't have to be charities but must be not-for-profit organisations, where any surplus they make is used to further their organisation's objects. Surpluses must not be used to pay dividends or other rewards and EBs must not be controlled, directly or indirectly, by a local authority or an LO registered to pay landfill tax.

For further information on how to enrol with ENTRUST as an EB, see www.entrust.org.uk.

ENTRUST

Distributors of landfill communities funding are regulated by ENTRUST on behalf of HMRC. ENTRUST has the mandate to approve and enrol EBs, after which they are eligible to apply for funding. It does not allocate or have influence over the distribution of landfill tax monies.

EBs must ensure that landfill tax credit monies are spent in accordance with the landfill tax regulations and audit and verify the compliance of this activity. EBs' management and control of funds ensures that landfill tax monies are applied and spent in accordance with the regulations. ENTRUST's role is to provide guidance and regulate these bodies.

The Landfill Communities Fund

The Landfill Communities Fund (LCF) is a government scheme that provides funding for community or environmental projects in the vicinity of landfill sites. The LCF encourages landfill operators and environmental bodies to work in partnership to create environmental benefits and jobs, promote sustainable waste management, and undertake projects that improve the lives of communities living near landfill sites.

The following information is taken from ENTRUST'S website at: www.entrust. org.uk/home/facts-and-figures and www.entrust.org.uk/home/lcf/objectives.

Number of enrolled bodies with ENTRUST 2,727
Number of enrolled bodies that have received landfill tax funding 2,528

Since the start of the scheme in 1996:
Donations (contributions from landfill operators to EBs) £1,028,058,391
Total spend since 1996 by EBs on admin and projects £937,282,924
Total spend since 1996 by EBs on projects £804,669,063

Areas of work

To qualify for funding, the objective of an organisation's work must be physical works at an identified site within approximately 10 miles of a landfill site. ENTRUST assesses the proposals before work takes place.

The following objects describe areas of work that can be undertaken:

A – The remediation or restoration of land which cannot now be used because of a ceased activity that used to take place there.

B – The reduction, prevention or mitigation of effects of pollution that has resulted, or may result, from an activity which has now ceased.

C and CC – no longer used.

D – The provision, maintenance or improvement of a public park or other general public amenity.

DA – The conservation of a specific species or a specific habitat where it naturally occurs.

E – The repair, maintenance or restoration of a place of worship or a place of architectural importance.

F – The provision of financial, administrative or other similar services by one organisation enrolled with ENTRUST to another.

Object A
The remediation or restoration of land which cannot now be used because of a ceased activity that used to take place there.

The work must be on a single site something once took place that now stops it being used, e.g. the site may have been contaminated in some way. The principle is that the person who polluted the land must now not own or operate from the land. Any orders that the current landowner is under from the relevant environmental agency must not be fulfilled by using LCF funding.

You will be asked to demonstrate:

- the ceased activity
- who carried it out
- when it stopped
- that the person who polluted the land will not benefit (financially or through obligations being met)
- how the ceased activity caused or is causing pollution.

Object B
The reduction, prevention or mitigation of effects of pollution that has resulted, or may result, from an activity which has now ceased.

You must be able to demonstrate that the pollution identified in the works you propose is directly linked to helping mitigate, prevent or reduce pollution.

You will be asked to demonstrate the same criteria as for Object A.

Objects C and CC – removed on 1 April 2003.

Object D

The provision, maintenance or improvement of a public park or other general public amenity.

The primary intent of this objective must be for the general public's benefit for leisure or recreation. The site where the work takes place must be open and accessible to the general public. The intention must not be to generate profit and the site where the work will take place must be within 10 miles of a landfill site.

You will be asked to demonstrate that:

- the amenity will directly benefit the general public and that they will have open access to, or use of, the amenity
- it is somewhere where the general public can go, join or use without any limit or restrictive use (through cost or rights of access) being in place
- the amenity is within 10 miles of a landfill site
- the intent of the project is not to derive income
- the site is a single location
- the costs of the project relate to the actual physical improvement, maintenance or provision of the identified amenity, rather than its management or administration.

Object DA

The conservation of a specific species or a specific habitat where it naturally occurs.

The primary intent of this objective must be for the conservation of identified species or habitats. The costs of the work you undertake must be directly related to the identified species or habitat and the place where it naturally occurs.

You will be asked to demonstrate:

- the identified species or habitats that will be conserved by the project
- that all the costs of the works relate to the conservation of the identified species or habitats
- that the costs of the works you propose relate solely to the place where the species or habitat naturally occurs.

[The LCF advises that the species or habitat in question is listed in a biodiversity action plan – a strategy prepared for an area aimed at conserving and enhancing biological diversity – and that you involve the designated lead partner in the project.]

Object E

The repair, maintenance or restoration of a place of worship or a place of architectural importance.

The primary intent of this objective is to maintain, repair or restore a place of worship, or a building or structure that must have listed status or equivalent where the general public can access the building. This objective does not allow works to private residences.

You will be asked to demonstrate that:

- the building or structure is open and accessible to the general public
- the works you propose are to repair, restore or maintain the building or structure
- all the costs of the works relate to the actual building or structure.

Object F

The provision of financial, administrative or other similar services by one organisation enrolled with ENTRUST to another.

This objective allows one enrolled EB to provide certain services to another EB. It may not provide them to an organisation that is not enrolled with ENTRUST. These services may include core administrative or similar services to assist in the running of the other EB.

You will be asked to demonstrate that:

- your EB is going to provide a service to another EB, or you are going to pay a contractor to provide a service to another EB
- you are not simply transferring money to another EB to cover its administration costs.

How to apply

There are two ways of receiving funding from the LCF:

- from an organisation that distributes the monies on behalf of a landfill operator. These are commonly known as distributive environmental bodies (DEBs)
- directly from an LO.

You are far more likely to receive money via a DEB than you are directly from an LO.

Distributive environmental body funders

This is likely to be the most successful route to funding. These grant-making bodies are responsible for most of the money that landfill operators give and they distribute funds on their behalf.

DEBs must make sure your expenditure complies with the landfill tax regulations and ENTRUST guidelines. Your organisation will therefore need to meet certain conditions about the way it spends any landfill tax money. There is a high level of demand for funding and a DEB is likely to set strict criteria. Each has its own application form and guidelines.

If you decide to apply for funding through a DEB you might first need to enrol with ENTRUST. You should check the particular DEB's criteria and see if it is willing to fund your work before you contact ENTRUST. For a list of DEBs, see www.entrust.org.uk/home/lcf/funders-directory.

Landfill operators as direct funders

This is a less likely source of funding, although you might be able to find LOs that will give landfill tax money directly to your organisation. LOs have to be registered with HMRC to participate. A list of LOs is available to download from HMRC's website at customs.hmrc.gov.uk.

If you plan to apply directly to an LO, you will need to enrol your organisation as an environmental body with ENTRUST.

In Scotland, you should request details from the Scottish Environment Protection Agency (SEPA), see www.sepa.org.uk. See information on SEPA later in this chapter.

Contributing third parties

LOs do not get 100% tax relief for the amount they give to the scheme, some may require you to find an independent contributing third party (CTP), which will reimburse the LOs up to 10% of the award to cover this cost. The amount you might have to find from a third party contributor will depend on your funding route.

If you apply for money from distributive environmental bodies (DEBs)

The DEBs will explain how much you need to find from a third party. The third party's reimbursement should, ideally, be paid directly to the LOs who gave the landfill tax money to the DEBs.

If you apply for money from LOs

You might have to find a third party to reimburse up to 10% of the sum the LOs provide. For example, if you apply to LOs for £10,000, you might need to find someone to reimburse the LOs up to £1,000.

Multiple CTPs

There can be more than one CTP that makes up the 10% you will need to find. CTPs are very diverse and include major plcs, local authorities, groups, clubs, statutory bodies and individuals. They can come from the private, public or voluntary sector and some are charities.

Who cannot be a CTP?

A CTP must not:

- gain a unique benefit from the project going ahead
- be made up from LCF monies.

For further details on these points, please consult section 7 of the Benefit Rules from the EB Guidance Manual at: www.entrust.org.uk/home/guidance-library/guidance.

Open information about CTPs

ENTRUST needs to know the identity of CTPs so that it can regulate the scheme effectively. EBs must tell their LOs the name and address of the CTP that will be making a payment, and the sum to expect. LOs have been separately instructed to record information about contributing third parties and submit it to ENTRUST.

Sometimes LOs will find a contributing third party and, in those circumstances, the LOs must pass on the name and address to the EBs being supported when money is passed to the EBs.

LCF monies cannot be used as the CTP amount. Any monies provided for the CTP payment must be proven as sourced from other monies, and accounted for separately. It is ENTRUST guidance that any organisation holds LCF funds in a separate bank account from other monies.

Northern Ireland Environment Agency

The Northern Ireland Environment Agency (NIEA) takes the lead in advising on, and implementing, the government's environmental policy and strategy in Northern Ireland. Activities are undertaken which promote the government's key themes of sustainable development, biodiversity and climate change.

Its overall aims are to:

- protect and conserve Northern Ireland's natural heritage and built environment
- control pollution
- promote the wider appreciation of the environment and best environmental practices.

Waste management

The Land and Resource Management Unit (LRM) is responsible for implementing waste management legislation and policy and promoting a more sustainable approach to dealing with waste in Northern Ireland, in order to make a major contribution to safeguarding the environment and promoting resource efficiency and economic growth.

For further information see NIEA's website: www.ni-environment.gov.uk/waste-home.htm.

Scottish Environment Protection Agency

The Scottish Environment Protection Agency (SEPA) is Scotland's environmental regulator. Its main role is to protect and improve the environment.

SEPA is a non-departmental public body, accountable through Scottish ministers to the Scottish Parliament. It advises Scottish ministers, regulated businesses, industry and the public on environmental best practice.

Specialist areas include chemistry, ecology, environmental regulation, hydrology, engineering, quality control, planning, communications, business support and management functions.

SEPA monitors and informs on Scotland's environment, publishes a wide range of publications and environmental reports, is responsible for delivering Scotland's flood warning system and helping to implement its national waste strategy and, with the Health and Safety Executive controlling, the risk of major accidents at industrial sites.

Waste management

SEPA has a statutory duty to protect the environment and human health from the effects of waste management and disposal and it has the authority to enforce European compliance schemes. It also supports the Scottish government and other organisations delivering the 'national waste plan'. For further information on this strategic plan, visit http://www.scotland.gov.uk/Resource/Doc/47133/0009763.pdf.

> *The amount of waste going to landfill in Scotland has more than halved its 16 million tonne figure since 1994. A total of 7.23 million tonnes of controlled waste went to landfill in Scotland in 2006. However, the risk of increased greenhouse emissions means that further reductions still need to be made. Fly tipping is also a big problem in Scotland, with over 40,921 incidents reported in 2006–07 alone.*

> *Preventing and minimising waste are the most effective ways of easing its negative effects. However, waste can also be put to good use through reuse, recycling, composting and thermal treatment – a process that uses heat to treat and recover energy from waste.*

For further information see SEPA's website: www.sepa.org.uk/waste.aspx.

Environment Agency Wales

The Environment Agency Wales is the public body responsible for protecting the environment in Wales: from flood risk management and agriculture, to conservation and industry regulation. The Minister for the Environment, Sustainability and Housing sets annual priorities.

Waste management

> *'Wise About Waste: The National Waste Strategy for Wales' promotes a number of actions to improve the management of waste in Wales.*

> *These include measures to increase the use of recycled and composted materials by businesses and the public sector in Wales, a public sector waste minimisation campaign and an education campaign to raise awareness and understanding across Wales of the need to manage waste in a more environmentally friendly manner. It also includes moves to establish a 'centre of excellence in waste research' amongst further and higher education institutions in Wales.*

The future target for local authority recycling and composting of municipal wastes is 40% combined recycling and composting by 2009/10 with a minimum of 15% each of recycling and composting.

For further information see wales.gov.uk/about/strategy/publications/environmentcountryside/2096132/

Case study

Fife Environment Trust

Fife Environment Trust distributes LCF contributions made by two landfill operators (Fife Council and Scottish Power) to community projects within Fife. Grants range from £500 to £30,000.

Before applying an organisation must enrol as an environmental body and register the project with ENTRUST.

Fife squirrel projects

Red squirrels are endangered nationally, and Fife is no exception. Competition from grey squirrels and the squirrel parapox virus are the main threats; fragmentation of suitable habitat is also significant. However, Fife still has a relatively healthy population of red squirrels.

The projects' aims included protecting the red squirrel through increased public awareness and education, surveying and monitoring and implementing a conservation strategy focused around Fife's core red squirrel populations.

The Trust's awards enabled Fife Coast and Countryside Trust to employ a strategic officer to deliver two red squirrel conservation projects: Ladybank Woods in East Fife and Devilla Forest in West Fife. A separate, successful application was made for each of the two sites; both qualified for LCF support under Object DA: 'The conservation of a specific species or a specific habitat where it naturally occurs'.

LCF funding – £56,600 for two projects provided through Fife Environment Trust

The projects' aims are to:

- conduct systematic squirrel population research
- implement grey squirrel control measures

continued...

- facilitate public understanding of red squirrels
- encourage public use of the woods.

Work at Ladybank is now completed and the next stage of work will be carried out at Devilla Forest. A 2km woodland trail has been constructed along existing tracks at Ladybank Woods and a system of ropes and squirrel bridges has been created to enable viewing. Interpretation panels, woodland sculptures, waymarkers and other communication and education materials have been installed. Links with local schools are being developed and there are regular organised educational visits, with information packs available.

Red squirrel population surveys at the site are contributing to wider studies of the species, its dispersal and interaction with grey squirrels. Community participation is at the core of the project and a volunteer training programme has been set up in partnership with the local agricultural college and community groups to help deliver the project. There is even a dedicated Fife Squirrel Project website: www.fiferedsquirrels.co.uk.

Case study

SITA Trust

SITA Trust currently allocates LCF funding through three main programmes. Enhancing Communities is aimed at community improvement projects, Greenprints provides conservation volunteering opportunities for young people, and Enriching Nature supports UK biodiversity conservation projects.

Enriching Nature is an England-wide programme; applications are welcomed for projects within 10 miles of any registered landfill in England. Projects should focus on a species or habitat that has been identified as a priority by the UK Biodiversity Action Planning process. SITA Trust can fund physical improvements as well as monitoring and research at specific sites.

To ensure the Trust supports the best projects, the regional fund managers visit all qualifying applicants to discuss their proposal. They then get technical advice from assessment panels, made up of biodiversity experts from some of the nation's most respected conservation organisations and authorities, before reporting to the Trust's board.

continued ...

Sparrows back to London

This three-year research project aims to establish the effectiveness of different methods of amenity landscape management for trying to save the much-loved house sparrow from its present dramatic population decline.

RSPB researchers successfully bid to SITA Trust's Enhancing Nature programme in 2008. The project qualified under Object DA: 'The conservation of a specific species or a specific habitat where it naturally occurs'.

The RSPB is now working in partnership with six London local authorities to establish whether long grass, wildflower meadows or arable flowers provide the best food source for these endangered birds.

The study is being conducted at 16 sites. First, a baseline survey of sparrow populations, current land management practice and food availability is carried out. This is followed by a trial, in close partnership with landowners, of different land management techniques. The results are tested against control sites. Parallel to this is a programme of education and outreach work to encourage people to support sparrows in their gardens.

LCF funding – £167,725 provided through SITA Trust's Enriching Nature programme

The project's aims are to:

- investigate the best land management techniques for providing food sources for sparrows
- educate people about supporting sparrows in their own gardens
- ultimately, help to halt the sparrow's recent population decline in the UK.

The trials are now in their early stages and will take three years to complete. While the primary aim is to help sparrows, the RSPB hopes that the new habitats that spring up across the capital's public spaces and gardens will be good news for all sorts of native wildlife.

Case study

Biffaward

Biffaward is a multi-million pound environment fund managed by the Royal Society of Wildlife Trusts (RSWT), which uses landfill tax credits donated by Biffa Waste Services.

Biffaward's main grants programme – community funding category, provides support of between £5,000 and £50,000 to projects that provide and improve community facilities. Applications are welcomed throughout the year. Applicants must first register their project with ENTRUST.

Tardebigge Community Hall Car Park, Worcestershire

The aim of this project was for the community to cooperate in improving access to its popular community hall and the surrounding countryside by creating a multi-purpose countryside access point, with parking near the new hall, road access and sympathetic lighting, landscaping and planting.

The rural setting and nearby Grade II listed church meant planning restrictions were quite stringent and included a requirement for grasscrete surfacing, which made the project more expensive. Fortunately the funding application was successful.

The project qualified for LCF support under Object D: 'The provision, maintenance or improvement of a public park or other general public amenity'.

LCF funding – £50,000 provided through Biffaward

The project's aims are to:

- improve access to a popular community amenity
- create a point of access to encourage use of the surrounding countryside
- involve local volunteers in the work
- ensure the project remains sympathetic to the rural setting.

The community hall was already well used, but the new car park, complete with a disabled access ramp, is much appreciated, especially by disabled visitors such members of the stroke club, which uses the premises. Other groups such as the Brownies have a lot of equipment, so a proper car park is very welcome. The car park should contribute much to the long-term viability of this popular facility as well as opening up access to the surrounding environment.

continued...

Aberlleiniog Castle, Anglesey

Aberlleiniog Castle is a Scheduled Ancient Monument in east Anglesey built around 1088. When Menter Môn Trust acquired the castle in 2003 it was in a state of advanced ruin and in danger of collapse. The LCF money helped towards the total project cost of £175,000 to preserve this significant example of Norman architecture. The specialist team of local archaeologists, heritage construction contractors and stonemasons numbered and photographed all the stones before dismantling and then gradually rebuilding entire sections of the walls and towers. The building project qualified for LCF support under Object D: 'The provision, maintenance or improvement of a public park or other general public amenity'.

A second, separately funded, project at the site created and improved public access to the woodland surrounding Aberlleiniog Castle using sustainably produced, locally sourced materials.

Woodland management schemes were planned and implemented and 6 hectares of native broadleaf woodland were created. This part of the project qualified for LCF support under Object DA: 'The conservation of a specific species or a specific habitat where it naturally occurs'.

Anglesey is presently one of the least wooded counties in Britain.

LCF funding – £32,421 towards building restoration and £9,080 towards managing and improving access to the surrounding woodland from Mentor Môn Trust

The project's aims are to:

- preserve a building of national historical importance
- improve access to the site and surrounding woodland using local resources
- open up the castle to visitors and groups of all ages.

Repair and restoration of the castle is now complete. A trial archaeological dig has uncovered interesting finds such as clay pipe stems, pottery and a coin from around 1700. The woodland access project has been a success, with new footpaths, timber bridges, boardwalks and waymarkers in use. New areas of woodland have been planted with the help of local schoolchildren.

The project has also created a community coordinator role to work with local people and encourage them to get involved as volunteers on the site. Many

continued ...

individuals and groups have visited the site and it has featured in the BBC Wales programme 'Secret Wales'.

The project also benefited from successful funding bids to the Heritage Lottery Fund Wales, and Cadw, the organisation responsible for preserving Wales' heritage environments. For further information see www.mentermon. com.

Case study

Staffordshire Environmental Fund

Staffordshire Environmental Fund provides funding throughout the county. It has over 10 years' experience of grantgiving and is accredited by ENTRUST.

The Fund registers all projects with ENTRUST on behalf of the grant applicants.

Central Forest Skate Park, Stoke-on-Trent

The area of land in the north of the county was the site of a former coalmine. Its redevelopment was a key part of the North Staffordshire 'Greening-for-Growth' regeneration scheme.

The skate park was designed and built to international standards to help attract skaters from all over the country in an area hit hard by the decline of the local primary industry. It was also intended to provide an outlet for local young people's energies and help keep them away from other potentially disruptive activities.

The project qualified for LCF support under Object D: 'The provision, maintenance or

improvement of a public park or other general public amenity'.

LCF funding – £50,000 provided through Staffordshire Environment Fund

The project's aims were to:

- reclaim a former industrial site
- provide a facility of international standard for local, national and international use

continued...

- improve the local environment by focusing skateboarders away from practising elsewhere
- form a key part of wider regeneration activity at the site.

The wonderful new facility was launched with fireworks, and skateboarding teams demonstrating their skills. The skate park, one of the largest in Europe, incorporates many of the features skaters look for in a normal urban environment, such as steps and handrails, and is proving extremely popular. It forms a major part of a wider new space in the centre of Stoke that includes pathways, green spaces with lighting, CCTV and nature trails. There are plans to make the area into a major outdoor activity centre to accommodate a variety of sports facilities as well as bike trails and additional footpaths and trees.

For further information see www.staffs-environmental.co.uk.

The case studies are adapted from ENTRUST's website. For further information see www.entrust.org.uk/home/lcf/project-case-studies.

11 **Winning company support**

Why apply to companies?

Although charitable giving by companies is not as significant as that of individuals, government or grant-making charities, it is still a funding source that should be considered both on local and national levels.

Before applying to companies you should understand why and how they give. Their support will be different from that of other funders. They are ultimately responsible to their shareholders and answer to them as to how they spend any surplus profits. They will not be motivated primarily by philanthropy or by a desire to see new and pioneering voluntary activity. In many cases, they will be looking to generate goodwill, market their goods and services and improve their image and their economic position in relation to their competitors, whether at a local, regional or national level.

There is, however, among some businesses a desire to be seen to be giving something back to their communities or society in general. Some companies have now set up their own charities which, while having close ties to and receiving assets from the company, are a separate legal entity. Whether these foundations are truly independent of the company in their giving is a matter of debate but they are self-governing and set up for charitable purposes for the benefit of the public.

The relationship you have with any company that donates to your cause, whether by cash, gifts in kind, staff time or other resources is a two-way association. While you will be pleased to receive funding, staff time or gifts in kind, the company will also benefit from the good publicity, awareness of local issues which it may not have previously had and a boost in morale for its staff. As with any relationship, your group needs to be selective about which companies it approaches: you need to feel some pride in the association you're about to establish and which may last a long time. Research the company's website, or any other information with this in mind.

How much do companies give?

Company giving is not easy to quantify. Companies can help in a number of ways, including products and services for free, staff time, secondments, advertising, low-cost or free use of facilities, expertise, free equipment and money. In its research for *The Guide to UK Company Giving*, DSC assessed the total community contributions of nearly 500 featured companies to be £808 million, of which £500 million was in cash support (2007/08 figures).

In 2007/08, the top 300 corporate donors gave around £638 million in total community contributions, £492 million of which was cash support. This total support represents 0.38% of these companies' pre-tax profits and accounts for nearly 99% of company giving in the UK. Indeed, the top 25 companies give around 37% of the total corporate support available (or £298 million in community contributions).

Ten good reasons to apply to companies

- Their employees are connected with your organisation.
- They are local and looking for good publicity.
- They have a particular interest in environmental issues.
- Your event will be good for staff to take part in.
- You know the chief executive or personnel officer, or someone in the marketing department helps out in your group.
- Your group uses their particular product.
- You're asking for something that's easy for them to give.
- They've given to you before.
- Your activities help their business.
- They like you.

continued...

Ten good reasons to think again about applying

- You know nothing about the company.
- It is not successful.
- It is not located in your area.
- Its business is not connected in any way with your aims.
- It has a stated policy of never giving to unsolicited appeals.
- You have received well-publicised sponsorship from a rival firm.
- You are asking for £10,000; the company's total budget is £500.
- Its policies, product, image, etc. is not compatible with your work.
- Your supporters would be against having its support.
- Its charitable giving is already fully committed for the next two years.

Why companies give

Some companies give because they see the benefit that will come to them from being seen to be a good corporate citizen. The more they see the donation as a business opportunity for them, the more likely they are to work with you. The onus is on you to give them good reasons to support your organisation.

These are some of the main reasons why companies give.

Creating goodwill

Companies want to be seen as good corporate citizens in the communities where they operate and as caring by society at large.

Cause association

Companies like to be associated with causes which relate to, or are potentially impacted by, their business. For example, mining and extraction companies might support environmental projects; banks, economic development projects; retailers and insurance companies, projects working with young people and crime prevention; and so on. One motive for this might be to enhance their image, but it could also help build contacts and gain market intelligence and therefore increase sales and consequently profits.

Government pressure

There can be pressure put on companies from the government to support particular initiatives which contribute to government policy.

Expectation

There can be peer pressure among companies in a particular sector of business where each company is concerned to see that the quantity and quality of its giving is appropriate to its status as a company.

Staff development

Employee volunteering and secondment to the voluntary sector is a good way for companies to develop their staff and also promotes good staff morale.

Personal interest

It can be very helpful if the chair or other senior directors are interested in your cause (and perhaps support it personally). Even with some large companies that have well-established policies and criteria for their giving, you are more likely to be successful if you can persuade a friend of the managing director to ask on your behalf, even if it does not exactly fit into the company's criteria. Often, you do not need to do the asking yourself; the key is to find the right person to do it for you. Recruiting an eminent local businessperson onto your fundraising committee and persuading them to approach their colleagues saves you time and resources and raises more support; peer to peer asking is often the most effective way to influence a company's giving.

A history of giving

Some companies have a long history of philanthropy and continue to give, following their traditions.

Persistence

Persistence can pay: if a charity persists in its approach to a company eventually the company may not want to keep refusing a worthwhile cause. Although if you are turned down you should consider whether you can improve your application, ask through another method or ask for something else.

Tax reasons

Giving to a charity can be done tax-effectively. This will be an added benefit for the company, but seldom a determining factor.

Privately-owned or family-controlled companies

Privately-owned or family-controlled companies' giving is often little different from personal giving. For public companies, where it is the shareholders' funds that are being given away, the company will want to justify its charitable support. You can help them to do this by telling them not just why you want the money, but why supporting you should be of interest to them. You can also tell them about any benefits they will get in return for their money and about the impact that their donation will make on your work.

Remember too that companies like thanks, recognition and good publicity for their support, whether in newsletters, your annual report, by having their branding on your materials, or through media coverage.

Case study

The Environment Campaign at Business in the Community

...aims to inspire, support and challenge companies to continually improve their impact on the environment. Whether your business is just beginning to understand its climate impact, or whether it is already taking action, you can benefit from reading further examples of responsible business practice.

During autumn 2008 leading companies in Yorkshire and Humber with best practice examples of environmental management opened their doors to businesses from across the region. Two examples are given below.

Croda International plc Best Practice 'Opening Doors' event – November 2008

In conjunction with Business in the Community and Carbon Action Yorkshire, leading companies with best practice examples of environmental management are opening their doors to businesses from across the Yorkshire and Humber region. Croda's Hull site was the location of the third visit in this series. Businesses came to share

continued...

best practice solutions to common environmental issues, followed by a site tour to see the issues and solutions firsthand.

Croda is a world leader in natural based speciality chemicals, which are sold to virtually every type of industry. The company has approximately 4000 employees, working at 43 sites in 36 countries. The Hull site produces lubricants based on rape seed oil and Croda works with UK-based farmers to grow rape seed oil.

Rape seed is crushed by a partner company; the meal is sold as animal feed and the oil is delivered by barge via the river Hull to the Croda site. There are a number of energy intensive processes on site as certain components from the oil are heated in order to remain fluid.

Croda's energy management programme on site started in 2000. Areas of focus were capital investment projects, equipment maintenance and culture change. Initial capital investment projects included steam raising plants, investing in new technology such as a gas economiser, and also investment in equipment to measure utilities usage.

Croda also found ways of cutting out process stages and increasing plant throughputs which in turn cut energy usage. Other site efficiencies have also improved – waste to landfill is down and process yields have increased.

Since 2000, improvements have meant that site usage of electricity has reduced by around 40% and gas usage has reduced by 60%. With such dramatic increases in energy prices over recent years, Mark Robinson, Operations Director, said 'I question whether we would still have been in existence without the changes'.

After the quick win efficiencies were made, Croda started to look at what they could do next, and electricity from wind became an attractive proposition. After several years of planning and addressing numerous considerations (including visual and noise implications, shadow flicker, analogue TV signals, mobile phones, ecology, archaeology, aviation) Croda was given the go-ahead to site a 125m tall, 2MW capacity wind turbine on the Hull site, generating on average the equivalent of the annual electricity usage of approximately 600 houses.

continued...

After all the hard work of getting the wind turbine in place, Croda now generates 40% of the site electricity requirement. Plus Croda can export electricity back to the local electricity grid.

Croda continues to look for innovative new ways to improve their energy management and, therefore, environmental impact.

Croda's Hull site is an excellent example of how investment in new technologies can not only reduce your environmental impact but can also provide serious financial benefits.

Marshalls plc Best Practice 'Opening Doors' event – September 08

Marshalls plc is the UK's leading manufacturer and supplier of innovative hard landscaping materials such as concrete and natural stone building products. Water is an integral part of the manufacturing process and therefore a key environmental impact for the Brookfoot manufacturing site. Using around 100,000 cubic metres of water per year in all its processes, with just a few simple measures, Marshalls has reduced its mains water intake by over 66% and production of effluent by 93%.

Marshalls has been recognised by Yorkshire Water as leading the way in reducing water usage, so much so that the Brookfoot site only relies on Yorkshire Water for 20% of its water, the remaining 80% coming from recycling and harvesting water. The local community welcomes the changes as there are now no adverse effects on water pressure in the village during peak swilling down periods.

Richard Marshall, Business Unit Manager at Brookfoot, said 'In terms of water sustainability, as with any issue, you either do something or do nothing. Doing something gave Brookfoot an overall saving of over £145,000.'

Site staff at Brookfoot are constantly seeking ways to reduce waste generated and an ultimate aim of zero waste to landfill. A waste stream 'road-map' has been developed detailing projects in the pipeline and progress against the measures. Reviewed every six weeks, this is a valuable tool for tracking progress against new schemes and ideas. One particular success story has been surrounding the use of smaller waste collectors for the more obscure items of waste. Traditionally, larger businesses have found it difficult to engage with smaller

continued . . .

contractors but Marshalls has found that by being flexible, solutions can generally be worked out to suit everyone's needs.

Marshalls has also developed a system of dust recovery and a method of re-using this in the product. In total the site recycles 2,500 tonnes per annum.

With so many 'wins' surrounding resource efficiency, Marshall's Brookfoot site is an excellent example of how environmental measures can work for you and your business.

These two events were delivered by Business in the Community in partnership with Carbon Action Yorkshire, Yorkshire Forward's programme aimed at accelerating the development of a lower carbon economy in the Yorkshire and Humber region.

This extract was taken from BITC's website www.bitc.org.uk.

It's not all about money

A common mistake when thinking about company giving is to see it as only about raising money. While some companies can and do give large sums to voluntary organisations, the majority will not. You have to think clearly about why you are approaching them, what benefits they will receive from being linked with your group, and whether you can ask for something other than financial help which the might be more likely to give.

Applying for support from companies is time consuming and can be frustrating. More groups than ever before are chasing very limited company resources.

On the upside, when you are successful, you can have a new source of support that has lots of spin-offs: important contacts; work experience opportunities; management committee members; use of company facilities; in-house expertise provided free or at low cost; staff time; and so on.

What companies like to support

There are trends in what companies like to support. For example, in the 1980s, AIDS/HIV and homelessness were not generally supported, but today companies do support these causes. The following are some of the areas that companies find attractive:

- **important local projects in the areas where the company has a significant presence.** Business in the Community organises 'Seeing is Believing' – events for business leaders, when it takes them to visit local projects to see problems at first hand and explain how they can make a significant contribution.
- **activities that relate to their product** – for example, a cereal manufacturer might be drawn to a project promoting health and fitness.
- **economic development projects** – companies like economic development projects because a flourishing economy benefits business. Shell, for example, supports LiveWIRE, an award scheme for new enterprise, and the STEP programme, which provides undergraduates with work experience during the summer vacation.
- **environmental projects.** United Utilities, through its United Futures partnership with the Groundwork Trust, will provide funding for a number of environmental projects in local communities across the UK.
- **educational projects.** Companies like educational projects because education and training are an investment in future employees.
- **events, competitions and other activities** attract keen public interest or mass participation, such as Comic Relief's Red Nose Day or BBC Children in Need Appeal.
- **initiatives that have the backing of very prominent people.** Who knows who is always important in getting support from companies. The Prince's Trust is able to capitalise on this in its fundraising 'finding that doors open for them without having to be pushed'.

What companies don't like to support

There are certain areas that UK companies will generally not support:

- **local appeals outside areas where they have a business presence** – there is no business reason for them to do this
- **purely denominational appeals for religious purposes**, although they may support social projects run by religious bodies
- **mailed appeals** that are printed and sent to hundreds of companies
- **controversial campaigns** that might bring them bad publicity
- **overseas development work**, unless the company has a business presence in that country, when support will more likely come from a local subsidiary – although some companies do support emergency and aid appeals on the basis that these are the sort of issues that their staff are interested in.

The different types of company that give

Multinational companies

Most multinational companies have global giving programmes, generally tied to areas where they have or are developing business interests. Some multinational companies have an international structure for managing their giving, with budgets set for each country and a common policy for the sorts of activity they are interested in supporting. With others, community involvement policy remains a purely local matter for company management in the country concerned, although some have tried to transfer projects and ideas from one country to another.

Leading national companies

The giving of leading companies is well documented in the *Guide to UK Company Giving*, published by DSC. This gives information on the scale and scope of the company giving programmes of the top 500 corporate donors, with enough information to be able to identify those companies that might be interested in supporting you.

The leading national companies will often support large national charities as well as having their own sponsorship schemes, making smaller donations to local charities, and sponsoring events in the area where they are headquartered or where they have a major business presence.

Community Mark

Business in the Community has established the CommunityMark, a national standard which recognises business excellence in community investment. It was created in consultation with representatives from the London Benchmarking Group, National Council for Voluntary Organisations, Charities Aid Foundation, the Office of the Third Sector and Volunteering England.

It is open to companies in the UK of all sizes and from all sectors. Companies need to demonstrate the long-term positive impact that they are having in their communities.

The CommunityMark provides companies with a self-assessment method of benchmarking their community investment, with the process being complemented by 'additional feedback from community partners and relevant employee volunteers', this feedback is however, selected by the company itself.

Companies that attain the CommunityMark are required to disclose only *part* of their CommunityMark submission and some supporting documentation 'in order to ensure confidence in the rigour of the submission process and substantiate the company's achievements for the benefit of stakeholders'. In this respect their giving is in some respects, less transparent than the former Per-Cent Club (which the CommunityMark replaces), where companies were encouraged to give at least 1% of their pre-tax profits.

'Surveys and referee feedback undergo a first round assessment and scoring by a trained assessor from Business in the Community, during which the assessor will conduct a 15 minute phone call with the most senior person with responsibility for Community. Initial assessments are then reviewed by a second assessor before being taken to an internal moderation group. This self-assessment and scoring process is validated externally by AD Little.

'The CommunityMark Independent Approvals Panel (IAP) was formed to provide independent and transparent validation of the CommunityMark process. Membership is representative of CommunityMark stakeholders and combines individual skills and expertise of public, private and third sectors. The IAP is asked to advise and challenge the CommunityMark Assessment Team on any inconsistencies in CommunityMark applications.'

Companies that achieve the CommunityMark should have demonstrated excellence across each of the following five principles in their approach to community investment:

- Identify the social issues that are most relevant to your business and most pressing to the communities you work with.
- Work in partnership with your communities leveraging your combined expertise for mutual benefit.
- Plan and manage your community investment using the most appropriate resources to deliver against your targets.
- Inspire and engage your employees, customers and suppliers to support your community programmes.
- Measure and evaluate the difference that your investment has in the community and on your business. Strive for continual improvement.

Case study

The Code for Sustainable Homes

The Code for Sustainable Homes is a world leading all-round measure of environmental sustainability, ensuring that new homes deliver significant improvements in key areas such as carbon dioxide (CO_2) emissions and water use.

- The government's objective for the Code is for it to become the single national standard for the design and construction of homes, and that it drives a step-change in sustainable home building practice.
- The aim is to make the system of gaining a Code assessment as simple, transparent and rigorous as possible, and one which inspires confidence in Code assessors, home builders, product manufacturers and, crucially, consumers.
- The Code supersedes EcoHomes and lifts the standards required for energy and water consumption.

The government has indicated its intention to use the Code as the basis of future changes in Building Regulations Part L (1A), proposing it as a route map for new homes to become net-zero carbon by 2016.

The Code defines six levels of environmental sustainability:

- level 1 is set just above current 2006 building regulations
- level 6 is 'net-zero carbon' for homes in use, including appliance and occupant energy use.

An increasing proportion of credits us needed to satisfy each level, of which a mandatory proportion are energy and water, reflecting the growing importance of climate change and availability of potable water.

The Code for Sustainable Homes Route Map

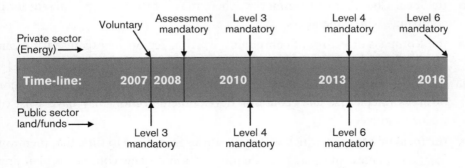

255

Larger local companies

In any city or region there will be large companies that are important to the local economy. They will often feel a responsibility to support voluntary action and community initiatives in those areas, and value the good publicity this provides. If yours is an important project, make it part of your fundraising strategy to develop a good relationship with the larger companies in your area.

There are also companies with a regional remit. The water, electricity and ITV's regional television operators all have a specific geographical area within which they operate, even if they are part of a multinational company; their community support will be confined within these regional boundaries.

Smaller national companies

The larger companies, because of their size but also because their giving is well documented, are often overwhelmed with requests for support. But there are also companies that are less well known and with smaller budgets for giving which receive far fewer approaches. There are also newly floated companies whose giving will only really develop once they have become public. Such companies can provide opportunities for the enterprising fundraiser.

Smaller local companies

Smaller, local companies (known in European jargon as small and medium-sized enterprises, or SMEs) are often overlooked. Almost everyone targets the large companies because good information is available. However, there is a wide range of local companies, from manufacturers on trading estates to accountants and solicitors in the high street. Many of these firms are privately owned, and the approach will often be through the managing director or senior partner. The best sources of information on what companies exist in your area are:

- **the local Chamber of Commerce**, where most of the more prominent local companies will be members
- **the Kompass directory of companies**, which is regionally organised and can now be searched online
- **the local council**: the business department might produce a list of major business ratepayers. The economic development section may have a list of major employers
- **the local newspaper**, which will carry stories from time to time that mention local companies, and may provide information on new companies planning to set up in the area
- **you**: by identifying local companies that it could just be worth approaching.

It is likely that most of the smaller companies you approach will not have a donations policy in place (if they give at all), and may well make their decisions on the basis of the personal interests of their managing director or senior partners. Some may never have made a charitable donation before and may not know about the related tax advantages available to them, so be prepared to tell them about these opportunities.

Some of these companies may prefer to give in kind – for example, a prize for a raffle or advertising in a souvenir brochure for a fundraising event. It might be easier to approach these companies for this sort of support in the first instance, and later on, once they have given something, persuade them to make a cash donation.

Small- and medium-sized businesses will react quickly to economic conditions. When business is falling, their concerns will be for their staff, and not giving money to charities.

Staff time is also at a premium as numbers are small and people are usually stretched with their workload. Staff volunteering schemes are therefore unlikely to be entered into.

Charitable giving is far more likely to be led by the enthusiasms of the partners or directors, but is also likely to be responsive to causes where staff are involved. One local business gives the following advice:

- Match your request to what the business can afford. If a project is too large and the business can only give a small donation it will see its contribution as being swallowed up and not making any difference at all.
- Lengthy letters take up too much time to consider. It's much better if they're simple, succinct and concise.
- Letters should be typed rather than handwritten.
- A good track record gives the appeal credence.
- Corporate giving is not just about money – partners tend to give of their time and skills through involvement, more so than cash.
- Telephone to make things happen. If this is daunting, either delegate the contact work to someone else (perhaps someone on your management committee who already has links with business people) or increase your confidence with training.

Venture philanthropy

The end of the last century and the early years of this have seen the growth of a new economy based on the IT revolution (the internet, mobile phones, etc.) and also on new ways of delivering utilities and other services to consumers. Many of these companies are too busy developing their business to put any real effort into philanthropy. But some – as well as their founders, who now rank among Britain's leading rich – are attracted by the concept of 'venture philanthropy', a US concept, which involves a much more hands-on approach to giving. They are prepared to invest substantially in one or more key projects which have the potential to make a real difference and be replicated, providing support over a longer timeframe and becoming personally involved in the development of the project. Venture philanthropy is a way of supporting organisations through the provision of management and technical support in addition to financial resources.

Examples of venture philanthropy

SHINE

Support and Help in Education (SHINE) was set up by a group of city people as a vehicle for their philanthropy. Focusing on literacy and numeracy projects, support is given to disadvantaged, disengaged and challenged children and young people (7 to 16 years) in Greater London and Manchester.

Impetus Trust

Impetus Trust is a pioneer of venture philanthropy in the UK. Impetus offers donors the means to make the biggest difference with their money by enabling charities to achieve a positive change in their performance.

Impetus operates by providing long-term financing of charities' infrastructure, hands-on management support and capacity building delivered through projects run by volunteer associates. Its website includes the selection criteria and guidelines; however, due to the Trust's high-involvement approach, it invests in only a small number of charities each year.

It seeks to apply private, equity-style investment management methodologies in the charitable sector. It looks for ambitious, growth-minded charities led by strong management teams who can use Impetus' capital and business advice to build the infrastructure they need to implement their charitable visions.

Impetus has invested in 11 such charities to date, thereby touching the lives of more than 160,000 individuals.

The School for Social Entrepreneurs is a useful source of information on developments in venture philanthropy from a UK perspective.

Who decides and who to write to

Larger companies will have a manager who is responsible for dealing with charitable appeals, although a donations committee (which includes senior management) may have the final say. The largest companies may also employ specialist staff to assess the applications and make recommendations.

Some companies such as Richer Sounds (The Persula Foundation) or Lloyds TSB (Lloyds TSB Foundation for England and Wales) operate an independent foundation which sets policy and decides on applications.

With medium-sized and smaller companies, it is nearly always the most senior executive who decides. You should write in the first instance to the person who deals with charitable appeals. Make sure that you have the name and job title correct. If you have a top-level contact, or if one of your members or volunteers is an employee of the company, then use them.

Getting started

You should try to find out as much as you can about the company and about its possible interest in supporting your project, but remember that:

- companies generally have less well defined policies than grant-making charities, although you can often determine a pattern to their giving
- the chance of an application 'out of the blue' getting substantial support is low
- companies are more conservative in their giving, and are less likely to support innovative projects (at least until they get established) or anything that is risky or controversial
- company policies change more frequently than those of grant-making charities, because of mergers, takeovers, or a fall or rise in profits, so ensure your research is up to date. Consulting a directory, or even having a copy of the company's annual report and accounts is not enough; it may have been taken over since then. Check the financial press and internet on a regular basis.

Research tips

Research is important, not just into policies, but also into contacts. Here are some tips.

1) Find out what, if any, previous contact you have had with companies, any previous fundraising approaches you have made, and with what success.

2) Identify and match possible funders with various aspects of your work. In particular, try to find any local companies that are known for their generosity and might have an interest in supporting environmental concerns.

3) Find out whether any of your management committee, volunteers or supporters have any personal contact with the companies you plan to approach – and whether they know people who have credibility in the business world who can help you do the asking.

4) Enlist a senior business leader to assist you with your fundraising. This can be someone to serve as chair of a development or fundraising committee, or just to contact a few colleagues and sign a few letters.

5) Contact Business in the Community to find out about its membership or to help you identify local companies through its regional network.

Ethical issues

Receiving support from companies can be problematic if the business values or practice of the company conflict with what your organisation stands for. There are two approaches:

- Some organisations will accept money from anyone, on the basis that the money can be used to do good – this can be risky.
- Others define certain types of company that they will not accept support from. Tobacco, alcohol, gambling, armaments, mining/oil industries, polluters and companies operating overseas that underpay their workforce are all areas of business activity that can cause problems.

An ethical stance is of particular importance where the work of the charity is directly connected with the issue or where the relationship is high profile. Groups promoting health would find it hard to accept money from a tobacco or alcohol company; peace and international relations organisations have similar problems with arms manufacturers; and so on.

Decide your ethical policy before approaching companies. It should be agreed by the management committee and minuted. You might want to define and agree a policy in consultation with everyone in your organisation, although sometimes this can be contentious and create divisions. If you think this is likely, it might be better to treat each decision on an ad hoc basis while moving towards some sort of consensus on policy.

Sometimes the issues are clear cut. It is relatively easy, for example, for a health charity to decide whether to accept money from a tobacco company, or a youth charity from a drinks company. The product relationship with the cause is clear, and all the charity has to do is agree a position on the issue.

There are organisations that chart the ethical behaviour of companies and which can provide you with the information you need to formulate an ethical donations policy.

- EIRIS (Ethical Investment Research Services) researches companies on the FT All-Share Index. Its main aim is to advise on socially responsible investment. A charge is made for its services.

- Ethical Consumer Research Association produces *Corporate Critic*, which rates over 50,000 companies on their ethical performance at www.corporate critic.org.

Ten ideas for getting support from companies

1) Put yourself in the position of the company. Why should it want to give its shareholders' funds to you? Why should it choose your charity, rather than any of the other organisations that make contact? Think about the benefits the company will get from supporting you and mention these in your appeal letter. If you are looking for sponsorship, then these benefits should be at the heart of your proposal.

2) Suggest something specific for the company to support, and in your letter say why it should be interested. It is often best to think of something quite small if you are approaching the company for the first time.

3) Use all the contacts you have in the company to help get your project supported. Do you know the chair, the managing director or any other senior member of staff who may be able to put in a good word for you? Perhaps if you telephone, you can get into conversation with the chair's personal assistant so that they become interested and enthusiastic about your cause.

continued...

261

4) Think of all the ways in which the company could help. Cash might not be the best way for the company to give support. Might it be easier to ask for staff time, perhaps giving you some expertise you lack? Or the use of a vehicle? Or access to company staff to circulate an appeal or volunteer in some other way for your group? It is likely that everyone else will be asking for cash. The company may find it easier to give in kind, but once it has done so and got to know you and your work, cash support may be available next time.

5) Consider whether there is a senior executive of the company (the more senior the better) who might become a trustee of your charity – or serve on a fundraising or development committee. They can bring new ideas, good organisation and a wealth of business contacts to your organisation that will be worth many times the value of a donation. Such an invitation, even if refused, may be seen as flattering. If this level of involvement is too much, a request for advice may succeed.

6) Do you have any volunteers who also work for the company? They may be able to help you 'from the inside', and it will do you no harm if you mention their support for your organisation in your appeal letter, though you must remember to check that they are happy to be mentioned first.

7) Don't assume that every company will give. Make parallel approaches to a number of companies.

8) Consider who might be the best person to make the approach or sign the letter. It may not be you but could be a senior business executive from another company which has already supported your organisation generously. Their endorsement of your work can provide a comfort factor for other companies.

9) Every time you buy anything from a company, ask for a discount. This will save you money, but it is also a way of getting them to support you.

10) Check if the company is registered for payroll giving and, if it is, ask if you can promote your cause to employees. You will find more on payroll giving in Chapter 7 *Raising Support From the Public*.

The kind of help companies give

There is a variety of ways in which companies can support charities:

- A cash donation (usually a one-off grant).
- Support in kind, which includes: giving company products or surplus office equipment; and making company facilities available, including meeting rooms or printing or design facilities.
- Secondment of a member of staff to work with the charity, where a member of the company's staff helps on an agreed basis while remaining employed (and paid) by the company.
- Offering work experience to a charity beneficiary or student at an educational institution.
- Contributing a senior member of staff to the charity's management board.
- Providing expertise and advice or training.
- Encouraging and making it easy for employees to volunteer.
- Organising a fundraising campaign among employees, including encouraging employees to give through payroll giving.
- Sponsorship of an event or activity.
- Sponsorship of promotional and educational materials.
- Sponsorship of an award scheme.
- Cause-related marketing, where the company contributes a donation to the charity in return for each product sold in order to encourage sales.
- Advertising in charity brochures and publications.

Companies will always receive more applications than they will have set the budget to respond to. Community involvement budgets have not expanded in line with demands for support and many companies now focus their grantmaking quite narrowly. Some larger companies will have set up small grants' schemes in regions or towns where they have a major factory or business presence. Some have matching schemes, where they match money collected or donated by employees. Some will have developed special grants programmes and others will have a 'charity of the year' for their major donation and as a focus for encouraging staff involvement.

Cash donations

This is the most obvious way that a company can be asked to support your organisation, but also the most expensive for them, so most cash donations are small (under £250), although some companies will match their employees' fundraising. You are more likely to be successful if you offer a 'shopping list' of specific items, rather than a vague request for general support.

In the entries at the end of this chapter we try to give an idea of the range of grants available from the large companies and what they like to support. This varies greatly from company to company. Some will have well-defined policies which work in a similar way to grant-making charities. They know what they want to give to, and what they do not. Guidelines are often publicised and applications may be handled by staff with job titles such as corporate affairs director or head of external affairs.

However, the majority of companies – especially the smaller ones – will have an informal approach. Here, any applications will be looked at by anyone from the personnel officer to the managing director, or her/his secretary. They will not necessarily have any special insight into the voluntary sector and they will be doing the community support task on top of their work, and so may have to fit it into the odd Friday afternoon a month. They do not have the time to work through piles of paper or attend lengthy meetings to get to know the issues you are facing and the work you are doing.

A good number of companies will operate on the basis of the chair's six favourite charities and if you are not on the list, you will have to find a way in, as the company giving policy will already be fixed. Inevitably, if you are successful with this sort of company, you may be successful with others, as part of company giving works on spreading the word.

You might stand more chance of success if you can tie your application in with an event or celebration. Anniversaries are useful; your 50th year or your 500th member, which you may be able to find a company to tie in with. It will be particularly attractive if you have a time limit to your fundraising – this gives those working in the supporting company a definite target to work for.

Tax and company giving

The 2000 Finance Act made giving tax-effectively straightforward for companies.

Donations

The company simply pays the full donation to the charity under Gift Aid and then deducts the total amount of its charitable donations from its pre-tax profit calculations at the end of the year. The level of benefit a company can receive in return is restricted on a sliding scale according to the amount of the donation, up to a maximum of £250 in benefits.

Business expenditure

Any expenditure by a company which is wholly and exclusively for business purposes is also deductible against corporation tax liability. This will cover most sponsorship and advertising payments to charity.

Shares

Companies are able to get tax relief for gifts of certain shares and securities to charity. See the HM Revenue & Customs website www.hmrc.gov.uk for more information.

Gifts in kind

Giving things rather than money is often easier for a company. The value of the gift to the charity will always be much more than the cost to the company. Companies might give:

- products for use by the charity
- products as prizes or as lots to be auctioned
- old stock and ends of lines for resale in charity shops
- professional and technical advice *pro bono* (without charge)
- staff time
- facilities such as meeting rooms, conference facilities or training.

If a company donates articles that it makes or sells in the course of its trade, or an article that it has used in its trade (this can include computers and furniture), then this can be treated as a tax-deductible business expense. The 'book value' of donated items (value as given in the accounts) is written off before the donation is made (un-saleable or damaged stock, ends of lines, etc.) also attract full tax relief. There are organisations which act as 'clearing houses' for gifts in kind, such as Kind Direct (formerly Gifts in Kind UK).

What kind of gift is a gift in kind?

Gifts in kind are donations of items or services, rather than the money to buy them. One community investment director with widespread experience of companies and voluntary organisations suggested the following list.

- Donation of coach/airline/ferry tickets.
- Advertising on company websites.
- Use of surplus storage/sports facilities.
- Donation of hotel accommodation.
- Use of telephones for helplines.
- Design and printing of leaflet/poster.
- Donation of surplus food/drinks.
- Access to information on customer demography/attitudes/preferences.
- Vacant sites for recreation projects.
- Free loan of plant, equipment, scaffolding, marquees, portaloos.
- Donation of rubble, tarmac, topsoil.
- Free advertising space on temporarily unused sites.
- Charity leaflet/appeal in a regular business or customer mailshot.
- Free servicing of vehicles.

Some practical tips on how to set about getting support in kind

Make a list of everything you need

In other words, create a 'wish list'. This can include services as well as products (such as the design for a leaflet you plan to produce).

Go through the list and try to identify companies that might have what you require

Personal knowledge is useful but you might also want to use business directories to widen your choice.

Make contact

Writing a letter can act as an introduction but you will probably need to follow it up with a phone call or personal visit. State your request, saying that it is for a charity and

continued ...

---

indicating how well used it will be and how important it is to your user group and your organisation's future. If the company doesn't want to donate, it might be able to give you a discount.

Be positive and enthusiastic

It can be very difficult for the company to refuse if it knows what you want and how important it is for you and the local community. It will always cost the company far less to donate the item than it would cost you to purchase it.

Say thank you

If you are successful in gaining company support, report back on the difference the donation has made. Send it your annual report and later, perhaps try to recruit the company as a cash donor.

Employee volunteering and secondments

A major resource that companies can offer is their staff time and this can be provided in a number of ways.

Employee volunteering

Many of the large companies encourage their staff to volunteer, usually out of office hours, on the basis that this enhances the skills of their employees and promotes good community relations. Some companies make matching donations to the projects their employees are involved with. *Cares* is a national campaign run by Business in the Community that aims to engage employees in their communities through volunteering.

Professional skills

Banks, law firms, accountants, advertising and PR companies can all encourage staff to give their professional skills free of charge or to become trustees.

Secondment

This is where the company loans you a member of staff full time for an extended period. There needs to be a good reason why the company would do this, as it is an expensive form of support.

Employee volunteering is not only valuable in itself, but is strategically important since you will be building a relationship with a member of staff who can then act as an intermediary in asking the company for other forms of support at a later date.

267

Asking companies to advertise

Companies will sometimes take an advertisement in a publication – possibilities include:

- your annual report
- programmes produced specifically for fundraising events
- conference folders, pads and pens
- leaflets aimed at your service users and others
- posters, including educational wall charts.

However, you do need to think through whether you actually want an advertisement or company logo to appear prominently on your materials.

Advertising can be broken down into two categories:

Goodwill advertising

Where the primary purpose of the advertiser is to support a charity and to be seen supporting a good cause; this creates goodwill for the company rather than selling its products.

Commercial advertising

Where the advertiser wishes to reach the audience that the charity's publication goes to, and the decision is made for purely financial considerations.

What are you offering to advertisers?

Before trying to sell the advertising, you need to recognise what you are offering. If it is goodwill advertising, then the prestige of the event, the nature of the audience, the location and any celebrities who will be present will be major incentives. Price is less of an issue than the work of the charity, although the advertiser will want to know the circulation and readership of the publication, any special characteristics of that readership and any particular connection between it and the advertiser's product. If it is commercial advertising, these details become much more significant.

Pricing the advertising

The first consideration when pricing the advertising is the format of the publication. A lavish souvenir brochure is different from an annual report, and this in turn is very different from a single colour newsletter produced on your computer. There are two factors to consider when deciding the cost of the advertising.

- How much you want to raise? Divide this target by the number of pages of advertising to get a page rate.
- How much are advertisers prepared to pay? For commercial advertising this is especially important. Try to define the value of your audience to them.

Once you have decided a page rate, then you can then set prices for smaller spaces that are slightly higher than pro rata. For example, if the page rate is £250, then a half page might be priced at £150, a quarter page at £85, and eighth page at £50. You can ask for higher sums for special positions, such as the back cover, the inside front cover and facing the contents page. For a regular publication, you could offer a series discount for taking space in several issues.

You might consider producing a rate card which contains all the information that the advertiser needs to know, including:

- deadline for agreeing to take space
- deadline for receipt of artwork and address where it is to be sent
- publication size
- print run
- use of colour on cover and inside pages (four-colour, two-colour, black and white)
- page rates, including special positions, size of advertising space, and whether VAT is chargeable
- payment details.

A simple brochure or covering letter which sets out the reasons for advertising is useful, but posting copies out will generate little response. The way to sell advertising is on the telephone, where you make a call to follow up a letter you have sent. For larger advertisers, you might try to arrange a personal visit. The majority of people you approach will probably say 'no' but your job is to persuade a significant proportion to buy a space.

Business sponsorship

Sponsorship needs to be carefully defined. It is not a donation and the fact that you are a charity is largely irrelevant, it is a business arrangement. The charity is looking to raise funds for its work and the company wants to improve its image, promote and sell its products or entertain its customers.

The sponsor's contribution is usually money, although it could be a gift of goods (such as gardening equipment), or services (such as free transport), or professional expertise (such as promotion or marketing consultancy), or the use of buildings (such as an exhibition centre), or free promotion (such as media coverage in a newspaper).

Many companies will provide much more in sponsorship than they would as a donation, but only so long as the commercial benefits warrant it. Developing links with the major national and local corporate sponsors could be an investment in your future that is well worth making now.

Most sponsors are commercial companies. There are four main options for sponsorship:

Businesses that want to promote themselves

Businesses want to promote themselves to create a better image or generate awareness in the local communities where they operate. This includes those companies with an 'image problem' – for example, mining and extraction companies associated with the destruction of the environment that want to project a cleaner image by being associated with a conservationist cause.

Businesses that want to introduce or promote a product or service

This could include a new brand of trainers or shampoo, or a supermarket opening in the area. Public awareness is important if a product or service is to get accepted, so companies may be open to proposals that give a product or service more exposure.

Companies looking for entertainment opportunities

Companies look for entertainment opportunities to influence customers, suppliers, regulators, the media and other opinion formers. They may be interested in sponsoring a concert, a theatrical event, an art exhibition or a sporting event, which would provide them with an appropriate entertainment opportunity and the opportunity to meet and mingle.

Companies that are committed supporters of your organisation

You may be able to offer them something that they would like to sponsor, even if it is partly for philanthropic reasons.

What are companies looking for?

Organisations should be able to offer at least some of the following:

A respectable partner

An organisation to be associated with that has the right image.

A real partnership

What involvement is being looked for from the sponsor and how well does this opportunity meet its needs?

A proven track record and a professional approach

Your proven track record would preferably be in securing and delivering sponsorships. Have you as the applicant approached the business of getting sponsorship in a professional way, and can you demonstrate a similar professionalism in the running of the organisation?

An interesting project and initiative

The project should be interesting at least to the company management and possibly also company staff. Does the sponsorship represent a new initiative, something that would not happen without the company's support? Is it interesting and lively?

Continuity

Is there scope for a continuing relationship (over the next few years), or is the activity or event just a one-off?

Genuine value for money

What are the benefits and how much money is being asked from the sponsor? How does this rate as compared with other possible sponsorships that the company might consider? The relationship of cost to return and the importance of the return to the company are the dominant factors affecting the decision to sponsor.

Visibility

How 'visible' will the event be, and what specific publicity and PR benefits will accrue to the sponsor? Will the company name be given a high profile?

Appropriateness

Is the activity or event appropriate to the sponsor? Also, are you approaching the right company?

Targeted audience

This could lead to direct marketing, for example, by providing the company's fair trade coffee at your group's annual awards ceremony.

Other tangible benefits

For example, good publicity; media coverage; a link with brand advertising; entertainment opportunities for company directors and staff; access to leaders; involvement of company employees or retirees; and training or experience for employees.

Why companies like sponsorship

- It helps them get their message across.
- It can enhance or change their image.

- It can reach a target audience very precisely.
- It can be very cost-effective advertising or product promotion.
- Further marketing opportunities may develop from the sponsorship.
- It generates good publicity for the sponsor, often of a kind that money can't buy.
- It generates an awareness of the company within the local community in which the company operates and from where it draws its workforce and customers.
- Sponsors can entertain important clients at the events they sponsor.

What can be sponsored?

There is an extremely wide range of things that can be sponsored, including:

- cultural and sporting events
- mass participation fundraising events, such as a marathon or fun run
- the publication of a report or a book, with an attendant launch
- the production of fundraising materials, leaflets and posters, or the sponsorship of a complete fundraising campaign
- conferences and seminars, especially to specialist audiences (such as doctors) where promotional material can be displayed
- vehicles, where the acknowledgement can be painted on the side
- equipment such as cars or computers produced by the company
- competitions, awards and prizes
- scholarships, bursaries and travel grants.

The bulk of corporate sponsorship money goes to sport, with motor racing, golf, tennis, athletics, football and cricket all receiving huge amounts. These offer extensive media coverage, good opportunities for corporate entertainment and an association with a popular activity.

The arts is another big recipient of sponsorship – business support for the arts runs at around £150 million a year. Arts sponsorship is promoted by Arts & Business, which describes itself as acting 'as a crucible where businesses and arts organisations come together to create partnerships to benefit themselves and the community at large'.

As a charity you will not be competing for a share of these budgets; however, social sponsorship is much smaller by comparison and is a growing area. The 'market' is less crowded and there are all sorts of imaginative ways in which companies can sponsor events and activities run by charities.

Who to approach

The company

You need to be selective when you decide on which companies to approach and then find out who you should contact within the company. The choice of company will depend upon what connection you have with them.

- Have they supported you before?
- Do they have a stated interest in the environment?
- Are they local to your community?
- Are you consumers of their service or product?
- Do they need better publicity in the community and could you offer that with a link?
- Do your activities contribute to improving the business environment?
- Is the company a large employer in the area with an interest in the current and future workforce?

The person

Once you have decided on the company, you will need to find out how it is organised and who makes any decisions about charitable giving. Where a company has a number of branches or operating units throughout the country these may have some autonomy in grant decisions. There is usually a maximum amount that they can decide, over which the application will be passed to the next level, regional or national. If you can find this out beforehand it will save time in the long run.

You need to tailor your request to the level you are asking at and which budget it might come from, it may not necessarily be from the company's charitable giving budget but possibly marketing or personnel. Once you have established the budget source and level, you will then need to find the right person to talk and write to. Many organisations find this the frustrating part. There is no short cut if you have no inside knowledge of the company.

Be prepared to spend time on the company's website or the telephone, particularly if the company has no decided policy on giving. If there is no policy, there is not likely to be a name on the website or at reception. You may have to go through a number of different departments and repeat your request a number of times before you find someone who knows what the company can help with. With all 'cold' applications you must have a name to write to and the right job title.

Send a summary proposal to see if it generates any interest and follow this up with a phone call a few days later to try and arrange a meeting. There may be an advertising agency or marketing consultant who will introduce sponsorship opportunities to sponsors. They will sometimes charge you a fee; more usually they will receive a commission from the sponsor. It depends who retains them, and in whose interests they are acting.

Getting sponsorship – ten practical tips

1) Before you begin, think about an ethical code. Are there some companies you wouldn't wish to be associated with?

2) Identify the right person in the company to contact. You need their name and job title. This will often be the marketing manager.

3) Stress the benefits of the sponsorship to the potential sponsor. This should be done often and as clearly as possible and backed up with statistics or other supporting information.

4) The size of the payment will be dependent upon the value of the sponsorship to the sponsor, not the cost of the work for you.

5) Help companies use their own resources to make the sponsorship work. Suggest, for instance, that they might like a picture story in their house magazine or in the trade press. Most are very keen to impress their colleagues and their rivals, but few think of this without prompting.

6) Sponsorship, especially long-term deals, is all about working together. Promise only what you know you can deliver, and always try to deliver a little bit more than you promised.

7) Remember that most sponsorship money comes in sums of under £10,000 and that you are planning a local, not an international event.

8) Get into the habit of reading adverts. Look particularly at local papers and trade press. Who has got money to spend on promotion? What kind of image are they trying to promote? Who are they trying to reach? How can you help them?

9) Mention another company that supports you. One satisfied sponsor can help you get another.

10) Keep trying. It is hard work but sponsorships can be really valuable.

Your sponsorship package

It is not enough to offer 1,000 contacts to a company if it sponsors your event. Most of them may be irrelevant to the company. You need to say which 1,000 people will be involved and how.

Think of each group that you reach in some way. Estimate an annual number for each. The following are general groups of people to get the process started but there may be more specialised areas that you are in contact with. Some groups will overlap. The more you can define your different groups of contacts, and the more information you can give about them, the more help it will be to you and potential sponsors.

Group	Number
Adults	....
Men	....
Women	....
Young adults	....
Teenagers	....
Children	....
Consumers	....
(what, how and where people buy – drinks, clothes, transport, which shops, areas, etc.)	
Businesses	....
(who do you use for products, services, etc.?)	
Schools	....
Clubs	....
Employed	....
Unemployed	....
Trainees	....
Agencies	....
Local authority	....
Central government departments	....
Quangos	....
Health authority	....
Learning and Skills Council	....
Other	....

Contractual issues

Sponsorship involves giving something in return for the money you are receiving, so you need to agree terms through a contract. This can be set out in a legal agreement (for larger sponsorships) or in the form of a letter. You need to be clear about the following factors.

How long the arrangement will run

Is it for one year – requiring you to find a new sponsor next year – or can you get a commitment for several years? What happens at the end of this period – does the sponsor have a first refusal on the following year's event? Most successful sponsorships last for several years, and the benefit builds up over the sponsorship period. But companies don't like being tied to sponsoring something indefinitely – their sponsorship programme would begin to look stale.

The fee to be paid, and when the instalments are due

What benefits are to be delivered in return for the fee. These should be specified as clearly as possible, so that you know precisely what you are contracted to deliver.

Whether VAT is chargeable

This will depend on whether your organisation is registered for VAT and the extent of the benefits offered to the sponsor. If VAT is chargeable, this should be discussed at the outset, and the fee agreed should be exclusive of VAT.

Who will pay for what costs

Who pays for the additional publicity the sponsor requires is something that is often forgotten. There needs to be a clear agreement as to who is responsible for what, so you can ensure that everything is covered and there are no misunderstandings later on.

Who is responsible for doing what

You will need to clarify who will do the public relations, who will handle the bookings, who will invite the guests, whose staff will receive the guests, and so on.

Any termination arrangements

In the event of the activity having to be cancelled.

Who is responsible for managing the sponsorship

You should have a named person on both sides.

Whether the sponsor is a 'commercial participator'

Under the terms of the Charities Act 2006, when the requirements of the Charities Act will apply.

If everything is written down and agreed, there will be fewer problems later – and it ensures that everything has been properly thought through at the outset.

Joint promotions and cause-related marketing

Many larger charities are involved in promotional activity to help market a commercial product – this is often known as cause-related marketing (CRM). This can bring in large amounts of money and expose the name of the charity (and sponsor) to literally millions of people. The same idea on a smaller scale can also be adapted for use by local charities through local promotions.

Commercial promotions can include, for example, on-pack and licensing promotional deals, affinity credit cards, competitions and awards and the use of phone lines. What they have in common is that they present an opportunity to raise money for your cause and to project your charity to new audiences, but they require that you work with the company and on its terms to achieve this.

This arrangement benefits both the charity and the commercial partner. It differs from sponsorship in that you are promoting the company's product or service (in return for a payment) as the primary purpose of the arrangement. But, as with sponsorship, you will need to make a business case for it.

Getting started with promotions

Joint promotions are quite difficult to arrange and you must first talk about the possibility of your developing promotional links with companies with someone who has experience of this or with a marketing or advertising agency (but be careful of the cost).

You need to decide whether you are the type of charity that can expect a commercial link of this sort. It has been generally accepted that national household-name charities and those addressing popular causes (such as helping children) are more likely to benefit from this area of fundraising than the less well-known charities or those addressing less 'popular' causes.

You should take the initiative yourself by contacting companies that might be interested in your work. You can also contact promotion agencies (that are not retained by you) to make them aware of the opportunities you are offering which they could include when appropriate in their sales pitch to companies.

If you are approached by a promotional agency pitching for business, this does not mean that anything is certain. It may be working independently, hoping that a good idea that involves your charity can then be sold to a company. In nine out of ten situations, these ideas come to nothing, and you may find you have put in considerable effort without getting any payback.

Issues with sponsorships and joint promotions

Sponsorship involves a close working relationship with a company. Therefore you will need to be sure when you enter into any sponsorship agreement that this relationship will benefit your organisation and will not damage your charity's reputation. With commercial promotions the relationship is even closer. The charity is actively promoting the products of the company, so it is important that the product you are associated with is good value and good quality. With both arrangements it is important that you have no ethical problems in associating with that company. You should develop an ethical donations policy before you apply for any sponsorship or suggest a joint promotion – agreeing in advance which types of company you are happy to work with and which you are not. (See *Ethical issues* on page 260)

There is also the question of who will benefit most from the arrangement. How much you should expect to receive from a sponsorship or commercial promotion is also a difficult question. It may be worth a great deal to them to be linked with you. Any negotiation should start from what you think the association is worth to them. Your need for money should not dim the value of your commercial worth.

Finally, there are important legal issues arising from the 1992 Charities Act (and still applicable following the Charities Act 2006). The 1992 Act defines a 'commercial participator' as 'any person who carries on for gain a business which is not a fundraising business but who in the course of that business engages in any promotional venture in the course of which it is represented that contributions are to be given to or applied for the benefit of a charity'. In other words, high street shops often promote products on the understanding that part of the sale price will go to charity – for example charity Christmas cards published commercially state explicitly that for each pack sold a certain sum will go to charity. The Act also covers advertising and sales campaigns or other joint promotions by companies with charities. If the activity falls within the provisions of the Act, this then requires:

- a written agreement in a prescribed form between the charity and the commercial participator
- the public to be informed how the charity will benefit from its involvement, which shows what part of the proceeds or profits are to be given to the charity. This is a matter for professional advice.

The Charity Commission also suggests that trustees should consider the following points before allowing the charity's name to be associated with a particular business or product.

- The relationship is appropriate and will not damage the particular charity or the good name of charity as a whole.

- The proposed fundraising venture is a more effective way of raising money than others that might be considered and the terms of the arrangement are generally advantageous to the charity.

- The arrangement is set out in some detail and kept under review, such that the charity's name is not misused or improperly exploited, and that the charity has the right to prevent future use of its name if the arrangement proves unsatisfactory. It may be worth taking legal advice in drawing up the terms of the arrangement.

Which companies support environmental organisations?

There are a large number of prospective supporters of environmental projects in the corporate sector. Potentially any company can give to your organisation so long as:

- you make a connection between you and them
- you show the company good commercial reasons for supporting you
- the company does not have a stated exclusion on support for environmental organisations.

Following are details of 20 companies identified from the 2008 research for DSC's *The Guide to UK Company Giving* as having expressed a preference for supporting environmental projects. They represent a cross-section of the various types of environmental-related causes that companies support, but are in no way an exhaustive list. There may be many more opportunities for support from companies that are based near you and we encourage you to seek these out.

Although companies, the larger ones in particular, are keen to detail the steps they have taken to improve their own environmental impact, they are less forthcoming about the types and amount of support they give to environmental organisations.

For this reason it is difficult to state with any certainty which of the listed companies is the 'best' for supporting groups concerned with the environment. Indeed, of the £12 million given in total cash donations by these companies, information on the proportion allocated to environmental projects was not always available.

As such, each entry gives the company's latest annual cash donations figure and, where available, that for total community contributions, which includes in-kind support and employee volunteering. It also attempts to give some indication of how much of the total cash support went towards environmental projects. In some instances this has been provided by the company. In the main, however, we have had to calculate a figure based on listed beneficiary groups (where provided), stated support policy and past experience.

Due to this, in certain cases it is probable that we have understated the level of a company's support for environmental groups, while in others it has not been possible to give any guide at all.

Allianz Insurance plc

Contact
Fran Everist, Community Affairs
Consultant, 57 Ladymead, Guildford,
Surrey GU1 1DB
Tel: 01483 568 161; Fax: 01483 300 952;
email: fran.everist@allianzcornhill.co.uk;
website: www.allianz.co.uk

Year end: 31/12/2008

Turnover: £1.5 billion

Pre-tax profit: £130 million

Nature of business
The group undertakes all classes of
insurance business. It has 13 UK
branches.

Main UK locations
Brentford, Liphook, Guildford, Bristol,
Tunbridge Wells.

Cash donations: £239,000 (2008)

Grants for the environment: £25,000

Community support policy

Allianz Insurance plc transacts all classes
of general insurance business in Great
Britain.

Allianz's charitable support policy is to
consider all applications for support and
to provide help where appropriate. There
is a preference for charities where the
business is located (Guildford, London,
Tunbridge Wells, Bristol, Brentford and
Liphook), and in which a member of staff
is involved.

Allianz's website states that:

*In 2008, Allianz launched a nationwide
fund with the Community Foundation
Network. The Allianz Fund has been
established to benefit communities in the
areas close to the company's offices (see
above). The fund supports projects that
build capacity and skills within the
community through training and
development. Other fund criteria include
disadvantaged people, older people, drugs
and the environment.*

Support is also provided through the
Allianz Fund at the Surrey Community
Foundation.

In 2008, the company made donations of
£238,618 (2007: £146,000).
Environmental projects which conserve
or improve biodiversity or which
improve community access to and
awareness of the environment are
supported, an example being the £1,026
awarded to the Normandy Community
Therapy Garden. The centre uses
horticulture as a medium to change
people's lives on a daily basis, and offers
vocational training and social
therapeutic horticulture in order to
improve self-esteem and confidence. Part
of the grant was used towards installing
an automatic irrigation system for the
garden.

In kind support

Non-cash support is given in the form of
gifts in kind and may take the form of
one or more of the following:

- donation of surplus office furniture
  or equipment
- donation of in-house design and
  print services
- use of office space for meetings
- donation of the expertise and time of
  a relevantly qualified employee
- teams of volunteers
- items for raffles and auctions
- donation of unwanted paper and
  stationery to schools and community
  groups.

Employee-led support

Allianz operate a 'Helping Hands'
scheme as part of its community
investment programme. This scheme
marries teams of employees with local
charities and community groups in need
of help.

Staff are also involved in mentoring students and businesses in the Surrey area.

Payroll giving

The company operates the Give As You Earn scheme to which the company adds 10%.

Exclusions

No response to circular appeals. No support for advertising in charity brochures, appeals from individuals, the arts, medical research, overseas projects, political appeals, religious appeals, sport or local appeals not in areas of company presence.

Applications

For further details please contact the correspondent.

Information available

Further tailored advice for applicants is available from the company on request.

BAA Airports Ltd

Contact
Caroline Nicholls, Director BAA Communities Trust, 1st Floor., Heathrow Point West, 234 Bath Road, Hayes UB3 5AP
Tel: 020 8745 9800;
email: caroline_nicholls@baa.com;
website: www.baa.co.uk

Year end: 31/12/2007

Turnover: £2.247 billion

Pre-tax profit: £747 million

Nature of business
BAA plc owns and operates seven UK airports: Heathrow, Gatwick, Stansted, Aberdeen, Edinburgh, Glasgow and Southampton. Each airport is run by a separate operating company.

Main UK locations
Heathrow, Gatwick, Edinburgh, Glasgow, Southampton, Stansted, Aberdeen.

Cash donations: £1.4 million (2007)

Grants for the environment: £500,000

Community support policy

BAA Airports Ltd is one of the world's leading airport company's and owns seven UK airports (London Heathrow, London Gatwick and London Stansted, Aberdeen, Edinburgh, Glasgow and Southampton).

The company has its own charitable trust, The BAA 21st Century Communities Trust (Charity Commission no.1058617), which gives grants in the areas surrounding the company's airports. Support is concentrated on projects which will be of community benefit and that are mainly concerned with education, youth development and the environment.

A smaller BAA charitable trust, specifically linked to the Gatwick area, also gives grants for environmental purposes. Applications to the Gatwick Airport Community Trust (Charity Commission no. 1089683) should be addressed: c/o Public Affairs, 7th Floor Destinations Place, Gatwick Airport RH6 0NP. Alternatively, call Rosamund Quade on 01892 826088.

In 2007 (the latest year for which figures are currently available), cash contributions from the company totalled £1,376,238 of which £569,796 went to the BAA Communities Trust. During the same year the trust made grants totalling £566,430 , generally in the range of £2,000 to £10,000 each, although some larger amounts were given. Recipients included: Groundwork – Thames Valley (£30,000); Environment Education Project (£19,800); Whitecrook Park Project – Glasgow (£15,000); and The Forest Schools Programme (£10,575).

During 2008, the BAA Communities Trust in partnership with Green Corridor, an environmental charity, launched an education programme to get local students thinking about the environment. The programme was supported with a £20,000 grant from the trust.

BAA Community & Environment Awards

Launched in January 2009, the BAA Community & Environment Awards for schools, voluntary organisations and community groups, provides grants of up to £2,500 six times per year. The awards focus on five themes: 'reduce, re-use, recycle'; 'climate change and energy'; 'protecting and enhancing our environment'; 'bringing communities together'; and, 'developing skills'. It is expected that around £100,000 will be available for awards in 2009.

If you have an idea for a small project that will cost less than £5,000, then to find out more, or to receive an application form, contact Louise Morris on 01895 839855 or email louiseM.morris@groundwork.org.uk. You can also visit www.baa.com/charitablesupport for details.

Further information regarding the support given to environmental projects in the vicinity of each of BAA's seven airport operations can be found by visiting the appropriate website. Links to each of these are available at: www.baa.com

Employee-led support

The company matches employee giving on a pound for pound basis, and employee fundraising to a maximum of £250. Staff are also given time off to volunteer.

Payroll giving

The company operate the Payroll Giving in Action and the Give As You Earn schemes.

Exclusions

No support is given to circular appeals, advertising in charity brochures, animal welfare, appeals from individuals, the arts, elderly people, fundraising events, heritage, medical research, overseas projects, political appeals, religious appeals, science/technology, sickness/disability, or sport.

Applications

Applicants are advised to contact the community relations manager at their local airport:

BAA Aberdeen: Aberdeen Airport, Dyce, Aberdeen AB21 7DU (0870 040 0006; Fax: 01224 775845).

BAA Edinburgh: Edinburgh Airport EH12 9DN (0870 040 0007; Fax: 0131 344 3470).

BAA Gatwick: Gatwick Airport RH6 ONP (0870 000 2468).

BAA Glasgow: Glasgow Airport, St Andrews Drive, Paisley PA3 2SW (0870 040 0008; Fax: 0141 848 4769).

BAA Heathrow: Heathrow Airport, 234 Bath Road, Hayes UB3 5AP (0870 000 0123; Fax: 020 8745 4290).

BAA Southampton: Southampton Airport SO18 2NL (0870 040 0009; Fax: 023 8062 7283).

BAA Stansted: Stansted Airport, Enterprise House, Bassingbourne Road, Stansted CM24 1QW (0870 000 0303; Fax: 01279 662066).

Information available

Written guidance is provided in letter form in response to requests. The company also produces a social responsibility report.

The Body Shop International plc

Contact
Lisa Jackson, Principal – Body Shop Foundation, Watersmead, Littlehampton BN17 6LS
Tel: 01903 731 500; Fax: 01903 726 250; website: www.thebodyshopfoundation.org

Year end: 29/12/2007

Turnover: £329.5 million

Pre-tax profit: £43.4 million

Nature of business
The Body Shop is a multi-local, values-led, global retailer. The group sells skin and hair care products through its own shops and franchised outlets in 47 markets worldwide.

Main UK locations
Glasgow, Littlehampton.

Cash donations: £675,000 (2007)

Grants for the environment: £250,000

Community support policy
Grants are given through The Body Shop Foundation (Charity Commission no. 802757) which is funded by the company and has since 1989 supported a variety of issues. The foundation works in three main areas, namely:

- animal protection
- human rights
- environmental protection.

It aims to support organisations at the forefront of social and environmental change, support groups with little hope of conventional funding and support projects working to increase public awareness. The foundation is currently running the following grants programmes: global main grants programme; regional funding panels – Asia Pacific; UK & Republic of Ireland; Europe, Middle East & Africa; and, The Americas; global small grants programme; and local community grants programme – Littlehampton and Southwark areas.

In 2008, the company donated £675,000 to the foundation.

The Body Shop Foundation
In 2008 the foundation made grants totalling nearly £620,000 of which £440,000 went towards supporting animal and environmental protection causes. Major beneficiaries included: Amazon Rain Forest Foundation (£50,000); Tropical Forest Trust (£40,000); Global Action Plan (£21,000); BioRegional Development Group (£20,000); Global Green Grants, Green Map System, NCSA – Environmental Protection UK and Stop Climate Chaos (£10,000 each); Green Light Trust (£9,800); and CleanupUK (£5,500).

In kind support
Gifts in kind club
The club closed in 2008 following doubts about its future.

Employee-led support
Employees are encouraged to take an active role in their local communities. At the UK global head office, employees are entitled to six days of volunteer time, supporting local projects and causes as individuals and as business teams.

Exclusions
The foundation does not:

- sponsor individuals
- fund sporting activities or the arts
- sponsor or support fundraising events, receptions or conferences.

In addition, no donations can be made to promote religious causes or political campaign causes, although the foundation may work with religious or political organisations on partnership projects and fund raise with organisations that have a political or religious foundation for causes that support its values and principles.

No donations can be made to, nor funds raised for, organisations linked to animal testing, organisations advocating violence or discrimination or in other ways promoting behaviour inconstant with the foundation's principles.

Applications

The Body Shop International and The Body Shop Foundation no longer accept unsolicited applications for funding.

However, in exceptional circumstances the company may respond to a humanitarian emergency and make a special donation to a public appeal, but such a donation must have the approval of the CEO.

Information available

The company produce a comprehensive annual report, as well as the twice yearly publication, *Charity Matters*.

Cadbury plc

Contact
Alexandra Law, Community Investment Officer, Cadbury House,
Uxbridge Business Park, Uxbridge
UB8 1DH
Tel: 01895 615 000; Fax: 01895 615 001; website: www.cadbury.com

Year end: 31/12/2008

Turnover: £5.384 billion

Pre-tax profit: £400 million

Nature of business
Cadbury's principal activity is the manufacture and marketing of confectionery.

Main UK locations
Bournville, Maple Cross, Hertfordshire.

Cash donations: £507,000 (2008)

Total contributions: £1,054,515

Grants for the environment: £100,000

Community support policy

Cadbury's community investment can be a mixture of money, the time and skills of its people and/or gifts in kind. A wide range of resources can be given in kind. These include product donations, use of meeting rooms and other facilities, as well as access to training and other specialist materials.

As the needs of communities vary from region to region and country to county, Cadbury's investment is not prescriptive. Local business units decide how much money, time and skills or gifts in kind they will invest, using the *Growing community value around the world* guidelines to measure and manage their community investments.

Most requests for charitable donations in the UK are channelled through the Cadbury Foundation (Charity Commission no. 1050482) – the company's charitable trust in the UK. This has no endowment but is funded by grants from the company each year.

Grants are given mainly in support of organisations working with education and enterprise, health, welfare or the environment. National charities and local groups around its sites (in Birmingham, Bristol, London (Hackney) and Sheffield) may be assisted.

In 2008, Cadbury made a total community investment in the UK of just over £1 million, of which about £500,000 was in cash donations. This figure appears not to include the annual grant the company makes to the Cadbury Foundation (see below).

Cadbury Foundation

In 2007, the latest year for which accounts are available, the foundation received a donation of £755,000 from the company. The foundation in turn made grants totalling nearly £835,000. Grants to environmental organisations totalled £65,000. Beneficiaries in the UK included: Groundwork (£30,000) and the Soil Association (£16,000).

In kind support

Cadbury businesses donate a wide range of resources in kind including:

- products
- materials and promotional items
- equipment and furniture.

Education

Regular links are maintained with schools through work experience, work shadowing, collaborative projects and provision of school packs. A number of schools are now assigned a 'Links Manager' in order that the business can support their work.

Employee-led support

The company seeks to increase employee participation in community activities. Team challenges are effectively team-building and personal development activities which are performed by staff for the benefit of good causes. Various opportunities have been offered for staff to get involved, including: mentoring individual pupils, coaching and organising team sports, providing business and management advice and support to head teachers and community managers.

Earthwatch

Since 2005, Cadbury's have been working in partnership with Earthwatch on a biodiversity programme in Ghana. To date this has provided the opportunity for 78 employees from around the world to participate in the programme.

Cash-Match

Employees' fundraising efforts are acknowledged through a Cash-Match scheme up to a usual limit of £100 for an individual and up to £200 for team events. Employees have been cash-matched for activities ranging from raffles to sponsored show jumping.

Payroll giving

The 'Pennies from Heaven' scheme is available to employees wishing to make tax-effective donations to a charity of their choice.

Exclusions

In view of the policy of concentrating grants behind selected projects, most ad hoc appeals have to be declined and are therefore not encouraged.

The foundation does not support: requests for commercial sponsorship, help with funding of individuals' education and training programmes, purchase of advertising space, involvement in fundraising projects, travel or leisure projects, donation of gifts in kind (including company products), regional projects unless in the locality of company operations.

Normally support has not been given for projects outside the UK since it is policy to provide support through local businesses in the many countries around the world where Cadbury has operations.

Applications

As indicated above, appeals outside the criteria defined are not encouraged, as most grants are committed in advance on an ongoing basis.

However, if you are able to answer 'Yes' to all the below, then it may be possible for the foundation to consider your organisation for funding:

- is the project promoting education, enterprise or employability within a group or groups of people?
- would your client base be considered at risk or socially excluded?
- are you located in geographical proximity to one of our major UK operations (e.g., Birmingham, Sheffield, Bristol, London (Hackney))?

■ are some of our employees already involved?

Please write to the correspondent at:

Cadbury Foundation
Cadbury House
Uxbridge Business Park
Uxbridge
UB8 1DH.

If you are seeking sponsorship, advertising, fundraising or requests for donations or gifts-in kind (including our products) please contact your local business.

Carillion plc

Contact
Richard Tapp, Director of Legal Services, Chairman to the Appeals Committee,
24 Birch Street,
Wolverhampton WV1 4HY
Tel: 01902 422 431; Fax: 01902 316 165; website: www.carillionplc.com

Year end: 31/12/2008

Turnover: £5.2 billion

Pre-tax profit: £115.9 million

Nature of business
Providing expertise in commercial and industrial building, refurbishment, civil engineering, road and rail construction and maintenance, mechanical and electrical services, facilities management and PFI solutions.

Main UK locations
Wolverhampton, Leeds, Manchester, Liverpool, London, Bristol, Brentford, Glasgow.

Cash donations: £129,000 (2008)

Total contributions: £967,583

Grants for the environment: £30,000

Community support policy
Carillion's community involvement benefits one of the following groups: charities, not-for-profit organisations representing economically and socially disadvantaged groups, schools and youth organisations, environmental, development and cultural groups, organisations which aid social economic regeneration, campaigns addressing specific community needs and social enterprise.

Furthermore, the charitable objective should be close to or have some connection with the group and its objectives, whilst the subject matter should be tangible and be able to reflect the support given by the group, i.e. the group should receive some public recognition.

The value of investment includes staff time spent in community involvement activities or on full or part-time secondments, provision of professional services, gifts in kind, use of facilities and loan of assets as well as financial contributions such as cash donations and payments or sponsorships.

In 2008, the company made cash donations of £129,000 (2007: £150,000). The main beneficiaries were: The Wildlife Trust; British Occupational Health Research Foundation; Beacon Centre for the Blind; and The Prince's Trust.

Carillion participate in and arrange various events in line with the focus areas of its 'Making Tomorrow A Better Place' theme. These range from work with local communities, charities and enhancing the natural environment to recycling products that would otherwise have been sent to landfill. A range of case studies are provided on its website under the headings of: 'Sustainable Communities and Workforce'; 'Natural Resource Protection and Environmental Enhancement'; and 'Climate Change and Energy'.

In kind support

This can include staff time spent in community involvement activities or on full or part-time secondments, provision of professional services, gifts in kind, use of facilities and loan of assets.

Employee-led support

Carillion businesses work closely with schools on raising awareness of the dangers of construction sites; staff conduct tours for children around sites during construction phases, helping them in CV writing and providing school work placements.

Payroll giving

The company operate a payroll giving scheme.

Applications

In writing to the correspondent.

Information available

The company produces a Social Responsibility Report. Its website contains comprehensive details of its community activities.

CEMEX UK Operations Ltd

Contact
Chief Administrator for Charities, CEMEX House, Coldharbour Lane, Thorpe, Egham TW20 8TD
Tel: 01932 568 833; Fax: 01932 568 933; website: www.cemex.co.uk

Year end: 31/12/2007

Turnover: £978.7 million

Pre-tax profit: £56.2 million

Nature of business
Principal activities: production and supply of materials for use in the construction industry.

Main UK locations
Rugby, Barrington, South Ferriby, Rochester, Egham.

Cash donations: £202,000 (2007)

Grants for the environment: £100,000

Community support policy

CEMEX is a global building solutions company and leading supplier of cement, ready-mixed concrete and aggregates.

Support from the company for environmental projects is available through three avenues: CEMEX UK Foundation; CEMEX Community Fund; and Rugby Group Benevolent Fund.

CEMEX UK Foundation: The activities of the foundation cover a number of key areas including the company's 'Charity of the Year' (2007: Butterfly Conservation), supporting employees volunteering and matched funding of employees fundraising efforts.

CEMEX Community Fund: Operating under the Landfill Communities Fund, support is available for projects within three miles of a CEMEX quarry or landfill. Grants range from £1,000 to £15,000 for projects which:

- provide and maintain public parks and amenities when the work protects the social, built and/or natural environment

- repair, or restore buildings or structures which are of religious, historical or architectural interest.

Rugby Group Benevolent Fund: Smaller scale support is available through this scheme for initiatives local to the Rugby site. See **Applications** for contact details.

Community contributions

The latest 2007 annual report and accounts for CEMEX UK Operations declared a charitable donations figure for the year of £202,105 (2006: £14,567).

The company's website provides comprehensive details of some of the projects it has been involved in. For example:

Rehabilitating offenders: During 2007 CEMEX UK worked with a leading environmental regeneration charity, Groundwork, to support former offenders. To help them back to work, the former offenders assisted with a restoration project and learnt woodland management skills at Stanwell Quarry. The project aimed to provide the social and employment skills necessary for offenders to join or re-enter the workplace following a prison sentence.

Educational projects: Again in partnership with Groundwork (Hertfordshire), CEMEX UK supported educational projects, such as one with Green Lanes Primary School in Hatfield, where pupils studied quarrying, and learnt how the industry has influenced the local and wider environment.

Conservation issues: For 14 years CEMEX UK has published an annual conservation book with leading not-for-profit organisations to highlight conservation issues and support fundraising programmes. In 2007, it signed a memorandum of understanding and published 'Birds & People' with BirdLife international. Through this book CEMEX UK hope to raise awareness amongst the public of the importance of bird conservation, and of the fact that declining bird populations are primarily due to habitat loss; something the company is working to redress in the UK as part of our quarry restoration programmes.

Under the Landfill Tax Credit scheme donations totalling £180,000 were made in 2006/07. Details of the beneficiaries and how to apply are available at: www.cemexcf.org.uk

In kind support
Environment
CEMEX has worked with the Wildlife Trust and Suffolk Wildlife Trust in restoring quarry sites from which it is no longer extracting aggregates. These provide both nature reserves and leisure facilities for the local community.

Employee-led support
The company foundation not only supports employees in their volunteering activities on behalf of the charity of the year, but also, to a lesser extent, where employees are giving their own time on behalf of a local community or charitable organisation.

For appropriate activities and charities matched funding may also be given up to a maximum of £250 per employee.

Exclusions
No support for circular appeals, animal welfare, appeals from individuals or advertising in charity brochures.

Applications
In writing to the correspondent. All appeals are considered by a monthly committee which decides what to support.

Applicants wishing to establish whether they meet the company's proximity criteria can now visit: cemexlocations.co.uk

For further information about applications to the Rugby Benevolent Fund, please contact Ian Southcott, UK Community Affairs Manager at CEMEX House in Rugby.

Deep Sea Leisure plc

Contact
Heather Taylor, Forthside Terrace, North Queensferry, Inverkeithing, Fife KY11 1JR
Tel: 01383 411 411;
website: www.blueplanetaquarium.com
Year end: 31/10/2008
Turnover: £7.359 million
Pre-tax profit: £1.949 million

Nature of business
Owner and operator of public aquarium visitor attractions.

Main UK locations
Ellesmere Port.

Cash donations: £6,800 (2008)

Grants for the environment: £3,000

Community support policy

Deep Sea Leisure provides small scale support to charities working with children, the disabled, animal welfare and the environment. There is some preference for Scottish-based organisations.

In 2008, the company made grants to 12 organisations totalling £6,801 (2007: £11,918). Although relatively small in size, many grants appear to be recurrent. Beneficiaries included: Amphibian Ark (£1,464); Riding for the Disabled – Dunfermline (£1,175); Hearing Dogs for Deaf People (£967); Oxfam (£572); The Shark Trust (£453); and Marine Conservation Society (£180).

Past beneficiaries have included: Keep Scotland Beautiful (£991); Scottish Wildlife Trust (£576); SSPCA (£399); Seahorse Trust (£352); PADI Project Aware (£218); and The Scottish Fisheries Museum Trust (£173).

Applications

In writing to the correspondent. However, please be aware that there is a limited budget and that many of the current grant recipients are supported regularly.

Duchy Originals Ltd

Contact
(See **Applications**),
The Old Ryde House,
393 Richmond Road, East Twickenham
TW1 2EF

Tel: 020 8831 6800;
website: www.duchyoriginals.com

Year end: 31/03/2008

Turnover: £4,058,234

Pre-tax profit: £151,717

Nature of business
The ownership and management of a range of premium organic food and drink products under the 'Duchy Originals' brand.

Cash donations: £743,000 (2007)

Grants for the environment: £200,000

Community support policy

The Duchy Originals company was launched in 1990 by HRH the Prince of Wales and in 1999 made its first profits which were donated to the Prince's Charities Foundation. This support continues, as does the company's commitment to long term sustainability.

The Prince's Charities Foundation

Founded in 1979 the foundation was established by the Prince to enable him to help support a variety of charitable causes and projects. Besides benefiting from the profits of Duchy Originals, the foundation also receives support from Highgrove shops and other social enterprises within The Prince's Charities.

The foundation's website states: *[It] receives an ever-increasing number of requests for assistance. Donations are made to an extensive variety of causes working with environmental issues, health and hospices, community and welfare, education, heritage, the built environment and charities supporting servicemen and women.*

Although the company did not make a donation to the foundation in 2008 (the latest year for which accounts are available) it did so consistently over the previous four years.

In 2008 the foundation had an income of £23.3 million, mainly from commercial trading operations, with £5.5 million coming from what was described as 'miscellaneous donations'. grants during the year totalled £22.7 million and were broken down as follows:

- culture (£19.3 million)
- environment (£1.6 million)
- medical welfare (£705,000)
- education (£553,000)
- other (£531,000)
- children and youth (£80,000)
- overseas aid (£19,000).

Beneficiaries of environmental grants of over £10,000 each included: Accounting for Sustainability (£325,00); The Prince's Foundation for the Built Environment (£277,000); The Rainforest Project (£228,000); Northumberland Wildlife Trust (£87,000); The Soil Association (£35,000); and Cambrian Mountains Initiative and The National Trust (£13,000 each).

Further information about the work of The Prince's Charities Foundation can be found in the trust section of this guide on page 181.

Applications

In writing to: The Trustees, The Prince's Charities Foundation, Clarence House, St James's, London SW1A 1BA (Tel: 020 7930 4832).

ERM Group Holdings Ltd

Contact
Stuart Keeling, ERM Foundation UK, 2nd Floor, Exchequer Court, 33 St Mary Axe, London EC3A 8AA Tel: 020 3206 5200; Fax: 020 3206 5440; website: www.erm.com

Year end: 31/03/2008

Turnover: £317.981 million

Pre-tax profit: £12.684 million

Nature of business
The principal activities of the group are the provision of environmental, social, risk and health and safety consulting services.

Cash donations: £111,000 (2008)

Grants for the environment: £75,000

Community support policy

ERM (Environmental Resources Management) was established in the UK in 1971 and has eight offices in London, Aberdeen, Bristol, Edinburgh, Leeds, Manchester, Oxford and Swansea.

In order to help the company and its staff support and contribute to environmental projects at home and in the developing world, the ERM Foundation UK (Charity Commission no. 1113415) was established in March 2006. On its website, the company states that:

The ERM Foundation UK supports environmental and community projects near each of our offices ensuring ERMers are able to participate in projects. ERMers are encouraged to nominate charities and projects that they feel would benefit from both our professional expertise and the support the ERM Foundation can bring.

Support for these causes is given through appropriate charitable, educational and scientific means and can include pro-bono as well as financial assistance. Projects have ranged from programmes to help inner city teenagers experience life in the National Forest to promoting household resource conservation.

In 2008, the group made donations to charity of £111,000 (2007: £138,000) of which £73,000 (2007: £60,000) went to the ERM Foundation UK.

The ERM Foundation UK

For the year ending 31 March 2007, the foundation had an income of around £311,000. Although no grants were made during the year, examples of projects recently supported by the company/

foundation were given on its website. These included those listed below.

The London Orchard Project: through the creation of mini-orchards across London the project aims to promote food security and reduce carbon emissions. The foundation has raised funds to purchase trees and staff have given their time to teach the skills needed to plant, maintain and harvest fruit trees.

C S Lewis Nature Reserve: financial support was given to help the Berkshire, Buckinghamshire and Oxford Wildlife Trust improve and preserve this Oxford-based nature reserve.

Earth Restoration Service (ERS): financial support was provided by the foundation in order that ERS could establish a School Tree Nurseries programme. This aims to help schools establish a tree nursery in their grounds and then plant saplings on suitable land in the community. The success of the programme has led to it being expanded to include over 50 schools.

Gunnersbury Triangle, London: through the establishment of a long-term relationship with the London Wildlife Trust, the foundation has provided volunteer time and some consultancy services to the organisation. This enabled an annual open day to take place at Gunnersbury Triangle and the organisation of a summer children's programme.

In kind support

Company staff may provide their skills and knowledge on a pro-bono basis to appropriate environmental and sustainability projects.

Employee-led support

Staff are supported by the foundation in their volunteering efforts.

Applications

In writing to the correspondent.

Esso UK Ltd

Contact
Community Affairs Assistant
UK Public Affairs
ExxonMobil House, Mailpoint 8,
Ermyn Way, Leatherhead KT22 8UX
Tel: 01372 222000; Fax: 01372 223222;
website: www.esso.co.uk

Year end: 31/12/2007

Turnover: £12.98 billion

Pre-tax profit: £1.339 billion

Nature of business
Principal activities: the exploration for, production, transportation and sale of, crude oil, natural gas and natural gas liquids; the refining, distribution and marketing of petroleum products within the UK.

Main UK locations
Leatherhead, Fawley, Fife, Aberdeen.

Cash donations: £500,000 (2007)

Total contributions: £1.5 million

Grants for the environment: £100,000

Community support policy

Esso's website explains that:

It is ExxonMobil's [Esso's parent company] policy to be a good corporate citizen wherever we do business. In the UK, we support the local communities around our key business locations. Our focus is on employee volunteering, education, environmental and neighbourhood projects.

The company directs its support to the neighbourhoods around its key business locations. As a result its community programme is based on the needs and wants of the people in those areas. Emphasis is placed, therefore, on: education (particularly the teaching of science, technology, maths and environmental concerns), and the environment. ExxonMobil employees and their families are also encouraged to participate in community initiatives through the VIP (Volunteer Involvement Programme) scheme.

ExxonMobil proactively plans its programmes and likes to establish long-term working partnerships with the organisations it works with in the voluntary sector. Almost all funds are committed at the beginning of the year, therefore unsolicited requests are rarely supported. There is a preference for voluntary organisations working in the areas of Leatherhead, Fawley, Fife and Aberdeen.

In 2007, Esso UK Ltd invested around £1.5 million in the community of which £500,000 was in cash donations. Only limited information was available about those organisations that received funding from the company. However, the following statement regarding its support for environmental issues is taken from the company's website:

ExxonMobil has a long-standing history of environment-related community work. We encourage the involvement of local people in activities aimed at improving their local environment, maximising energy efficiency and managing waste through recycling. We also have an ongoing commitment to make all of our operations more energy efficient. To complement this commitment, we also support energy efficiency initiatives in the community.

We also work closely with CREATE (Centre for Research, Education and Training in Energy), a government and industry supported organisation, which is dedicated to the promotion of energy-saving education in UK schools and colleges. Energy savings have a positive effect on reducing carbon emissions, so it's important for everyone to be encouraged to use energy more efficiently.

In kind support

The following is also taken from the website:

Education

'*The ExxonMobil Link Schools programme is now reaching out to about 35 schools around our key operating locations. This is delivered by organisations including Learning Through Landscapes who encourage schools to look at the potential their school grounds have for learning and enjoyment, and CREATE who are using their experience and expertise to help shape the programme and to offer schools a package of support including advice, materials and resources.*

Employee-led support

Volunteering

In 2006, we launched the ExxonMobil Energy Challenge, recruiting volunteers to provide practical advice to low-income householders on ways they can reduce their fuel costs. The volunteers visit vulnerable households and community venues, offering tips on ways to conserve energy and to keep homes warm. They also help people to apply for available grants and benefits. The initiative is being carried out in partnership with Community Service Volunteers (CSV), National Energy Action (NEA) and Energy Action Scotland (EAS).

Through our Volunteer Involvement Programme (VIP) we encourage employees and their families to contribute their time, talent and energy to local charities and non-profit organisations. To assist and recognise their efforts, we provide contributions to the organisations that our employees and their families support

Payroll giving

The company operates the Payroll Giving in Action scheme.

Exclusions

No response to circular appeals. No grant support for advertising in charity brochures, animal welfare, appeals from individuals, medical research, overseas projects, political appeals, religious appeals, or sport.

Applications

The company responds to all appeals received, but in view of the policy outlined above unsolicited appeals are very rarely successful.

Lafarge Aggregates & Concrete UK

Contact
Charity Advisor, Communications Department, PO Box 7388,
Granite House,
Watermead Business Park, Syston,
Leicester LE7 1WA
Tel: 0116 264 8000; Fax: 0116 269 8348;
website: www.lafarge-aggregates.co.uk

Year end: 31/12/2006

Turnover: £460.764 million

Pre-tax profit: £16.823 million

Nature of business
Supplier of asphalt, aggregate and concrete products.

Main UK locations
Leicester.

Cash donations: £820,000 (2006)

Grants for the environment: £300,000

Community support policy

Lafarge Aggregates & Concrete UK has a robust community relations programme which includes: community grants; community events; employee involvement; and education.

There are two ways local charities and community organisations can apply for grants: Lafarge charitable donations and the Landfill Communities Fund. Regarding the latter, Lafarge has produced a leaflet [downloadable from their website] to explain what the fund is and how local groups can apply for a wide range of community and environmental projects situated within 10 miles of a landfill site and close to a Lafarge Aggregates & Concrete UK operational site.

In 2007, the company donated more than £820,000 to community projects around the UK. No specific details regarding the beneficiaries were available.

As well as employing in-house restoration specialists, Lafarge work on various restoration projects in partnership with a number of environmental organisations, including: Berkshire, Buckinghamshire and Oxfordshire Wildlife Trust; Durham Wildlife Trust; Goodquarry.com; National Memorial Arboretum; and Whitby Natural World. In total, Lafarge is a member of 17 county wildlife trusts, enjoys active relationships with many conservation groups and is the guardian of two National Nature Reserves (NNRs), as well as actively managing 30 Sites of Special Scientific Interest (SSSIs), 17 of which are former quarries.

In kind support

Education

Lafarge Aggregates & Concrete UK is committed to developing relationships with schools close to our sites. The company also supports national education initiatives such as Enterprise Week.

Schools and other education groups are welcome to visit Lafarge's operational sites including hard rock and sand & gravel quarries, landfill and recycling centres and Readymix plants. Tours of its head office in Leicestershire are also available. Your local Lafarge site manager is also available to speak to your class in school. Tours are dependent on weather and safety factors. To organise a visit or speaker, please contact the site manager directly. Or, contact the head office on 0116 264 8251.

Environment

Lafarge works in partnership with a number of organisations such as wildlife trusts, national conservation organisations and local community groups on quarry restoration projects.

Employee-led support

The following is taken from Lafarge's website:

Lafarge encourages its employees to get involved in community activities, from speaking about geology, wildlife and biodiversity to local groups, to fundraising for local causes.

If you'd like one of our experts to speak at your meeting or event, or would like to let us know about your fundraising activities, please contact us by writing to:

Community Involvement
Communications Department
Lafarge Aggregates & Concrete UK
PO BOX 7388
Granite House
Watermead Business Park
Syston
Leicester
LE7 1WA.

Exclusions

Local appeals not in areas of company presence.

Applications

The following is taken from the company's website:

Charitable donations programme

Charities and community organisations are encouraged to apply for a cash or materials donation. To be eligible for consideration, your organisation must be located within three miles of an operational Lafarge Aggregates & Concrete UK site or be otherwise affected by our operations – please contact Lafarge's charity advisor for further information. To find out which Lafarge Aggregates & Concrete UK site is nearest you, please refer to the 'Location finder' on our website.

All requests for cash or materials donations must be made in writing, with details of your organisation and/or project. If you are requesting a materials donation, please indicate the type and quantity of material, when it is needed and if you require delivery or will be collecting the material.

We endeavour to respond to all requests within 14 working days.

Lush Cosmetics Ltd

Contact
Sophie Pritchard, Charitable Giving Manager, 29 High Street, Poole BH15 1AB
Tel: 01202 667 830;
email: charitypot@lush.co.uk;
website: lushcharitypot.co.uk

Year end: 30/06/2008

Turnover: £153.177 million

Pre-tax profit: £19.431 million

Nature of business
The production and retail of cosmetic products.

Cash donations: £482,000 (2008)

Grants for the environment: £40,000

Community support policy

Lush's support for charitable organisations has grown nearly ten-fold in the last three years, especially so since the launch of its 'Charity Pot' in 2007 and its continuing expansion in the UK and abroad.

Lush state: *'We decided to prioritise those charities which really struggle to secure funding, where relatively small donations make a huge difference. Therefore, many of our grants have gone to small, grassroots organisations and especially those working for causes which find it hard to raise funds'*. With this in mind, support is mainly directed towards animal welfare, environment and conservation, and humanitarian concerns.

Lush's 'Charity Pot' contains hand and body lotion produced from fairly traded cocoa butter and almond oil and is sold in its various retail outlets. Every penny the consumer pays for the product (excluding the VAT which the UK government receives) goes into the Lush Charity Pot Fund which is then used to support a variety of charities, good causes and campaign groups. Since its launch in April 2007, Lush has donated a total of over £267,000 to 58 charities and other good causes both here in the UK and overseas.

According to its latest annual report and accounts, donations to charitable organisations in 2008 amounted to £428,000 worldwide. Beneficiaries included: Sumatra Orang Utan Society; Kipungani Schools Trust in Kenya; Dorset Wildlife Trust; Beirut for The Ethical Treatment of Animals (BETA); The Gordon Charitable Trust; Transport 2000; and Plane Stupid. More recently support has been given to the Fresh Start Foundation and Wherever the Need.

Further information about each of these and other charities Lush has supported can be found on their website.

Employee-led support

Payroll giving
The Charities Aid Foundation's Give As You Earn scheme is in operation.

Applications

To tell Lush about interesting charities or projects which you'd like to nominate for their support in future, please email: charitypot@lush.co.uk

The Manchester Airport Group plc

Contact
Mrs Wendy Sinfield, Community Relations Manager, Wythenshawe, Manchester M90 1QX

Tel: 0871 271 0711; Fax: 0161 489 3813; email: community.relations@ manairport.co.uk; website: www.manchesterairport.co.uk
Year end: 31/03/2009
Turnover: £371.3 million
Pre-tax profit: £54.2 million
Nature of business
International airport operation.

Main UK locations
Manchester.
Cash donations: £100,000 (2009)
Total contributions: £639,000
Grants for the environment: £20,000

Community support policy

The Manchester Airport Group (MAG) focuses its community work on the areas closest to Manchester Airport and gives priority to those with the greatest social and economic need. A significant proportion of its funding is provided via the Manchester Airport Community Trust Fund (Charity Commission no. 1071703) which receives an annual donation from the company (see below).

The group's other airports at Bournemouth and East Midlands have smaller community funds which support environmental initiatives. A fund does not appear to exist at Humberside Airport, although help may be available to local groups. Further information on community relations at each of these airports can be found at: www.magworld.co.uk

Manchester Airport Community Trust Fund

The following is taken from the trust's website:

[The trust] is a registered charity and was established to promote, enhance, improve and protect both the natural and built environment in our local community.

In 2009/10, the airport is contributing £100,000 which is further enhanced by income from fines imposed on airlines when their aircraft exceed our noise limits. These funds are then used to support neighbourhood and community projects throughout the area of benefit which covers a 12-mile radius of the Airport, concentrating on the areas most exposed to aircraft noise.

The trust will fund projects that enhance, protect and conserve the natural and built environment. It will consider applications for projects which:

- *encourage tree planting, forestation, landscaping and other works of environmental improvement or heritage conservation*

- *promote or advance social welfare for recreation and sport and leisure, with the object of improving the conditions of life for those living or working in, or visitors to, the area of benefit*

- *provide better appreciation of the natural and urban environment and ways of better serving, protecting and improving the same. This may include education and training*

- *promote the use of the natural environment as a safe habitat for flora and fauna of all kinds*

- *in the opinion of the trustees are within the Trust's charitable purposes.*

Projects must be for the benefit of the whole community, or a substantial section of it, and not groups of an exclusive nature.

In 2007/08 the trust received a donation of £100,000 from Manchester Airport and a further £39,000 as a result of noise fines levied at the airport. The trust awarded 71 grants totalling nearly £145,000. Beneficiaries of grants for environmental purposes included those to: Friends of Hesketh Park (£5,000); Friends of Torkington Park (£3,750); Wythenshawe Community Farm (£3,800); and Friends of Bernadette's Eco Gardens (£530).

In kind support

Through a network of 'Community Champions' established right across its business, members of staff are encouraged to get involved in volunteering in local projects. Recent examples include: reading mentoring, mock interviews, 'World of Work' days, and the Airport Academy project – an employment and training programme helping unemployed people living in the Manchester South Regeneration areas and, particularly, in Wythenshawe.

Employee-led support

The company has an active employee volunteering scheme and allows employees company time off in which to volunteer.

Exclusions

No support for appeals from individuals, commercial organisations, organisations which have statutory responsibilities such as hospitals or schools (unless the project is clearly not a statutory responsibility), those working for profit, or for organisations outside of the trust boundary.

Applications

Charities and schools in communities in close proximity to Manchester airport which do not qualify for funding from the trust fund may apply for prizes for fundraising by contacting the correspondent.

Grant applications to the Manchester Airport Community Trust Fund should not be made without first reading the policy guidelines. These, along with an application form, are available upon request from the Fund Administrator at the address given below. You can also get an application form and further information on-line from www.manchesterairport.co.uk

The Administrator
Manchester Airport Community Trust
   Fund
Community Relations
Manchester Airport
Manchester
M90 1QX

Tel: 0161 489 5281 (An answerphone is available for out-of-hours enquiries)

Fax: 0161 489 3467

Email: trust.fund@manairport.co.uk

Trustees meet quarterly. You should return your completed form to the administrator no later than the first Friday of March, June, September or December for consideration by the trustees the following month.

If you are successful you will usually receive a cheque a month after the trustees' meeting. You must send the trust fund original invoices/receipts for the works or goods you purchased within three months of receiving your grant cheque.

The National Farmers Union Mutual Insurance Society Ltd

Contact
James D Creechan, Secretary to the trust, Tiddington Road, Stratford upon Avon, Warwickshire CV37 7BJ
Tel: 01789 204211;
email: nfu_mutual_charitable_trust@nfu mutual.co.uk;
website: www.nfumutual.co.uk

Year end: 31/12/2008

Pre-tax profit: £685 million

Nature of business
Insurers.

Main UK locations
Stratford upon Avon.

Cash donations: £260,000 (2008)

Grants for the environment: £100,000

Community support policy
The National Farmers Union Mutual Insurance Society Ltd's (NFU Mutual) corporate responsibility programme has a number of strands to it. These range from substantial support for the farming community, through to an associated charitable trust, localised support, employee fundraising and a payroll giving scheme.

As a member of Business in the Community, the company coordinates its programme of support activities under four of BitC's corporate social responsibility headings: community; environment; workplace and market place.

In 2008, NFU Mutual declared charitable donations in the UK of £260,000 (2007: £261,700) of which £250,000 was paid to The NFU Mutual Charitable Trust (Charity Commission no. 1073064). The company also makes small-scale donations through its Community Giving Fund which helped 89 causes during the year.

In addition to the above. in 2009 NFU Mutual are offering a donation of £10 to Garden Organic when a member takes out an NFU Mutual insurance policy. Garden Organic is the national charity for organic growing, with a mission to inspire, encourage and support individuals and groups to grow organically.

The NFU Mutual Charitable Trust
In 2008, the trust had a total income of £264,000 and made grants totalling £165,000. Support is directed towards education, the relief of poverty in agriculture, rural development and insurance.

13 organisations benefited from grant support, including: Farming and Countryside Education (£22,000); Royal

Agricultural Benevolent Institution (£17,000); Agrifood Charities Partnership (£10,000); and The Arthur Rank Centre (£5,000).

Employee-led support

Employees are encouraged to fundraise on behalf of charity. It is not known if these sums are matched by the company.

Payroll giving

A recent campaign has nearly doubled the number of staff partaking in the scheme offered by the company.

Applications

In writing to the correspondent of the trust.

Enquiries regarding support from the NFU Community Giving Fund should be directed in the first instance to Beth Wells, Corporate Communications Executive on 01789 202173 or email: beth_wells@nfumutual.co.uk

Northumbrian Water Group

Contact
The Community Relations Manager, Abbey Road, Pity Me, Durham DH1 5FJ
Tel: 0870 608 4820;
website: www.nwl.co.uk

Year end: 30/03/2009

Turnover: £641.2 million

Pre-tax profit: £168.8 million

Nature of business
Northumbrian Water Group plc is one of the UK's 10 water and sewerage businesses. The company and its subsidiaries work in three related areas: the supply of water and waste water services within the UK; international water management; and a range of supporting technical and consultancy services.

Main UK locations
Durham.

Cash donations: £135,000 (2009)

Grants for the environment: £50,000

Community support policy

The following is taken from the company's website:

NWG gives not only money but also time and facilities to help its communities. These activities are mainly targeted to support projects which make the areas served better places in which to live, work or invest. The key elements of the programme include:

- *an extensive community involvement programme supporting the work of community foundations and encouraging voluntary time through the 'Just an hour' scheme and funding through 'Cheque it out'*

- *health and environmental campaigning, including our innovative 'Water for health' initiative*

- *educational programmes which range from curriculum support to 'Back to Business' where NWL is a lead partner in a pilot scheme to link schools and businesses*

- *environmental partnerships and campaigns where, as well as being a member of many environmental organisations, NWL has developed some key partnerships to help the conservation and biodiversity of our sites, for example, with the Essex Wildlife Trust at Hanningfield*

- *regional support for local community organisations and support for our adopted charity, WaterAid.*

Environmental

Small grants for environmental purposes are distributed via the region's community foundations, such as the Community Foundation serving Tyne & Wear and Northumberland, Tees Valley Community Foundation and County

Durham Foundation. For example, £300 was granted to Satley Residents Association to fund the Wild Bird Feeding Station at Satley Marwood Social Centre and £200 to Friends of Prudhoe Woods.

Key partnerships have also been developed by Northumbrian Water to help the conservation of biodiversity on its sites. Its contribution to the partnerships includes funding project officers. Current partnerships include: Northumberland Wildlife Trust (Kielder and Bakethin); Durham Wildlife Trust; Essex Wildlife Trust (Hanningfield); Broads Authority (Lound and Trinity Broads); and Davy Down Trust.

In kind support

The company gives additional support through gifts in kind, joint promotions and encouraging employee volunteering.

Up to 2008, over £225,000 has been provided for water coolers in schools. Over 500 have been supplied to date in over 300 schools.

Employee-led support

An employee volunteering scheme launched in 2002, Just an hour, encourages employees to spend an hour of work time a month providing support to community or environmental initiatives. In 2008, 23% of employees participate in the scheme, giving over 5,431 hours to the community.

The 'Care for safety' scheme, which encourages employees to reduce accidents and associated lost time, has triggered payments totalling £49,890 for our nominated charities: Great North Air Ambulance Service, Mencap's Dilston College, RNLI, St Teresa's Hospice and East Anglia's Children's Hospices.

Exclusions

No support for circular appeals, local appeals not in areas of company presence, large national appeals or overseas projects (other than support for WaterAid).

Applications

In writing to the correspondent.

Tate & Lyle plc

Contact
The Corporate Social Responsibility Manager, Sugar Quay, Lower Thames Street, London EC3R 6DQ
Tel: 020 7626 6525; Fax: 020 7623 5213; website: www.tate-lyle.co.uk

Year end: 31/03/2009

Turnover: £3.553 billion

Pre-tax profit: £113 million

Nature of business
Principal activities are the processing of carbohydrates to provide a range of sweetener and starch products and animal feed; and bulk storage. The company's UK sugar refinery is in London.

Main UK locations
Burton-on-Trent, Hull, Newham, Merseyside, Selby.

Cash donations: £674,000 (2009)

Total contributions: £895,000

Grants for the environment: £120,000

Community support policy

Tate & Lyle's main areas of charitable support are education and causes close to where the company operates or those in which an employee is involved. Main locations are Newham, Merseyside, Avonmouth, Hull, Burton-on-Trent and Selby.

The company guidelines for funding and support are:

- education 50%
- environment 25%
- health 15%
- arts 10%.

Each year around 300 organisations are supported, ranging from long-established charities to fledgling community organisations. Community support takes many forms, depending on the needs of the organisation, and includes funding, employee volunteering, consultancy, donation of products and equipment and, for selected partners, free use of the company's warehousing, office accommodation and meeting room facilities.

In 2008/09 worldwide community contributions totalled £895,000 of which £674,000 was in cash donations. The actual community spend on environmental issues was 18% of the total.

UK organisations supported during the year included: Community Links; Community Food Enterprise; Richard House Children's Hospice; and East London Business Alliance.

In kind support

Education

The company's main education activities are the major literacy programmes, Reading is Fundamental and the Newham Literacy Programme.

Non-cash support has also been given to education business partnerships.

Enterprise

The company supports Business in the Community and the East London Partnership.

Secondments

Applications for secondments to enterprise agencies are considered, and executives throughout the group are encouraged to participate in local educational systems.

Employee-led support

The company operates an employee volunteering scheme.

Education

Links are developed with local schools and colleges offering work experience and work shadowing.

Payroll giving

The company operates the Give As You Earn scheme.

Exclusions

No support is given to circular appeals, advertising in charity brochures, individuals, purely denominational (religious) appeals, local appeals not in areas of company presence, animal welfare, political appeals, sport or large national appeals.

Applications

In writing to the correspondent.

Total UK Ltd

Contact
Kate Munro, Corporate Communications Manager, 40 Clarendon Road, Watford WD17 1TQ
Tel: 01923 694000; Fax: 01923 694400; website: www.total.co.uk

Year end: 31/12/2008

Turnover: £7.219 billion

Pre-tax profit: £148 million

Nature of business
The refining, distribution and sale of petroleum products and lubricants.

Main UK locations
Milford Haven, London, Watford, Redhill, Immingham, Stalybridge, Aberdeen.

Cash donations: £370,000 (2008)

Grants for the environment: £100,000

Community support policy

There is a preference for local charities in areas of company presence (i.e. Aberdeen, Watford, Immingham, Milford Haven, Redhill and Stalybridge), appeals relevant to company business, or those which have a member of company staff involved. Preferred areas of support are the arts, youth, education, enterprise/ training, environment/heritage, medical research and science/technology.

Supports is also given to national charities (e.g., via 'Charity of the Year'), while at a local level, regional offices, refineries and service stations organise 'Fun Days' on behalf of a chosen charity.

Charitable donations in 2008 amounted to £370,000 (2007: £540,000). Past beneficiaries have included: Royal Scottish National Orchestra; National Galleries of Scotland; Young People's Trust for the Environment; and, Disaster Emergency Committee. The national charity CLIC Sargent appears to receive yearly support from the company.

UK Green School Awards

The Total UK website explains how:

The Green School Awards, organised by the Young People's Trust for the Environment (YPTE), were launched in 2006 to encourage cross-curricular work on the environment in primary schools and stimulate interest in both conventional and alternative energy sources.

The awards enable teachers to bring the environment into many areas of study across the national curriculum for England, Wales and Scotland.

Participating schools develop projects which compete for regional awards, with regional award winners then going on to a National Green School Awards final ceremony. Prizes range from £500 to £5,000

Total Foundation

This French-based charity has supported over 150 projects in 40 countries since its inception 15 years ago. The foundation was allocated 50 million euros for its fourth financial period 2008–2012 and supports the community, culture and the environment. Further details are available at: foundation.total.com

In kind support

The company provides the use of facilities such as postage and photocopying.

Employee-led support

Payroll giving

The company operates the Give As You Earn Scheme.

Exclusions

No support for circular appeals, advertising in charity brochures, animal welfare, appeals from individuals, elderly people, fundraising events, overseas projects, political appeals, religious appeals, sickness/disability, social welfare or sport.

Applications

In writing only to the correspondent for those organisations located near to Total refining and marketing facilities (please refer to the list of 'preferred locations'). For organisations based near to Total's exploration and production facilities in Aberdeen, please contact: Sandra McIntosh, Public Affairs & Corporate Communication Department, Total E&P plc, Crawpeel Road, Altens, Aberdeen AB12 3FG (Tel: 01224 297000).

Information available: The company produce a Corporate Social Responsibility Report.

Toyota Motor Manufacturing (UK) Ltd

Contact
Susan Wilkinson, External Affairs Department, Burnaston, Derbyshire DE1 9TA
Tel: 01332 282121;
website: www.toyotauk.com
Year end: 31/03/2008

Turnover: £2.774 billion

Pre-tax profit: £9.254 million

Nature of business
Car and engine manufacture.

Main UK locations
Burnaston, Deeside.

Cash donations: £257,000 (2008)

Grants for the environment: £50,000

Community support policy

Since the start of production in 1992 Toyota has contributed to a variety of local and national community causes. The focus of support is based around four main areas – environment, children, education, and health. In addition, employee involvement in the community is encouraged and, where suitable, financial support is given to employee fundraising activities or to local community organisations in which employees play an active role. Local charitable events are regularly supported through the donation of raffle prizes and vehicles.

In 2007/08, the company made charitable donations of £349,330 (2006/07: £256,541). These donations comprised:

- £40,102 to charities involved in conserving the environment and promoting environmental preservation and awareness

- £17,733 to charities involved in medical research

- £291,495 to local charities involved in a range of activities in the communities surrounding Burnaston and Deeside.

Toyota Manufacturing UK provides grants of up to £1,000 for successful projects in the fields of the environment, children, education and health within its local communities.

These grants are intended for the purchase of long-term tangible equipment and resources up to the value of £1,000.

The following is taken from the company's website:

Environmental education
Environmental awareness and education are key to a sustainable future. To raise awareness of our responsible manufacturing techniques and holistic approach towards the environment we have been a premier sponsor of the Conkers Environmental Discovery Centre since it opened in 2001. CONKERS, the award winning environmental attraction based in South Derbyshire which offers a unique mix of indoor and outdoor experiences. Our partnership with Conkers provides us with a unique opportunity for us to demonstrate our environmental responsibility to a diverse audience in an engaging manner through interactive exhibits and display graphics.

In kind support

Toyota engineers visit four secondary schools in Derbyshire, Staffordshire and Flintshire each week to work alongside pupils on a variety of real-life engineering challenges. Toyota has supported the national Young Engineers programme since 2000. The programme runs clubs in schools and colleges across the UK and aims to inspire young people to recognise the importance and excitement of a future career in engineering.

Employee-led support

Employee involvement in the community is encouraged and, where suitable, financial support given.

Employee fundraising efforts are matched by the company up to a maximum of £250 per activity.

Payroll giving
A payroll giving scheme is in operation.

Exclusions

No support for advertising in charity brochures, animal welfare, appeals from individuals, the arts, enterprise/training, fundraising events, overseas projects, political or religious appeals, science/technology, social welfare, sport, or local appeals not in areas of company presence. No response to circular appeals.

Applications

A self-screening eligibility form and an application form are posted on the company's website. If your organisation meets the eligibility criteria, please forward your completed application form to the correspondent.

All applications submitted are fully assessed on a monthly basis and a reply is forwarded to the applicant.

Unilever UK

Contact
Community Affairs Team,
Unilever House, Springfield Drive,
Leatherhead KT22 7GR
Tel: 01372 945000;
website: www.unilever.co.uk

Year end: 31/12/2007

Turnover: £32.15 billion

Pre-tax profit: £4.147 billion

Nature of business
Unilever is one of the world's leading suppliers of fast moving consumer goods in food, household and personal care products. Its brands include Knorr, Hellmans, PG Tips, Birds Eye, Wall's Ice Cream, Sure, Persil, Comfort, Cif, Dove, Lynx and Colman's.

Unilever UK is based in a number of sites around the UK. The head office is in Walton on Thames, and it is from here that UK Community Involvement is managed.

Main UK locations
Bedford, Walton on Thames, Lowestoft, Purfleet, London, Manchester, Port Sunlight, Windsor, Kingston on Thames, Burton on Trent, Crumlin, Bebington,

Warrington, Crawley, Leeds, Hull, Ipswich, Gloucester

Cash donations: £1 million (2007)

Total contributions: £6.34 million

Grants for the environment: £200,000

Community support policy

The company's community involvement takes many forms, from direct funding for national projects to employee volunteering support for local community initiatives.

Unilever is increasingly focusing on longer term partnerships, in some cases lasting up to 25 years. This means that while Unilever invests a great deal in community involvement, budgets are often fully committed years in advance, with funding for major projects only becoming available when an existing project comes to an end.

In order to maximise the impact of Unilever UK's community investment programme, its efforts are focused on the following key areas:

- sustainable development – in the areas of water, agriculture and fisheries
- the arts – focused on visual arts
- education – in the form of school governance and leadership
- health – focused on nutrition and healthy lifestyles.

Note: Most of the projects in the Unilever Community Investment Programme are researched and identified by its in-house community investment team. Unsolicited funding applications are not, therefore, normally encouraged.

In 2007, Unilever made total community contributions in the UK of £6.6 million. This was broken down as follows:

- charitable donations: £1.0 million
- community investment: £1.24 million
- commercial initiatives in the community: £4.1 million

■ management costs: £0.25 million.

Environmental projects and organisations supported by Unilever include: Forum for the Future; Mersey Basin Campaign; and Sussex Wildlife Trusts.

In kind support

The main areas of non-cash support are secondments, employee time and occasional donations of stock (although these are normally made to In-Kind Direct, please see the 'Sponsorship' section, below).

Education

Education is a key area of support, particularly for employee volunteering, and a number of sites participate in reading and number partner schemes. Unilever has moved away from the funding and provision of curriculum based educational resources, although selected resources such as From Field to Fork (a KS 3&4 resource focused on plant science, nutrition and sustainability) continue to be funded on an ongoing basis. Unilever also invests heavily in supporting current and retired staff who volunteer as school governors, with a monthly email briefing, regional seminars and a high profile annual conference which attracts leading figures from the world of education.

Sustainable development

Unilever is committed to sustainable development and this is reflected in the UK by the significant support provided to a number of key organisations and campaigns. Unilever has a 25 year commitment to providing support to the Mersey Basin Campaign and is a Foundation Corporate Partner of the Forum for the Future, the UK's leading sustainable development charity.

Health and nutrition

Unilever provides significant funding to both the British Nutrition Foundation and the British Skin Foundation. It has also worked with the Anaphylaxis Campaign to raise the awareness of food allergy issues.

Employee-led support

Numerous Unilever employees give time in assisting local schoolchildren with their reading and writing skills. Also, since 1990, through the Unilever Governors' network, support has been given to employees who volunteer to be school governors.

Payroll giving

The company operates the Give As You Earn scheme.

Exclusions

Under no circumstances is support given to political parties or to organisations with primarily political aims. Unilever makes a declaration to this effect in the Annual Report and Accounts that binds Unilever and all its operating units. Support is not given to churches or denominational charities. This does not exclude support for charities with a religious connection whose work is ecumenical. Support is not given to individuals to undertake studies, gap year trips, social work or for any other purposes.

Applications

Projects supported by Unilever's community investment programme are mostly researched and identified by its in-house community investment team.

Unsolicited applications are not therefore encouraged as less than 1% of unsolicited applications sent to the UK head office generally receive support.

Unilever asks that you use the 'Contact Us' section of the Unilever UK website to ensure that your request is directed to the correct person.

Information Available: Unilever UK's website www.unilever.co.uk contains information about its community involvement activities as well as more general information on its approach to managing corporate responsibility issues.

United Utilities Group plc

Contact
Jan Potter, Haweswater House, Lingley Mere Business Park, Great Sankey, Warrington WA5 3LP Tel: 01925 237 000; Fax: 01925 237 066; email: jan.potter@uuplc.co.uk; website: www.unitedutilities.com

Year end: 31/03/2009

Turnover: £2.435 billion

Pre-tax profit: £568.7 million

Nature of business
A multi-utility supplying water/waste water services, electricity, gas and telecommunications worldwide.

Main UK locations
Warrington.

Cash donations: (See text below)

Total contributions: £4,262,520

Community support policy

The following overview is taken from the 'Supporting the Community' section of United Utilities website:

Over the last year [2007/08], we have conducted a wide ranging review of our approach to corporate responsibility. The review covered everything from our corporate responsibility strategy down to the partnerships we have developed with community organisations.

As a result, we are placing greater emphasis on two particular areas:

- *climate change, where the water sector faces tougher challenges than most other industries*

- *developing and attracting the skills we need to successfully meet the future challenges of running our business.*

We continue to support our employees' activities by providing volunteering opportunities, match-funding and community grants for those that volunteer in their own time.

As in previous years the company quotes conflicting figures for its UK community investment. Its annual report and accounts for 2008/09 state that it made charitable donations of £4.3 million, whilst its 2009 corporate responsibility report states that its total community investment was £3.1 million. Whichever of these figures is accurate, they include 'cash, time and in kind help'. Significant support was given to United Utilities official partners: Groundwork – to regenerate neighbourhoods; and Mersey Basin Campaign – the Water Framework Directive.

As part of the company's strategy in managing biodiversity on its operational sites, it works with a variety of partners such as Wildlife Trusts, Royal Society for the Protection of Birds and the Moors for the Future project. United Utilities also helps to deliver the Cumbria Biodiversity Action Plan's 'Wealth of Wildlife' project, which supports work on woodland and hay meadow habitats. (see: www.wildlifeincumbria.org.uk/wow).

In 2008/09, as part of the ongoing management of its larger land estates across the North West, United Utilities invested over £1.3 million. For 2009/10 its projected spending on this is nearly £1.5 million and covers access, biodiversity, woodland, estates business and boundary and access infrastructure.

In kind support

Education
United Utilities have a range of free teaching packs and videos, which support the National Curriculum, developed jointly with teachers and its community partners. The company provide teacher inset days and are

involved with a number of new education initiatives.

For general information, please contact the education liaison service:

Tel: 01257 425550 Fax: 01257 423364
Email: education@uuplc.co.uk

Employee-led support

United Utilities match funds employees' fundraising efforts on behalf of charitable organisations up to a maximum of £250 per application.

Payroll giving

The company offer its employees the Charities Trust payroll giving scheme.

Exclusions

No support for appeals from individuals, religious appeals or political appeals.

Applications

In writing to the correspondent.

Information available: The group publishes a social and environmental impact report.

12 Raising money from local authorities

Summary

This chapter provides an insight into the workings of local government. The practical tips will enable you to approach departments within your local authority and develop a funding relationship with appropriate contacts. Details of grant programmes and how the funds are administered locally are included. Helpful examples based on our own experience and research findings also appear throughout the chapter.

Background

Where the money comes from

Local government is an important source of income for many people working to raise money for the benefit of their local community. Local authorities are funded through central government grants, council tax and business rates. They set budgets for the coming year, some of which are earmarked for the voluntary and community sector (VCS). Funds are generally distributed by way of grants but, increasingly, also through service delivery contracts. Local authorities also administer some grant programmes on behalf of central government departments.

Empowerment of local government

Local government has remained high on the political agenda since 2006. There have been a number of government white papers that have aimed to empower local government by changing the dynamic of the relationship that exists between local and central government.

As central government is responsible for setting the national agenda, it could be seen that it has a tendency towards increasing its own political responsibilities at the expense of local government, while local government has, in turn, relied heavily on central government to lead the way concerning domestic policy initiatives.

Some recent legislation has focused on shifting the balance of power between the two levels of government. The 2007 Sustainable Communities Act has been a major catalyst, setting in law local government's new rights and areas of responsibilities. (For further information see Chapter 15 *Fundraising for environmental campaigns.*)

Strong and Prosperous Communities[1] and The Balance of Power: Central and Local Government[2]

These two recent White Papers focused on the future role and structure of local government and the need to give people more say on local public services and action. The major changes resulting from the papers' recommendations include:

- devolution of power from central to local government
- development of communication between central and local government
- clarification of existing powers for both local and central government
- encouragement of local financial autonomy
- increased power for local people and communities
- encouraging local authorities to play a leading role in the development of local strategic partnerships (LSPs) and the coordination of service delivery plans, which places new responsibilities on local authorities to make connections between community needs and services
- greater attempts to understand the level of support local government needs from the centre to carry out its responsibilities, i.e. creation of new laws.

The White Papers aimed to strengthen local government's powers and responsibilities by encouraging local authorities to become autonomous, with

---

[1] Communities and Local Government, *Strong and Prosperous Communities*, (October, 2006).

[2] House of Commons Report, Communities and Local Government Committee, *The Balance of Power: Central and Local Government*, (May, 2009).

the expectation that this would increase local independence throughout decision making processes and increase accountability within local budgets. The VCS welcomed these initiatives as they place local people and local politicians in a stronger position to improve facilities in their communities, which, hopefully, will lead to greater local democracy.

The documents can be downloaded from www.communities.gov.uk/ publications/localgovernment/implementationplanprogress (*Strong and Prosperous Communities*) and www.publications.parliament.uk/pa/cm200809/ cmselect/cmcomloc/33/33i.pdf (*The Balance of Power: Central and Local Government*).

Local government and accountability

Comprehensive area assessment (CAA)

In the current climate, all areas of government spending, including spending in local government, are coming under high levels of public scrutiny. CAA, launched in April 2009, measures how effectively public bodies are managed and how well they provide public services to their local communities.

The annual assessment, which takes place in November, is carried out by the Audit Commission, the Care Quality Commission, HMI Constabulary, HMI Prisons, HMI Probation and Ofsted. The Audit Commission has overall responsibility. The individual inspectorates have been given new duties to cooperate with each other and to manage the burden of inspection on individual organisations within relevant sectors.

The new approach to assessment and inspection is expected to reduce the number of automatic rolling inspections, making for a more proportionate number in the future. However, government recognises that in certain situations regular inspections should be maintained as usual to protect the needs of vulnerable groups, for example children and young adults.

The importance of CAA for the VCS is that it shows whether progress is being made to develop a thriving voluntary sector, whether VCS expertise feeds into decision making, and whether the sector is able to play a full role in delivering services for the wider community, including disadvantaged and vulnerable groups.

The Audit Commission anticipates that a new website *oneplace* will be up and running by December 2009. According to the Audit Commission:

The new oneplace website will feature the results of the comprehensive area assessment (CAA), based on the collective assessment of six independent inspectorates. It will show how organisations and service providers are doing on the issues that matter most in their local area. It will highlight where things are going well, where there may be problems and how councils and their partners are working together to improve quality of life for residents.

For further details of this website see: www.audit-commission.gov.uk/localgov.

Duty to involve

As of April 2009 local authorities now have what is called a 'duty to involve'. Under this duty, local government are now obliged to consult with a representative group of local people (including groups defined by age, race, gender and ethnicity) on a range of local decisions. This is important for voluntary and community sector organisations (VCOs) who want to get more involved in local decision making, particularly concerning local government functions, as they can be called upon as representatives to voice the concerns of their local communities and its residents.

Local frameworks

The next section looks at how local government works in partnership with the VCS. It also explains how local authorities are structured and how fundraisers should approach them for funding.

Local strategic partnerships (LSPs) and local area agreements (LAAs)

Since Labour's inception, central government has created a multitude of local area strategies which has, as you might expect, brought many VCOs into a closer working relationship with their local authority, since these initiatives are governed by boards with voluntary sector representation.

LSPs are local partnerships between local authorities, local representatives of statutory bodies such as the NHS and the police, the private sector and the voluntary sector. The LSP agrees a vision for the future of the area, called a sustainable community strategy. It informs the negotiation of LAAs, whose priorities are agreed between all public sector working agencies and central government, to be achieved locally over a three-year period.

LAAs are designed to rationalise the many area-based funding streams and their associated targets and budgets, reduce bureaucracy and give local communities greater control over how resources are deployed to meet local priorities. They set out the local priorities that have been negotiated between all the main public sector organisations in an area, local government and central government.

The ideas behind them are to:

- recognise that local services should reflect what local people want
- give more flexibility to local authorities and other public sector organisations in how they deliver services for local people
- make local authorities and other public services more accountable to local people
- reduce red tape and improve value for money
- enable local people to get more involved in decisions about local services.

You can obtain details of what the priorities are in your area by visiting www.localpriorities.communities.gov.uk.

LSPs are the mechanism through which community strategies are developed and regeneration and development money is delivered, and will reduce the number of initiatives and partnerships in any given area.

How local government is organised

Local government structure

You may find it easier to prepare your application to your local authority if you understand how it is structured and whom you need to get to know. There are two main ways that local governments are organised, depending on where you live – one-tier or two-tier systems. There have been several reforms over the past 40 years that have lead to different arrangements in different areas.

1. **County and district councils.** Most areas in England have two levels of government: a county council and a district council. These parts of the country are known as shire areas.
2. **County councils.** These cover large areas and provide most of the public services, including education, social services, public transport and libraries. They are divided into several districts.
3. **District councils.** These cover smaller areas and provide more local services, such as council housing, leisure facilities, local planning and waste

collection. A district council with borough or city status is called borough council or city council instead of district council, but this doesn't change its role.

4. **Unitary authorities.** In England's larger towns and in some smaller counties, there is just one level of government, called a unitary authority or a metropolitan district council, which is responsible for all local services. Some towns have their own directly elected mayor.

   In London, each borough is a unitary authority, but the Greater London Authority (the Mayor and Assembly) provides Londonwide government, and has responsibility for certain services including transport and the police.

   Unitary authorities may be called borough council, city council, county council, district council, or just council.

5. **Town and parish councils.** In some parts of England there are also town and parish councils, covering a smaller area. They are responsible for services such as allotments, public toilets, parks and ponds, war memorials and local halls and community centres. They are sometimes described as the third tier of local government.

Restructured unitary authorities

In 2008, Communities and Local Government accepted proposals from a few local authorities to form into unitary authorities. After final parliamentary approval, on 1 April 2009, 10 unitary authorities were created: five from counties (Cornwall, County Durham, Northumberland, Shropshire and Wiltshire) and five from districts (Bedford, Central Bedfordshire, Cheshire East, Cheshire West and Chester).

Fundraisers should be aware that after the reorganisation process responsibility for VCS funding may be allocated within alternative departments or areas within your local council. Therefore, it is best to establish where (if at all) the voluntary and community sector liaison unit is located within these restructured unitary authorities.

Joint services

Some local authorities share services covering a wider area, such as the police, the fire service and public transport. This may be done to avoid splitting up services when council structures are changed, or because some councils are too small to run an effective service on their own.

It is important for fundraisers to be aware of the organisational structure of their local authority and know which decision makers have responsibilities in line with their organisation's priorities.

Understanding local authorities

Each local authority is individual in the way that its departments are organised. In most cases the majority will have departments delivering services focusing on the following areas that are particularly relevant to fundraisers

- culture and leisure
- education and learning
- social welfare and health (including children and young adults)
- environment
- community and living.

However, please note that not all council departments will have budgets for making grants. In order to find out how your local council is organised it is usually best to visit their website first.

Don't think of your local authority just as a source of possible grant aid – it may also provide information and advice, for example, access to funding information portals. Check out links on their website; most local council websites conform to a generic structure which provides a list of links to the main departments (as mentioned earlier) and they also have specific links aimed at the VCS, for example, Swindon Borough Council has the following links that are relevant to the VCS in their area:

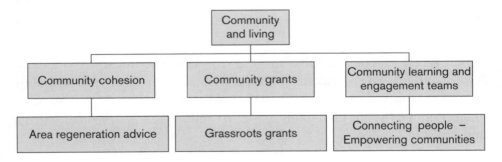

Our research into local government funding (which lists all available local government funding programmes through DSC's subscription website www.governmentfunding.org.uk) found that local government websites were better than others. Some provided extensive information, such as advice on writing a fundraising application and easily accessible application forms and guidance notes, while others were difficult to navigate, often making it hard to find the relevant information, if it existed at all.

Many high quality local authorities' websites provide clear and accessible information on other areas of their work that relates to the VCS, including copies of the local Compact agreements, local area agreements (LAAs) and a list of the council's funding priorities for the coming period. It is unlikely that any council today will not have information on one or more of the three areas just mentioned, either online or by request from the appropriate council contact. These three areas are important for the VCS and may have a significant affect on a VCO's fundraising strategy. Therefore, it is best to keep track of any changes in these areas and find out from your council how you can become involved and have some influence where and when it is appropriate.

If, however, your council does not provide any of the information just mentioned, your best option is to concentrate on developing a connection with a department whose work is applicable to your own and make contact with them (see the next section for a list of possible contacts).

What to do next?

If internet based research proves to be fruitless and you are still unsure how your local authority is structured, ring or arrange a visit to your local councillor's office, and ask about your local authority and how it works. You could do this in any case, as it would be a useful introduction for your organisation. The chief executive's department should have a directory of local councillors' contact numbers.

For grants and other forms of advice and help there are a number of local government officers who are responsible for providing information and support services that are relevant to your organisation. Many local authorities have specialist grants officers and sometimes voluntary sector liaison officers whose main role is to provide funding information, support and advice to VCOs. The person or team dealing with VCS grants may have a number of titles; the following is not a comprehensive list but will give you some idea of who to ask for.

- grants officer
- voluntary sector liaison officer
- economic development manager
- regeneration funds manager
- lead officer for the community and voluntary sector
- policy and partnerships manager

- policy officer
- delegated grants team
- policy and partnerships team.

Establishing whether your council employs these types of officers or teams is the first avenue fundraisers should explore. Council representatives will be able to tell you how much (if anything) is available and how it is spent.

Some councillors may be able to lobby on your behalf. Some attend parish council meetings, and may use these meetings as a sounding board to find out about local priorities. If your organisation's name is given a good review here more note may be taken of your organisation's work at a district level. While this is important, you should also find out the names of the councillors serving on relevant committees, particularly the chair. Try to enlist the support of your local councillors, whichever party they represent, and find out about their interests.

You may also need to develop working relationships with officers dealing with regeneration, employment and training and with links to European Structural Funds (see Chapter 14 *Raising money from Europe*). The government offices for the regions and the regional development agencies have key roles in these areas, and any contacts you can develop will be helpful. However, officers in your local authority may also be able to give you advice and direct you to relevant officers in the regional bodies.

Establishing a relationship

Local authorities are no different to other types of funders, such as trusts and foundations, in that personal relationships count. You need to build a relationship with your local authority, as you would any other potential supporter.

As with any other area of government funding, it is not enough to demonstrate that you are doing good and important work; you must also show that your work delivers against the priorities set by the local government funders you are applying to, which they look for in order to meet their own targets and objectives.

It may help to find out what other councils are doing. If your council is spending very little on your particular area of work, it may be useful to be able to underline this point by making suitable comparisons with other similar areas. Although this will probably not help you much in the short term (as it would be unlikely that your council could increase its budget) it may be something it takes forward in the future.

State your case

Once you have identified the councillors and council officers whose support you need, it is advisable to spend time interesting them in your organisation. Inviting them to events would be a good opportunity for them to meet your colleagues. If your organisation includes people with local influence persuade them to talk to some of the key councillors and officials about the value of your work.

It is advisable to prepare the ground in this way before you make any formal grant application, so that you have a fair idea of what will and will not be acceptable. Make sure that all those responsible for contacting and lobbying councillors are properly briefed: on the local importance of the organisation (backed up by figures, analysis, etc.); how your work relates to the council's policies and priorities; and on what the council can do to help. If councillors receive conflicting or muddled statements from a variety of sources, this can do considerable damage to your case.

You may find it difficult to prioritise spending time in meetings or on phone calls with representatives of statutory bodies. However, keep in mind that in any community, even in large urban areas, a relatively small number of people make the majority of decisions across all sectors. They may wear many different hats, for example, chief executives of local businesses, primary care trusts, police and even councillors may also be trustees for local charities.

Try to establish relationships that give you access – to be able to advance your cause, find out important information and have a level of influence on decisions where it is appropriate. If you are an unknown quantity, whether on an official or unofficial basis, this will be much more difficult.

Finally, you need to be clear about what you do and what you need and then make sure that the people that matter in the local authority become equally clear about this. You will need to be clued up on the local authority's priorities and what they are looking for from the relationship. This will take time and effort, but it usually pays dividends.

Demonstrating the value of your project

What features of your project make it attractive to your local authority? How do any of the following apply to your organisation or project?

- fits in with local government priorities (essential)
- local benefits
- regional benefits
- large number of different groups can benefit (outline which)
- community run; participation of local residents
- innovative approach
- addresses special needs
- matching funds raised
- established track record
- excellence
- sound finances
- includes 'hard to reach' groups
- fills a gap or augments local government service provision
- a number of different bodies/organisations are involved (name which)
- established and enthusiastic membership
- large number of benefits from a small grant (what benefits?)
- what local support you have
- good publicity for the local authority
- value for money
- others (get your team together to list possible options).

Other types of support

Support in kind

Local councils may be able to offer you support in kind (as well as cash grants), such as: second-hand office equipment and furniture; free or low rent premises; help with transport maintenance; staff secondments; and access to the council bulk-purchasing scheme, which may offer lower prices than elsewhere. Each area will be different, but here are some examples of how local government might be able to offer support:

- advice
- equipment – to buy or to loan
- salaries

- running costs – heating, lighting and so on
- project start-up costs
- training
- buildings
- transport
- refurbishment
- sessional hours
- sports and arts activities
- help with programme development
- access to other funders and programmes
- publicity
- endorsement
- rate relief.

Community Assets Programme

The £30 million Community Assets programme aims to empower communities by encouraging the transfer of underused local authority assets to local organisations. The fund provides grants for refurbishment of local authority buildings, to ensure that high-quality spaces and facilities are transferred to VCS ownership.

The refurbishment of assets and their transfer to the VCS aims to achieve the following outcomes:

- Local VCOs have greater security and independence, and are better able to meet the needs of the communities they serve.
- Communities have more access to better facilities that respond to their needs.
- There is more effective partnership working between local authorities and the VCS.

The Community Assets Programme is now administered by BIG. For more information please refer to the BIG website: www.biglotteryfund.org.uk.

Rate relief

Local authorities can also give valuable indirect support to local charitable organisations through rate relief. The level of relief varies, but the mandatory rate is 80% and the discretionary allowance can be up to 100%. The amount will be governed by the authority's policy and may depend upon the type of organisation. Rate relief is only given if you apply, and cannot be given retrospectively.

Contact your local authority for further details of its policy and how to apply. Claim while you can as there is an ongoing review of local government discretionary rate relief.

Locally administered grant programmes

Central government grant schemes that have a specific focus on local people can sometimes be administered by independent grant administrators who distribute funding to different local areas who may be eligible for support. The following are examples of such schemes.

Young Roots

Young Roots is administered by the Heritage Lottery Fund (HLF), which is responsible to the Department for Culture, Media and Sport. It aims to involve 13–25 year-olds in finding out about their heritage, developing skills, building confidence and promoting community involvement.

HLF encourages organisations to contribute as much as they can either as cash, non-cash contributions (for example, donated materials) or volunteer time. Grants can usually be made between £3,000 and £25,000 and projects should be completed within 18 months of receipt of funding.

Young Roots' projects should stem directly from young people's interests and ideas and must be delivered through a partnership. Youth groups must work with at least one heritage partner (for example, a local wildlife trust or museum) to deliver the project.

Historic Buildings, Monuments and Designed Landscapes

The Historic Buildings, Monuments and Designed Landscapes programme provides grants for the repair and conservation of historic buildings, monuments and designed landscapes in England. Grants are primarily offered for urgent repairs or other work required within two years to prevent loss or damage to important architectural, archaeological or landscape features. The grants are managed by English Heritage (EH).

This total value of the fund is approximately £8 million; the maximum grant is £10,000. Projects are usually funded for two to three years.

For further information contact the appropriate English Heritage regional office (for details see www.hlf.org.uk).

For general HLF grant enquiries contact grants@english-heritage.org.uk.

Landscape Partnerships

Landscape Partnerships supports schemes led by partnerships of local, regional and national interests which aim to conserve areas of distinctive landscape character throughout the UK. Each scheme should be based around a portfolio of smaller projects, which together provide a varied package of benefits to an area, its communities and visitors.

Grants can range between £250,000 and £2 million. Organisations applying for less than £1 million will need to provide at least 10% of the scheme costs from their own or other sources. For grants of £1 million or more, at least 25% of the scheme costs must be provided.

Parks for People

The Parks for People programme began as a joint initiative between BIG and HLF, but is now the full responsibility of HLF.

The programme aims to regenerate public parks[3] of national, regional or local heritage value for the enjoyment and recreation of local people. Funding is available for not-for-profit organisations that own or manage a public park.

Parks for People funds activities such as:

- the creation of a community history of the park and local area
- heritage activities designed with young people – possibly through schools and colleges
- horticultural demonstrations and workshops
- recording and measuring biodiversity

---

[3] For this programme, the term 'public park' means an existing designed urban or rural green space, the main purpose of which is for informal recreation and enjoyment. It includes parks, gardens, squares, walks and promenades.

- heritage trails and talks for all
- heritage courses and workshops for adults
- historical re-enactments and community drama and music.

Capital work is also supported, for example, for repairing and restoring landscapes and built features, improving access and providing community facilities.

The total fund value for Parks for People is approximately £90 million; the scheme is able to offer grants between £250,000 and £5 million. At least 5% of the funding must come from the organisation's own resources. A further 25% of project costs should come from partnership funding, which can be in either cash or non-cash contributions.

For further information see HLF's website www.hlf.org.uk.

General grant funding from local authorities

Most local authorities can give grants through specific departments; however, many have a general grant-giving programme. Local authority grants to the VCS tend to be discretionary, but can still have a wide remit, funding a range of purposes and a variety of organisations. In most cases, this type of support is usually called a 'Small Grants Programme', 'Community Fund' or 'Community Chest Fund.'

Such programmes are flexible and will consider funding a variety of projects that will be of general benefit to the local community, in order to attract as many types of projects as possible. Grant guidelines will usually outline a number of priority areas for funding, for example, health and wellbeing, arts and leisure or local environmental initiatives. This leaves a lot of scope for VCOs to be considered successfully for this type of funding.

Local funding is generally administered on a rolling basis, opening for application either once or a number of times a year, depending on the local authority's budget. As with any other type of grant programme or fund, each has its own annual budget. If you apply towards the end of the financial year there may be little or no money available for your request, meaning that you will have to wait until the next year's budget is set.

Grants tend to be relatively small, in some cases less than £1,000. Many local organisations might be aware of the particular fund so there may be a lot of competition for limited funding. As with any application, it is best to discuss the details of a project with a relevant grants officer, who should also be able to tell you how funding is available and the deadlines for applications.[4]

Case study

Greenwich Pride Awards

The Greenwich Pride Awards is an example of a small community grants programme with an environmental focus.

Greenwich Pride Award projects must provide local environmental improvements; however, added benefits can feature in any of the following areas:

- health improvement skills
- training and empowerment
- local community engagement
- school/biodiversity
- educational projects.

Grants of up to £1,500 are available for VCS groups that fulfil the programme's eligibility criteria. Funding can be for capital and equipment purchase, labour or any other costs associated with the project. Grants are one-off; ongoing costs will not be supported.

Greenwich Pride is a rolling programme and applications can be received at any time. An assessment panel meets quarterly. Applicants will be advised about the outcome of their bid within two weeks of a panel meeting.

The criteria for applications are flexible to attract as many creative environmental ideas as possible. Previous projects have included creating murals, launching a Neighbourhood in Bloom competition and transforming an area of derelict land into a community wildlife garden.

Advice and support on developing projects is available from the strategic development staff. For further information see www.greenwich.gov.uk and search for Greenwich Pride.

---

[4] Sometimes local community foundations (CF) may administer funding on behalf of local authorities. It is worth checking what additional schemes your local CF has to offer; to find your nearest one see www.communityfoundations.org.uk.

Looking for extra support

Local Compacts

The vast majority of relationships between local bodies and VCOs exist at local level. Local Compacts are now widely recognised and form part of many local authorities' frameworks for working in partnership with the local VCS.

Local Compacts work from the same values and commitments as the national Compact, which provides the framework for local Compact negotiations between the VCS, local government and other public bodies. They are specific to the area where they apply, which can lead to variations in the quality and effectiveness of agreements.

In 2009, the national Compact underwent a complete 'refresh' to reflect the changing laws and practices that have emerged in the 11 years since the Compact was formed. This will undoubtedly have an effect on many existing local agreements – local organisations should try to find out about their local authority's progress and whether the agreement seems to be functioning as it should.

Further information, including case studies, an information bank, and a register of local Compacts can be found online at www.thecompact.org.uk.

External funding support teams

Many local authorities now employ 'external funding support teams' as part of their voluntary sector liaison departments. This type of support may not be available in every local authority[5] or may fall under a different name. However, where available they can help VCOs identify and apply for financial support in many areas, from statutory support to grant-making charities. Birmingham City Council is one city council that employs such a team.

---

[5] If this is the case contact your local council for voluntary service, rural community council or equivalent body to find out what support it may be able to offer.

Birmingham City Council

The External Funding Support Team

Department: Adults and Communities Directorate

In general the External Funding Support Team:

- advises you on available funding to match your ideas or initiatives
- provides you with a funding search report
- advises your project team on bidding criteria
- advises you on what funding bodies look for from applicants
- signposts to other services of support and information.

Particular considerations

Apart from information particular to your council, there are criteria that all councils are likely to use when considering your proposal. You should take the following into account at an early stage:

- How well does your organisation's work and objectives fit in with your council's stated policies and priorities?
- Are there any organisations in the area doing similar work? If so, do they receive local government funding? Are there sound reasons why the authority should fund your organisation as well as, or instead of, those it is already funding?
- How successful are you? Is your work of a high calibre? What evidence can you provide to support this? How many people do you serve? How many of them come from the local authority area? Are there other ways in which you can demonstrate local community support, such as membership or local fundraising?
- How well organised are you in terms of financial and administrative control? Are you reliable? Is your work endorsed through grants from other official bodies?
- How strongly do local people feel about you? Would local opposition be strong if you were forced to disband from lack of funds?

Remember, local authorities are like other funders in what they want to know from you:

- What do you want to do?
- Why do you want to do it?
- How will you make it happen?
- Who will be accountable?
- What difference will the work make to the local area?
- What do you want from the local authority?
- What will happen when the grant is spent?

In other words, your local authority will look to see if you:

- have identified a clear need
- have produced a good and workable plan
- have costed your work
- will be able to measure the value and outcomes of your work
- have prepared an exit strategy.

Think differently

When you meet with people from your local authority, don't talk about funding, talk about collaboration. Council officials don't see themselves as being there to underwrite your core costs year in, year out or even to provide only financial support, and they will have their own views on what service provision they want to see in the area. Show how you understand their priorities and concerns and how your work fits into these, rather than expect them to support you to do whatever you want to do.

Media coverage

While you are talking privately to council officers and councillors you should also be directing your efforts at your local media to reinforce your message. Items on local radio and in the local paper about the importance and quality of your work, and reviews and interviews in which you outline future plans of benefit to the community, should also have an effect on councillors' opinions.

Maintain regular contact

Whatever support you are looking for, you should be talking regularly to council officers and councillors, especially those connected to your area of work. Keep them informed of your activities throughout the year, not just when it's grant application time. Establishing relationships shouldn't be just about funding; if it is you will find them more difficult to maintain and you won't be maximising other potential benefits.

Getting information

The Local Government Association produces some very useful factsheets about local authorities' structures and responsibilities, which are available online. The funding advice officer in your local council for voluntary service, rural community council or equivalent should be able to give you contacts and information on funding programmes.

Give acknowledgements and personal thanks

Like other funders, local authorities should be thanked for their support and acknowledged appropriately. Local authorities appreciate credit and recognition for their contribution to a project. Tell them how you will publicise their grant and generally help people to view them in a positive way.

Some final dos and don'ts

Do:

- find out how your local authority works
- find and contact key local officers
- build good relationships with local councillors across the political spectrum
- find out about and understand authority/department priorities
- think creatively about your project
- use local media to raise your profile
- attend meetings regularly
- be clear and to the point
- keep well informed about changes in criteria/priorities
- be persistent
- budget realistically
- show 'value for money'
- find out about application procedures and deadlines
- plan ahead
- research fully. Demonstrate the benefits of your project to the council and its community as well as to your own user group.

Don't:

- leave talking to councillors and officers until you need money
- limit your project to one narrow departmental interest
- forget in kind support from your local authority
- be modest about what you can offer
- let information become out of date
- plan in the short term – look to the future
- waffle
- take local authority support for granted
- think that if the local authority has funded you once it will always continue with its support
- give up.

13 Raising money from government

Introduction

In recent years the voluntary or 'third' sector has been high on the political agenda and consequently government is now a major funder for voluntary organisations. The voluntary sector is currently funded by central government grant programmes totalling £1.4 billion (*The Funders' Almanac 2008*, DSC). There is a range of government funding available for voluntary organisations working for environmental causes, specifically aimed at projects involving the environment or that have a broad scope, making them applicable to environmental projects and organisations.

Government funding is an avenue that organisations should explore. However, as this chapter will highlight, it operates in a very different way to other sources of funding detailed in this guide. As always with fundraising, getting money from government begins with being able to access relevant and appropriate funding information, followed by the determination to see it through to fruition.

To help organisations approach and hopefully access government funding, this chapter will:

- outline recent developments in government policy and the way this influences funding cycles
- distinguish and identify the different types of funding from government
- suggest ways of accessing support specific to voluntary organisations working with a focus on environmental impact.

What does government have to offer?

Types of government funding

The type of funding your organisation applies for will depend very much on its size, capacity, what you require funding for and the level of relationship you are willing to have with government. There are many different relationships and many potential opportunities for funding which bring their different demands and responsibilities.

Funding options

Loan schemes

These are usually low interest and generally repayable over a longer period than a grant. They are to support the increase of an organisation's capacity or the development of social enterprise.

Direct grants

Direct grants are most commonly awarded by central government or its agencies (see below) and can range from a one-off small grant to large grants awarded for up to five years.

Grant in aid

This is given to individual voluntary organisations on an annual review basis and is increasingly characterised as 'strategic funding'.

Contracts

Contracts with government, which occur most extensively at a local authority level.

Areas of government

- **Central** – funding is administered directly from the department or departmental directorate.
- **Agencies** – funding is administered by non-departmental public bodies (NDPBs) or other executive agencies appointed by central government.
- **Regional** – funding is channelled through government offices for the regions and regional development agencies (see page 341).
- **Local** – local partnerships of various types and funding distributed by local authorities.

Identifying which departments or agencies are most relevant to your organisation and the work that you do is the first step in approaching funding from central government and NDPBs. Within government, there are likely to be a number of government departments, agencies and public bodies interested in working with your organisation. However, potential funders may not be those most obvious to environmental organisations but relevant because you fulfil one of their policy objectives. For example, environmental organisations but relevant because you fulfil one of their policy objectives. For example, if your work involves young volunteers, you may be eligible for a grant from the v Match Fund, see page 338.

Some things you should know about government funding

Government funding can be quite complex and unpredictable so it's important to know what to expect. If you are thinking of applying for funding from any of the sources and types of government funding explained above, there are a number of things you need to bear in mind:

- **Funding programmes can change frequently.** In contrast to grant-making charities, which tend to maintain a relatively stable funding 'identity', government funds come and go with shifting 'political winds' (*Funders' Almanac*, page 45 DSC). Criteria and priorities may vary from year to year, or the fund may only be available for a year or two and then disappear or change into something quite different.

- **Different funders and funding programmes associated with government are not coordinated and funding is distributed in different ways.** The design of funding programmes varies between and even within departments.

- **Funding announcements are commonly made at very short notice**, and you typically have less than six weeks to put together an application – keeping up to date with government policies and their objectives is a good way to predict announcements and prevent a panic when relevant funding streams occur.

- **For most programmes the number of applicants is far greater than the funding can support**. Typically only between 5 and 20% of applicants will be successful (*The Complete Fundraising Handbook*, page 180 DSC).

- **Because funds are public money, there are usually extensive monitoring and reporting requirements which can be time consuming and difficult to manage**. However, there are smaller grants available which do not have such demanding requirements. The Cabinet Office's Grassroots Grants, for example, is an open programme with minimal reporting requirements (details of these grant programmes are outlined in the 'What's available?' section on page 335).

It's all about objectives

With government funding from any level it is not enough for you to show that your organisation is doing good and important work. You must be able to demonstrate that the work falls within the government department's own strategies and helps it to meet those aims and objectives. The key point is well stated by John Marshall

> *Government grants are primarily designed to meet departmental policy objectives and programme outcomes. These should of course be reflected in the published criteria for grants. Applications are, therefore, expected to demonstrate clearly how they will help departments achieve their objectives. Too many applicants seem to assume that the core work of their organisation is reason enough to secure a government grant. I am afraid that no matter how effective or important the work of your organisation, you need to show how it meets the objectives of the funder.*

> *The Complete Fundraising Handbook*, DSC, page 180

It is advisable to put some time into finding out whether there are any departmental objectives (as well as national) that are relevant to your organisation and/or project. For example, one of the Department of Energy and Climate Change's objectives (see page 334) includes protecting and enhancing the natural environment. Tying your work in with a particular policy that fits with your aims is recommended when promoting your organisation and/or project and is a good approach to take when applying for government grants. Be prepared to tailor your application around government or departmental objectives, without letting them compromise your own.

Policy

As explained in the quote above, funding from government is shaped by its objectives. Therefore, it is important to be alert to changes and developments within government policies and structures. The remits, and sometimes even the names of departments change, new funding programmes will emerge and existing ones alter accordingly. It is important to keep up to date with policy changes, but some key areas to be aware of are outlined in the following section.

Key policy areas and why they are important

The Office of the Third Sector (OTS)

OTS was created at the centre of government in May 2006 as part of the Cabinet Office to drive forward the government's role in supporting the voluntary sector, and bring together sector-related work from across government. OTS has a number of funding streams specifically targeted at the voluntary sector but is also a good way to keep track of changes and developments within government that are relevant to the voluntary sector. The easiest way to do this is to sign up to OTS's newsletter, which you can do on its website, see www.cabinetoffice.gov. uk/third_sector.

Capacitybuilders

Capacitybuilders is an NDPB funded by the OTS. Capacitybuilders exists to help create a more effective third sector by working to improve support for third sector organisations. The resulting national support services opened at the beginning of April 2008 and aim to improve infrastructure of the voluntary and community sector through the following workstreams: campaigning and advocacy; collaboration; equalities and diversity; income generation; leadership and governance; marketing and communications; modernising volunteering; performance management; and responding to social change. For more information see www.capacitybuilders. org.uk.

Futurebuilders

The Futurebuilders' initiative aims to increase the participation of voluntary and community sector organisations in the delivery of public services, primarily through loans and some grant-based finance. The fund focuses on five themes, deemed to be areas of public services in need of improvement: community cohesion, crime, education and learning, health and social care; and support for children and young people. For more information see www.futurebuilders-england.org.uk

The Small Organisation Tender Fund helps finance tendering costs or capacity building work – such as legal costs, advice from procurement specialists, financial expertise and bidding staff costs – to help small organisations win specific public sector contracts.

Grants will be offered on a first come, first served basis for up to 10% of a contract value, up to a maximum of £15,000. Contracts being tendered for must hold a minimum value of £30,000.

For the purposes of the Small Organisation Tender Fund, a 'small organisation' is defined as one with an annual turnover of less than £250,000. Applicants must also have been trading for a minimum of one year.

Other Futurebuilders' initiatives include the Full Investment Fund, which primarily provides low-interest loans to enable organisations to develop so that they can compete for service delivery contracts from statutory bodies, and the Tender Fund, which offers three-year, interest-free loans to community and voluntary sector organisations that need relatively small sums to help them tender successfully for public service delivery contracts.

Futurebuilders England, a consortium of voluntary sector organisations, administered the first phase of the £150 million Futurebuilders Fund following its launch in 2004. The Adventure Capital Fund (ACF) is managing the second phase of the Futurebuilders Fund from 1 April 2008 to 31 March 2011, with an additional £65 million of government funds. The second phase of Futurebuilders will open up a fund to bids from third sector organisations delivering *any* public service.

Key pieces of environmental legislation

Climate Change Act 2008

In October 2008 a new central government department was formed, the Department for Energy and Climate Change (DECC). DECC brought the Climate Change Bill through parliament, leading to the Climate Change Act.

The Act affects all sectors and aims to create a new approach to managing and responding to climate change in the UK. Two key aims underpin the Act:

- to improve carbon management and help the transition towards a low-carbon economy in the UK
- to demonstrate UK leadership and commitment to reducing global emissions internationally.

More information is available from the DECC website: www.decc.gov.uk.

Defra's third sector strategy

Third sector strategies signal central government departments' commitment to working with the third sector (which includes voluntary and community organisations, charities, non-governmental organisations (NGOs), cooperatives and mutuals and social enterprises).

As part of its strategy, Defra (the Department for Environment, Food and Rural Affairs) supports:

- 'Every Action Counts', a consortium of 29 third sector organisations providing advice and support to third sector organisations looking to reduce their impact on the environment, tackle climate change and improve their local area.

- Keep Britain Tidy (KBT), whose aim is to improve local environmental quality (such as litter, detritus, water courses, dog fouling and fly-tipping) and related behaviour (such as graffiti, abandoned vehicles and fly-posting). KBT's campaign, the 'Big Tidy Up', encourages groups to organise a clean up of their local area. The campaign is targeted at all sections of society, from schools, community groups and councils, to businesses and individuals. For more details or to register your organisation see www.thebigtidyup.org. The website also enables groups to profile their event and encourage others to join.

More information about Defra's third sector strategy is available at www.defra.gov.uk.

What's available?

This section gives you an overview of government funding programmes available, to illustrate the variety of funding types to pursue and to point you in the right direction. To remain current and as useful as possible the chapter will outline trends and signpost organisations to possible funding areas for environment projects, rather than acting as a directory of available grant schemes. As mentioned earlier government funding is likely to change with shifting political winds, and although the majority of the grants programmes listed here are likely to be around for the foreseeable future, it is important to keep a tab on changes.

Central government funding

The government departments with central responsibility for funding environment work are Defra and the DECC. Other departments also contribute, particularly the Department for Business Innovation and Skills and, for international projects, the Foreign and Commonwealth Office and the

Department for International Development (DFID). Some funding programmes are voluntary sector specific, others will include public sector and sometimes private sector organisations. The Office of the Third Sector at the Cabinet Office offers a range of funding opportunities targeted at the voluntary sector.

Trends in central government funding

- The period funding is offered for can range from one-off grants to grants lasting five years and more. The most common funding length is one to three years. Most funds also open on a yearly or multi-year basis, though this should not be relied upon.

- Applying for government grants is generally a lengthier process than with other grant-giving bodies. Organisations considering applying for government grants should allow sufficient time and resources. For this reason it is essential to get hold of as much information as possible about the grant and read all guidelines thoroughly.

- Applications are now often a two-stage process, with an initial short 'expression of interest' form. This should mean that less time is spent applying for funds for which organisations are ineligible or unsuitable. If the department/administrator approves the project outlined in the first stage, applicants are then invited to submit full bids.

- A growing trend in central government is to target funding at specific deprived areas, which is often administered through local authorities or non-departmental government organisations, such as community foundations. The aim is to give grants in the areas where they are most needed. The Home Office launched its last two voluntary and community sector grant schemes in this way.

Grant schemes

General

Adventure Capital Fund and Adventure Capital Fund – Business Development Grants

Awarding department: Cabinet Office

The Adventure Capital Fund (ACF) offers a range of investments and support to develop community-based enterprises. The aim of ACF is to fill the investment gap that faces community enterprise organisations, and to increase investment-readiness of community organisations wishing to move to greater sustainability through enterprise. The Business Development Grant is targeted at community enterprises in their early stages of development to improve their investment readiness and sustainability through developing their skills and capacity.

Futurebuilders and Futurebuilders Tender Fund (managed by ACF)

Awarding department: Cabinet Office

The Futurebuilders initiative aims to increase the sector's delivery of public services by providing funding primarily in the form of loans. The idea is that low-interest loans enable the organisation to develop sufficiently to become 'investment ready', meaning that they are able to compete for service delivery contracts from statutory bodies. Futurebuilders is unique in that applicants are not required to fill out an application form. Futurebuilders also offers a Tender Fund of interest-free three-year loans of between £3,000 and £50,000 to community and voluntary sector organisations that need relatively small sums to help them tender successfully for specific public service delivery contracts.

As of April 2009 Futurebuilders had made £380 million worth of investments, ranging from £300 to £2 million.

Futurebuilders also launched a Small Organisation Tender Fund at the beginning of 2009, offering grants to small third sector organisations that need small sums of money to help them tender successfully for specific public sector contracts. The fund operates on a rolling basis; however, a limited pot of £220,000 is available.

Communitybuilders

Awarding Department: Department for Communities and Local Government

Communitybuilders offers loans, grants and business support. There are three different strands to this programme:

- The **Development** element of the Fund is for organisations that need to develop foundations around governance, financial systems, leadership and core functions in order to become more sustainable. Business support and grants of £2,000 are available for staff development and training. The aim is to develop organisations to such a level that they can qualify for investment.

- The **Investment** element of this fund is for organisations who are ready to develop, grow and expand their role within the community. Investment will consist primarily of loans between £50,000 and £2,000,000 offered at 5% for an initial three year period of a ten year loan term.

- The **Feasibility** element of the Fund is for organisations that have ideas and need assistance with project development. Business support of up to 5 days and grants of up to £20,000 are available to use towards project development

337

of a growth plan. Grants of up to £75,000 and 30 days of support will also be available for larger projects. The aim is to develop organisations to such a level that they can qualify for investment.

Funding cycle: ongoing

Contact information: tel: 0191 2692278; email: info@communitybuildersfund. org.uk; website: www.communitybuildersfund.org.uk

v Match Fund
Awarding Department: Cabinet Office

v aims to inspire more investment in youth volunteering and help charities to involve young volunteers in their work. v are prioritising investing in projects that focus on engaging young people who have never volunteered before, including hard-to-reach and under-represented groups. Through the v Match Fund, v will match up to 100% of new investment from the private sector to fund projects which create volunteering opportunities for 16–25 year olds in England.

Funding cycle: ongoing

Contact information: tel: 020 7960 7019; email: matchfund@wearev.com; website: www.vinspired.com

Environment
Bio-energy Infrastructure Scheme
Awarding department: Department for Environment, Food and Rural Affairs

The scheme provides grants to help the development of the supply chain required to harvest, process, store and supply biomass to heat, combined heat and power (CHP) and electricity end-users. Grants are available for producer groups and businesses that are small or medium-sized enterprises based in England and supply biomass within Great Britain.

Funding cycle: annual and multi-year rounds

Contact information: tel: 01355 593 800; email: help@beis.org.uk; website: www.defra.gov.uk

Countdown 2010 Biodiversity Action Fund 2008–11
Awarding department: Department for Environment, Food and Rural Affairs

The fund supports projects that will help achieve the UK government's commitment to halt the loss of biodiversity by 2010 through supporting the recovery of priority species and habitats in England. It is aimed at voluntary sector conservation groups carrying out projects which directly contribute to the conservation of UK Biodiversity Action Plan (BAP) priority habitats and species. The scheme is funded by Natural England.

Funding cycle: multi-year rounds

Contact information: tel: 01733 455415; email: countdown2010@natural england.org.uk; website: www.naturalengland.org.uk

Rural Community Buildings Loan Fund

Awarding department: Department for Environment, Food and Rural Affairs

The fund is administered by Action with Communities in Rural England (ACRE) on behalf of Defra. Loans are usually between £1,000 to £20,000 and can be used for acquiring or renovating village halls.

Funding cycle: ongoing

Contact Information: tel: 01285 653477; email: acre@acre.org.uk; website: www.acre.org.uk

Low Carbon Buildings Programme (LCBP): Phase 2

Awarding department: Department of Energy and Climate Change

Phase 2 supports the installation of microgeneration technologies for organisations in the UK public and not-for-profit sectors. Grants are available for the purchase and installation of solar thermal hot water, solar photovoltaics, wind turbines, ground source heat pumps, automated wood pellet stoves and wood fuelled boiler systems. The LCBP grants are managed by the Building Research Establishment.

Funding cycle: ongoing

Contact information: tel: 08704 23 23 13; email: info@lcbpphase2.org.uk; website: www.lowcarbonbuildingsphase2.org.uk

Bio-energy Capital Grants Scheme

Awarding department: Department of Energy and Climate Change

The scheme aims to promote the efficient use of biomass for energy by stimulating the early deployment of biomass fuelled heat and biomass combined heat and power projects. The scheme is aimed at businesses, organisations and charities in the commercial, industrial and community sectors in England that are considering investing in biomass fuelled heat and/or combined heat and power projects, including anaerobic digesters. Capital grants are awarded towards the cost of equipment in complete installations.

Funding cycle: multi-year rounds

Contact information: tel: 0870 190 1900; email: biocapitalgrants@aeat.co.uk; website: www.decc.gov.uk

Landfill Communities Fund

Awarding department: HM Revenue & Customs (HMRC)

The principle of the Landfill Communities Fund (LCF) is that it offsets some of the negative impacts of landfill sites by allowing landfill operators to pay a proportion of their landfill tax liability to not-for-profit organisations that deliver benefits to the general public, biodiversity or the environment. LCF aims to create significant environmental benefits and jobs, promote sustainable waste management, and undertake projects that improve the lives of communities living near landfill sites. LCF is regulated by ENTRUST on behalf of HMRC.

For more information see Chapter 10.

International

Strategic Programme Fund – Low Carbon, High Growth

Awarding department: Foreign and Commonwealth Office (FCO)

The Strategic Programme Fund is the FCO's largest programme budget. It supports the FCO's strategic objective to 'promote a low carbon, high growth, global economy' and its purpose is to promote action on global issues in areas relating to the UK's foreign policy objectives. Funding is available for regional and global projects.

Funding cycle: annual and multi-year rounds

Contact information: tel: 020 7008 3263; email: spflchg@fco.gov.uk; website: www.fco.gov.uk

Congo Basin Forest Fund (CBFF)

Awarding department: Department for International Development

CPFF is a multi-donor fund set up to avoid deforestation, and contribute to poverty alleviation, in the Congo basin forests. The CBFF is available for innovative, high quality projects, of any size, that will contribute to achieving the fund's objectives.

Funding cycle: annual rounds

Contact information: email: cbfSecretariat@dfid.gov.uk; website: www.cbf-fund. org

Agencies (NDPBs)

As well as central government departments there is a substantial number of public bodies that manages funding programmes relevant to the voluntary sector – the key is to distinguish those that are most relevant and therefore likely to fund your organisation. Like central departments they disburse funds according to their strategies.

The official definition of an NDPB is 'a body which has a role in the process of national government, but is not a government department or part of one, and which accordingly operates to a greater or lesser extent at arm's length from ministers'.

Some examples of NDPBs working for the environment:

- **Natural England** to advise the government on the natural environment
- **Action with Communities in Rural England (ACRE)** to support rural communities
- **The Environment Agency** to protect and improve the environment and promote sustainable development.

Regional funding

Regional development agencies (RDAs) are financed through a single programme budget (the 'Single Pot'). This pooled budget consists of government departments' funding to RDAs, the majority being supplied by the Communities and Local Government (CLG).

The funding, once allocated, is available to the RDAs to spend as they see fit in order to achieve the regional priorities.

Regional development agencies

EEDA (East of England RDA)
www.eeda.org.uk

East Midlands Development Agency
www.emda.org.uk

London Development Agency
www.lda.gov.uk

One North East (North East of England RDA)
www.onenortheast.co.uk

Northwest RDA
www.nwda.co.uk

SEEDA (South of England RDA)
www.seeda.co.uk

South West RDA
www.southwestrda.org.uk

ADVANTAGE (West Midlands RDA)
www.advantagewm.co.uk

Yorkshire Forward
www.yorkshire-forward.com

Government offices for the regions operate as the voice of central government, through nine offices across England. Government offices should have dedicated voluntary and community sector liaison officers in each region. They manage significant spending programmes on behalf of their sponsor departments, including some European funds.

Government offices for the regions

Government Office for the East of England
www.goeast.gov.uk

Government Office for the East Midlands
www.goem.gov.uk

Government Office for London
www.gos.gov.uk/gol

Government Office for the North East
www.go-ne.gov.uk

Government Office for the North West
www.gos.gov.uk/gonw

Government Office for the South East
www.go-se.gov.uk

Government Office for the South West
www.gosw.gov.uk

Government Office for the West Midlands
www.go-wm.gov.uk

Government Office for Yorkshire and the Humber
www.gos.gov.uk/goyh

Local funding

Whilst, as a general rule, central government departments support national work or initiatives with a national significance, and leave the funding of local and community activities to local government, in recent years they have initiated a number of time-limited programmes. Although there are few of them, and they are under-resourced, the application process for these schemes tends to be less complicated.

Community Development Foundation's Grassroots Grants

In August 2008 £130 million of small grants and endowments were made available to strengthen independent grant-making capacity for voluntary groups with an evidenced income of less than £30,000 per annum. This funding is administered by the Community Development Foundation (CDF) and distributed by Local Funders. Applicants are invited to contact their relevant Local Funder for details on applying for the small grants programme. Applications for this fund are accepted on a rolling basis.

For further information, see: www.cdf.org.uk

Local authorities

Nearly all local authorities make grants to the local voluntary and community sector, but each one will organise budgets, administration and support differently according to local conditions and resources.

Most local authorities employ third sector liaison officers (TSLOs) to give advice and support on their funding. By contacting the TSLO you should be able to get a good idea of the type of funding available for your organisation. Even if this does not result in an immediate funding opportunity, it is important to develop effective relationships with such contacts and other influential figures where feasible.

Local councils for voluntary service (CVS), rural community councils (RCCs) or specialised funding advice agencies should also have contact details and local authority funding information.

The DCSF local authority address finder can be found at www.dcsf.gov.uk/local authorities/index.cfm?action=authority. The www.governmentfunding.org.uk site managed by DSC has a local authority funder finder.

To find your nearest CVS go to the National Association for Voluntary and Community Action www.navca.org.uk.

To find information on RCCs go to www.acre.org.uk and for more information on local authorities see Chapter 12 *Raising money from local authorities*.

Getting information and using websites

For strategy documents and more information
www.thecompact.org.uk
www.everychildmatters.gov.uk
www.skillsactive.com
www.sportengland.org

www.direct.gov.uk
This government information service site provides an index of sites, including departments, councils, NHS Trusts and NDPBs.

www.gnn.gov.uk
This is the government's official news service that contains all press releases from central and regional government as well as NDPBs.

Although the quality and accessibility of information on these websites and the regularity of updates varies, they contain information on government policy and recent press releases.

www.governmentfunding.org.uk
This site, managed by Directory of Social Change, has been developed to help fundraisers navigate the maze of funding available from central and local government. The site contains the following features.

- A searchable database of information on funding from local, regional and national government for the voluntary sector, together with downloadable application forms and guidance. It also provides information on independent grant administrators and regional and European funding.
- A personalised user profile, with the option to save searches and grant information, and receive email alerts on new and updated schemes which match criteria selected by the user.
- A news page containing important news articles from the sector press, with a searchable archive.
- A comprehensive help and advice section which contains general funding help, including an A–Z index of key terms and links to other relevant sites.

- An A–Z section listing 150 outcomes with details of grants schemes it has available.
- Funder ratings compiled by DSC researchers and governmentfunding.org.uk subscribers to let you know what to expect from each of the government funders listed on the website.

Other websites you can use to search for government and other funding opportunities include:

www.info4local.gov.uk
www.open4funding.info
www.grantsonline.org.uk
www.grantnet.com
www.supply2.gov.uk

14 Raising money from Europe

Introduction to European funding

The European Union (EU) provides a huge amount of money for social and economic development, mainly in its 27 member states. Most funding of interest to the voluntary sector in the UK is channelled through regional structures such as regional development agencies (RDAs), learning and skills councils (LSCs) and other co-financing organisations.

Getting money from Europe can be a long, slow and painstaking process. Guidance and procedures can be complicated and there can be a long time lag between submitting an application and receiving a grant. The internet is perhaps the most useful research tool when you are dealing with European funding. There is an enormous amount of information published on the main Europa website – ec.europa.eu – and one of your difficulties will be navigating through it all.

Small groups can find it difficult to complete an application for EU funding because of lack of resources. You might want to consider partnering with another organisation, one with better resources or more experience in making applications to Europe.

This chapter aims to demystify the areas around European funding by providing an overview, details of the funds available, how to apply, the issues surrounding funding and tips on how to be successful. The glossary on page 363 will help you through the proliferation of departments, organisations, acronyms and jargon.

Overview of EU funding

Each year, the EU agrees its budget. The budget year runs from 1 January to 31 December. When applying for funds you need to keep up to date and make contact as early as possible, ideally a full year in advance. The budget is adopted in December but it will have been under discussion for the whole of the preceding year and so it is never too early to begin your research. Where matching funds are required, you need to make sure that these are committed before you apply.

Grants, funds and programmes by EU policy

- Agriculture
- Audiovisual and media
- Communication
- Competition
- Conference interpretation
- Consumers
- Culture
- Development
- Economic and financial affairs
- Education, training and youth
- Employment and social affairs
- Energy
- Enlargement
- Enterprise
- Environment
- External relations
- External aid
- External trade
- Fisheries
- Fighting fraud
- Freedom, security and justice
- Humanitarian aid
- Human rights
- Information society
- Public health
- Regional policy
- Research and innovation
- Sport
- Statistics
- Transport

Funding is split into three areas:

Structural funds

The most important of these are the European Regional Development Fund (ERDF) and the European Social Fund (ESF), which is of particular interest to voluntary organisations. These funds are controlled by each individual member state government and administered regionally.

Budget line funding

There are 'budget lines' which offer opportunities for voluntary organisations to apply for funding, although eligibility is not necessarily limited to the voluntary sector. These budgets are controlled by officials in Brussels operating within one of the Directorates General (see page 356) of the EC.

To an extent, decisions on funding can be influenced by MEPs (Members of the European Parliament) in Strasbourg, who can lobby on your behalf. All applications for budget line funding must have a significant transnational dimension and UK-only projects are rarely considered.

Contract and research funding

This is for specific work which the EC wishes to commission, on behalf of either itself or of another government. It is usually put out to tender and can support research across a range of issues in the areas of health, environment, socio-economic affairs, energy, transport and medicine. There are also opportunities to host EC conferences and events.

The structural funds

There are several structural streams, with funding for the voluntary and community sector available from the ERDF and the ESF. The funds help to deliver the EU's cohesion policy, which aims to narrow the gaps in development and economic performance among the regions and the EU member states.

The Third Sector European Network (TSEN) is the body that brings together the voluntary and community sector support agencies in all nine English regions. These agencies provide technical assistance and encourage the development of voluntary and community sector projects to fulfil the objectives of the structural funds. For further useful information please refer to the National Council for Voluntary Organisations' website: www.ncvo-vol.org.uk/sfp/funding?id=2138.

European Regional Development Fund

The ERDF aims to reduce social and economic disparities between regions of the EU and is therefore only available in certain areas of the UK. It is essentially concerned with business growth and economic regeneration and invests in projects to improve innovation, the environment and infrastructure. Therefore, environmental organisations are well placed to apply for ERDF. Communities and Local Government manages the ERDF in England.

Under the 2007–13 programming period the ERDF, the ESF and the Cohesion Fund (a financial instrument of EU regional policy that aims to help reduce the development inequalities among regions and member states) contribute to three objectives set down by the EU:

- convergence
- regional competitiveness and employment
- European territorial cooperation.

The convergence objective covers regions whose gross domestic product (GDP) per capita is below 75% of the EU average and is aimed at accelerating their economic development. It is financed by the ERDF, the ESF and the Cohesion Fund. The priorities under this objective are human and physical capital, innovation, knowledge society, environment and administrative efficiency. The outermost regions (see Glossary on page 365) benefit from a special ERDF funding.

Outside the convergence regions, the regional competitiveness and employment objective aims at 'strengthening competitiveness and attractiveness, as well as employment, through a two-fold approach. First, development programmes will help regions to anticipate and promote economic change through innovation and the promotion of the knowledge society, entrepreneurship, the protection of the environment and the improvement of their accessibility. Second, more and better jobs will be supported by adapting the workforce and by investing in human resources'.

The European territorial cooperation objective will 'strengthen cross-border cooperation through joint local and regional initiatives, transnational cooperation aiming at integrated territorial development, and interregional cooperation and exchange of experience'.

The ERDF's four main priorities are:

1) promoting innovation and knowledge transfer, including research and development and building links between higher education institutions and businesses
2) stimulating enterprise and supporting successful business, including support for small and medium-sized enterprises and social enterprises

3) ensuring sustainable development, production and consumption, including encouraging take-up of renewable energy and building a better environment

4) building sustainable communities, including support for social enterprise, increasing the attractiveness of deprived areas and improving access to employment and public services.

Since 2000, England has benefited from over £3.4 billion of ERDF investment, with a further £2.5 billion being invested for the 2007–13 round of programmes.

Major projects which have benefited from ERDF investment include the regeneration of the King's Dock in Liverpool (£48 million) and the Eden Project in Cornwall (£12.8 million). Without this investment, these projects and many like them would not have happened.

Who can apply?

ERDF is aimed at economic regeneration projects promoted primarily by the public sector. This involves:

- government departments
- RDAs
- local authorities
- further and higher education establishments
- other public bodies
- voluntary sector organisations.

This doesn't exclude the private sector, which promotes and helps to fund high quality projects that meet ERDF objectives. Generally, ERDF grants are not given to profit-making private sector companies, but in certain circumstances the fund can be used to help develop small and medium-sized enterprises (SMEs). Private sector companies are encouraged to present applications in partnership with a public sector body.

Match funding

The ERDF programme will potentially contribute up to 50% of the costs of each project. The remaining project costs need to be provided by 'match funding'. This canbe made up of entirely public or entirely private funds from sources such as:

- RDAs
- local authorities
- government funding streams
- other public bodies
- the private sector.

How to apply for ERDF

ERDF has multiple bidding rounds, which will have separate calls for proposals, grant details and application deadlines. To apply for ERDF investment, contact the RDA for your region. The RDA can advise you on the application process, including giving advice on the potential of projects and their eligibility for ERDF funding.

Management of the funds

The RDAs are responsible for delivering the 2007–13 round of programmes on the ground. They work in partnership with Communities and Local Government (CLG) and representatives from across the programme area, ensuring the programmes are implemented effectively.

CLG provides the framework for how ERDF programmes should be delivered, reporting to ministers and the EC. The European Policy and Programmes Division oversees the management of ERDF.

Programme monitoring committees and secretariat

Although the structure and management arrangements vary in detail, each region has a programme monitoring committee and a secretariat to oversee ERDF investment. The monitoring committees are chaired by the regional director of the government office – or in the case of London, the Mayor – and draw their membership from government departments and a wide range of regional partners. These usually include:

- RDAs
- local authorities
- higher and further education institutions
- environmental bodies
- the voluntary and private sectors
- members of the business community.

The committees guide the programme for their region and monitor and assess its implementation.

European Social Fund

As one of the EU's structural funds, ESF promotes sustainable economic growth across the EU and enhance economic and social cohesion primarily through employment. So although ESF funding is spread across the EU, most money goes to those countries and regions where economic development is less advanced.

In 2007, the EU launched a new round of ESF programmes for the seven years to 2013. The new programme will invest £4.6 billion in 2007–13 of which £2.3 billion will come from the ESF and £2.3 billion will be national funding.

Objectives

The 2007–13 ESF programme has two primary objectives:

- The convergence objective aims to develop areas where the economy is lagging behind the rest of the EU. In England, only Cornwall and the Isles of Scilly benefit from ESF funding under this objective.
- The regional competitiveness and employment objective covers all areas outside the convergence objective areas. The whole of England is covered by this objective, except Cornwall and the Isles of Scilly.

Each region has an allocation of ESF money to fund projects. Allocations are based on regional employment and skills needs – for example, the numbers of people not in work and who do not have good qualifications. The ESF allocations are matched with a similar amount of national funding.

ESF regional allocations 2007 to 2013

Cornwall and the Isles of Scilly	£153 million
Merseyside	£158 million
South Yorkshire	£139 million
East of England	£174 million
East Midlands	£188 million
Gibraltar	£2.6 million
London	£371 million
North East	£180 million
North West (excluding Merseyside)	£254 million
South East	£173 million
South West (excluding Cornwall and the Isles of Scilly)	£109 million
West Midlands	£282 million
Yorkshire and the Humber (excluding South Yorkshire)	£163 million

---

Priorities in the 2007–13 ESF programme

The priorities are designed to focus spending on specific activities and to ensure that it reaches people in most need of support. There are two main priorities in England:

- **Priority 1** is 'extending employment opportunities'. It supports projects to tackle the barriers to work faced by unemployed and disadvantaged people. About £1.2 billion of ESF money is available for this priority.

- **Priority 2** is 'developing a skilled and adaptable workforce'. It supports projects to train people who do not have basic skills and qualifications needed in the workplace. About £670 million of ESF money is available for this priority.

There are similar priorities in the convergence area of Cornwall and the Isles of Scilly, where about £50 million of ESF money is available to tackle barriers to employment, and £80 million of ESF money to improve the skills of the local workforce.

In addition, technical assistance funds are available to finance the preparation, management, monitoring, evaluation, information and control activities of the programmes operations, together with activities to reinforce the administrative capacity for implementing the funds at national and regional levels.

Target groups

In Priority 1 resources are focused on helping people who are unemployed or have become inactive in the labour market. In particular, it focuses on people who are most likely to face disadvantage or discrimination. Key target groups include:

- people with disabilities and health conditions
- lone parents
- people aged over 50
- people from minority ethnic communities
- people without good qualifications
- young people not in education, employment or training.

In Priority 2 resources are focused on people in the workforce who lack basic skills or good qualifications. In particular, it focuses on those who are least likely to receive training. It also supports training for managers and employees in small firms. Priority 2 aims to help people gain relevant skills and qualifications needed for their career progression and for business growth and innovation in the information industry.

Management of the funds

The Department for Work and Pensions has overall responsibility for ESF funds in England. Each region has its own ESF allocation to fund projects to address its regional jobs and skills needs, within the framework of the two priorities in the England ESF programme.

At the regional level, ESF funds are distributed through public agencies. These are often LSCs, RDAs and/or local authorities.

How to apply

Any public, private or third sector organisation that is legally formed, and able to deliver ESF provision can apply for funding to a Co-financing Organisation (CFO). Individuals and sole traders cannot apply.

CFOs make ESF available through a process of open and competitive tendering. You do not have to find your own 'match funding' as CFOs are responsible for both the ESF and match funding.

ESF Community Grants

Community Grants is a new programme which aims to support small voluntary and community organisations to engage with local communities and deliver a range of skills and employment support activities, through the provision of grants up to £12,000. The scheme is designed to make ESF more accessible to organisations without the capacity to apply for the main structural funds.

The grants aim to support a quality outreach provision, providing an essential stepping stone for unemployed and economically inactive participants to find employment or progress to further learning.

To find out your region's contact detail for this programme, please visit www.esf.gov.uk/regions/regional_esf_frameworks.asp.

Tips on making applications to Europe

Don't expect clarity

Procedures vary from one office to another and even published guidelines change from time to time. Careful research is well worth the time and effort involved. You should refer to the relevant websites to ensure that your application meets with any changes and thus amend your application accordingly before finalising it.

Match funding is a crucial element to an ESF application

Many organisations fall at the point where they are unable to secure match funding. You should make sure that it is going to be available for your project and find out all the regulations surrounding it from the funder you approach. Make it clear where any co-funding will come from and how much will be available.

Don't be intimidated by the jargon and concepts

Many of the programmes use abstract language and talk about overarching goals such as 'developing a European sense of identity'. This sounds like a grand aim but it could be fulfilled by something as simple as an exchange trip. Make sure you take the time to look at the kind of projects each programme has funded in the past. A list of funded projects is published on an annual basis (usually in June) by each directorate and is available on their websites.

Talk about ideas, not money

Officials are there to develop their programme areas, not yours. You should be prepared to understand the wider picture, discuss your ideas and adapt them to meet their interests as well as yours for those budget lines and programmes where there are no clearly set out guidelines.

Don't be in a hurry

Take a long-term approach. Expect to be talking to officials early in one year in the hope of getting money in the next year. Sometimes it can take far longer. Response times in some departments are very protracted. In other words, plan ahead.

Note and observe all deadlines

Think partnership

This is becoming increasingly important for projects. It takes more time, but adds strength to your application.

continued ...

Consider using an expert to help you make your initial approach

There are a number of people based in Brussels and elsewhere who specialise in this sort of work. There are also a number of liaison groups that can advise you, such as the European Citizen Action Service (ECAS) www.ecas-citizens.eu.

Make your proposal succinct and absolutely clear

A well thought through and clearly articulated proposal is much more likely to convince the reader. Make sure you have provided all the accessory information required.

Don't underestimate the red tape

Ensure that you begin nothing before you have a signed contract, and make sure everything is fully documented.

Ask for advice and information from your regional government office or regional development agency

It will coordinate the funding in your area on behalf of the responsible government department (which in turn is coordinating it on behalf of the EU).

It's basic advice...

...but store your copy application securely and back it up.

Budget line funding

Funding for the environment is also available through budget line funds, which are distributed directly from the European Commission through Directorates General (see below). Most budget line funding is targeted at organisations operating at a European level, rather than local, regional and national organisations.

In the European Union, the staff of the main institutions (Commission, Council and Parliament) are organised into departments known as Directorates General (DG). Each department is accountable for specific tasks or policy areas. Although there is a DG for the environment, it is still essential to determine which DG your project best fits under (it may be more than one).

There are therefore two ways for environmental groups and organisations to access money from these funds: through the designated environment funding stream and through schemes held under other DG that have different priorities, but hold environment in their objectives.

Funding available from the Directorate General for the Environment

The four priorities of the DG for the Environment between 2002 and 2012 are:

- climate change
- nature and biodiversity
- environment, health and quality of life
- natural resources and waste.

There are two types of funding available from the DG for the Environment: project funding through programmes including LIFE+, and operating grants. The Commission also organises procurement tenders, which can be found on the Europa website ec.europa.eu/grants/index_en.htm website.

In 2005 the World Wide Fund for Nature published a useful handbook on EU funding for the environment for 2007–13 on behalf of the Commission. *EU funding for environment* is available at assets.panda.org/downloads/eufundingforenvironmentweb.pdf

LIFE+ programme

The European Union and some candidate and neighbouring countries support environment and nature conservation projects through LIFE+. In 2009 250 million was available for new projects under three headings: nature and biodiversity; environment policy and governance; and information and communication:

- **Nature and biodiversity** supports projects that contribute to the implementation of the EU's Birds and Habitats Directives and to the EU's goal of halting the loss of biodiversity. The maximum co-financing rate can be 75%, but is normally 50%.
- **Environment policy and governance** supports technological projects that offer significant environmental benefits, for example process or efficiency improvements. This part of LIFE+ so helps projects that improve the implementation of EU environmental legislation, build the environmental policy knowledge base, and develop environmental information sources through monitoring (including forest monitoring). Projects can be co-financed up to a level of 50%.

- **Information and communication** provides up to 50% co-financing for projects that spread information about environmental issues, such as climate change and conservation. This strand of LIFE+ can also support forest fire prevention awareness and training campaigns.

For more information go to ec.europa.eu/environment/life/funding/lifeplus.htm.

Who can apply for funding?

LIFE will co-finance innovative environmental schemes and biodiversity projects in the EU and certain third countries (all other country-relationships to the EU). The programme is open to NGOs, national authorities and the private sector.

LIFE projects database

The database provides an invaluable source of information about each project, including a description, beneficiary contact details and links to projects' home pages. Users can carry out a 1search to find projects in specific Member States or with a specific profile, in order to find a partner or exchange information and experience.

The database is available at ec.europa.eu/environment/life/project/Projects/index.cfm

How to apply for funding

An annual call for proposals for each heading is published each spring, with an autumn deadline for submission of proposals. You need to check the LIFE website regularly for updates and announcements.

All projects have to be submitted to the national contact points. The current national contact for the UK is:

Thomas HUDSON
UK Beta Technology Ltd
Area 1B
Barclay Court, Doncaster Carr
UK – Doncaster DN4 5HZ
Tel.: +44 1302 322 633; +44 7501 463 316 (mobile)
Fax: +44 1302 388 800
Email: tom.hudson@betatechnology.co.uk

Operating grants to European environmental NGOs

Operating grants are the main funding stream available to voluntary organisations as they are targeted specifically at European environmental NGOs.

As part of the LIFE programme outlined above, these grants support 'operational activities of NGOs that are primarily active in protecting and enhancing the environment at European level and involved in the development and implementation of Community policy and legislation'.

Who can apply for funding?

Organisations must be non-profit making and independent environmental NGOs. They must also be active at a European level (i.e. have activities and members in at least three EU Member States).

How to apply

The operating grants are awarded on an annual basis. Calls for proposals are published once a year on the DG Environment web page. You can also email env-ngo@ec.europa.eu for further information.

Funding opportunities from other Commission Directorate General

- Research projects with an environment component (cordis.europa.eu/fp7/home_en.html)
- Grants in the field of energy (ec.europa.eu/energy/grants/index_en.htm)
- Calls for projects and proposals in the field of education and training ec.europa.eu/dgs/education_culture/calls/grants_en.html*
- The youth in action programme (ec.europa.eu/youth/youth-in-action-programme/doc443_en.htm)

How to access the budget lines

Read the handbook on grant management

Since 1999, all DGs must meet the minimum standard set by the *Vade-mecum on Grant Management*. The purpose of this document is to provide a clear reference guide for all those involved in grants at any stage of their process, whether it be drawing up, proposing or evaluating programmes or processing individual applications. The document was produced in 1998 and has not been updated since; however, it still holds useful and relevant information (see website: ec.europa.eu/justice_home/funding/expired/guidelines/2002/vademecum_subv_2000_en.pdf).

Research thoroughly

Find out as much information as you can about which budget lines, programmes and actions will connect to your project. The internet is an invaluable research tool when dealing with Europe, with an enormous amount of information available on the main Europa website. Lists of current grants, previous grants and projects that have already been funded are also available through the individual DG websites, such as education, energy and environment (website address at end of chapter). You may also find it useful to get in touch with other organisations that are applying for funding, or that have already received funding, to learn from their experiences.

Make contact

Once you have identified a budget line or lines, make initial contact with the relevant DG, for example Environment, by telephone, fax or email; any of these methods is acceptable during initial stages. Establish whether your project fits in with the conditions of the programme by asking for written conditions and criteria. You can also ask for application deadlines and information on how soon after the deadline a decision might be made. The 'call for proposals' is published in the Official Journal of the EU, however by that time, there may only be a few months left in which to submit an application. For this reason, it is important to find out which calls for proposals are in the pipeline so that you can prepare a draft in advance.

At this stage, you may decide whether you want to submit a firm application or a brief outline of your proposal. Firm proposals are more appropriate if you are applying to a large funding programme with tight restrictions. If this is not the case, it is acceptable to submit an outline of your proposal that you can discuss with the relevant officials, whom you may be able to meet in either Brussels or the UK. This can be arranged at a relatively low cost and can give you the chance to explain your ideas fully and find out their priorities and any special requirements. Although this may seem like a far-fetched idea, it is in fact common practice; officials are accustomed to being seen in their offices and are happy to discuss potential applications.

After you have discussed your ideas and obtained all the relevant information, you will then be required to submit a formal application. At this stage, you may encounter difficulties, as it can take over a year for a decision, by which time your needs may have altered. Officials are aware of this issue and if you are in contact with them, they will usually tell you about the latest deadlines.

Lobby

It may be worthwhile lobbying MEPs, if you can find one who takes an interest in your project. Although they don't have any authority over the budget, their interest alone can be a powerful influence over officials. This should be approached with caution however, as lobbying can be viewed by officials as interference.

After your application is approved

Once you have agreement from the appropriate DG to support your project, you will be asked to sign a contract with the EC with a number of conditions. Possibly the most difficult are the financial reporting requirements. You should always get professional advice about the problems of fluctuating exchange rates, which can leave you with either less or more money to spend than you had planned for. Also make sure that you only charge for expenses that were included in your original project budget. If changes to this become necessary, get agreement from the EC first; you do not want to be put in the position of having to refund money. Finally, it may appear obvious, but it is extremely important that you submit your report and evaluation on time and in the required format, particularly if you expect to be applying for EU funding again.

If your application is not approved

As with other sources of funding, the DGs receive more applications than they can accept, so failure need not mean that your project was completely unsuitable. You can ask for feedback, for information about successful applications, and for the percentage of successful applicants. You may be able to revise your proposal and try again under a different heading or under the same heading the following year.

Issues around European funding

Contract funding

European funding is usually contract funding, not grant funding. If your project application is approved, you must do what you said in the application. If you use the money for activity not detailed in the application form you may be deemed to be in breach of contract and will have to pay back any European monies claimed.

Co-financing

European funds rarely pay 100% of the costs of running a given project. The money given to top up the European money is known as match funding or co-financing. Until recently, it has been the responsibility of organisations to secure match funding from another source in order to obtain European funding. However, the majority of ESF funding in England is now distributed in a system known as co-financing. Under co-financing, government offices for the regions distribute ESF funding via a variety of intermediary bodies, such as LSCs, Jobcentre Plus, Connexions Partnerships, Business Link, RDAs and some local authorities. These organisations are responsible for finding the match funding which they then combine with their ESF allocations to create a single funding stream.

A European dimension

Many of the budget line funds are conditional on you working in partnership with like-minded organisations in other member states. In most cases you will be expected to name these transnational partners in your application. The implication is that you should build relationships with like-minded organisations across Europe even before you consider submitting a proposal. Go to conferences, use email, and develop contacts by joining any relevant European networks and liaison groups. If you do not have a transnational partner, you can also ask officials of the relevant DG to help you find one.

Delays in decision making and payments

Applications can take a long time to process. For budget line funds this can be as long as a year. For ESF funds a delay of three months is not unusual. You are strongly advised not to start your project until formal approval has been received. Different European funding streams have different payment systems. The relevant guidance notes should give you details. However, be aware that the reality does not always follow the theory. Payments may be delayed for a number of reasons, the most common being that the claimant organisation has not provided all the required information.

Glossary

Call for proposal

This is an invitation for candidates to submit their proposals for action. They are published on the DG websites and also in the Official Journal of the European Union.

Candidate countries

Candidate countries are those which have been granted candidate status and are undergoing accession negotiations to join the EU. Current candidate countries are Turkey, Croatia and Macedonia, which were all granted candidate status in 2005.

Directorate General (DG)

The Directorates are essentially the government departments of the EU. They are each headed by a director general and are responsible for a specific area of European policy.

EEA

The European Economic Area (EEA) was created in 1994 to allow countries of the EFTA (see below) to participate in the European single market without joining the EU. The contracting countries to this agreement are three of the four members of the EFTA: Iceland, Lichtenstein and Norway, and the 27 member states of the EU.

EFTA

The European Free Trade Association (EFTA) is an intergovernmental organisation created to promote free trade and economic integration to benefit its four member states: Iceland, Liechtenstein, Norway and Switzerland.

ENGO

European non-governmental organisation. For example, a body active at European level in the youth field.

Europa

Europa is the name of the EU's website and its address can be found in the contacts section at the end of this chapter. It has a huge range of information and guidance available on all aspects of the EU's activity. To navigate to the area on grant funding from the main page go to Services then Grants and then choose the relevant area. You can also view the programmes by going to the relevant DG website.

European Commission (EC)

The EC is a politically independent body based in Brussels, responsible for upholding the interest of the EU as a whole. It carries out the day-to-day running of the EU, including preparing legislation, overseeing the budget and implementing the decisions of the Parliament and Council. There are currently 27 Commissioners (one for each member state), who are supported by approximately 25,000 European civil servants organised under different departments (the Directorates General).

Intergovernmental organisations

An intergovernmental organisation is an organisation made up of sovereign states, such as the European Union and the United Nations.

Member states

Member states are the 27 countries which acceded to the EU since its inception in 1951. These countries are: Austria, Belgium, Bulgaria, Cyprus, Czech Republic, Denmark, Estonia, Finland, France, Germany, Greece, Hungary, Ireland, Italy, Latvia, Lithuania, Luxembourg, Malta, Netherlands, Poland, Portugal, Romania, Slovakia, Slovenia, Spain, Sweden, United Kingdom.

New Neighbourhood Policy

The European Neighbourhood Policy was developed in 2004 in order to strengthen stability and security in the EU during the accession of new countries and to counteract any division between the widening EU and its border countries.

The New Neighbourhood Policy applies to countries that are immediate neighbours of the EU by land or sea: Algeria, Armenia, Azerbaijan, Belarus, Egypt, Georgia, Israel, Jordan, Lebanon, Libya, Moldova, Morocco, Occupied Palestine Territories, Syria, Tunisia and Ukraine. Although Russia falls into this category geographically, it is covered by a different policy.

Official Journal of the EU

The Official Journal of the EU is a periodical published every working day in all official languages of the EU. It includes information on legislation, notices and a supplement for public procurement and can be accessed online at the following website: www.eur-lex.europa.eu/JOIndex.do.

Outermost regions

There are seven outermost regions: Guadeloupe, French Guiana, Martinique, and Réunion (the four French overseas departments), the Canaries (Spain), and the Azores and Madeira (Portugal). These regions are distinguished by their low population density and considerable distance from mainline Europe. Their specific location makes them European bridgeheads for fostering trade with their non-EU neighbours, most of which are less developed countries.

Programme countries and neighbouring partner countries

Programme countries are the 27 countries of the original EU accession (see Member states on page 364).

Partner countries are broken down into four categories: Neighbouring Partner Countries, South East Europe and Caucasus, Mediterranean Partner Countries and Other Countries of the World.

Technical Assistance Office

Technical Assistance Office is a term that was previously used for the Education, Audiovisual and Culture Executive Agency.

Third countries

Third countries is a term given to all other country-relationships to the EU, outside the 27 member states. This includes all of the neighbouring partner countries.

15 **Fundraising for environmental campaigns**

The voluntary sector has a long history of engaging in campaigning activities and is often uniquely placed to voice the concerns of unheard minorities. This chapter explores ways in which voluntary and community sector (VCS) organisations can use the tools and resources available to them in order to campaign effectively.

What is environmental campaigning?

The Charity Commission defines campaigning as raising awareness and making efforts to educate or involve the public by mobilising their support on a particular issue, or to influence or change public attitudes. The Commission's definition includes activities which ensure existing laws are observed.

Of course, the scope, scale and style of each campaign are as diverse as the groups organising them. Fundraising for a single issue campaign, maybe saving a local wood, will clearly be very different to the methods employed in funding a large-scale international campaign. What you want to do and how you want to do it will be the key to how you go about fundraising and who you decide to approach for assistance.

Examples of environmental campaigning activity include:

■ a campaign against banks investing in unethical sources
■ a campaign to encourage schools, colleges and workplaces to buy and use fair-trade products

■ a campaign to encourage universities to switch to renewable power that doesn't contribute to climate change.

Funding for Sustainable Change, a research paper published jointly by DSC and NCVO supplements the Charity Commission's definition of campaigning. It identifies three key interpretations (from the Enabling Voice and Campaigning paper included in the Third Sector Review, (see page 368) which, it suggests, are representative of the activities that campaigning VCOs may become involved with:

Campaigning includes 'a range of activities by organisations to *influence* others in order to effect an identified and desired social, economic, environmental or political change.'

Advocacy is a general term used to describe 'lobbying and campaigning activities that attempt to *influence* public policy'.

Influence covers organisations that do not necessarily identify themselves as

'campaigners' despite carrying out a vital influencing role, such as creating new channels of influence for the public, in the public interest.[1]

Charity law: campaigning and political activity

Charities and voluntary sector organisations have always played a vital role in effecting environmental change in the UK. This has mainly been achieved through campaigning at a local and national level to change public opinion on a huge array of issues, from climate change to labelling the source of food correctly.

The Commission defines political activity as that which is aimed at securing, or opposing, any change in the law or in the policy or decisions of decision makers, including governments, at home or abroad. It includes activity aimed at preserving an existing piece of legislation where a charity opposes its repeal or amendment. Such activity can only be undertaken in support of the charity's purposes.

---

[1] Amy Rosser and Sarah Shimmin, *Funding for Sustainable Change: Exploring the extent to which grant-making trusts fund campaigning, advocacy and influence,* (2007), p. 3.

There was, for many years, confusion over whether the law allowed charities to be actively involved in campaigning and political activity. This uncertainty, coupled with the intangible nature of campaigning, has made it a particularly difficult area in which to raise funds.

However, in March 2008 the Charity Commission sought to clarify the situation by updating its guidance. The Charity Commission document (*CC9 Speaking Out*) gives comprehensive guidance on what is and is not acceptable under charity law.

Any charity's campaigning or political activities should support its charitable purposes and be well balanced, likely to succeed and not party political. Charities can also comment publicly on social, economic and political issues if they are related to its objects or the way in which the charity carries out its work. Whilst political activity can be a significant part of a charity's work, it cannot be the only way in which a charity pursues its purposes. It should also be noted that some charities cannot campaign or engage in any political activity because their governing document precludes it.

The Charity Commission's new guidance has helped to clarify the position regarding campaigning as a charitable activity, and funding providers are beginning to recognise this and respond accordingly. The government has also become more aware of the valuable experience the VCS can bring to policy debates and the need to support VCS organisations which are engaged in campaigning activities.

The following sections highlight some recent developments, including the latest Third Sector Review, the Compact and the Sustainable Communities Act, which may prove useful tools for environmental campaigning organisations.

The Third Sector Review: enabling voice and campaigning

The government has acknowledged the important role that VCOs play in effecting social change through campaigning activities. Since the 2007 Third Sector Review (TSR) identified 'voice and campaigning' as one of the government's five key priorities, campaigning has come back into VCS popular consciousness.

The TSR included a joint paper from NCVO and the Sheila McKechnie Foundation: *Understanding the Role of Government in Relation to Voice and Campaigning* (Cabinet Office, 2007), which focused on the issues surrounding campaigning activity and the roles of campaigners and funders in the voluntary sector.

The paper's main aim was to assess the needs of the campaigning sector. It also aimed to understand and clarify the government and the sector's positions, respectively, as funders and organisations in receipt of funding. The government is called on to facilitate an environment in which VCOs are able to provide 'voice to citizens and to campaign'. The report suggests that the government should support better engagement with the VCS and ensure a diverse range of voices are heard in all consultations.

The report's authors also call on the government to reinforce its commitment to the principles of the Compact (see page 324), that charities should be free to campaign regardless of any funding relationship they might be engaged with statutory funders.

Although there have been significant improvements, such as increased government funding opportunities and clearer application processes, there is still a long way to go before the hurdles presented by campaign fundraising become a thing of the past.

Campaigning and the Compact

The Compact, formally known as 'the Compact on Relations between Government and the Voluntary and Community Sector in England' was established in 1998. It is an agreement between the government and the third sector on how they can best improve their working relationship and work together for 'mutual advantage and community gain'. It applies to:

- central government departments, including government offices for the regions
- executive non-departmental public bodies that have a relationship with the voluntary and community sector
- a range of organisations in the voluntary and community sector.

The Compact's main purpose is to create a set of guidelines that help bring about a cultural shift in the behaviours that affect the working relationship between the government and the VCS. Its intention is to create a situation of equal partnership between the two parties.

Making it work for you

With regard to campaigning, using the Compact can be a way of giving your cause more influence when it comes to making an impact with local and central government. Through the Funding and Procurement Code the government agrees to consult with the VCS. If this hasn't been the case with a certain issue, you could refer to the Compact code (in which the government has agreed to work mutually with the VCS) as a way of gaining some leverage for your campaign.

The Compact also commits the government to the idea that charities should be free to campaign regardless of any funding relationship. However, there is some debate about just how equal this Compact partnership can be, given that the government is inherently more powerful in its position as a funder.

Sustainable Communities Act 2007

Background

The Sustainable Communities Act 2007 is designed to empower people by encouraging more involvement in local decision making processes. It was the result of a five-year campaign led by Local Works, a coalition of over 90 organisations.

The Act works from the principle that 'local people know best what needs to be done to promote the sustainability of their area, but sometimes they need central government to act to enable them to do so'.[2] It gives local people a channel through which to tell local and central government what can be done to prevent their local areas declining.

The Act is relatively new and so it is likely to be some time before it is proven to be effective. There has already been some criticism that the government has failed to follow the ethos of the Act in not publishing local public spending reports, thereby undermining one of its most significant objectives, of transparency.

How it works

The Act involves what Local Works (which is campaigning to promote the use of the Sustainable Communities Act) has described as a 'double devolution' process.. First of all, central government has a legal obligation to assist local authorities in promoting the sustainability of their local areas. Local authorities will be invited to make suggestions to the Secretary of State on how this can be achieved, which means that your local authority has the power to suggest what the government should do. Secondly, the Act states that your local authority cannot make its recommendations to the Secretary of State without the involvement of 'local people'. It has an obligation to set up representative panels

---

[2] *Sustainable Communities Act 2007: A Guide*, Communities and Local Government, 2008, p 3

that include underrepresented groups such as people from minority ethnic backgrounds, young people and older people.

Each local authority has the choice to opt in. According to Local Works, if your local authority has not opted in, you are within your rights to challenge this and ask that it implements the Act into its working practices. (Please refer to Local Works guidance for further details–www.localworks.org.)

The definition of sustainable communities in the Act is deliberately broad. It covers the following four areas:

- environmental
- local economies
- social inclusion
- democratic involvement.[3]

'Environmental' sustainability could cover anything from local renewable energy to protecting green spaces and so is likely to be the most profitable area for many organisations.

Making it work for you

Firstly you need to find out whether the Act is operating in your area. According to the Local Works website, at the time of writing 117 local authorities has agreed to use the Act.

Case study

Woodland Trust

The Woodland Trust has been quick to see the potential of the Sustainable Communities Act in protecting local woods and green spaces and is currently running a campaign to encourage local groups to get their council to opt in to the Act. Help is available on the website (see below), including draft letters, advice on proposals and a five step plan for taking action. For more information see www.woodlandtrust.org.uk/en/campaigns/woods-for-people/sustainable-communities.

---

[3] www.localworks.org/?q=node/5#28

The full Act and its associated guides can be found at the following websites:

- Local Works: www.localworks.org
- Unlock Democracy: www.unlockdemocracy.org.uk
- Communities and Local Government: www.communities.gov.uk.

In summary

This section has highlighted some important developments such as the Sustainable Communities Act and the Compact, which can be useful tools for campaigning organisations. This progress has made funding more accessible as grantmakers follow the trend towards greater support for campaigning organisations, as the next section will show.

Sources of funding

This section gives an overview of the main sources of funding available to charities and other voluntary sector groups involved in environmental campaigning. The information provided is not comprehensive but gives an indication of the types of funding streams and programmes available. It can help you to understand key trends and identify popular sources of funding for projects that include a campaigning element.

Environmental funding is an area that is constantly changing, as new issues will always arise and priorities will continually shift. There are many ways in which funding can be raised for environmental causes, and many types of funding streams are available, from one-off small grants to three-year strategic funding contracts.

Membership

Membership is usually the core income that contributes to the financing of a campaign. If managed well, it can act as a stable and recurrent funding stream that can allow a campaign greater freedom of movement.

A membership subscription for a campaign can range from a couple of pounds for a local campaign to £400 to join a professional association which provides benefits to its members, e.g. the British Medical Association.

The price of a membership subscription is generally determined by three factors:

- the level of services offered
- what members can afford
- how the campaign uses the membership.

The most important matter to consider when setting up a membership is to make sure the subscription income covers the cost of servicing the membership. If your subscription income is too low, you can run into difficulties by having to subsidise your membership.

General public

Raising money from the general public can be a lucrative source of income, as a variety of opportunities are available. Examples include:

- direct mail
- telephone fundraising
- public collections
- trading, sales and merchandising
- benefits and events.

More information is available on raising money from the general public in Chapter 7 *Raising support from the public.*

Grant-giving organisations

Charitable and non-charitable trusts and foundations and companies can provide large amounts of funding for campaigning activities.

Grant-making charities

When applying to grant-making charities, it is important to check whether your campaign fits within their objectives and priorities. In 2007 the estimated number of grant-making charities in the UK was 8,800[4] and although most will give grants to a wide range of causes, many will only make grants within a specific field, such as conservation of the environment or third world development.

Some charities will only give to a restricted geographical area, or nationally but with a preference for the area they are based in, so if you are a local organisation, try local grant-givers first.

Many grant-making charities are also more willing to fund a specific, usually one-off, cost rather than supporting core running costs. Things to check when matching your application to the most appropriate charity include:

---

[4] *Grantmaking by UK Trusts and Charities,* Association of Charitable Foundations and Charities Aid Foundation, 2007. Information taken from www.acf.org.uk/uploaded Files/Publications_and_resources/Publications/0416B_TrustAndFoundationBriefingPaper.pdf on 20.07.09

- its policy and field of work
- its beneficial area
- the type of costs supported
- the level of grant given.

Most grant-making charities are registered with the Charity Commission and are restricted to making grants for charitable purposes, but not necessarily only to registered charities. Provided their governing document doesn't preclude it, they can usually award grants to campaigns, as long as the money is spent on a purpose which is charitable in law.

Identify which areas of your work are charitable and apply for funding from grant-making charities for this work. This can free up other sources of income to finance non-charitable areas of your work, such as some political activities.

Non-charitable grant-making trusts

A small number of grantmakers have declared non-charitable purposes in order to remain free to fund political or campaigning activity. The Joseph Rowntree Reform Trust and the Barrow Cadbury Fund are two examples.

The Joseph Rowntree Reform Trust

The Joseph Rowntree Reform Trust is a non-charitable trust and gives funding only to non-charitable, political and campaigning activities being carried out in the UK. Previous environmental projects supported include the UK Chagos Support Association, towards the cost of developing a resettlement strategy to enable the Chagossians to return to their islands, and the Campaign Against Depleted Uranium to continue its campaigning work.

The trust does not have specific grants programmes, but 'maintains a longstanding interest in promoting democratic reform and defending civil liberties'. Grants are usually distributed in two financial brackets: grants of up to £5,000, which are considered at any time; grants of over £5,000, which are considered by the directors at their quarterly meetings.

Details of recent grants made by the trust, deadlines, application forms and contact details can be found on its website: www.jrrt.org.uk.

The Barrow Cadbury Fund

The Barrow Cadbury Fund is the non-charitable branch of the Barrow Cadbury Trust. The two organisations share the same board and secretariat and the same interests, with the Barrow Cadbury Fund giving grants to projects that the charitable side of the trust cannot fund. All information provided on the Barrow

Cadbury Trust's website (www.bctrust.org.uk) concerning eligibility criteria, deadlines and so on also applies to the Fund.

The Fund supports grassroots, user-led projects, favouring ideas that are 'innovative and visionary... that are likely to have a high impact on social change, either at a policy or practice level'. The main areas of interest are inclusive community work, young adults and criminal justice, and a global exchange programme. Further details on how your project could fit under these categories can be found at the Barrow Cadbury Trust's website, or through contacting the grants team at the head office:

Kean House
6 Kean Street
London
WC2B 4AS
Tel: 020 7632 9060
Email: general@barrowcadbury.org.uk.

Independent bodies

Network for Social Change

The Network for Social Change is, essentially, a community of wealthy individuals who administer grants through annual events, described as 'a collective committed to funding sustainability and social justice'.

The network operates three funding processes – the Main Funding Cycle, Major Projects and Fast Track Funding – through which funds are raised and allocated at its twice-yearly conferences.

Grants of up to £15,000 are distributed annually through the Main Funding Cycle under six categories: arts and education for change; economic justice; green planet; health and wholeness; human rights; and peace.

Smaller amounts of funding are also available, up to £5,000, under the Fast Track Funding scheme. The Major Projects' scheme supports projects that require larger amounts of funding.

Further information on the Network for Social Change can be found at thenetworkforsocialchange.org.uk.

The Big Lottery Fund (BIG)

Although actually a public authority, BIG is operated in a similar style to an independent foundation and maintains a distance from government. BIG gives grants to community groups and campaigning groups as well as to charities, as long as they are 'philanthropic or benevolent'. This means that they must be humanitarian or altruistic, strictly not-for-profit, and not dominated by purposes which are political or doctrinaire.

The following schemes are run by the National Lottery and are covered fully in Chapter 9, *Raising Money from the National Lottery*. Both schemes have been set up to support environmental projects and funding is available for campaigning in this area.

Changing Spaces: Access to Nature

This programme's main aim is to improve access and provide opportunities for people to enjoy nature, particularly young people, older people, people from black and minority ethnic groups and people with disabilities, focusing on projects that raise community awareness, increase active participation, include volunteers, and to those that provide education and learning opportunities. For further details see Chapter 9 *Raising money from the National Lottery*.

Changing Spaces: Community Sustainable Energy

This programme aims to help not-for-profit community-based organisations in England reduce their environmental impact through the installation of energy saving measures and microgeneration technologies. The scheme will also fund development studies that help community organisations to find out if a microgeneration and energy efficiency project will work for them. For further details see Chapter 9 *Raising money from the National Lottery*.

BIG runs a large number of funding programmes, many of which change, open and close frequently, so it is best to check the Fund's website (www.biglotteryfund.org.uk) for up to date information on what is currently available. For more information see Chapter 9 *Raising money from the National Lottery*.

Companies

Groups can also get funding for campaigning activities from companies; however as a general rule, less money is available than from grant-making charities and it tends to go to well-established, popular charities.

Companies have a history of supporting causes that are in line with their own interests. Whilst this has to be taken into consideration, it is also important to think about the credibility of your campaign and how this may be affected by gaining industry support. For example, a campaign to protect endangered sea-life funded by a major oil company is likely to prompt questions as to the integrity of a project.

As well as the obvious forms of funding such as donations and sponsorship, you should also look into the possibility of applying for support in kind. Many companies can make offers such as spare office space, equipment loans and staff secondments. For details of company giving see Chapter 11 *Winning company support.*

Central government

Both local and central government are viable sources of funding for campaigning projects.

Below are details of central government funds currently available to VCS groups with campaigning either as their main agenda or as part of wider criteria.

The first fund, Capacitybuilders Campaigning Fund, has now closed, however it has been included in this chapter due to its innovative nature.

Some government funding schemes do not spend their whole budget in the time-frame allocated and as a result, they re-open after their closing date has passed. It is worth checking on the Capacitybuilders website to see if this fund re-opens or a similar scheme is set up.

Capacitybuilders Campaigning Fund

Capacitybuilders is a non-departmental government body that aims to increase development and capacity within the third sector.

In May 2009 it was announced that Capacitybuilders would manage the government's new £750,000 campaigning programme – the first actively to help charities and other voluntary sector organisations carry out campaigning activity. The main aim will be to identify and support new ways that VCS groups can act as 'a strong voice for the most disadvantaged people in society'.

The programme will be developed and administered over two years, with packages of grants and other support services being provided to around 30 groups.

For further information or sign up to their newsletter refer to the Capacitybuilders website (www.capacitybuilders.org.uk), which gives details of this and other related funding programmes.

Strategic Programme Fund – Low Carbon High Growth

The Strategic Programme Fund (SPF) is the Foreign and Commonwealth Office's (FCO) largest programme budget. The Low Carbon, High Growth programme is a result of a merger between the SPF Climate Change and Energy and Growth programmes. Low Carbon, High Growth supports the FCO strategic objective to 'promote a low carbon, high growth, global economy'. Projects and campaigns in this area must demonstrate the ability to deliver transformational change at a county or sector-wide level, which the FCO suggests is difficult to achieve with small projects.

Local government

Although money may be available from local government for environmental campaigning, the procedures for applying aren't as clear cut as those for central government. Most local authorities operate a small grants scheme for VCS groups, and some will offer a grant scheme targeted at environmental work.

Your local authority should have a voluntary sector liaison officer who will be able to assist you in this; unfortunately not all of them do. If there isn't a liaison officer, contact the voluntary sector or community team. Find out if there are any small grants schemes relevant to your work, or look at the environment, voluntary sector and community and living sections of your authority's website for further information.

As with any other funder you approach, carry out some initial research into the viability of obtaining funding from your local authority. For example, what are your council's strategic priorities and how does its policy agenda fit with your work? Can your actions help it to achieve its goals, and how do the authority's goals fit in with your needs and agenda?

The Sustainable Communities Act (see page 370) is designed to empower local people to become more involved in decision making in their community. Although it does not give access to funding, it is an important avenue to becoming more involved, and building a positive working relationship, with your local authority, which could result in gaining future funding.

16 Environmental organisations and charitable status

Most grant-giving organisations, statutory bodies and the public are much more likely to give to charities which are registered, because they are subject to regulation.

In England and Wales the regulator of charities is the Charity Commission and in Northern Ireland the Charity Commission for Northern Ireland. All eligible charities must register with their regulating body. In Scotland all charities need to register with the Office of the Scottish Charity Regulator. Further details of these regulatory bodies are given later in this chapter.

There are benefits to being a registered charity, but it can also bring restrictions. This chapter looks at the pros and cons of being a charity, which organisations must by law be registered and how to go about this.

What are the benefits of being a charity?

The main advantages are that charities:

- can claim relief from tax on most income or gains and on profits from some activities
- can also claim tax repayments on income received on which tax has already been paid, including Gift Aid donations from individuals
- can take advantage of some special VAT exemptions
- will receive a mandatory 80% of business rate relief on premises, which can be increased to 100% at the discretion of the local authority

- that are VAT registered may be able to reclaim some of the VAT they are charged from HMRC
- are often able to raise funds from the public, grant-making charities and local government more easily than non-charitable bodies
- can seek advice and get information, including free publications, from their particualar regulator
- can formally represent and help to meet the needs of the community
- are able to give the public the assurance that they are being monitored and advised by a regulating authority.

What are the disadvantages of being a charity?

There are restrictions on what charities can do, both in terms of their work, and the ways in which they can operate:

- A charity must have exclusively charitable aims. Some organisations may carry out their aims by a range of activities, some charitable, some not. To become a charity, this type of organisation would have to stop its non-charitable activities. (The non-charitable activities can, of course, continue if carried on by a separate non-charitable organisation.) You will need to consider carefully if becoming a charity will severely restrict your planned activities. If so, charity registration may not be right for your organisation.
- There are limits to the extent of political or campaigning activities which a charity can take on.
- Strict rules apply to trading by charities.
- Trustees (i.e. the body of people administering and managing the charity) must not benefit from their position beyond what is allowed by law and is in the best interests of the charity.
- Charity trustees have signicant responsibilities and potential liabilities.
- Financial benefits from the charity which a trustee manages are not permissable unless they are specifically authorised by the governing document of the charity or by the Commission. Financial benefits include salaries, services and the awarding of business contracts to a trustee's own business from the charity. Similar problems arise where the spouse, relative or partner of a trustee receives such benefits. Trustees are, however, entitled to be reimbursed for reasonable out-of-pocket expenses, such as train fares to trustee meetings.

- Trustees need to avoid any situation where their personal interests conflict with their duties as trustees.
- Charity law imposes certain financial reporting obligations; these vary with the size of the charity.

What is a charity?

A body is a charity if it is established for exclusively charitable purposes and for the benefit of the public independently of government or commercial interests.

A charity's purposes are usually expressed in the objects clause of its governing document, for example, trust deed, constitution, memorandum and articles of association or rules.

What are charitable purposes?

'Charitable purposes' are those set out in the Charities Act 2006:
1) the prevention or relief of poverty
2) the advancement of education
3) the advancement of religion
4) the advancement of health or the saving of lives
5) the advancement of citizenship or community development
6) the advancement of the arts, culture, heritage or science
7) the advancement of amateur sport
8) the advancement of human rights, conflict resolution or reconciliation or the promotion of religious or racial harmony or equality and diversity
9) the advancement of environmental protection or improvement
10) the relief of those in need, by reason of youth, age, ill-health, disability, financial hardship or other disadvantage
11) the advancement of animal welfare
12) the promotion of the efficiency of the armed forces of the Crown or of the police, fire and rescue services or ambulance services
13) other purposes recognised as charitable under the existing law and any new purposes which are similar to another prescribed purpose.

Educational charities

Many youth organisations have educational objects. These are some of the areas they may cover.

- Formal education in schools and colleges.
- Scholarship funds.
- Vocational training and work experience.
- Sports organisations for young people, provided there is open access and training for all members.
- Arts organisations for young people such as youth theatre groups or bands.

To be an educational charity there must be some element of study or training and the subject must be of some educational worth. A young people's chess club has been held to be charitable, but a tiddlywinks club would be unlikely to qualify. Many youth clubs have been registered with objects to educate young people to develop their skills so as to develop their full potential as members of society.

Recreational charities

The Recreational Charities Act 1958 specifically included the provision of facilities for recreation 'or other leisure time occupation in the interest of social welfare' as being charitable. *This is provided that* the organisation is established for the public at large or for any disadvantaged group and is altruistic in nature, and the facilities provided are set up to meet certain social needs.

The organisation needs to be for a sufficient section of the public (see 'Assessing the public benefit of organisations applying to register as charities' on page 385. Other criteria apply and reference should be made to the Commission or OSCR (Office of Scottish Charity Regulator) to determine whether the organisation is charitable. Many organisations involved in outdoor activities will come within the Act.

Other charitable purposes

Organisations may also come within several other charitable purposes. Church groups or religious youth organisations for example may be charitable under the advancement of religion. Organisations coming under the prevention or relief of poverty would include those giving direct financial assistance or legal advice or providing housing to financially disadvantaged people.

Some non-charitable aims that are often presumed to be charitable

The following are examples of organisations or aims often assumed to be charitable, but which in fact are not.

- Individual sports clubs set up to benefit their members or promote excellence (as distinct from sports facilities open for everyone or provided for specific groups of people, such as young people, or as a method of promoting healthy recreation).

- The promotion of political or propagandist aims, or the promotion of a particular point of view (for more details please refer to booklet CC9, available on the Charity Commission's website).

- Aims that include arrangements where people running the organisation get significant personal benefit.

- Raising funds for other charities where the organisers do not have any say over how the funds are spent.

- Aims that promote friendship or international friendship, such as town twinning associations.

Appeals for funds

Fundraising is not a charitable object, it is simply an activity which can be undertaken to help achieve a charitable purpose. That purpose must fall within the charity's objects.

There are complex rules about fundraising and you may need to take professional advice. In the first instance you should refer to the Commission's booklet on fundraising – CC20, obtainable from the website.

The following points are considered good practice.

- Great care should be taken over the wording of a written appeal asking for money from the public. Organisations should make sure the aims for which the charity intends to use the money are accurately described.

- The record of a speech or broadcast may be regarded as evidence of the aims of an appeal. The organisers of that appeal cannot alter its aims to something not consistent with the terms under which donors were invited to contribute. Care should be given to the wording of any spoken appeal.

- If you want to raise money for a charity's general purposes, you must make this clear and avoid any suggestion that the money will be used for a more specific purpose.

- If an appeal is for a specific purpose, such as paying for or restoring a building, you should state what will happen to the money if either not enough, or too much, is raised.

See also Chapter 6 *Fundraising for projects*.

Public benefit

Under the Charities Act 2006, the Commission is required to issue guidance on public benefit. Statutory guidance on this is contained in the Commission's publication 'Charities and Public Benefit'. Anyone thinking of setting up and registering a new charity should familiarise themselves with this guidance and refer to the supplementary guidance on the public benefit of specific types of charity.

What is meant by 'the public benefit requirement'?

The public benefit requirement means that to be a charity, an organisation must be able to demonstrate that it is set up for aims that are charitable, and that its aims are, and will be, carried out for the public benefit. This applies to each of an organisation's aims; a charity cannot have some aims that are for the public benefit and some that are not.

Two key principles must be met in order to show that an organisation's aims are for the public benefit. Within each principle there are some important factors that must be considered in all cases. These are:

Principle 1: There must be an identifiable benefit or benefits

- It must be clear what the benefits are.
- The benefits must be related to the aims.
- Benefits must be balanced against any detriment or harm.

Principle 2: Benefit must be to the public, or a section of the public

- The beneficiaries must be appropriate to the aims.
- Where benefit is to a section of the public, the opportunity to benefit must not be unreasonably restricted by:
    - geographical or other restrictions or
    - ability to pay any fees charged.

- People in poverty must not be excluded from the opportunity to benefit.
- Any private benefits must be incidental.

Charity trustees' public benefit duties

Charity trustees have the following public benefit duties. They must:

- ensure that they carry out their charity's aims for the public benefit
- have regard to guidance the Commission publishes on public benefit (when they exercise any powers or duties where that may be relevant)
- report on their charity's public benefit in their trustees' annual report.

Anyone applying to register their organisation needs to understand that the charity trustees must be aware of, and fulfil, their statutory duties with regard to public benefit and public benefit reporting. This requirement is a continuing duty for charity trustees throughout the life of the charity; it is not just a requirement at registration.

Assessing the public benefit of organisations applying to register as charities

When considering whether an organisation's aims are for the public benefit, the Commission may assess its activities in order to:

- clarify its aims (i.e. understand the meaning and scope of the words used in its objects)
- decide whether those aims are charitable (i.e. that the aims fall within the descriptions of charitable purposes in the Charities Act 2006)
- ensure that the aims are or will or may be carried out for the public benefit.

In the case of an organisation applying to register as a charity, the Commission can consider relevant factual background information, such as asking for evidence of its current or proposed activities, in order to decide whether its aims are charitable and for the public benefit. Where it is not clear, the Commission will ask the organisation to provide further evidence. If the Commission is not satisfied that the public benefit requirement will be met, it may refuse registration, or may ask the applicant to amend the organisation's objects and/or activities to ensure it will meet the public benefit requirement before registration can proceed.

No organisation can be charitable if:

- its aims are illegal or could be said to further illegal aims under the law; or
- it is set up for the personal benefit of:
  - its trustees
  - its employees (other than in the case of relieving poverty – for example, there would normally be no reason why a firm or business should not operate a benevolent fund for its staff limited to the purpose of relieving poverty); or
  - other specific individuals; or
- it is created for political aims.

Different legal structures – governing documents

The governing document means any formal document which establishes a charity and which sets out its purposes and how it is to be administered. It may be a trust deed, constitution, memorandum and articles of association, will, conveyance, Royal Charter, Charity Commission Scheme or a simple set of rules.

A charity's governing document should contain information about:

- its registered name and any working name
- what it is set up to do (objects)
- how it will do those things (powers)
- who will run it (charity trustees)
- how the trustees will run it, including administrative provisions for meetings and proceedings, voting and financial procedures
- what happens if changes to the administrative and/or other provisions need to be made – except in the case of a charitable company, where company law makes provision (amendment provision)
- what happens if it wishes or needs to wind up (dissolution provision).

The governing document (formally referred to as the 'governing instrument'), is the charity trustees' 'instruction manual', as well as a legal document by which the charity is administered and managed. Charity trustees should refer to it regularly to remind themselves of the charity's purposes and how it should be run. Trustees and senior members of staff should be given a full copy of the governing document on appointment.

When questions arise over the running of the charity or a particular problem needs addressing, reference should be made to the governing document. You will often find that the document covers the point raised. Even if it does not, it is a useful first point of reference and should guide you in the right direction for your next steps.

The document should be clear and as simple as legal requirements allow. The Commission publishes model documents. If yours is not a model and you have found it difficult to follow, you should contact the Commission for advice on whether you can simplify it, perhaps by adopting a more straightforward document, or by amending your existing one. In some cases, e.g. where the organisation is run by a Charity Commission Scheme, the process of changing it will be more complicated and it may not be possible to make the provisions of your document any less complex, but you should ask the Commission's advice.

Main types of governing document

There are three main types of governing document:

- constitution or rules
- trust deed
- memorandum and articles of association.

The Commission provides model documents, free of charge, which contain administrative provisions suitable for each type of organisation. However, it is still necessary to insert the objects of the organisation and complete information, and to consider the suitability of the provisions generally to the individual circumstances of the organisation. The models are available on the Commission's website or by calling Charity Commission Direct on 0845 300 0218.

Where there is an umbrella body, it will expect a level of affiliation from any new local charity. This means that it wishes to be approached by individual groups that intend to establish a charity under its umbrella, rather than local groups applying directly to the Commission for registration.

The Charity Law Association (CLA) also produces suitable model governing documents but a charge is made. To order copies of these email the CLA administrator at admin@charitylawassociation.org.uk.

Charitable incorporated organisations (CIOs)

Many trustees of unincorporated charities feel they require the protection of incorporation and, in the past, they have opted for their charity 'adopting' a new structure to become a charitable company limited by guarantee. In this way, their liability becomes limited (with strict provisos concerning negligence and fraud). The charitable company is however subject to both charity and company law and the impact of this on a former non-incorporated charity requires more expertise, time and resources.

The purpose of the CIO is to provide a legal framework for charities which seek the protection and practicality of incorporation but without their having to meet the regulatory and reporting requirements of both company and charity law.

Following the 2006 Act, the Commission has prepared draft documents for two specific types of organisation, although at the time of writing (July 2009) these had not yet been published:

- a charity which would formerly have operated under a constitution and which has a membership – referred to as the 'Association' model
- a charity which would formerly have been governed by a will, trust deed or declaration of trust and which would have been referred to as a trust and whose body of members is not distinct from its charity trustees – referred to as the 'Foundation' model.

The new CIO will not be suitable for all charities and for many, the legal requirements will be considered still too onerous for the size of their organisation – they will remain as unincorporated organisations. However, the CIO does provide a legal framework within which many medium-sized organisations can work and grow.

The model documents are perhaps more wordy than most would have hoped, the idea behind them being to simplify, but they need to include provisions which would affect companies and unincorporated organisations and those which have come about simply because of the new structure.

Charity trustees should take some time to consider which form of governing document they choose, taking into consideration the nature of their work and the provisions they will need to run it both at the start and as it develops. They should also avoid taking on provisions that are too much for their capacity and resources.

Who regulates charities?

In England and Wales

The Charity Commission (the Commission) is established by law as the regulator and registrar for charities in England and Wales.

It regulates by:

- securing compliance with charity law and dealing with abuse and poor practice
- enabling charities to work better within an effective legal, accounting and governance framework, keeping pace with developments in society, the economy and the law
- promoting sound governance and accountability.

One of the Commission's responsibilities is to maintain a register of charities. The rules regarding charity registration in England and Wales have changed. From April 2007, charities with a gross annual income exceeding £5,000 that are not legally excepted or exempt from registration are required by law to register. Gross income means all the money the organisation has received in a financial year from all sources.

Trustees of charities with income exceeding £10,000 in their last financial year are required to complete and submit an annual return. Charities with income above £25,000 need to submit an annual report and accounts. All required submissions must be made within 10 months of the end of the charity's financial year.

Charities with an annual income of £10,000 or less do not have to submit an annual return or a copy of their trustees' annual report and accounts but are required to keep their register details up to date. To ensure these details are up to date and to confirm that they are still operating, the Commission requests smaller charities to submit an annual update form.

Charities with yearly incomes over £10,000 must by law send to the Commission their accounts and report every year within 10 months of the end of their year-end. The Commission now names charities that have seriously defaulted on these legal obligations on its 'Defaulting Charities' finder facility.

The Commission provides advice and guidance to charities. Its helpful website includes information on all the services it offers, including a staffed contact centre, website information and publications. Commission staff visit several hundred larger charities every year, promoting effective governance, with the information gathered contributing to policy development and to Commission publications. The Commission also modernises charities by making schemes by which it may amend, replace or amplify a charity's governing document. There is also a programme of Regulatory Reports which highlights good practice.

In Northern Ireland

Before the introduction of the new charity legislation in Northern Ireland, there was no local registration of charities and only limited control of how charities were run. Usually charities applied to HMRC for tax benefits and received a reference number.

The Charity Commission for Northern Ireland (CCNI) is a non-departmental public body, funded by grant-in-aid from the Department for Social Development. It was established under the Charities Act (NI) 2008 and became operational on 27 March 2009.

Its mission is to introduce a regulatory framework for the charitable sector in Northern Ireland, in line with developments in the rest of the UK and Ireland. This will provide a structure and process through which charities can demonstrate their contribution to society, the public can be assured regarding how charities are spending any donations and government can assist in better governance of the charity sector.

The new provisions will enable people to see how charities are spending their income and allow government to help charities manage themselves better, encouraging best practice.

The CCNI will maintain a register of charities andevery institution which is a charity under the law of Northern Ireland will have to be registered.

The register will include:

- the name of the charity
- if the charity is a legally designated religious charity, a statement to that effect
- such other particulars of, and such other information relating to, the charity as the CCNI thinks fit.

The CCNI has agreed its programme of work for the remainder of 2009 and beyond as it begins to discharge its statutory responsibilities.

A 'commencement order' will be introduced by September 2009 which will bring forward the following provisions:

- the meaning of charitable purpose and public benefit test
- the charities register

- the charity tribunal
- the Commission's investigatory powers.

The CCNI has agreed a timetable for registration and monitoring of local charities. The first registrations will start in April 2010 and charities will be expected to make their first returns in April 2011. These will include information on both financial performance and charitable activities.

In Scotland

The Office of Scottish Charity Regulator was established in December 2003 and published a statutory register of all 'live' charities for Scotland on 1 April 2006. Prior to this, an index of charities was maintained by HMRC.

All charities which work partly or wholly in Scotland must register with the OSCR and provide the following details for publication on the register:
- the name of the charity
- the principal office or the name and address of one of the charity trustees (unless OSCR is satisfied it is necessary to protect an individual or the charity's premises)
- the charity's purposes
- certain other information (including whether it is a designated religious charity or national collector).

The register is available for public inspection at OSCR's principal office and on its website.

Charities entered into the Scottish Charity Register are required to submit an annual return and accounts to OSCR. Charities with an annual gross income of £25,000 or above are also required to submit a supplementary monitoring return. These documents must be submitted to OSCR within nine months of the financial year-end. If these documents have not been received by the deadline OSCR will take the following action:
- Immediately after the deadline for submission a charity's individual entry on the Scottish Charity Register will indicate that the annual return is 'overdue'.
- Ten weeks after the deadline the annual return status of the charity's entry in the Scottish Charity Register will change from 'active' to 'passed to compliance' to indicate that the charity has been referred to the compliance support team.
- Charities that have still not provided an annual return, including the supplementary monitoring return if appropriate, and/or accounts within six months of the deadline for submission will be listed as defaulting charities and published on a page on OSCR's website.

Charities will be removed from this page once the required documents have been received, checked and passed as complete. The Annual Return Status of the charity's entry in the Scottish Charity Register will then change back to 'active'.

Consequences of continued non-submission of the required documents

Under section 45 of the Charities and Trustees Investment (Scotland) Act 2005, OSCR has powers to appoint an accountant to prepare accounts for a charity. Should OSCR make use of this power as a consequence of continued non-submission of the required documents, the charity's trustees would be personally liable for any costs incurred by OSCR and the expenses of the person of preparing the accounts.

Charities that do not provide OSCR with the required documents within 12 months of the deadline for submission may be considered for removal from the Scottish Charity Register.

Contact details for all three regulators are included in *Useful contacts and sources of information* (page 409).

How do you register as a charity?

In order to be registered as a charity, the Charity Commission must be satisfied that your objects are charitable. It will also want evidence of how you intend to operate within those objects and what your activities are and that they don't conflict with your stated purposes, and it will also check that your governing document is appropriate for your charity. The procedure is as follows:

1) In England and Wales, write to or telephone the Charity Commission for a copy of its charity registration pack. This includes information on setting up a charity and guidance booklets as well as an application form. The application pack is very useful and you should read the guidance and information carefully and follow the procedures outlined. Tell the Commission if you intend to use an agreed or approved model constitution, as a special application form will be available for these cases and, everything else being acceptable, it should quicken the process.

   In Northern Ireland, the draft timetable for the first registrations of charities indicates that this will take place around April 2010 and full details regarding applying for charity registration should be provided on the CCNI's website. If you are considering registering a charity in Northern Ireland before that date you should contact:

Department of Social Development
Voluntary and Community Unit
Lighthouse Building
1 Cromac Place
Gasworks Business Park
Ormeau Road
Belfast BT7 2JB

Telephone: 028 9082 9425
Fax: 028 9082 9431
Textphone: 028 9082 9446
email: vcu@dsdni.gov.uk

In Scotland, the OSCR does not provide an application pack or advise on the setting up of charities.

For information and guidance about setting up a charity based in Scotland, or which operates in Scotland you should contact the Scottish Council for Voluntary Organisations:

SCVO
Mansfield Traquair Centre
15 Mansfield Place
Edinburgh EH3 6BB

Telephone: 0131 556 3882
Email: enquiries@scvo.org.uk
Website: www.scvo.org.uk

2) Establish your organisation either by executing and stamping the trust deed, adopting the constitution at a members' meeting or incorporating the company.

3) Send all the required documentation (listed in the pack) to the appropriate regulator for consideration.

4) If all the documentation and the information you provide on your activities is acceptable, the charity will be registered and you will receive written confirmation and your charity registration number. If not, the regulator may call for additional information or require amendments to the governing document. If it considers that your activities and purposes are charitable but the wording of your document does not reflect this and precludes the organisation from registration you will be advised how to address this. If it considers that your activities and purposes are not exclusively charitable (even if your stated purposes are), it will give you reasons for rejecting your application.

- If you are a branch or a local group of a national organisation you should first approach your national body, which will usually have an approved model constitution that has been agreed with the regulator.
- For a model trust deed, constitution or memorandum and articles of association contact the Commission, the SCVO or the Charity Law Association – see *Useful contacts and sources of information* on page 409. These models do not include objects clauses.

17 Tax and tax benefits

There is a legal requirement to pay taxes due regardless of status, (i.e. whether a charity, company, other organisation or individual) and whether or not we are asked to by HM Revenue & Customs (HMRC). Although tax issues can be highly complex, the penalties, if we get them wrong, can be severe and not knowing or understanding the law is not considered an excuse by HMRC.

You might need to take specialist advice, especially at an early stage. For example, if you are planning a major fundraising campaign, you may go over the VAT threshold for the first time. This will affect not just that particular appeal but all your other activities as well. Or if you organise an event that generates a surplus, the profit may be taxed (usually to corporation tax) and there is the chance that either VAT will need to be levied on the price charged or VAT incurred in putting on an event will not be recoverable.

On a positive note, there are some tax benefits available to UK charities, for example, tax relief on income and gains, and on profits from *some* activities, as well as claiming tax back on income received on which tax has already been paid, for example on bank interest and Gift Aid donations.

In order for your charity to benefit from the tax benefits available, you must be recognised by HMRC as 'a charity for tax purposes' (this is a different process than registering as a charity with the Charity Commission, the Charity Commission for Northern Ireland or the Office of the Scottish Regulator).

HMRC has a very informative and helpful website which includes a guide on how to apply for recognition as a charity for tax and Gift Aid purposes – www.hmrc.gov.uk/charities – and you should refer to this in the first instance.

It is not possible to cover all aspects of tax issues in relation to charitable organisations in this one chapter. Here we offer an overview of the following subjects.

- Tax advantages
- Corporation tax

- Exemptions from corporation tax – trading income
- VAT
- Charity lotteries
- Gift aid
- Payroll giving
- PAYE
- Donation vouchers

Tax advantages

Registered charities:

- do not normally have to pay income/corporation tax (in the case of some types of income), capital gains tax, or stamp duty, and gifts to charities are free of inheritance tax
- pay no more than 20% of normal business rates on the buildings which they use and occupy to further their charitable aims
- can get special VAT treatment in some circumstances
- can reclaim tax made on tax-effective donations (gift aid).

Corporation tax

Corporation tax is a tax on the trading profits of companies and other business organisations (including charities). Even though the profit is only a surplus to be retained by the charity, in some cases it is still subject to tax.

Charity exemptions from corporation tax – trading income

Trading income is a term used to describe activities which involve the provision of goods or services to customers on a commercial basis (as opposed to donated income and investment income). When deciding whether a trade exists, it is of no relevance to HMRC that you do not intend to make a profit or that you intend profits to be used only for charitable purposes.

Trading is not itself a charitable purpose, but charities can and do trade, either to fulfil a charitable purpose or simply to raise funds.

Any profits your charity generates from trading activities are taxable but a range of tax exemptions is available depending on the nature of your trading activities.

Your charity may be able to benefit from one or more of the three main reliefs available to reduce or exempt tax on the profits from trading activities. These are:

- a primary purpose trading exemption
- an exemption for trades conducted mainly by charitable beneficiaries
- a small trading exemption.

Primary purpose trading exemption

In order to discover what the primary purposes of your charity are, look at the objects clause in the governing document (the trust deed, memorandum & articles of association, constitution etc.).

If your charity's trading activities are carried out in the course of meeting your primary purpose (your objects) then this is known as primary purpose trading.

The profits from primary purpose trading are exempt from corporation tax (or income tax in the case of charitable trusts). This exemption from tax is only available if the profits are applied solely to the purposes of the charity. However, the sales that have given rise to those profits will be regarded as a business activity for the purposes of determining liability for VAT.

Examples

Where environmental projects are concerned an example might be running courses designed to raise awareness in local businesses about recycling and sustainable energy. The provision of such courses for a fee would count as primary purpose trading and would be exempt. This is because the activities are fulfilling the objects of the charity.

Activities ancillary to the primary purpose trade

Some activities that are not strictly primary purpose trading but which could not exist without the primary purpose trade, can also be exempted, as 'activities ancillary to the primary purpose trade'.

Example

A college providing places at a crèche for the children of students in return for payment.

An exemption for trades conducted mainly by charitable beneficiaries

If the work in connection with your trading activities is mainly carried out by beneficiaries of your charity then the profits generated can be exempt from tax as long as those profits are used solely for the charity's charitable purposes. For example, the sale of goods made by people with disabilities (as part of their therapy or training) and then sold to the public would be exempt.

However, be very careful to work out exactly who are the beneficiaries of the charity. Consulting the objects clause of your charity's governing document is the starting point.

Workers do not need to be exclusively charitable beneficiaries; other workers acting in a supervisory or voluntary capacity are acceptable so long as charitable beneficiaries do *most* of the work.

PAYE (see page 406) and National Minimum Wage rules must still be applied to any paid employees (including those who are charitable beneficiaries).

The small trading exemption

This exemption can be claimed against the profits from any trading activities that are not otherwise exempt and where the trading turnover falls within certain limits.

These limits are set in relation to the turnover from small trading in comparison with the overall income of your charity (including income from this trade) and are subject to change in the future.

The following advice is provided by HMRC and is current at the time of writing (July 2009). However, as with all tax matters, figures need to be calculated using up-to-date information, so you should refer to HMRC's website when assessing your income for tax purposes.

> *From April 2000 there is a statutory exemption for the profits of 'small trading' carried on by a charity that are not otherwise already exempt. Before charities consider whether this particular exemption applies, they may first want to consider whether the Extra Statutory Concession (ESC C4) for fundraising events applies.* [Please refer to this sub-heading on page 401].

> **How does the small trading exemption apply?**
> *The small trading exemption applies to the profits of all trading activities that are not already exempt from tax, provided:*
>
> ■ *the total turnover from all of the activities does not exceed the annual turnover limit, or*
>
> ■ *if the total turnover exceeds the annual turnover limit, the charity had a reasonable expectation that it would not do so, and*
>
> ■ *the profits are used solely for the purposes of the charity.*
>
> *The small trading exemption does not apply to VAT.*

Calculation of the annual turnover limit

The annual turnover limit is:

- *£5,000, or*

- *if the turnover is greater than £5,000, 25 % of the charity's total incoming resources, subject to an overall upper limit of £50,000.*

This table illustrates the application of these rules:

Total incoming resources of the charity	Maximum permitted turnover
Under £20,000	£5,000
£20,001 to £200,000	25% of charity's total incoming resources
Over £200,000	£50,000

For the purpose of this limit, 'total incoming resources' means the total receipts of the charity for the year from all sources (grants, donations, investment income, all trading receipts, etc), calculated in accordance with normal charity accounting rules (whether the income would otherwise be taxable or not).

Examples

Example 1

A charity sells Christmas cards to raise funds. This trading is not primary purpose nor does it fall to be considered under ESC C4 because it is not raising income from a fundraising event.

- *Assume this is the only taxable trading activity.*

- *The turnover from the Christmas cards amount to £4,500 in the year.*

- *Any profits will be exempt from tax, because the turnover does not exceed £5,000.*

Example 2

- *A charity has a turnover from non-primary purpose trading of £40,000 for the year.*

- *Its total incoming resources for the year are £160,000 (including the £40,000 turnover).*

- *Profits will be exempt from tax because the turnover from the non-exempt trading does not exceed either:*
  - *25% of the total incoming resources (£160,000 @ 25% = £40,000), or*
  - *the overall upper limit of £50,000.*

Example 3
- *A charity has turnover from non-primary purpose trading of £40,000 for the year.*
- *Its total incoming resources only amounted to £150,000.*
- *The £40,000 turnover exceeds the annual turnover limit (£150,000 @ 25 %= £37500).*
- *However, the profits on sales* may *still be exempt from tax for this year if the charity had a reasonable expectation at the start of the year that the turnover would not exceed the limit.*

Example 4
- *A charity has turnover of £60,000 for the year.*
- *Its total incoming resources only amounted to £150,000.*
- *The turnover exceeds the overall upper limit of £50,000.*
- *The profits on sales* may *still be exempt from tax for this year if the charity had a reasonable expectation at the start of the year that the turnover would not exceed that limit.*

The reasonable expectation test
If the total turnover of taxable trading does exceed the limits, profits may still be exempt if the charity can show that, at the start of the relevant accounting period, it was reasonable for it to expect that the turnover would not exceed the limit. This might be because:
- *the charity expected the turnover to be lower than it turned out to be, or*
- *the charity expected that its total incoming resources would be higher than they turned out to be.*

HMRC Charities will consider any evidence the charity may have to satisfy the reasonable expectation test.

Example:
- *the charity may have carried on the activity for a number of years and may therefore be able to show that the turnover increased unexpectedly compared with earlier years*

- *the charity might have started carrying out the trading activity during the year in question and might be able to show that the turnover was higher than it forecasted*

- *the charity's total incoming resources might be lower than it forecast, for example, because the charity did not receive a grant for which it had budgeted.*

The type of evidence needed to demonstrate the levels of turnover and incoming resources which were expected might include:

- *minutes of meetings at which such matters were discussed*

- *copies of cash flow forecasts*

- *business plans and previous years' accounts.*

If the charity expects to be regularly trading at or around the small trading exemption limits, it might be better for the charity to consider using a trading subsidiary company.

For further guidance see HMRC's website: www.hmrc.gov.uk.

This information is taken from: www.hmrc.gov.uk/charities/guidance-notes/annex4/sectionb.htm#19.

Extra Statutory Concession ESC C4

You can also take advantage of 'Extra Statutory Concession C4' if your trading activities are connected only with fundraising events:

Certain events arranged by voluntary organisations or charities for the purpose of raising funds for charity may fall within the definition of 'trade' in Section 832 ICTA 1988, with the result that any profits will be liable to income tax or corporation tax. However, tax will not be charged on such profits provided:

1) *the event is of a kind which falls within the exemption from VAT under Group 12 of Schedule 9 to the VAT Act 1994 and*

2) *the profits are transferred to charities or otherwise applied for charitable purposes.*

The fact that an activity is exempt from VAT, and that any profit will not be taxed, does not necessarily mean that charities can undertake the activity directly rather than through a trading company.

To get tax relief for trading activities not covered by these exemptions, your charity may also want to consider conducting all or part of its trading activities from a subsidiary trading company and transferring any profits back to the charity as a corporate gift aid donation.

Further information about the direct tax treatment of trades carried on by charities can be found on HMRC's website.

VAT

VAT law uses the concept of 'business', which has a broad definition. As a general rule, if your charity is making a charge for an activity then it is in business for VAT purposes. Its charitable status has no bearing on whether you are in business for VAT purposes. Once registered for VAT your charity will be subject to the normal VAT requirements of any other business.

If your charity is carrying on a business activity you need to consider whether that activity is taxable or exempt from VAT. If your charity is engaged in taxable business activities you are subject to VAT registration thresholds in the same way as any other business.

In certain cases the charity will need to register for VAT and charge VAT on what it sells. VAT registration is compulsory if your total trading income (across all funds and projects) exceeds the current VAT registration level, and penalties will be charged if your charity doesn't register for VAT as soon as required. In calculating the total trading income you can exclude sales which, if you were VAT registered, would be VAT exempt.

If your charity's income is more than £68,000 (2009/10 figure), work out how much of this is trading income. This means being very clear whether funding agreements are grants or contracts. Then deduct items that would be VAT exempt.

You will find information on exempt goods and services at www.hmrc.gov.uk/ vat/reclaim-exempt.htm#1. Items that are exempt from VAT include:

- insurance, finance and credit
- education and training
- fundraising events by charities
- subscriptions to membership organisations
- selling, leasing and letting of commercial land and buildings – but this exemption can be waived.

Exempt supplies are not taxable for VAT, so you do not include sales of exempt goods or services in your taxable turnover for VAT purposes. If you buy exempt items, there is no VAT to reclaim.

If the total comes to more than about £60,000, you will need to watch the position carefully. If it goes over the threshold you must register for VAT within a month. Note that all income, primary purpose and trading for fundraising counts for the VAT threshold.

If you do this calculation and realise that your charity went over the VAT threshold some time ago, but you haven't registered, then a 'retrospective registration' will be needed. In other words, on the form VAT1, where you give the date from which the charity needs to be registered, this may be several years in the past. This can give rise to complex issues such as the need to re-invoice past work or, if this is not possible, previous income may have to be treated as VAT inclusive – which could prove to be very expensive. The charity may have to submit retrospective VAT returns and repay the VAT amount due. The charity would also be liable to VAT penalties unless the trustees could persuade HMRC that they had a 'reasonable excuse' for not realising the position at the time. In these circumstances you would need specialist help.

However, in some cases, charities making a retrospective registration where they are able to re-invoice work (for example, to a local authority) have found they are able to reclaim substantial VAT on past expenditure, which more than covers the cost of professional help. However, the level of monitoring trading income should be such that the organisation should not get into this position.

If you conclude that you do not need to register, you can ignore VAT issues in relation to income, but in that case you should remember to allow for all expenditure at prices including VAT. (If a charity has some trading income, but is below the threshold, it is possible to register for VAT voluntarily but there are few cases where it would be advantageous to do so. Voluntary registration is worth considering where most or all of the sales would be zero-rated, for example, if the charity derives substantial income from charity shops selling donated goods, or from sales of books and publications).

VAT registration is done through the relevant HMRC VAT registration office for your area, by completing and returning form VAT1. Charities that do have to register for VAT are usually VAT partially exempt because the grants and donations side is non-VATable, which makes the VAT issues more complex.

Where an organisation is VAT registered, it must charge VAT at the appropriate rate on everything sold. The implications of VAT depend on your customer, in some cases this is an added financial burden, in others they may be able to reclaim the VAT.

Once you register, you will have to charge VAT in the future on all full rated supplies at the standard rate (for example on catering) and do a quarterly VAT return to HMRC. The good news is that you can 'offset' some VAT you have to pay against the VAT you charge. The other point to note is that you may well have a range of activities, some of which may be exempt from VAT, some full rated and some outside the scope. In any case, you will probably need a VAT specialist to help you, at least in the early stages.

When planning your fundraising, it is worth thinking about the VAT situation. If you are planning major building alterations, is there a way of recovering some or all of the VAT? Will your fundraising mean you go over the VAT threshold anyway? Is there a way around this (such as organising payments so that you do not receive more than the limit for VAT-able income in any one financial year)?

For more information or advice on any of these matters please see the detailed guidance notes on the HMRC website, www.hmrc.gov.uk/charities. 'CWL4' is an excellent leaflet produced by HMRC and also available from its website.

Brief guidance on the VAT issues relating to admission charges for cultural charities is available on the Charity Commission website on www.charity commission.gov.uk.

Charity lotteries

Tax exemption for profits from charity lotteries

There are detailed statutory regulations about the conduct of charity lotteries including accounts, age restrictions, the maximum price of tickets, the application of resulting profits and the amounts which may be paid out in prizes and deducted for expenses. You are advised to consult the appropriate local authority, the Gambling Commission and HMRC for further information and advice.

Generally, profits from lotteries organised by charities for fundraising purposes are exempt from tax as long as all current statutory requirements and both the following conditions are met:

- the lottery is promoted and conducted with a lottery operating licence
- all the proceeds are used for the charitable purposes of the charity.

For detailed information on tax and charity lotteries please refer to the following websites:
www.hmrc.gov.uk/CHARITIES/tax/trading/exemptions.htm#5
www.gamblingcommission.gov.uk/Client/detail.asp?ContentId=259

Contact details for the Gambling Commission and HMRC are given in *Useful contacts and sources of information* on page 409.

Gift Aid

Gift Aid is a scheme to encourage individuals and businesses to donate more money to charity.

Under the scheme, UK charities can claim back the basic rate tax already paid on gifts of money received from individuals who pay or have paid UK tax.

The scheme also allows UK companies to make gifts of money to charity before any tax is deducted.

Key requirements of the Gift Aid Scheme:

- Gift Aid only applies to donations of money.
- Gift Aid donations from individuals must be supported by a valid 'Gift Aid declaration'.
- You can give donors modest tokens of appreciation (called 'benefits') in order to acknowledge a gift but there are strict limits on their value.
- Your charity must keep adequate records to support any claims for Gift Aid repayments and of any benefits provided to donors.
- Donations and/or tax repayments received through the Gift Aid scheme must only be used for charitable purposes.
- Donations that give a right of admission to view a charity's property and some other particular types of donation must follow special rules to qualify for Gift Aid.

For further information and useful examples of gift aid, please refer to HRMC's website, www.hmrc.gov.uk/charities/gift_aid/index.htm.

Payroll giving

Payroll giving is a unique way for people to give regularly to charity. It allows employees, or occupational pensioners, to give money to any UK charity directly

405

from their pay, before tax is deducted. This means that it costs the donor less and charities get more. It offers a regular flow of income and the money can be used as core funding.

Payroll giving also provides an opportunity to educate donors and potential donors. Unless donors wish to remain anonymous, you can send them regular newsletters about your charity's input into the community, so they see that their gifts are valuable, thus helping to reinforce their decision to choose your organisation. Equally, if your charity is helping a company to promote the scheme, it is a unique opportunity to talk to a captive audience.

Payroll giving provides unique access to corporate networking. The opportunity is also there for you to get to know your donors.

For free additional guidance about payroll giving, promotional materials and useful links visit www.payrollgivingcentre.org.uk, operated by the Institute of Fundraising.

PAYE

PAYE (Pay As You Earn) is the system that HMRC uses to collect income tax and national insurance contributions (NICs) from employees' pay as they earn it; this includes the directors of limited companies.

If you employ and pay staff, you will have to deduct tax and NICs from your employees' pay each pay period and pay Employer's Class 1 NICs if they earn above a certain threshold. You pay these amounts to HMRC monthly or quarterly and need to send the correct amount on time or you may be charged interest.

Employers' responsibility for PAYE

As an employer you have a legal obligation to operate PAYE on the payments you make to your employees if their earnings reach the national insurance lower earnings limit (LEL). You use the employee's tax code and national insurance category letter to work out how much income tax and NICs to deduct from their pay and how much Employer's Class 1 NICs you owe on their earnings. You must send the correct amount on time each month, although you may be able to send the amounts due every quarter if your average monthly payments are likely to be less than £1,500. For further details of the current LEL, the date for online and postal payments and whether you can send payments quarterly, please refer to HMRC's website.

What payments does PAYE apply to?

PAYE is applied to all the payments that an employee receives as a result of working for you, including:

- salary and wages
- overtime, shift pay and tips – unless these are paid directly to your employee or they come out of an independent tronc (an arrangement for the pooling and distribution to employees of tips, gratuities and/or service charges in the hotel and catering trade)
- bonuses and commission
- certain expenses allowances paid in cash
- statutory sick pay
- statutory maternity, paternity or adoption pay
- lump sum and compensation payments – such as redundancy payments – unless they're exempt from tax
- non-cash items such as vouchers, shares or premium bonds – you apply PAYE to the cash value of such items.

To check the current PAYE and NIC rates and limits please refer to the HMRC website, which includes a link to the current information.

PAYE on expenses and benefits

Employees are also taxed through PAYE on benefits in kind, such as a company car, medical insurance and other benefits. As an employer you will have to pay Class 1A NICs on some benefits. However you don't pay these contributions under the PAYE system – you do so separately at the year end.

PAYE is also applied to any expenses allowances that you pay to your employees – unless they are covered by a dispensation. A dispensation allows you to make the payments free of tax and NICs and can cut out a lot of form filling and other paperwork.

Other deductions under PAYE

As well as deducting income tax and NICs from your employees' pay each pay period, you might also use the PAYE system to deduct other items, such as:

- student loan repayments
- employees' pension contributions
- payments under an attachment of earnings order
- repayment of a loan you've made to an employee.

Pay statements

You are required to give each of your employees a pay statement – or payslip – at or before the time that you pay them. This can be in either paper or electronic format but it must show certain items, including each employee's gross pay (before tax), any deductions and the net amount payable after the deductions have been made. If you don't give your employees an itemised payslip they could complain to an employment tribunal.

At the end of each tax year you must give employees a summary of their pay and deductions on form P60. This must be in paper format.

Getting started with PAYE

When you pay your employees for the first time you must check whether you need to operate PAYE and register as an employer with HMRC. You can register as an employer by email or by calling the New Employer Helpline on 0845 60 70 143.

You can also contact your local HMRC Customer Advice Team for free confidential advice or to find out about workshops and presentations to help you with PAYE and payroll.

For more detailed information on the topics listed above, key dates, current rates and limits, forms and useful links to other guidance, please visit www.hmrc.gov.uk/paye/intro-basics.

CAF and other vouchers

If someone gives you a donation using a Charities Aid Foundation (CAF) voucher – or another charity voucher – you cannot reclaim any tax on these. This is because the donor has already made a gift aid donation to CAF and CAF has then reclaimed the tax. Tax cannot be reclaimed twice.

Conclusion

You need to make sure that you get the payment of taxes right. HMRC will not be swayed by the fact that your committee is made up of willing volunteers who did not know the law – if tax is due you will have to pay it. It should also be stressed that it is vital to keep up to date with any changes; amendments often happen with little publicity and the onus is on you to be aware of all the current information. This chapter should have alerted you to the main areas of possible concern. The message is that if you are not sure, refer to HMRC at an early stage and if necessary get specialist advice.

Useful contacts and sources of information

Here are some sources of information and advice, many of which are referred to in the chapters of the guide. The list is in alphabetical order and a brief description of the organisations is given, with information taken from their websites.

Arts Council England

Arts Council England is the national development agency for the arts in England, distributing public money from government and the National Lottery.

14 Great Peter Street
London SW1P 3NQ

Tel: 0845 300 6200
Fax: 020 7973 6590
Textphone: 020 7973 6564
Email: enquiries@artscouncil.org.uk
Website: www.artscouncil.org.uk

BBC Children in Need

'Our mission is to positively change the lives of disadvantaged children and young people in the UK. Our vision is a society where each and every child and young person is supported to realise their potential.'

Although Children in Need focuses on children and young people, environmental projects with this beneficiary class would be eligible to apply.

If you're applying for a grant or need advice on any aspect of fundraising for BBC Children in Need, get in touch with your local office (details below).

For general enquiries, please use the form online or call 0345 609 0015.

National offices

England and general helpline

BBC Children in Need Appeal
PO Box 1000
London W12 7WJ

Tel: 020 8576 7788

Scotland

BBC Children in Need Appeal
BBC Scotland
G10, 40 Pacific Drive
Glasgow G51 1DA

Tel: 0141 422 6111

Northern Ireland

BBC Children in Need Appeal
Broadcasting House
Ormeau Avenue
Belfast BT2 8HQ

Tel: 028 9033 8221

Wales

BBC Children in Need Appeal
Broadcasting House
Llandaff
Cardiff CF5 2YQ

Tel: 029 2032 2383

Regional offices

North – Newcastle

BBC Children in Need Appeal
Broadcasting Centre
Barrack Road
Newcastle NE99 2NE

Tel: 0191 232 1313

North – Manchester

BBC Children in Need Appeal
Room 2010

New Broadcasting House
Oxford Road
Manchester M60 1SJ

Tel: 0161 244 3439

North – Leeds

BBC Children in Need Appeal
BBC Broadcasting Centre
2 St Peter's Square
Leeds LS9 8AH

Tel: 0113 224 7155

Central – Norwich

BBC Children in Need Appeal
BBC East
The Forum
Norwich NR2 1BH

Tel: 01603 284 774

Central – Nottingham

BBC Children in Need Appeal
BBC Nottingham
London Road
Nottingham NG2 4UU

Tel: 01159 021851

Central – Birmingham

BBC Children in Need Appeal
Level 10, BBC Birmingham
The Mailbox
Birmingham B1 1RF

Tel: 0121 567 6707

South and West – Bristol

BBC Children in Need Appeal
Broadcasting House
Whiteladies Road
Bristol BS8 2LR

Tel: 0117 974 6600

South and West – Plymouth

BBC Children in Need Appeal
Broadcasting House
Seymour Road
Mannamead
Plymouth PL3 5BD

Tel: 01752 234588

London and South East

BBC Children in Need Appeal
Room 735, South East Block
Bush House
Strand
London WC2B 4PA

Tel: 020 7557 0389
Email for all enquiries:
pudsey@bbc.co.uk
Website: www.bbc.co.uk/pudsey

Big Lottery Fund (BIG)

'We are committed to bringing real improvements to communities, and to the lives of people most in need.'

1 Plough Place
London EC4A 1DE

Tel: 020 7211 1800/0300 500 5050
Textphone: 0845 6 02 1659
Fax: 020 7211 1750
Website: www.biglotteryfund.org.uk

For funding information or general enquiries call the BIG advice line on 0845 4 10 20 30 or email general.enquiries@biglotteryfund.org.uk.

Strategic grants office

4th floor
Pearl Assurance House
Friar Lane
Nottingham NG1 6BT

Tel: 0115 934 2950
Textphone: 0115 934 2951

412

Fax: 0115 934 2952

Email: strategicgrants@biglotteryfund.org.uk

Northern Ireland office

For funding information or general enquiries call the BIG advice line on 028 9055 1455.

1 Cromac Quay
Cromac Wood
Belfast BT7 2JD

Tel: 028 9055 1455
Textphone: 028 9055 1431
Fax: 028 9055 1444

Scotland office

For funding information or general enquiries call the BIG advice line on 0870 2 40 23 91 or email enquiries.scotland@biglotteryfund.org.uk.

1 Atlantic Quay
1 Robertson Street
Glasgow G2 8JB

Tel: 0141 242 1400
Textphone: 0141 242 1500
Fax: 0141 242 1401

Wales offices

For funding information or general enquiries call the BIG advice line on 01686 611 700 or email enquiries.wales@biglotteryfund.org.uk.

Newtown office

2nd Floor
Ladywell House
Newtown
Powys SY16 1JB
Tel: 01686 611700
Textphone: 01686 610205
Fax: 01686 621534

Cardiff office

6th Floor
1 Kingsway
Cardiff CF10 3JN

Tel: 029 2067 8200
Textphone: 0845 602 1659
Fax: 029 2066 7275

England regional offices

East Midlands

For funding information or general enquiries call the BIG advice line on 0845 4 10 20 30 or email enquiries.em@biglotteryfund.org.uk.

4th Floor
Pearl Assurance House
Friar Lane
Nottingham NG1 6BT
Tel: 0115 872 2950
Fax: 0115 872 2990

West Midlands

For funding information or general enquiries call the BIG advice line on 0845 4 10 20 30 or email enquiries.wm@biglotteryfund.org.uk.

Big Lottery Fund, Birmingham Centre
Apex House
3 Embassy Drive
Edgbaston
Birmingham B15 1TR
Tel: 0121 345 7700
Textphone: 0121 345 7666
Fax: 0121 345 8888

East of England

For funding information or general enquiries call the BIG advice line on 0845 4 10 20 30. For information about events that are happening in the East of England region email regionevents.ea@biglotteryfund.org.uk, or contact:

Big Lottery Fund
2nd Floor
Elizabeth House
1 High Street
Chesterton
Cambridge CB4 1YW

Tel: 01223 449000
Textphone: 01223 352041
Fax: 01223 312628

London

For funding information or general enquiries call the BIG advice line on 0845 4 10 20 30 or email general.enquiries@biglotteryfund.org.uk.

For information about the work of the London team, contact:

The London regional office
5th Floor
1 Plough Place
London EC4A 1DE

Tel: 020 7842 4000
Textphone: 0845 039 0204
Fax: 020 7842 4010

North East

For funding information or general enquiries call the BIG advice line on 0845 4 10 20 30 or email enquiries.ne@biglotteryfund.org.uk.

2 St James Gate
Newcastle upon Tyne NE1 4BE

Tel: 0191 376 1600
Textphone: 0191 376 1776
Fax: 0191 376 1661

North West

For funding information or general enquiries call the BIG advice line on 0845 4 10 20 30 or email general.enquiries@biglotteryfund.org.uk.

There is no separate email address for the North West

Big Lottery Fund
10th Floor
York House
York Street
Manchester M2 3BB

Tel: 0161 261 4600
Textphone: 0161 261 4647
Fax: 0161 261 4646

South East

For funding information or general enquiries call the BIG advice line on 0845 4 10 20 30. For more information on events in the South East email southeastevents@biglotteryfund.org.uk.

4th Floor
Dominion House
Woodbridge Road
Guildford
Surrey GU1 4BN

Tel: 01483 462900
Textphone: 01483 568764
Fax: 01483 569764

South West

For funding information or general enquiries call the BIG advice line on 0845 4 10 20 30 or email general.enquiries@biglotteryfund.org.uk.

Beaufort House
51 New North Road
Exeter EX4 4EQ

Tel: 01392 849700
Textphone: 01392 490633
Fax: 01392 491134

Yorkshire and the Humber

For funding information or general enquiries call the BIG advice line on 0845 4 10 20 30 or email enquiries.yh@biglotteryfund.org.uk.

3rd floor Carlton Tower
34 St Pauls Street
Leeds LS1 2AT
Tel: 0113 224 5301
Textphone: 0113 245 4104
Fax: 0113 244 0363

BRE Trust

The BRE Trust (formerly the Foundation for the Built Environment) is a charitable company whose objectives are, through research and education, to advance knowledge, innovation and communication in all matters concerning the built environment for public benefit.

Room 5 Building 1
Bucknalls Lane
Garston
Watford
Herts WD25 9XX

Tel: 01923 664598
Fax: 01923 664089
Email: secretary@bretrust.org.uk
www.bretrust.org.uk

British Youth Council

'All young people across the UK will have a say and be heard.'

The British Youth Council (BYC) is led by young people, for young people, aged 26 and under, across the UK. It provides training and volunteering and campaigning activity, both locally and globally. Environmental projects with a youth focus will be eligible to apply to BYC.

The Mezzanine 2
Downstream Building
1 London Bridge SE1 9BG

Tel: 0845 458 1489
Fax: 0845 458 1847
Email facility available online
Website: www.byc.org.uk

Business in the Community (BitC)

'Business in the Community inspires, engages, supports and challenges companies to continually improve the impact they have on society and the environment through their responsible business programme, sometimes referred to as corporate social responsibility (CSR).'

BitC works through four areas: community, environment, marketplace and workplace. It has more than 850 companies in membership and represents one in five of the UK private sector workforce; it also convenes a network of global partners.

137 Shepherdess Walk
London N1 7RQ

Tel: 020 7566 8650
Email: information@bitc.org.uk
Website: www.bitc.org.uk

417

Charities Aid Foundation (CAF)

CAF's mission is: 'An integrated customer-focused organisation for donors and charities that stimulates giving, social investment and the effective use of funds.'

25 Kings Hill Avenue
Kings Hill
West Malling
Kent ME19 4TA

Tel: 01732 520 000
Fax: 01732 520 001
Email: enquiries@cafonline.org
Website: www.cafonline.org

Charity Commission for England and Wales (the Commission)

'Mission:

The Charity Commission is the independent regulator for charitable activity

- enabling charities to maximise their impact
- ensuring compliance with legal obligations
- encouraging innovation and effectiveness
- championing the public interest in charity to promote the public's trust and confidence'

The Charity Commission has four offices:

London: 30 Millbank, London SW1P 4DU
Liverpool: 12 Princes Dock, Princes Parade, Liverpool L3 1DE
Taunton: Woodfield House, Tangier, Taunton, Somerset TA1 4BL
Newport: 8th Floor, Clarence House, Clarence Place, Newport NP19 7AA

The Commission provides an online knowledge base for the most frequently asked questions raised by customers and this is continually updated – go to www.charity-commission.gov.uk.

Email: enquiries@charitycommission.gsi.gov.uk.

If you experience difficulties accessing the online facility you should call 0845 300 0197.

If you would rather speak to an advisor you can call Charity Commission Direct – see below. You can write to the Commission at:

Charity Commission Direct
PO Box 1227
Liverpool L69 3UG

Tel: 0845 3000 218

Staff are available to take calls between 8.00am–8.00pm from Monday to Friday and 9.00am–1.00pm on Saturdays (except national holidays).

There is also a Textbox service on 0845 3000 219 for hearing impaired callers.

The centralised fax number is: 0151 703 1555

A comprehensive range of guidance documents is available to download from the Commission's website: www.charity-commission.gov.uk.

The Commission advises that it is not always necessary to seek legal advice for issues you need clarifying and it is advisable to contact the Commission in the first instance.

If you do need legal advice, make sure you find a solicitor who specialises in charity law.

Information about suitable solicitors is available from the Charity Law Association – details given below.

Charity Commission for Northern Ireland

The Charities Act (Northern Ireland) 2008 will create a new body – the Charity Commission for Northern Ireland – which will have Commissioners and staff. It will establish a compulsory charity register of all charities operating in Northern Ireland and provide a charity test of what is and is not a charity. It will also put in place new requirements for all public collections. All of this will allow better supervision, control and support of charities.

Secretariat
Charity Commission for N.I.
3rd Floor Lighthouse Building
1 Cromac Place
Gasworks Business Park
Ormeau Road
Belfast
BT7 2JB

Tel: 028 9082 9449
Fax: 028 9082 9431
email: admin@charitycommissionni.org.uk

Charity Law Association

'The Charity Law Association was established at the end of 1992 with the aim of enabling those who advise on or use charity law to meet together, to exchange ideas and intelligence and to use their experience and expertise for the benefit of the charity sector.

'To ensure that it is free to promote any changes to charity law which appear to its members, based on their expertise in the field, to be necessary or desirable the Association is not itself a charity.

'The Association works closely with the Charity Commission and is now consulted by government and others in connection with charity law issues.

'The Association currently has over 850 members, including many of the country's largest charities and most leading charity lawyers.'

10 Tavistock Close
Rainham
Kent ME8 9HR

Tel: 01634 373253
Email: admin@charitylawassociation.org.uk
Website: www.charitylawassociation.org.uk

Comic Relief

'Comic Relief's vision is a just world free from poverty.'

Comic Relief was set up in 1985 by comedians who wanted to do something to help others. It now has two major fundraising campaigns: Red Nose Day and Sport Relief.

Comic Relief UK
5th Floor
89 Albert Embankment
London SE1 7TP

Tel: 020 7820 5555
Fax: 020 7820 5500
Minicom: 020 7820 5579
General enquiries info@comicrelief.org.uk
Website: www.comicrelief.com

Community Foundation Network (CFN)

'Community Foundation Network represents the community foundation movement in the UK. Our aim is to help clients create lasting value from their local giving through the network of community foundations.

'Community foundations are charities located across the UK dedicated to strengthening local communities, creating opportunities and tackling issues of disadvantage and exclusion. Community foundations target grants that make a genuine difference to the lives of local people. They manage funds donated by individuals and organisations, building endowment and acting as the vital link between donors and local needs, connecting people with causes, and enabling clients to achieve far more than they could ever by themselves.'

Details of all local community foundations can be found on the network's website – www.communityfoundations.org.uk.

Community Foundation Network
Arena House
66–68 Pentonville Road
London N1 9HS

Tel: 020 7713 9326
Fax: 020 7713 9327
Email: network@communityfoundations.org.uk
Website: www.communityfoundations.org.uk

Companies House

Main office

Companies House
Crown Way
Maindy
Cardiff CF14 3UZ

Edinburgh

Companies House
4th floor
Edinburgh Quay 2
139 Fountainbridge
Edinburgh EH3 9FF

London

Companies House Executive Agency
21 Bloomsbury Street
London WC1B 3XD

Tel: 0303 1234 500
Minicom: 029 2038 1245
Email: enquiries@companies-house.gov.uk
Website: www.companieshouse.gov.uk

Council for Environmental Education (CEE)

'The Council for Environmental Education (CEE) is a national membership body for organisations and individuals in England committed to environmental education and education for sustainable development.

'CEE works with and for its membership to develop policy, enhance practice and enable members to work more effectively together.'

Its website gives details of CEE's work, member organisations and current news. The information centre provides access to CEE's database on events, training, funding and learning resources.

94 London Street
Reading RG1 4SJ

Tel: 0118 950 2550
Fax: 0118 959 1955
Website: www.cee.org.uk

Department for Culture, Media and Sport (DCMS)

This government department aims 'to improve the quality of life for all through cultural and sporting activities, to support the pursuit of excellence and to champion the tourism, creative and leisure industries'.

Department for Culture Media and Sport
2–4 Cockspur Street
London SW1Y 5DH

Tel: 020 7211 6200 (open 9.30am–4.30pm) Monday to Friday

Email: enquiries@culture.gov.uk
Website: www.culture.gov.uk

Directory of Social Change (DSC)

'Directory of Social Change (DSC) is an independent charity with a vision of an independent voluntary sector at the heart of social change. We achieve this by providing essential information and training to the voluntary sector to enable charities to achieve their mission.

'Our independent status and well respected research means we can challenge and create debate around government policy, trust funding, and other issues which threaten the independence of smaller charities. We are in touch with over 20,000 charities annually through our conferences and training on fundraising, management, organisational and personal development, communication, finance and law.

'We also publish a wide variety of resources for charities, including our well-known UK fundraising guides, directories and websites. We were started in 1974 and our 45 staff are based in London and Liverpool.

'Our mission is to be an agent connecting givers, influencers and service deliverers.

'We believe that the activities of voluntary and community organisations are crucial, both to the causes they serve and the social environment in which they operate.'

24 Stephenson Way
London NW1 2DP

Tel: 08450 77 77 07
Fax: 020 7391 4804
Email: enquiries@dsc.org.uk
Website: www.dsc.org.uk

For publications that may be useful to readers of this guide, please see DSC publications at the end of this section.

Europe in the UK – Information Network

The website for this network brings together contact details for organisations in the UK regions, from local authorities to universities, business support agencies to libraries, who find it useful to work together on European issues to serve the needs of their customers more effectively. You can find full details of the Europe Direct drop-in centres which are spread throughout the UK and are designed to help members of the public get basic information about what the EU does and how it works.

The site also aims to raise awareness of how the European Union affects the UK and to demonstrate how its citizens can both benefit from, and influence, what happens at a European level.

The website gives details of where in your area one can find out more about Europe, whether you want to know about funding initiatives, comparative statistics or up-to-date information on EU decisions.

Website: www.europe.org.uk

European Union – Education, Audiovisual and Culture Executive Agency

The Education, Audiovisual and Culture Executive Agency (EACEA) is a public body of the European Commission operational since January 2006.

The role of EACEA is to manage European funding opportunities and networks in the fields of education and training, citizenship, youth, audiovisual and culture.

The Agency's mandate covers a variety of Europe and worldwide opportunities for organisations, professionals and individuals, at all ages and stages of life. Seven key community programmes have been partly or fully delegated to the EACEA: Lifelong Learning, Erasmus Mundus, Tempus, Culture, Youth in Action, Europe for Citizens and Media, as well as several international Cooperation Agreements in the field of higher education.

Education, Audiovisual, and Culture Executive Agency
Avenue du Bourget 1
BE-1140 Brussels

General Executive Agency information tel: +32 2 29 75615
General email: eacea-info@ec.europa.eu

Gambling Commission

The Gambling Commission was established in October 2005 taking over the role previously played by the Gaming Board for Great Britain in regulating casinos, bingo, gaming machines and lotteries.

The Gambling Commission has responsibility for the regulation of betting and remote gambling; helping to protect children and vulnerable people from being harmed or exploited by gambling; and for advising local and central government on issues related to gambling.

Alphabetical index of funders